# DYING OF FRIGHT

## Masterpieces of the Macabre

BY LES DANIELS

Illustrated by Lee Brown Coye

**CHARLES SCRIBNER'S SONS**
**NEW YORK**

**Library of Congress Cataloging in Publication Data**

Main entry under title:
Dying of fright.

Includes biographical notes.
  1. Horror tales, American.   2. Horror tales, English.
I. Daniels, Les, 1943-
PZ1.D77   [PS648.H6] 823'.0872   75-43969
ISBN 0-684-14624-X

1 3 5 7 9 11 13 15 17 19 MD/C 20 18 16 14 12 10 8 6 4 2

Printed in the United States of America

# Acknowledgments

For "The Call of Cthulhu" by H. P. Lovecraft and "A Visitor from Egypt" by Frank Belknap Long:
  Permission granted by Arkham House Publishers, Inc., Sauk City, Wisconsin
For "The Graveyard Rats" by Henry Kuttner:
  Copyright 1948, 1969 by Henry Kuttner, reprinted by permission of Harold Matson Co. Inc.
For "Rope Enough" by John Collier:
  Copyright 1951 by John Collier, reprinted by permission of Harold Matson Co. Inc.
For "They Bite" by Anthony Boucher:
  Originally published in UNKNOWN WORLDS; Copyright © 1943, 1971 by William A. P. White
For "Homecoming" by Ray Bradbury:
  Copyright 1955 by Ray Bradbury, reprinted by permission of the Harold Matson Co. Inc.
For "The House in Goblin Wood" by Carter Dickson:
  Permission granted by John Dickson Carr
For "The Man Who Never Grew Young" by Fritz Leiber:
  Copyright 1947 by Fritz Leiber, reprinted by permission of Robert P. Mills
For "Born of Man and Woman" by Richard Matheson:
  Copyright 1955 by Richard Matheson, reprinted by permission of Harold Matson Co. Inc.

# Contents

# Introduction

*Dying of Fright* is intended to present, within the pages of one volume, some of the best work by the best writers who have devoted themselves to the creation of frightening fiction. Several of the stories are famous, others not so familiar, but all are among the finest ever written.

The choices have been guided by a decision to demonstrate the existence of a coherent and continuing tradition in Anglo-American terror tales. To that end, the selections have been limited to those written in English and to those authors who have produced a considerable body of work in the field. The occasional piece produced by a writer who usually creates more conventional fiction is a story that is likely to remain an isolated incident rather than an important influence, and translations have traditionally proven treacherous as representations of the spirit expressed in the original language.

There is, of course, room for controversy about the selections. Critics and theorists have attempted without much success to arrive at a standard for judging fiction in this genre. Despite the popularity of horror stories, professional experts on literature seem incapable of accounting for their appeal and usually ignore such work until the passage of time has demonstrated its durability.

The only lasting criterion was established by Edgar Allan Poe, a major critic who was also a major creator. Poe judged stories by their effect, that is, by their ability to make a strong emotional or perhaps even spiritual impact on the reader. This goes against the grain of modern academic theory; one critic has even labeled this method of perceiving merit as "the affective fallacy" and has chosen, like most of his colleagues, to appreciate only that literature which is structured to provide a sufficient amount of intellectual ambiguity. One serious scholar, in his study called *The Fantastic*, was able to come to grips with the genre only by narrowing it down to those very few tales which teeter on the borderline between realism and fantasy, thus remaining ambiguous enough to allow for elaborate structural analysis.

Yet sinister and supernatural stories do not make their primary appeal to the intellect, and they can only be judged subjectively, by the results they produce in the reader. If they are frightening, they succeed; if not, then they fail. Even more than with most artistic endeavors, their merits are a matter of taste, and the only obvious way to achieve an even apparently objective opinion is to wait for the general agreement of readers and writers in the field. Still, no story has been included here solely on the basis of its reputation, unless it was felt to be a genuinely affective experience and not just a landmark of literary history.

There are a number of important authors whose work might have been included in this collection and who at least deserve to be mentioned. These include such pioneering practitioners of the Gothic novel as Horace Walpole, Ann Radcliffe, Matthew Gregory Lewis,

Mary Shelley, and Charles Robert Maturin, although they tended to be less adept when dealing with the short story, a form that had not yet been perfected.

Later significant British writers in the field include E. F. Benson, Edward Bulwer-Lytton, Ramsey Campbell, Wilkie Collins, Basil Copper, John Keir Cross, Roald Dahl, Walter de la Mare, L. P. Hartley, Oliver Onions, M. P. Shiel, Robert Louis Stevenson, Bram Stoker, and H. Russell Wakefield.

Among the more important American authors are Nelson Bond, Stanley Ellin, Harlan Ellison, Shirley Jackson, Fitz-James O'Brien, Mary E. Wilkins-Freeman, and Edward Lucas White. An extraordinary number of talented American writers have been associated with the unique magazine *Weird Tales*. In addition to those whose stories appear in this book, the major contributors include August Derleth, Robert E. Howard, Carl Jacobi, C. L. Moore, H. Warner Munn, E. Hoffmann Price, Seabury Quinn, Clark Ashton Smith, Donald Wandrei, Manly Wade Wellman, and Henry S. Whitehead.

*Dying of Fright* is in part a supplement to the earlier *Living in Fear: A History of Horror in the Mass Media,* and that volume contains further information on many of the writers listed here.

The drawings in this book are the work of Lee Brown Coye, perhaps the most important living American illustrator in the domain of the macabre. His bold and dramatic designs seem to remain indelibly etched in the memory and have been praised by countless commentators. He has had several showings at the Whitney Museum, and one of his paintings is in the permanent collection of the Metropolitan Museum of Art. In addition to his popular illustrations, he produces paintings, sculpture, and scale models. Coye came to the field of frightening fiction through his association with the most important editor and publisher in the genre, August Derleth. They worked together on three important anthologies, *Sleep No More* (1944), *Who Knocks?* (1946), and *The Night Side* (1947). These led to Coye's association with *Weird Tales,* and he did many impressive illustrations and covers during the last decade of that magazine's appearance. More recently, he has done a number of jackets for books published by Arkham House, a firm that has printed limited editions of fiction by most of this century's best authors of supernatural stories. Coye has also done drawings for such important collections as H. P. Lovecraft's *Three Tales of Horror* (1967) and Manly Wade Wellman's *Worse Things Waiting* (1973).

In 1975, Coye received the Best Artist Award at the First World Fantasy Convention.

With an artist of this caliber adding his interpretations to tales by twenty-five of the finest authors in the genre, it is to be hoped that readers will find *Dying of Fright* among the very best anthologies of its kind.

# DYING
# OF
# FRIGHT

# Washington Irving

Washington Irving (1783–1859) is the first American man of letters to have gained international renown. In fact, he has been called the father of American literature, even though his reputation today rests almost entirely on two tales. These two narratives, "The Legend of Sleepy Hollow" and "Rip Van Winkle," both concerned with supernatural subjects, are often described as the first modern short stories in English.

Irving's father had served in the American Revolution under George Washington, whose name was given to the family's eleventh son. Irving planned a career in law, but he gradually drifted into journalism, and his first work appeared in his brother Peter's paper, the *Morning Chronicle*. His earliest book, a collection of essays called *Salmagundi* (1807), was written in collaboration with another brother. Irving's satirical *A History of New York, by Diedrich Knickerbocker* (1809) is one of the earliest examples of humor in American literature, and it brought him local fame. In fact, Irving's fictitious narrator is still a symbol of New York City. After serving as a staff officer in the War of 1812, and then editing a magazine in Philadelphia for a year, Irving went to England to represent the business interests of his brothers.

He stayed abroad for seventeen years. In London, he cultivated such acquaintances as Lord Byron and Sir Walter Scott, and it was there that he wrote his famous *Sketch Book* (1819). This group of essays and stories was first published in the United States, partly because Irving feared the reaction of European critics. When the book did appear in England, Irving was hailed for his wit and charm, finally overcoming the European conviction that there was no such thing as American culture. The English edition of the book was published through the efforts of novelist William Godwin, whose daughter Mary Shelley had recently written *Frankenstein*. Years later, Irving and the widowed Mrs. Shelley were to have a brief romance.

The *Sketch Book* was followed by another collection, *Bracebridge Hall* (1822), and by *Tales of a Traveller* (1824). The latter got comparatively bad reviews, apparently because it was so similar to the previous volumes, but critics now regard it as Irving's best book, even if it does not include anything as important as the *Sketch Book*'s "Sleepy Hollow" and "Rip Van Winkle."

In 1832, Irving returned to the United States and found himself a celebrity. He refused opportunities for such positions as mayor of New York, congressman, and secretary of the navy, but finally accepted the post of ambassador to Spain in 1842. His late works, principally factual, include a biography of Columbus, *A Tour of the Prairies* (1835), and *The Adven-*

*tures of Captain Bonneville* (1837). The exhausting task of preparing a formal biography of Irving's namesake is said to have hastened his death; the last volume of his *Life of Washington* appeared in 1859.

"The Adventure of the German Student" is a selection from *Tales of a Traveller*, one of a series of supernatural stories appearing in the first section of the book, "Strange Stories by a Nervous Gentleman." Most of them are parodies, of which the most amusing is "The Bold Dragoon," a story about a ghost who haunts a room by playing bagpipes while the furniture dances. "The German Student" is in a more serious vein; in fact, it is Irving's most terrifying tale. Considering its comparative antiquity, it is a remarkably modern performance, narrated in a crisp clear style that is free from the oratorical devices often expected of nineteenth-century fiction. Although it has its romantic side, the tale also includes some views on sexual morality suggesting that what many modern people consider "revolutionary" is actually as old as the French Revolution. The story, Irving wrote, was "founded on an anecdote related to me as existing somewhere in French," but he was never able to discover its source.

# THE ADVENTURE OF THE GERMAN STUDENT

# Washington Irving

On a stormy night, in the tempestuous times of the French revolution, a young German was returning to his lodgings, at a late hour, across the old part of Paris. The lightning gleamed, and the loud claps of thunder rattled through the lofty narrow streets—but I should first tell you something about this young German.

Gottfried Wolfgang was a young man of good family. He had studied for some time at Göttingen, but being of a visionary and enthusiastic character, he had wandered into those wild and speculative doctrines which have so often bewildered German students. His secluded life, his intense application, and the singular nature of his studies, had an effect on both mind and body. His health was impaired; his imagination diseased. He had been indulging in fanciful speculations on spiritual essences, until, like Swedenborg, he had an ideal world of his own around him. He took up a notion, I do not know from what cause, that there was an evil influence hanging over him; an evil genius or spirit seeking to ensnare him and insure his perdition. Such an idea working on his melancholy temperament produced the most gloomy effects. He became haggard and desponding. His friends discovered the mental malady preying upon him, and determined that the best cure was a change of scene; he was sent, therefore, to finish his studies amidst the splendors and gayeties of Paris.

Wolfgang arrived at Paris at the breaking out of the Revolution. The popular delirium at first caught his enthusiastic mind, and he was captivated by the political and philosophical theories of the day, but the scenes of blood which followed shocked his sensitive nature; disgusted him with society and the world, and made him more than ever a recluse. He shut himself up in a solitary apartment in the *Pays Latin*, the quarter of students. There, in a gloomy street not far from the monastic walls of the Sorbonne, he pursued his favorite speculations. Sometimes he spent hours together in the great libraries of Paris, those catacombs of departed authors, rummaging among their hoards of dusty and obsolete works in quest of food for his unhealthy appetite. He was, in a manner, a literary ghoul, feeding in the charnel-house of decayed literature.

Wolfgang, though solitary and recluse, was of an ardent temperament, but for a time it operated merely upon his imagination. He was too shy and ignorant of the world to make any advances to the fair, but he was a passionate admirer of female beauty, and in his lonely chamber would often lose himself in reveries on forms and faces which he had seen, and his fancy would deck out images of loveliness far surpassing the reality.

While his mind was in this excited and sublimated state, a dream produced an extraordinary effect upon him. It was of a female face of transcendent beauty. So strong was the impression made, that he dreamed of it again and again. It haunted his thoughts by day, his slumbers by night; in fine, he became passionately enamored of this shadow of a dream. This lasted so long that it became one of those fixed ideas which haunt the minds of melancholy men, and are at times mistaken for madness.

Such was Gottfried Wolfgang, and such his situation at the time I mentioned. He was returning home late one stormy night, through some of the old and gloomy streets of the *Marais*, the ancient part of Paris. The loud claps of thunder rattled among the high houses of the narrow streets. He came to the Place de la Greve, the square where public executions are performed. The lightning quivered about the pinnacles of the ancient Hôtel de Ville, and shed flickering gleams over the open space in front. As Wolfgang was crossing the square, he shrank back with horror at finding himself close by the guillotine. It was the height of the Reign of Terror, when this dreadful instrument of death stood ever ready, and its scaffold was continually running with the blood of the virtuous and the brave. It had that very day been actively employed in the work of carnage, and there it stood in grim array, amidst a silent and sleeping city, waiting for fresh victims.

Wolfgang's heart sickened within him, and he was turning shuddering from the horrible engine, when he beheld a shadowy form, cowering as it were at the foot of the steps which led up to the scaffold. A succession of vivid flashes of lightning revealed it more distinctly. It was a female figure, dressed in black. She was seated on one of the lower steps of the scaffold, leaning forward, her face hid in her lap; and her long dishevelled tresses hanging to the ground, streaming with the rain which fell in torrents. Wolfgang paused. There was something awful in this solitary monument of woe. The female had the appearance of being above the common order. He knew the times to be full of vicissitude, and that many a fair head, which had once been pillowed on down, now wandered houseless. Perhaps this was some poor mourner whom the dreadful axe had rendered desolate, and who sat here heartbroken on the strand of existence, from which all that was dear to her had been launched into eternity.

He approached, and addressed her in the accents of sympathy. She raised her head and gazed wildly at him. What was his astonishment at beholding, by the bright glare of the lightning, the very face which had haunted him in his dreams. It was pale and disconsolate, but ravishingly beautiful.

Trembling with violent and conflicting emotions, Wolfgang again accosted her. He spoke something of her being exposed at such an hour of the night, and to the fury of such a storm, and offered to conduct her to her friends. She pointed to the guillotine with a gesture of dreadful signification.

"I have no friend on earth!" said she.

"But you have a home," said Wolfgang.

"Yes—in the grave!"

The heart of the student melted at the words.

"If a stranger dare make an offer," said he, "without danger of being misunderstood, I would offer my humble dwelling as a shelter; myself as a devoted friend. I am friendless myself in Paris, and a stranger in the land; but if my life could be of service, it is at your disposal, and should be sacrificed before harm or indignity should come to you."

There was an honest earnestness in the young man's manner that had its effect. His foreign accent, too, was in his favor; it showed him not to be a hackneyed inhabitant of Paris. Indeed, there is an eloquence in true enthusiasm that is not to be doubted. The homeless stranger confided herself implicitly to the protection of the student.

He supported her faltering steps across the Pont Neuf, and by the place where the statue of Henry the Fourth had been overthrown by the populace. The storm had abated, and the thunder rumbled at a distance. All Paris was quiet; that great volcano of human passion slumbered for awhile, to gather fresh strength for the next day's eruption. The student conducted his charge through the ancient streets of the *Pays Latin*, and by the dusky walls of the Sorbonne, to the great dingy hotel which he inhabited. The old portress who admitted them stared with surprise at the unusual sight of the melancholy Wolfgang with a female companion.

On entering his apartment, the student, for the first time, blushed at the scantiness and indifference of his dwelling. He had but one chamber—an old-fashioned salon—heavily carved, and fantastically furnished with the remains of former magnificence, for it was of those hotels in the quarter of the Luxembourg Palace which had once belonged to nobility. It was lumbered with books and papers, and all the usual apparatus of a student, and his bed stood in a recess at one end.

When lights were brought, and Wolfgang had a better opportunity of contemplating the stranger, he was more than ever intoxicated by her beauty. Her face was pale, but of a dazzling fairness, set off by a profusion of raven hair that hung clustering about it. Her eyes were large and brilliant, with a singular expression approaching almost to wildness. As far as her black dress permitted her shape to be seen, it was of perfect symmetry. Her whole appearance was highly striking, though she was dressed in the simplest style. The only thing approaching to an ornament which she wore, was a broad black band round her neck, clasped by diamonds.

The perplexity now commenced with the student how to dispose of the helpless being thus thrown upon his protection. He thought of abandoning his chamber to her, and seeking shelter for himself elsewhere. Still he was so fascinated by her charms, there seemed to be such a spell upon his thoughts and senses, that he could not tear himself from her presence. Her manner, too, was singular and unaccountable. She spoke no more of the guillotine. Her grief had abated. The attentions of the student had first won her confidence, and then, apparently, her heart. She was evidently an enthusiast like himself, and enthusiasts soon understand each other.

In the infatuation of the moment, Wolfgang avowed his passion for her. He told her the story of his mysterious dream, and how she had possessed his heart before he had even seen her. She was strangely affected by his recital, and acknowledged to have felt an impulse toward him equally unaccountable. It was the time for wild theory and wild actions. Old prejudices and superstitions were done away; everything was under the sway of the "Goddess of Reason." Among other rubbish of the old times, the forms and ceremonies of marriage began to be considered superfluous bonds for honorable minds. Social compacts were the vogue. Wolfgang was too much of a theorist not to be tainted by the liberal doctrines of the day.

"Why should we separate?" said he, "our hearts are united; in the eye of reason and honor we are as one. What need is there of sordid forms to bind high souls together?"

The stranger listened with emotion; she had evidently received illumination at the same school.

"You have no home nor family," continued he; "let me be everything to you, or rather let us be everything to one another. If form is necessary, form shall be observed—there is my hand. I pledge myself to you forever."

"Forever?" said the stranger, solemnly.

"Forever!" repeated Wolfgang.

The stranger clasped the hand extended to her: "Then I am yours," murmured she, and sank upon his bosom.

The next morning the student left his bride sleeping, and sallied forth at an early hour to seek more spacious apartments, suitable to the change in his situation. When he returned, he found the stranger lying with her head hanging over the bed, and one arm thrown over it. He spoke to her, but received no reply. He advanced to awaken her from her uneasy posture. On taking her hand, it was cold—there was no pulsation—her face was pallid and ghastly.—In a word—she was a corpse.

Horrified and frantic, he alarmed the house. A scene of confusion ensued. The police was summoned. As the officer of police entered the room, he started back on beholding the corpse.

"Great heaven!" cried he, "how did this woman come here?"

"Do you know anything about her?" said Wolfgang, eagerly.

"Do I?" exclaimed the police officer, "she was guillotined yesterday."

He stepped forward, undid the black collar round the neck of the corpse, and the head rolled on the floor!

The student burst into a frenzy. "The fiend! the fiend has gained possession of me!" shrieked he; "I am lost forever."

They tried to soothe him, but in vain. He was possessed with the frighful belief that an evil spirit had reanimated the dead body to ensnare him. He went distracted, and died in a madhouse.

# Edgar Allan Poe

Edgar Allen Poe (1809–1849) is perhaps the most important and certainly the most tragic figure in American literature. The story of his unhappy life has been frequently repeated. His actress mother died of tuberculosis when he was hardly more than an infant, and he was taken in by the Allans, only to be disowned after the death of his beloved foster-mother. Soon after he married, his wife, Virginia, contracted the same disease, and after years of suffering, she too expired. In the midst of such constant misery, Poe attempted to establish himself as an author at a time when it was virtually impossible for an American to earn a living by writing. His life was spent in poverty and frustration; he had a drinking problem, and he once described himself as insane. And yet, despite his unhappiness, Poe steadfastly pursued his goal and achieved, at least posthumously, the recognition he deserved: a triumph over death as complete as any described in his supernatural stories.

His life and his work are often confused. His tales of terror have such an impact that commentators frequently attempt to explain them away as no more than symptoms of Poe's purportedly diseased personality. However, the classic stature of the stories indicates that they are something more. Although the popular image of Poe has undeniable romantic appeal, the fact is that he was no depraved degenerate, but rather an industrious and painstaking perfectionist in his chosen field. And even his choice of morbid themes was carefully calculated. He was well aware of the current popularity of the macabre and stated his case to the publisher of the first magazine he edited, the *Southern Literary Messenger.* Celebrated stories, Poe insisted, were characterized by "the ludicrous heightened into the grotesque: the fearful coloured into the horrible: the witty exaggerated into the burlesque: the singular wrought out into the strange and mystical." The accuracy of his assumptions may be judged by the fact that under his control the magazine increased its circulation sevenfold. Later he edited *Graham's Magazine,* and it became the first mass circulation periodical in American history.

His brilliant tales include many of the finest and most frightening ever written: "The Fall of the House of Usher," "Ligeia," "The Cask of Amontillado," "William Wilson," "The Black Cat," "The Tell-Tale Heart," "The Pit and the Pendulum," "A Descent into the Maelstrom," "The Facts in the Case of M. Valdemar," and "Hop-Frog" are among the best. In theory and in practice, he defined the short story as a literary form, and every author who has subsequently worked this form owes him a debt. In a mere handful of tales, beginning with "The Murders in the Rue Morgue," he created a new genre: the detective story. And his poetry and criticism, if less popular than the stories, are of equal historical importance.

There has been endless speculation on the question of where he got his ideas. Without sinking into spurious psychoanalysis, it can be noted that Poe developed his own method for plumbing his subconscious, discussed in "Marginalia." He trained himself to slip into a state near sleep, experience a dream, and then awaken instead of passing into complete unconsciousness. The impression thus received could be remembered and transformed into a tale.

"The Masque of the Red Death," perhaps the most poetic of his stories, first appeared in *Graham's Magazine* in May 1842. Its original title, emphasizing the disguise of the antagonist rather than the protagonist's party, was "The Mask of the Red Death." Set in the distant past in a distant land, it has the remoteness and yet the relevance of the finest fables, and it symbolizes in unforgettable fashion the sinister specter that haunts every living being.

# THE MASQUE OF THE RED DEATH

# Edgar Allan Poe

The "Red Death" had long devastated the country. No pestilence had ever been so fatal, or so hideous. Blood was its Avatar and its seal—the redness and the horror of blood. There were sharp pains, and sudden dizziness, and then profuse bleeding at the pores, with dissolution. The scarlet stains upon the body and especially upon the face of the victim, were the pest ban which shut him out from the aid and from the sympathy of his fellow-men. And the whole seizure, progress and termination of the disease, were the incidents of half an hour.

But the Prince Prospero was happy and dauntless and sagacious. When his dominions were half depopulated, he summoned to his presence a thousand hale and light-hearted friends from among the knights and dames of his court, and with these retired to the deep seclusion of one of his castellated abbeys. This was an extensive and magnificent structure, the creation of the prince's own eccentric yet august taste. A strong and lofty wall girdled it in. This wall had gates of iron. The courtiers, having entered, brought furnaces and massy hammers and welded the bolts. They resolved to leave means neither of ingress or egress to the sudden impulses of despair or of frenzy from within. The abbey was amply provisioned. With such precautions the courtiers might bid defiance to contagion. The external world could take care of itself. In the meantime it was folly to grieve, or to think. The prince had provided all the appliances of pleasure. There were buffoons, there were improvisatori, there were ballet-dancers, there were musicians, there was Beauty, there was wine. All these and security were within. Without was the "Red Death."

It was toward the close of the fifth or sixth month of his seclusion, and while the pestilence raged most furiously abroad, that the Prince Prospero entertained his thousand friends at a masked ball of the most unusual magnificence.

It was a voluptuous scene, that masquerade. But first let me tell of the rooms in which it was held. There were seven—an imperial suite. In many palaces, however, such suites form a long and straight vista, while the folding doors slide back nearly to the walls on either hand, so that the view of the whole extent is scarcely impeded. Here the case was very different; as might have been expected from the duke's love of the *bizarre*. The apartments were so irregularly disposed that the vision embraced but little more than one at a time. There was a sharp turn at every twenty or thirty yards, and at each turn a novel effect. To the right and left, in the middle of each wall, a tall and narrow Gothic window looked out upon a closed corridor which pursued the windings of the suite. These windows were of stained glass whose color varied in accordance with the prevailing hue of the decorations of the chamber into which it opened. That at the eastern extremity was hung, for example, in blue—and vividly blue were its windows. The second chamber was purple in its ornaments and tapestries, and here the panes were purple. The third was green throughout, and so were the casements. The fourth was furnished and lighted with orange—the fifth with white—the sixth with violet. The seventh apartment was closely shrouded in black velvet tapestries that hung all over the ceiling and down the walls, falling in heavy folds upon a carpet of the same material and hue. But in this chamber only, the color of the windows failed to correspond with the decorations. The panes here were scarlet—a deep blood color. Now in no one of the seven apartments was there any lamp or candelabrum, amid the profusion of golden ornaments that lay scattered to and fro or depended from the roof. There was no light of any kind emanating from lamp or candle within the suite of chambers. But in the corridors that followed the suite, there stood, opposite to each window, a heavy tripod, bearing a brazier of fire that projected its rays through the tinted glass and so glaringly illumined the room. And thus were produced a multitide of gaudy and fantastic appearances. But in the western or black chamber the effect of the fire-light that streamed upon the dark hangings through the blood-tinted panes, was ghastly in the extreme, and produced so wild a look upon the countenances of those who entered, that there were few of the company bold enough to set foot within its precincts at all.

It was in this apartment, also, that there stood against the western wall, a gigantic clock of ebony. Its pendulum swung to and fro with a dull, heavy, monotonous clang; and when the minute-hand made the circuit of the face, and the hour was to be stricken, there came from the brazen lungs of the clock a sound which was clear and loud and deep and exceedingly musical, but of so peculiar a note and emphasis that, at each lapse of an hour, the musicians of the orchestra were constrained to pause, momentarily, in their performance, to hearken to the sound; and thus the waltzers perforce ceased their evolutions; and there was a brief disconcert of the whole gay company; and, while the chimes of the clock yet rang, it was observed that the giddiest grew pale, and the more aged and sedate passed their hands over their brows as if in confused reverie or meditation. But when the echoes had fully ceased, a light laughter at once pervaded the assembly; the musicians looked at each other and smiled as if at their own nervousness and folly, and made whispering vows, each to the other, that the next chiming of the clock should produce in them no similar emotion; and then, after the lapse of sixty minutes, (which embrace three thousand and six hundred seconds of the Time that flies,) there came yet another chiming of the clock, and then were the same disconcert and tremulousness and meditation as before.

But, in spite of these things, it was a gay and magnificent revel. The tastes of the duke were peculiar. He had a fine eye for colors and effects. He disregarded the *decora* of mere fashion. His plans were bold and fiery, and his conceptions glowed with barbaric lustre. There are some who would have thought him mad. His followers felt that he was not. It was necessary to hear and see and touch him to be *sure* that he was not.

He had directed, in great part, the moveable embellishments of the seven chambers, upon occasion of this great *fête;* and it was his own guiding taste which had given character to the masqueraders. Be sure they were grotesque. There were much glare and glitter and piquancy and phantasm—much of what has been since seen in *Hernani.* There were arabesque figures with unsuited limbs and appointments. There were delirious fancies such as the madman fashions. There was much of the beautiful, much of the wanton, much of the *bizarre,* something of the terrible, and not a little of that which might have excited disgust. To and fro in the seven chambers there stalked, in fact, a multitude of dreams. And these—the dreams—writhed in and about, taking hue from the rooms, and causing the wild music of the orchestra to seem as the echo of their steps. And, anon, there strikes the ebony clock which stands in the hall of the velvet. And then, for a moment, all is still, and all is silent save the voice of the clock. The dreams are stiff-frozen as they stand. But the echoes of the chime die away—they have endured but an instant—and a light, half-subdued laughter floats after them as they depart. And now again the music swells, and the dreams live, and writhe to and fro more merrily than ever, taking hue from the many-tinted windows through which stream the rays from the tripods. But to the chamber which lies most westwardly of the seven, there are now none of the maskers who venture; for the night is waning away; and there flows a ruddier light through the blood-colored panes; and the blackness of the sable drapery appals; and to him whose foot falls upon the sable carpet, there comes from the near clock of ebony a muffled peal more solemnly emphatic than any which reaches *their* ears who indulge in the more remote gaieties of the other apartments.

But these other apartments were densely crowded, and in them beat feverishly the heart of life. And the revel went whirlingly on, until at length there commenced the sounding of midnight upon the clock. And then the music ceased, as I have told; and the evolutions of the waltzers were quieted; and there was an uneasy cessation of all things as before. But now there were twelve strokes to be sounded by the bell of the clock; and thus it happened, perhaps, that more of thought crept, with more of time, into the meditations of the thoughtful among those who revelled. And thus, too, it happened, perhaps, that before the last echoes of the last chime had utterly sunk into silence, there were many individuals in the crowd who had found leisure to become aware of the presence of a masked figure which had arrested the attention of no single individual before. And the rumor of this new presence having spread itself whisperingly around, there arose at length from the whole company a buzz, or murmur, expressive of disapprobation and surprise—then, finally, of terror, of horror, and disgust.

In an assembly of phantasms such as I have painted, it may well be supposed that no ordinary appearance could have excited such sensation. In truth the masquerade license of the night was nearly unlimited; but the figure in question had out-Heroded Herod, and gone beyond the bounds of even the prince's indefinite decorum. There are chords in the hearts of the most reckless which cannot be touched without emotion. Even with the utterly lost, to whom life and death are equally jests, there are matters of which no jest can be made. The whole company, indeed, seemed now deeply to feel that in the costume and bearing of the stranger neither wit nor propriety existed. The figure was tall and gaunt, and shrouded from head to foot in the habiliments of the grave. The mask which concealed the visage was made so nearly to resemble the countenance of a stiffened corpse that the closest scrutiny must have had difficulty in detecting the cheat. And yet all this might have been endured, if not approved, by the mad revellers around. But the mummer had gone so far to assume the type of the Red Death. His vesture was dabbled in *blood*—and his broad brow, with all the features of the face, was besprinkled with the scarlet horror.

When the eyes of Prince Prospero fell upon this spectral image (which with a slow and solemn movement, as if more fully to sustain its *rôle,* stalked to and fro among the waltzers) he was seen to be convulsed, in the first moment with a strong shudder either of terror or distaste; but, in the next, his brow reddened with rage.

"Who dares?" he demanded hoarsely of the courtiers who stood near him—"who dares insult us with this blasphemous mockery? Seize him and unmask him—that we may know whom we have to hang at sunrise, from the battlements!"

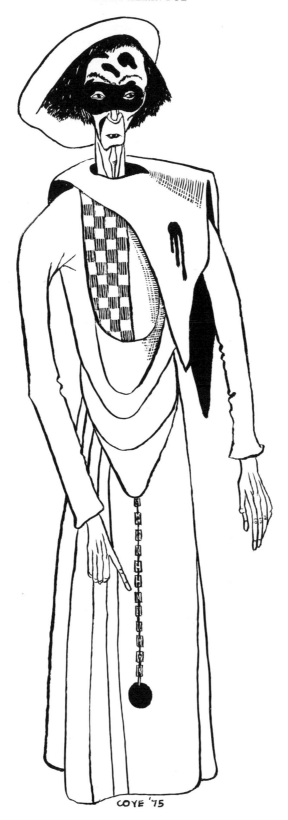

It was in the eastern or blue chamber in which stood the Prince Prospero as he uttered these words. They rang throughout the seven rooms loudly and clearly—for the prince was a bold and robust man, and the music had become hushed at the waving of his hand.

It was in the blue room where stood the prince, with a group of pale courtiers by his side. At first, as he spoke, there was a slight rushing movement of this group in the direction of the intruder, who at the moment was also near at hand, and now, with deliberate and stately step, made closer approach to the speaker. But from a certain nameless awe with which the mad assumptions of the mummer had inspired the whole party, there were found none who put forth hand to seize him; so that, unimpeded, he passed within a yard of the prince's person; and, while the vast assembly, as if with one impulse, shrank from the centres of the rooms to the walls, he made his way uninterruptedly, but with the same solemn and measured step which had distinguished him from the first, through the blue chamber to the purple—through the purple to the green—through the green to the orange—through this again to the white—and even thence to the violet, ere a decided movement had been made to arrest him. It was then, however, that the Prince Prospero, maddening with rage and the shame of his own momentary cowardice, rushed hurriedly through the six chambers, while none followed him on account of a deadly terror that had seized upon all. He bore aloft a drawn dagger, and had approached, in rapid impetuosity, to within three or four feet of the retreating figure, when the latter, having attained the extremity of the velvet apartment, turned suddenly and confronted his pursuer. There was a sharp cry—and the dagger dropped gleaming upon the sable carpet, upon which, instantly afterwards, fell prostrate in death the Prince Prospero. Then, summoning the wild courage of despair, a throng of the revellers at once threw themselves into the black apartment, and, seizing the mummer, whose tall figure stood erect and motionless within the shadow of the ebony clock, gasped in unutterable horror at finding the grave-cerements and corpse-like mask which they handled with so violent a rudeness, untenanted by any tangible form.

And now was acknowledged the presence of the Red Death. He had come like a thief in the night. And one by one dropped the revellers in the blood-bedewed halls of their revel, and died each in the despairing posture of his fall. And the life of the ebony clock went out with that of the last of the gay. And the flames of the tripods expired. And Darkness and Decay and the Red Death held illimitable dominion over all.

# Nathaniel Hawthorne

Nathaniel Hawthorne (1804–1864) is one of the great American authors and, unlike Poe, was recognized by his contemporaries. Poe himself called Hawthorne "a man of the truest genius," and Herman Melville dedicated *Moby Dick* to him, "in token of my admiration for his genius."

Such tributes, though, came after years of effort and doubt. All of Hawthorne's early short stories were published anonymously, partly because of his modesty, but also because publishers were reluctant to admit that he had written almost everything in their magazines. His two earliest tales, "The Hollow of the Three Hills" and "Alice Doan's Appeal," are both concerned with witchcraft, not too surprising a subject in view of the fact that his great-grandfather was a judge at the Salem witch trials. His first novel, the anonymously published *Fanshawe* (1828), is a Gothic piece portraying a young man obsessed with death. Hawthorne later came to despise this book, so much so that he attempted to have every copy destroyed. Yet the theme stayed with him; at his own death he left four incomplete novels, and two of them, *Septimus Felton* and *The Dolliver Romance,* deal with attempts to discover the secret of eternal life.

If none of his major novels is quite so single-mindedly sinister, a number of his shorter works dwell determinedly on death and damnation. Among the most famous of these are "Young Goodman Brown," "Rappaccini's Daughter," and that enigmatic parable "The Minister's Black Veil." Hawthorne never matches the feverish intensity of Poe; most of his tales are infused with melancholy, and they come closer to tragedy than to melodrama. His tales also show a strong tendency toward symbolism and allegory, modes that go in and out of fashion, and he has not been well served by efforts to make his most somber works a compulsory component of school studies. Still, his best work is chilling and compelling.

Hawthorne achieved recognition after a friend financed the publication of his *Twice-Told Tales* (1837), and real fame with the appearance of *The Scarlet Letter* in 1850. Previously, he had worked in several government positions, and he was later a United States consul in England, apparently a reward for writing the campaign biography of his college acquaintance President Franklin Pierce.

Hawthorne was fascinated with the authors of previous generations and had a special fondness for the Gothic novels of the eighteenth century, which had inaugurated the terror tale as a literary category. "Ethan Brand," from his 1851 collection *The Snow-Image and Other Twice-Told Tales*, is a brilliant distillation of Gothic ingredients, achieving in a few pages what had taken his predecessors volumes. His notebooks reveal that the story had been

13

in his mind for years before he composed it, and the subtitle, "A Chapter from an Abortive Romance," suggests that he had hoped to produce something more extensive. Yet nothing more is really necessary; Hawthorne's references to earlier events in the story are self-explanatory, and eliminating the details helps to prevent the extravagance and sentimentality of the eighteenth-century style. The central figure is still the same, though, a proud and tortured person possessed by the desire to defy the natural order of the universe. Such a character has origins in mythical figures like Prometheus and Faust and in more recent literary antecedents like Frankenstein and the tormented heroes of Lord Byron. The "Unpardonable Sin" that Ethan Brand seeks and finds may not be defined, but there seems little doubt that it is nothing more or less than the decision to seek out utter damnation.

# ETHAN BRAND

## Nathaniel Hawthorne

Bartram the lime-burner, a rough, heavy-looking man, begrimed with charcoal, sat watching his kiln at nightfall, while his little son played at building houses with the scattered fragments of marble, when, on the hillside below them, they heard a roar of laughter, not mirthful, but slow, and even solemn, like a wind shaking the boughs of the forest.

"Father, what is that?" asked the little boy, leaving his play, and pressing betwixt his father's knees.

"Oh, some drunken man, I suppose," answered the lime-burner, "some merry fellow from the barroom in the village, who dared not laugh loud enough within doors lest he should blow the roof of the house off. So here he is, shaking his jolly sides at the foot of Graylock."

"But, Father," said the child, more sensitive than the obtuse, middle-aged clown, "he does not laugh like a man that is glad. So the noise frightens me!"

"Don't be a fool, child!" cried his father, gruffly. "You will never make a man, I do believe; there is too much of your mother in you. I have known the rustling of a leaf startle you. Hark! Here comes the merry fellow now. You shall see that there is no harm in him."

Bartram and his little son, while they were talking thus, sat watching the same limekiln that had been the scene of Ethan Brand's solitary and meditative life, before he began his search for the Unpardonable Sin. Many years, as we have seen, had now elapsed, since that portentious night when the Idea was first developed. The kiln, however, on the mountainside, stood unimpaired, and was in nothing changed since he had thrown his dark thoughts into the intense glow of its furnace, and melted them, as it were, into the one thought that took possession of his life. It was a rude, round, tower-like structure about twenty feet high, heavily built of rough stones, and with a hillock of earth heaped about the larger part of its circumference; so that the blocks and fragments of marble might be drawn by cartloads, and thrown in at the top. There was an opening at the bottom of the tower, like an oven mouth, but large enough to admit a man in a stooping posture, and provided with a massive iron door. With the smoke and jets of flame issuing from the chinks and crevices of this door, which seemed to give admittance into the hillside, it resembled nothing so much as the private entrance to the infernal regions, which the shepherds of the Delectable Mountains were accustomed to show to pilgrims.

There are many such limekilns in that tract of country, for the purpose of burning the white marble which composes a large part of the substance of the hills. Some of them, built years ago, and long deserted, with weeds growing in the vacant round of the interior, which is open to the sky, and grass and wild flowers rooting themselves into the chinks of the stones, look already like relics of antiquity, and may yet be overspread with the lichens of centuries to come. Others, where the lime-burner still feeds his daily and nightlong fire, afford points of interest to the wanderer among the hills, who seats himself on a log of wood or a fragment of marble, to hold a chat with the solitary man. It is a lonesome, and, when the character is inclined to thought, may be an intensely thoughtful occupation; as it proved in the case of Ethan Brand, who had mused to such strange purpose, in days gone by, while the fire in this very kiln was burning.

The man who now watched the fire was of a different order, and troubled himself with no thoughts save the very few that were requisite to his business. At frequent intervals, he flung back the clashing weight of the iron door, and, turning his face from the insufferable glare, thrust in huge logs of oak, or stirred the immense brands with a long pole. Within the furnace were seen the curling and riotous flames, and the burning marble, almost molten with the intensity of heat; while without, the reflection of the fire quivered on the dark intricacy of the surrounding forest, and showed in the foreground a bright and ruddy little picture of the hut, the spring beside its door, the athletic and coal-begrimed figure of the lime-burner, and the half-frightened child, shrinking into the protection of his father's shadow. And when, again, the iron door was closed, then reappeared the tender light of the half-full moon, which vainly strove to trace out the indistinct shapes of the neighboring mountains; and, in the upper sky, there was a flitting congregation of clouds, still faintly tinged with the rosy sunset, though thus far down into the valley the sunshine had vanished long and long ago.

The little boy now crept still closer to his father, as footsteps were heard ascending the hillside, and a human form thrust aside the bushes that clustered beneath the trees.

"Halloo! who is it?" cried the lime-burner, vexed at his son's timidity, yet half infected by it. "Come forward, and show yourself, like a man, or I'll fling this chunk of marble at your head!"

"You offer me a rough welcome," said a gloomy voice, as the unknown man drew nigh. "Yet I neither claim nor desire a kinder one, even at my own fireside."

To obtain a distincter view, Bartram threw open the iron door of the kiln, whence immediately issued a gush of fierce light, that smote full upon the stranger's face and figure. To a careless eye, there appeared nothing very remarkable in his aspect, which was that of a man in a coarse, brown, country-made suit of clothes, tall and thin, with the staff and heavy shoes of a wayfarer. As he advanced, he fixed his eyes—which were very bright—intently upon the brightness of the furnace, as if he beheld, or expected to behold, some object worthy of note within it.

"Good evening, stranger," said the lime-burner. "Whence come you, so late in the day?"

"I come from my search," answered the wayfarer, "for, at last, it is finished."

"Drunk! or crazy!" muttered Bartram to himself. "I shall have trouble with the fellow. The sooner I drive him away, the better."

The little boy, all in a tremble, whispered to his father, and begged him to shut the door of the kiln, so that there might not be so much light; for that there was something in the man's face which he was afraid to look at, yet could not look away from. And, indeed, even the lime-burner's dull and torpid sense began to be impressed by an indescribable something in that thin, rugged, thoughtful visage, with the grizzled hair hanging wildly about it, and those deeply sunken eyes, which gleamed like fires within the entrance of a mysterious cavern. But, as he closed the door, the stranger turned towards him, and spoke in a quiet, familiar way that made Bartram feel as if he were a sane and sensible man, after all.

"Your task draws to an end, I see," said he. "This marble has already been burning three days. A few hours more will convert the stone to lime."

"Why, who are you?" exclaimed the lime-burner. "You seem as well acquainted with my business as I am myself."

"And well I may be," said the stranger, "for I followed the same craft many a long year, and here, too, on this very spot. But you are a newcomer in these parts. Did you never hear of Ethan Brand?"

"The man that went in search of the Unpardonable Sin?" asked Bartram, with a laugh.

"The same," answered the stranger. "He has found what he sought, and therefore he comes back again."

"What! then you are Ethan Brand himself?" cried the lime-burner, in amazement. "I am a newcomer here, as you say, and they call it eighteen years since you left the foot of Graylock. But, I can tell you, the good folks still talk about Ethan Brand, in the village yonder, and what strange errand took him away from his limekiln. Well, and so you have found the Unpardonable Sin?"

"Even so!" said the stranger, calmly.

"If the question is a fair one," proceeded Bartram, "where might it be?"

Ethan Brand laid his finger on his own heart.

"Here!" replied he.

And then, without mirth in his countenance, but as if moved by an involuntary recognition of the infinite absurdity of seeking throughout the world for what was the closest of all things to himself, and looking into every heart, save his own, for what was hidden in no other breast, he broke into a laugh of scorn. It was the same slow, heavy laugh that had almost appalled the lime-burner when it heralded the wayfarer's approach.

The solitary mountainside was made dismal by it. Laughter, when out of place, mistimed, or bursting forth from a disordered state of feeling may be the most terrible modulation of the human voice. The laughter of one asleep, even if it be a little child —the madman's laugh — the wild, screaming laugh of a born idiot—are sounds that we sometimes tremble to hear, and would always willingly forget. Poets have imagined no utterance of fiends or hobgoblins so fearfully appropriate as a laugh. And even the obtuse lime-burner felt his nerves shaken, as this strange man looked inward at his own heart, and burst into laughter that rolled away into the night, and was indistinctly reverberated among the hills.

"Joe," said he to his little son, "scamper down to the tavern in the village, and tell the jolly fellows there that Ethan Brand has come back, and that he has found the Unpardonable Sin!"

The boy darted away on his errand, to which Ethan Brand made no objection, nor seemed hardly to notice it. He sat on a log of wood, looking steadfastly at the iron door of the kiln. When the child was out of sight, and his swift and light footsteps ceased to be heard treading first on the fallen leaves and then on the rocky mountain path, the lime-burner began to regret his departure. He felt that the little fellow's presence had been a barrier between his guest and himself, and that he must now deal, heart to heart, with a man who, on his own confession, had committed the one only crime for which Heaven could afford no mercy. That crime, in its indistinct blackness, seemed to overshadow him. The lime-burner's own sins rose up within him, and made his memory riotous with a throng of evil shapes that asserted their kindred with the Master Sin, whatever it might be, which it was within the scope of man's corrupted nature to conceive and cherish. They were all of one family; they went to and fro between his breast and Ethan Brand's, and carried dark greetings from one to the other.

Then Bartram remembered the stories which had grown traditionary in reference to this strange man, who had come upon him like a shadow of the night, and was making himself at home in his old place, after so long absence that the dead people, dead and buried for years, would have had more right to be at home, in any familiar spot, than he. Ethan Brand, it was said, had conversed with Satan himself in the lurid blaze of this very kiln. The legend had been matter of mirth heretofore, but looked grisly now. According to this tale, before Ethan Brand departed on his search, he had been accustomed to evoke a fiend from the hot furnace of the limekiln, night after night, in order to confer with him about the Unpardonable Sin; the man and the fiend each laboring to frame the image of some mode of guilt which could neither be atoned for nor forgiven. And, with the first gleam of light upon the mountaintop, the fiend crept in at the iron door, there to abide the intensest element of fire until again summoned forth to share in the dreadful task of extending man's possible guilt beyond the scope of Heaven's else infinite mercy.

While the lime-burner was struggling with the horror of these thoughts, Ethan Brand rose from the log, and flung open the door of the kiln. The action was in such accordance with the idea in Bartram's mind, that he almost expected to see the Evil One issue forth, red hot, from the raging furnace.

"Hold! hold!" cried he, with a tremulous attempt to laugh; for he was ashamed of his fears, although they overmastered him. "Don't, for mercy's sake, bring out your Devil now!"

"Man!" sternly replied Ethan Brand, "what need have I of the Devil? I have left him behind me, on my track. It is with such halfway sinners as you that he busies himself. Fear not because I open the door. I do but act by old custom, and am going to trim your fire, like a lime-burner, as I was once."

He stirred the vast coals, thrust in more wood, and bent forward to gaze into the hollow prison house of the fire, regardless of the fierce glow that reddened upon his face. The lime-burner sat watching him, and half suspected this strange guest of a purpose, if not to evoke a fiend, at least to plunge bodily into the flames, and thus vanish from the sight of man. Ethan Brand, however, drew quietly back, and closed the door of the kiln.

"I have looked," said he, "into many a human heart that was seven times hotter with sinful passions than yonder furnace is with fire. But I found not there what I sought. No, not the Unpardonable Sin!"

"What is the Unpardonable Sin?" asked the lime-burner; and then he shrank farther from his companion, trembling lest his question should be answered.

"It is a sin that grew within my own breast," replied Ethan Brand, standing erect, with a pride that distinguishes all enthusiasts of his stamp. "A sin that grew nowhere else! The sin of an intellect that triumphed over the sense of brotherhood with man and reverence for God, and sacrificed everything to its own mighty claims! The only sin that deserves a recompense of immortal agony! Freely, were it to do again, would I incur the guilt. Unshrinkingly I accept the retribution!"

"The man's head is turned," muttered the lime-burner to himself. "He may be a sinner like the rest of us—nothing more likely—but, I'll be sworn, he is a madman, too."

Nevertheless, he felt uncomfortable at his situation, alone with Ethan Brand on the wild mountainside, and was right glad to hear the rough murmur of tongues, and the footsteps of what seemed a pretty numerous party, stumbling over the stones and rustling through the underbrush. Soon appeared the whole lazy regiment that was wont to infest the village tavern, comprehending three or four individuals who had drunk flip beside the barroom fire through all the winters, and smoked their pipes beneath the stoop through all the summers, since Ethan Brand's departure. Laughing boisterously, and mingling all their voices together in unceremonious talk, they now burst into the moonshine and narrow streaks of firelight that illuminated the open space before the limekiln. Bartram set the door ajar again, flooding the spot with light, that the whole company might get a fair view of Ethan Brand, and he of them.

There, among other old acquaintances, was a once ubiquitous man, now almost extinct, but whom we were formerly sure to encounter at the hotel of every thriving village throughout the country. It was the stage agent. The present specimen of the genus was a wilted and smoke-dried man, wrinkled and red-nosed, in a smartly cut, brown, bobtailed coat with brass buttons, who, for a length of time unknown, had kept his desk and corner in the barroom, and was still puffing what seemed to be the same cigar that he had lighted twenty years before. He had great fame as a dry joker, though, perhaps, less on account of any intrinsic humor than from a certain flavor of brandy toddy and tobacco smoke, which impregnated all his ideas and expressions, as well as his person. Another well remembered, though strangely altered, face was that of Lawyer Giles, as people still called him in courtesy; an elderly ragamuffin, in his soiled shirt sleeves and tow-cloth trousers. This poor fellow had been an attorney, in what he called his better days, a sharp practitioner, and in great vogue among the village litigants; but flip, and sling, and toddy, and cocktails, imbibed at all hours, morning, noon, and night, had caused him to slide from intellectual to various kinds and degrees of bodily labor, till at last, to adopt his own phrase, he slid into a soap vat. In other words, Giles was now a soap-boiler, in a small way. He had come to be but the fragment of a human being, a part of one foot having been chopped off by an ax, and an entire hand torn away by the devilish grip of a steam engine. Yet, though the corporeal hand was gone, a spiritual member remained; for, stretching forth the stump, Giles steadfastly averred that he felt an invisible thumb and fingers with as vivid a sensation as before the real ones were amputated. A maimed and miserable wretch he was; but one, nevertheless, whom the world could not trample on, and had no right to scorn, either in this or any previous stage of his misfortunes, since he had still kept up the courage and spirit of a man, asked nothing in charity, and with his one hand—and that the left one—fought a stern battle against want and hostile circumstances.

Among the throng, too, came another personage, who, with certain points of similarity to Lawyer Giles, had many more of difference. It was the village doctor; a man of some fifty years, whom, at an earlier period of his life, we introduced as paying a professional visit to Ethan Brand during the latter's supposed insanity. He was now a purple-visaged, rude, and brutal, yet half-gentlemanly figure, with something wild, ruined, and desperate in his talk, and in all the details of his gesture and manners. Brandy possessed this man like an evil spirit, and made him as surly and savage as a wild beast, and as miserable as a lost soul; but there was supposed to be in him such wonderful skill, such native gifts of healing, beyond any which medical science could impart, that society caught hold of him, and would not let him sink out of its reach. So, swaying to and fro upon his horse, and grumbling thick accents at the bedside, he visited all the sick chambers for miles about among the mountain towns, and sometimes raised a dying man, as it were, by miracle, or quite as often, no doubt, sent his patient to a grave that was dug many a year too soon. The doctor had an everlasting pipe in his mouth, and, as somebody said, in allusion to his habit of swearing, it was always alight with hell-fire.

These three worthies pressed forward, and greeted Ethan Brand each after his own fashion, earnestly inviting him to partake of the contents of a certain black bottle, in which, as they averred, he would find something far better worth seeking for than the Unpardonable

Sin. No mind, which has wrought itself by intense and solitary meditation into a high state of enthusiasm, can endure the kind of contact with low and vulgar modes of thought and feeling to which Ethan Brand was now subjected. It made him doubt—and, strange to say, it was a painful doubt—whether he had indeed found the Unpardonable Sin, and found it within himself. The whole question on which he had exhausted life, and more than life, looked like a delusion.

"Leave me," he said bitterly, "ye brute beasts, that have made yourselves so, shriveling up your souls with fiery liquors! I have done with you. Years and years ago, I groped into your hearts and found nothing there for my purpose. Get ye gone!"

"Why, you uncivil scoundrel," cried the fierce doctor, "is that the way you respond to the kindness of your best friends? Then let me tell you the truth. You have no more found the Unpardonable Sin than yonder boy Joe has. You are but a crazy fellow—I told you so twenty years ago—neither better nor worse than a crazy fellow, and the fit companion of old Humphrey, here!"

He pointed to an old man, shabbily dressed, with long white hair, thin visage, and unsteady eyes. For some years past, this aged person had been wandering about among the hills, inquiring of all travelers whom he met for his daughter. The girl, it seemed, had gone off with a company of circus performers, and occasionally tidings of her came to the village, and fine stories were told of her glittering appearance as she rode on horseback in the ring, or performed marvelous feats on the tightrope.

The white-haired father now approached Ethan Brand, and gazed unsteadily into his face.

"They tell me you have been all over the earth," said he, wringing his hands with earnestness. "You must have seen my daughter, for she makes a grand figure in the world, and everybody goes to see her. Did she send any word to her old father, or say when she was coming back?"

Ethan Brand's eye quailed beneath the old man's. That daughter, from whom he so earnestly desired a word of greeting, was the Esther of our tale, the very girl whom, with such cold and remorseless purpose, Ethan Brand had made the subject of a psychological experiment, and wasted, absorbed, and perhaps annihilated her soul, in the process.

"Yes," murmured he, turning away from the hoary wanderer, "it is no delusion. There is an Unpardonable Sin!"

While these things were passing, a merry scene was going forward in the area of cheerful light, beside the spring and before the door of the hut. A number of the youth of the village, young men and girls, had hurried up the hillside, impelled by curiosity to see Ethan Brand, the hero of so many a legend familiar to their childhood. Finding nothing, however, very remarkable in his aspect—nothing but a sunburnt wayfarer, in plain garb and dusty shoes, who sat looking into the fire as if he fancied pictures among the coals—these young people speedily grew tired of observing him. As it happened, there was other amusement at hand. An old German Jew traveling with a diorama on his back was passing down the mountain road towards the village just as the party turned aside from it, and, in hopes of eking out the profits of the day, the showman had kept them company to the limekiln.

"Come, old Dutchman," cried one of the young men, "let us see your pictures, if you can swear they are worth looking at!"

"Oh, yes, Captain," answered the Jew—whether as a matter of courtesy or craft, he styled everybody Captain—"I shall show you, indeed, some very superb pictures!"

So, placing his box in a proper position, he invited the young men and girls to look through the glass orifices of the machine, and proceeded to exhibit a series of the most outrageous scratchings and daubings, as specimens of the fine arts, that ever an itinerant showman had the face to impose upon his circle of spectators. The pictures were worn out, moreover, tattered, full of cracks and wrinkles, dingy with tobacco smoke, and otherwise in a most pitiable condition. Some purported to be cities, public edifices, and ruined castles in Europe; others represented Napoleon's battles and Nelson's sea fights; and in the midst of these would be seen a gigantic, brown, hairy hand—which might have been mistaken for the Hand of Destiny, though, in truth, it was only the showman's—pointing its forefinger to various scenes of the conflict, while its owner gave historical illustrations. When, with much merriment at its abominable deficiency of merit, the exhibition was concluded, the German bade little Joe put his head into the box. Viewed through the magnifying glasses, the boy's round, rosy visage assumed the strangest imaginable aspect of an immense Titanic child, the mouth grinning broadly, and the eyes and every other feature overflowing with fun at the joke. Suddenly, however, that merry face turned pale, and its expression changed to horror, for this easily impressed and excitable child had become sensible that the eye of Ethan Brand was fixed upon him through the glass.

"You make the little man to be afraid, Captain," said the German Jew, turning up the dark and strong outline of his visage from his stooping posture. "But look again, and, by chance, I shall cause you to see somewhat that is very fine, upon my word!"

Ethan Brand gazed into the box for an instant, and then, starting back, looked fixedly at the German. What had he seen? Nothing, apparently; for a curious youth, who had peeped in almost at the same moment, beheld only a vacant space of canvas.

"I remember you now," muttered Ethan Brand to the showman.

"Ah, Captain," whispered the Jew of Nuremberg, with a dark smile, "I find it to be a heavy matter in my show box, this Unpardonable Sin! By my faith, Captain, it has wearied my shoulder, this long day, to carry it over the mountain."

"Peace," answered Ethan Brand, sternly, "or get thee into the furnace yonder!"

The Jew's exhibition had scarcely concluded, when a great, elderly dog—who seemed to be his own master, as no person in the company laid claim to him—saw fit to render himself the object of public notice. Hitherto, he had shown himself a very quiet, well-disposed old dog, going round from one to another, and, by way of being sociable, offering his rough head to be patted by any kindly hand that would take so much trouble. But now, all of a sudden, this grave and venerable quadruped, of his own mere motion, and without the slightest suggestion from anybody else, began to run round after his tail, which, to heighten the absurdity of the proceeding, was a great deal shorter than it should have been. Never was seen such headlong eagerness in pursuit of an object that could not possibly be attained; never was heard such a tremendous outbreak of growling, snarling, barking, and snapping—as if one end of the ridiculous brute's body were at deadly and most unforgivable enmity with the other. Faster and faster, round about went the cur; and faster and still faster fled the unapproachable brevity of his tail; and louder and fiercer grew his yells of rage and animosity; until, utterly exhausted, and as far from the goal as ever, the foolish old dog ceased his performance as suddenly as he had begun it. The next moment, he was as mild, quiet, sensible, and respectable in his deportment as when he first scraped acquaintance with the company.

As may be supposed, the exhibition was greeted with universal laughter, clapping of hands, and shouts of encore, to which the canine performer responded by wagging all that there was to wag of his tail, but appeared totally unable to repeat his very successful effort to amuse the spectators.

Meanwhile, Ethan Brand had resumed his seat upon the log, and moved, it might be, by a perception of some remote analogy between his own case and that of this self-pursuing cur, he broke into the awful laugh which, more than any other token, expressed the condition of his inward being. From that moment, the merriment of the party was at an end; they stood

aghast, dreading lest the inauspicious sound should be reverberated around the horizon, and that mountain would thunder it to mountain, and so the horror be prolonged upon their ears. Then, whispering one to another that it was late—that the moon was almost down—that the August night was growing chill—they hurried homewards, leaving the lime-burner and little Joe to deal as they might with their unwelcome guest. Save for these three human beings, the open space on the hillside was a solitude, set in a vast gloom of forest. Beyond that darksome verge, the firelight glimmered on the stately trunks and almost black foliage of pines, intermixed with the lighter verdure of sapling oaks, maples, and poplars, while here and there lay the gigantic corpses of dead trees, decaying on the leaf-strewn soil. And it seemed to little Joe—a timorous and imaginative child—that the silent forest was holding its breath until some fearful thing should happen.

Ethan Brand thrust more wood into the fire, and closed the door of the kiln; then, looking over his shoulder at the lime-burner and his son, he bade rather than advised them to retire to rest.

"For myself, I cannot sleep," said he. "I have matters that it concerns me to meditate upon. I will watch the fire, as I used to do in the old time."

"And call the Devil out of the furnace to keep you company, I suppose," muttered Bartram, who had been making intimate acquaintance with the black bottle above mentioned. "But watch, if you like, and call as many devils as you like! For my part, I shall be all the better for a snooze. Come, Joe!"

As the boy followed his father into the hut, he looked back at the wayfarer, and the tears came into his eyes, for his tender spirit had an intuition of the bleak and terrible loneliness in which this man had enveloped himself.

When they had gone, Ethan Brand sat listening to the crackling of the kindled wood, and looking at the little spirits of fire that issued through the chinks of the door. These trifles, however, once so familiar, had but the slightest hold of his attention, while deep within his mind he was reviewing the gradual but marvelous change that had been wrought upon him by the search to which he had devoted himself. He remembered how the night dew had fallen upon him—how the dark forest had whispered to him—how the stars had gleamed upon him—a simple and loving man, watching his fire in the years gone by, and ever musing as it burned. He remembered with what tenderness, with what love and sympathy for mankind, and what pity for human guilt and woe, he had first begun to contemplate those ideas which afterwards became the inspiration of his life; with what reverence he had then looked into the heart of man, viewing it as a temple originally divine, and, however desecrated, still to be held sacred by a brother; with what awful fear he had deprecated the success of his pursuit, and prayed that the Unpardonable Sin might never be revealed to him. Then ensued that vast intellectual development, which, in its progress, disturbed the counterpoise between his mind and heart. The Idea that possessed his life had operated as a means of education; it had gone on cultivating his powers to the highest point of which they were susceptible; it had raised him from the level of an unlettered laborer to stand on a starlit eminence, whither the philosophers of the earth, laden with the lore of universities, might vainly strive to clamber after him. So much for the intellect! But where was the heart? That, indeed, had withered— had contracted—had hardened—had perished! It had ceased to partake of the universal throb. He had lost his hold of the magnetic chain of humanity. He was no longer a brother man, opening the chambers or the dungeons of our common nature by the key of holy sympathy, which give him a right to share in all its secrets: he was now a cold observer, looking on mankind as the subject of his experiment, and, at length, converting man and woman to be his puppets, and pulling the wires that moved them to such degrees of crime as were demanded for his study.

Thus Ethan Brand became a fiend. He began to be so from the moment that his moral nature had ceased to keep the pace of improvement with his intellect. And now, as his highest effort and inevitable development—as the bright and gorgeous flower, and rich, delicious fruit of his life's labor—he had produced the Unpardonable Sin!

"What more have I to seek? what more to achieve?" said Ethan Brand to himself. "My task is done, and well done!"

Starting from the log with a certain alacrity in his gait and ascending the hillock of earth that was raised against the stone circumference of the limekiln, he thus reached the top of the structure. It was a space of perhaps ten feet across, from edge to edge, presenting a view of the upper surface of the immense mass of broken marble with which the kiln was heaped. All these innumerable blocks and fragments of marble were red hot and vividly on fire, sending up great spouts of blue flame, which quivered aloft and danced madly, as within a magic circle, and sank and rose again, with continual and multitudinous activity. As the lonely man bent forward over this terrible body of fire, the blasting heat smote up against his person with a breath that, it might be supposed, would have scorched and shriveled him up in a moment.

Ethan Brand stood erect, and raised his arms on high. The blue flames played upon his face, and imparted the wild and ghastly light which alone could have suited its expression; it was that of a fiend on the verge of plunging into his gulf of intensest torment.

"O Mother Earth," cried he, "who art no more my mother, and into whose bosom this frame shall never be resolved! O mankind, whose brotherhood I have cast off, and trampled thy great heart beneath my feet! O stars of heaven, that shone on me of old, as if to light me onward and upward! Farewell all, and forever. Come, deadly element of Fire, henceforth my familiar friend! Embrace me, as I do thee!"

That night the sound of a fearful peal of laughter rolled heavily through the sleep of the lime-burner and his little son; dim shapes of horror and anguish haunted their dreams, and seemed still present in the rude hovel when they opened their eyes to the daylight.

"Up, boy, up!" cried the lime-burner, staring about him. "Thank Heaven, the night is gone, at last; and rather than pass such another, I would watch my limekiln, wide awake, for a twelvemonth. This Ethan Brand, with his humbug of an Unpardonable Sin, has done me no such mighty favor, in taking my place!"

He issued from the hut, followed by little Joe, who kept fast hold of his father's hand. The early sunshine was already pouring its gold upon the mountaintops, and though the valleys were still in shadow, they smiled cheerfully in the promise of the bright day that was hastening onward. The village, completely shut in by hills, which swelled away gently about it, looked as if it had rested peacefully in the hollow of the great hand of Providence. Every dwelling was distinctly visible; the little spires of the two churches pointed upwards, and caught a fore-glimmering of brightness from the sun-gilt skies upon their gilded weathercocks. The tavern was astir, and the figure of the old, smoke-dried stage agent, cigar in mouth, was seen beneath the stoop. Old Graylock was glorified with a golden cloud upon his head. Scattered likewise over the breasts of the surrounding mountains, there were heaps of hoary mist, in fantastic shapes, some of them far down into the valley, others high up towards the summits, and still others, of the same family of mist or cloud, hovering in the gold radiance of the upper atmosphere. Stepping from one to another of the clouds that rested on the hills, and thence to the loftier brotherhood that sailed in air, it seemed almost as if a mortal man might thus ascend into the heavenly regions. Earth was so mingled with sky that it was a daydream to look at it.

To supply that charm of the familiar and homely, which Nature so readily adopts into a scene like this, the stagecoach was rattling down the mountain road, and the driver sounded his horn, while Echo caught up the notes, and intertwined them into a rich and varied and elaborate harmony, of which the original performer could lay claim to little share. The great hills played a concert among themselves, each contributing a strain of airy sweetness.

Little Joe's face brightened at once.

"Dear Father," cried he, skipping cheerily to and fro, "that strange man is gone, and the sky and the mountains all seem glad of it!"

"Yes," growled the lime-burner, with an oath, "but he has let the fire go down, and no thanks to him if five hundred bushels of lime are not spoiled. If I catch the fellow hereabouts again, I shall feel like tossing him into the furnace!"

With his long pole in his hand, he ascended to the top of the kiln. After a moment's pause, he called to his son.

"Come up here, Joe!" said he.

So little Joe ran up the hillock, and stood by his father's side. The marble was all burnt into perfect, snow-white lime. But on its surface, in the midst of the circle—snow white, too, and thoroughly converted into lime—lay a human skeleton, in the attitude of a person who, after long toil, lies down to long repose. Within the ribs—strange to say—was the shape of a human heart.

"Was the fellow's heart made of marble?" cried Bartram, in some perplexity at this phenomenon. "At any rate, it is burnt into what looks like special good lime; and, taking all the bones together, my kiln is half a bushel the richer for him."

So saying, the rude lime-burner lifted his pole, and, letting it fall upon the skeleton, the relics of Ethan Brand were crumbled into fragments.

# J. Sheridan Le Fanu

Joseph Sheridan Le Fanu (1814–1873), one of the nineteenth century's most important authors of mystery and the supernatural, was known to his contemporaries as "The Invisible Prince." He wrote over a dozen novels and a number of short stories that make him a pivotal figure in the transition between the old-fashioned Gothic novel and the modern terror tale.

The Irish writer was trained as a lawyer, but he was more interested in writing and in time became the editor and publisher of several periodicals, notably the *Dublin University Magazine.* Among his best novels are *The House by the Churchyard* (1863) and *Uncle Silas* (1864), often described as the finest mystery novel of the nineteenth century, although many critics prefer *The Moonstone* by Wilkie Collins.

Le Fanu's influence on later British writers is incalculable. Literary historians have concluded that the stories posthumously collected in *The Purcell Papers* (1880) helped to inspire the plots of both Charlotte Brontë's *Jane Eyre* and Emily Brontë's *Wuthering Heights.* And Le Fanu appears to have had a profound effect on his more famous colleague and compatriot Bram Stoker. Le Fanu's fine vampire tale "Carmilla" was one of the sources for *Dracula,* a point made clear by certain details in the excised first chapter of Stoker's novel, which was later reprinted as a short story called "Dracula's Guest." Also, Stoker's popular tale "The Judge's House" bears a marked resemblance to Le Fanu's earlier "An Account of Some Strange Disturbances in Aungier Street," which also concerns a student in a house haunted by a rat and the spirit of a malevolent magistrate.

Le Fanu's collection *In a Glass Darkly* (1872) presented the character Dr. Hesselius, the prototype for the popular figure of the occult detective. One of these stories, "Green Tea," seems to have inaugurated the tradition of a protagonist using drugs as a method for experiencing supernatural manifestations. Le Fanu's general sense of style and structure influenced any number of later writers, notably M. R. James and W. F. Harvey. He also contributed to the idea that writers of weird fiction lead weird lives. Much of his work was composed by candlelight after midnight, when, waking in the small hours of the morning, Le Fanu sat up in bed imagining horrors and putting them down on paper.

Le Fanu's better tales include "Schalken the Painter," "Dickon the Devil," "Madam Crowl's Ghost," "The Haunted Baronet," and "Wicked Captain Walshawe, of Wauling." One of the very best, equal to the more celebrated "Carmilla" and "Green Tea," is "Squire Toby's Will," rescued from obscurity and reprinted in 1923 through the researches of M. R. James. "Squire Toby's Will" is a remarkable ghost story, one of the most inventive variations on the theme of a spirit seeking revenge. It is all the more frightening because the protagonist's crime is considerably smaller than the usual one of murder, yet he is haunted without mercy and with a multiplicity of methods that provides ample proof of Le Fanu's ingenuity and intensity.

# SQUIRE TOBY'S WILL

## J. Sheridan Le Fanu

Many persons accustomed to travel the old York and London road, in the days of stage-coaches, will remember passing, in the afternoon, say, of an autumn day, in their journey to the capital, about three miles south of the town of Applebury, and a mile and a half before you reach the Old Angel Inn, a large black-and-white house, as those old-fashioned cage-work habitations are termed, dilapidated and weather-stained, with broad lattice windows glimmering all over in the evening sun with little diamond panes, and thrown into relief by a dense background of ancient elms. A wide avenue, now overgrown like a churchyard with grass and weeds, and flanked by double rows of the same dark trees, old and gigantic, with here and there a gap in their solemn files, and sometimes a fallen tree lying across on the avenue, leads up to the halldoor.

Looking up its sombre and lifeless avenue from the top of the London coach, as I have often done, you are struck with so many signs of desertion and decay,—the tufted grass sprouting in the chinks of the steps and window-stones, the smokeless chimneys over which the jackdaws are wheeling, the absence of human life and all its evidence, that you conclude at once that the place is uninhabited and abandoned to decay. The name of this ancient house is Gylingden Hall. Tall hedges and old timber quickly shroud the old place from view, and about a quarter of a mile further on you pass, embowered in melancholy trees, a small and ruinous Saxon chapel, which, time out of mind, has been the burying-place of the family of Marston, and partakes of the neglect and desolation which brood over their ancient dwelling-place.

The grand melancholy of the secluded valley of Gylingden, lonely as an enchanted forest, in which the crows returning to their roosts among the trees, and the straggling deer who peep from beneath their branches, seem to hold a wild and undisturbed dominion, heightens the forlorn aspect of Gylingden Hall.

Of late years repairs have been neglected, and here and there the roof is stripped, and "the stitch in time" has been wanting. At the side of the house exposed to the gales that sweep through the valley like a torrent through its channel, there is not a perfect window left, and the shutters but imperfectly exclude the rain. The ceilings and walls are mildewed and green with damp stains. Here and there, where the drip falls from the ceiling, the floors are rotting. On stormy nights, as the guard described, you can hear the doors clapping in the old house, as far away as old Gryston bridge, and the howl and sobbing of the wind through its empty galleries.

About seventy years ago died the old Squire, Toby Marston, famous in that part of the world for his hounds, his hospitality, and his vices. He had done kind things, and he had fought duels: he had given away money and he had horse-whipped people. He carried with him some blessings and a good many curses, and left behind him an amount of debts and charges upon the estates which appalled his two sons, who had no taste for business or accounts, and had never suspected, till that wicked, openhanded, and swearing old gentleman died, how very nearly he had run the estates into insolvency.

They met at Gylingden Hall. They had the will before them, and lawyers to interpret, and information without stint, as to the encumbrances with which the deceased had saddled them. The will was so framed as to set the two brothers instantly at deadly feud.

These brothers differed in some points; but in one material characteristic they resembled one another, and also their departed father. They never went into a quarrel by halves, and once in, they did not stick at trifles.

The elder, Scroope Marston, the more dangerous man of the two, had never been a favourite of the old Squire. He had no taste for the sports of the field and the pleasures of a rustic life. He was no athlete, and he certainly was not handsome. All this the Squire resented. The young man, who had no respect for him, and outgrew his fear of his violence as he came to manhood, retorted. This aversion, therefore, in the ill-conditioned old man grew into positive hatred. He used to wish that d——d pippin-squeezing, humpbacked rascal Scroope, out of the way of better men—meaning his younger son Charles; and in his cups would talk in a way which even the old and young fellows who followed his hounds, and drank his port, and could stand a reasonable amount of brutality, did not like.

Scroope Marston was slightly deformed, and he had the lean sallow face, piercing black eyes, and black lank hair, which sometimes accompany deformity.

"I'm no feyther o' that hog-backed creature. I'm no sire of hisn, d——n him! I'd as soon call that tongs son o' mine," the old man used to bawl, in allusion to his son's long, lank limbs: "Charlie's a man, but that's a jack-an-ape. He has no good-nature; there's nothing handy, nor manly, nor no one turn of a Marston in him."

And when he was pretty drunk, the old Squire used to swear he should never "sit at the head o' that board; nor frighten away folk from Gylingden Hall wi' his d——d hatchet face—the black loon!"

"Handsome Charlie was the man for his money. He knew what a horse was, and could sit tó his bottle; and the lasses were all clean *wad* about him. He was a Marston every inch of his six foot two."

Handsome Charlie and he, however, had also had a row or two. The old Squire was free with his horsewhip as with his tongue, and on occasion when neither weapon was quite practicable, had been known to give a fellow "a tap o' his knuckles." Handsome Charlie, however, thought there was a period at which personal chastisement should cease; and one night, when the port was flowing, there was some allusion to Marion Hayward, the miller's daughter, which for some reason the old gentleman did not like. Being "in liquor," and having clearer ideas about pugilism than self-government, he struck out, to the surprise of all present, at Handsome Charlie. The youth threw back his head scientifically, and nothing followed but the crash of a decanter on the floor. But the old Squire's blood was up, and he bounced from his chair. Up jumped Handsome Charlie, resolved to stand no nonsense. Drunken Squire Lilbourne, intending to mediate, fell flat on the floor, and cut his ear among the glasses. Handsome Charlie caught the thump which the old Squire discharged at him upon his open hand, and catching him by the cravat, swung him with his back to the wall. They said the old man never looked so purple, nor his eyes so goggle before; and then Handsome Charlie pinioned him tight to the wall by both arms.

"Well, I say—come, don't you talk no more nonsense o' that sort, and I won't lick you," croaked the old Squire. "You stopped that un clever, you did. Didn't he? Come, Charlie, man, gie us your hand, I say, and sit down again, lad." And so the battle ended; and I believe it was the last time the Squire raised his hand to Handsome Charlie.

But those days were over. Old Toby Marston lay cold and quiet enough now, under the drip of the mighty ash-tree within the Saxon ruin where so many of the old Marston race returned to dust, and were forgotten. The weather-stained top-boots and leather-breeches, the three-cornered cocked hat to which old gentlemen of that day still clung, and the well-known red waistcoat that reached below his hips, and the fierce pug face of the old Squire, were now but a picture of memory. And the brothers between whom he had planted an ir-reconcilable quarrel, were now in their new mourning suits, with the gloss still on, debating furiously across the table in the great oak parlour, which had so often resounded to the banter and coarse songs, the oaths and laughter of the congenial neighbours whom the old Squire of Gylingden Hall loved to assemble there.

These young gentlemen, who had grown up in Gylingden Hall, were not accustomed to bridle their tongues, nor, if need be, to hesitate about a blow. Neither had been at the old man's funeral. His death had been sudden. Having been helped to his bed in that hilarious and quarrelsome state which was induced by port and punch, he was found dead in the morning,—his head hanging over the side of the bed, and his face very black and swollen.

Now the Squire's will despoiled his eldest son of Gylingden, which had descended to the heir time out of mind. Scroope Marston was furious. His deep stern voice was heard inveigh-ing against his dead father and living brother, and the heavy thumps on the table with which he enforced his stormy recriminations resounded through the large chamber. Then broke in Charlie's rougher voice, and then came a quick alternation of short sentences, and then both voices together in growing loudness and anger, and at last, swelling the tumult, the expostu-lations of pacific and frightened lawyers, and at last a sudden break up of the conference. Scroope broke out of the room, his pale furious face showing whiter against his long black hair, his dark fierce eyes blazing, his hands clenched, and looking more ungainly and de-formed than ever in the convulsions of his fury.

Very violent words must have passed between them; for Charlie, though he was the win-ning man, was almost as angry as Scroope. The elder brother was for holding possession of the house, and putting his rival to legal process to oust him. But his legal advisers were clearly against it. So, with a heart boiling over with gall, up he went to London, and found the firm who had managed his father's business fair and communicative enough. They looked into the settlements, and found that Gylingden was excepted. It was very odd, but so it was, specially excepted; so that the right of the old Squire to deal with it by his will could not be questioned.

Notwithstanding all this, Scroope, breathing vengeance and aggression, and quite willing to wreck himself provided he could run his brother down, assailed Handsome Charlie, and battered old Squire Toby's will in the Prerogative Court and also at common law, and the feud between the brothers was knit, and every month their exasperation was heightened.

Scroope was beaten, and defeat did not soften him. Charlie might have forgiven hard words; but he had been himself worsted during the long campaign in some of those skir-mishes, special motions, and so forth, that constitute the episodes of a legal epic like that in which the Marston brothers figured as opposing combatants; and the blight of the law-costs had touched him, too, with the usual effect upon the temper of a man of embarrassed means.

Years flew, and brought no healing on their wings. On the contrary, the deep corrosion of this hatred bit deeper by time. Neither brother married. But an accident of a different kind befell the younger, Charles Marston, which abridged his enjoyments very materially.

This was a bad fall from his hunter. There were severe fractures, and there was concussion of the brain. For some time it was thought that he could not recover. He disappointed these evil auguries, however. He did recover, but changed in two essential particulars. He had received an injury to his hip, which doomed him never more to sit in the saddle. And the rollicking animal spirits which hitherto had never failed him, had now taken flight forever.

He had been for five days in a state of coma—absolute insensibility—and when he recovered consciousness he was haunted by an indescribable anxiety.

Tom Cooper, who had been butler in the palmy days of Gylingden Hall, under old Squire Toby, still maintained his post with old-fashioned fidelity, in these days of faded splendour and frugal housekeeping. Twenty years had passed since the death of his old master. He had grown lean, and stooped, and his face, dark with the peculiar brown of age, furrowed and gnarled, and his temper, except with his master, had waxed surly.

His master had visited Bath and Buxton, and came back, as he went, lame, and halting gloomily about with the aid of a stick. When the hunter was sold, the last tradition of the old life at Gylingden disappeared. The young Squire, as he was still called, excluded by his mischance from the hunting-field, dropped into a solitary way of life, and halted slowly and solitarily about the old place, seldom raising his eyes, and with an appearance of indescribable gloom.

Old Cooper could talk freely on occasion with his master; and one day he said, as he handed him his hat and stick in the hall:

"You should rouse yourself up a bit, Master Charles!"

"It's past rousing with me, old Cooper."

"It's just this, I'm thinking: there's something on your mind, and you won't tell no one. There's no good keeping it on your stomach. You'll be a deal lighter if you tell it. Come, now, what is it, Master Charlie?"

The Squire looked with his round grey eyes straight into Cooper's eyes. He felt that there was a sort of spell broken. It was like the old rule of the ghost who can't speak till it is spoken to. He looked earnestly into old Cooper's face for some seconds, and sighed deeply.

"It ain't the first good guess you've made in your day, old Cooper, and I'm glad you've spoke. It's bin on my mind, sure enough, ever since I had that fall. Come in here after me, and shut the door."

The Squire pushed open the door of the oak parlour, and looked round on the pictures abstractedly. He had not been there for some time, and seating himself on the table, he looked again for a while in Cooper's face before he spoke.

"It's not a great deal, Cooper, but it troubles me, and I would not tell it to the parson nor the doctor; for, God knows what they'd say, though there's nothing to signify in it. But you were always true to the family, and I don't mind if I tell you."

"'Tis as safe with Cooper, Master Charles, as if 'twas locked in a chest, and sunk in a well."

"It's only this," said Charles Marston, looking down on the end of his stick, with which he was tracing lines and circles, "all the time I was lying like dead, as you thought, after that fall, I was with the old master." He raised his eyes to Cooper's again as he spoke, and with an awful oath he repeated—"I was with him, Cooper!"

"He was a good man, sir, in his way," repeated old Cooper, returning his gaze with awe. "He was a good master to me, and a good father to you, and I hope he's happy. May God rest him!"

"Well," said Squire Charles, "it's only this: the whole of that time I was with him, or he was with me—I don't know which. The upshot is, we were together, and I thought I'd never get out of his hands again, and all the time he was bullying me about some one thing; and if it was to save my life, Tom Cooper, by——from the time I waked I never could call to mind what it was; and I think I'd give that hand to know; and if you can think of anything it might be—for God's sake! don't be afraid, Tom Cooper, but speak it out, for he threatened me hard, and it was surely him."

Here ensued a silence.

"And what did you think it might be yourself, Master Charles?" said Cooper.

"I han't thought of aught that's likely. I'll never hit on't—*never*. I thought it might happen he knew something about that d——hump-backed villain, Scroope, that swore before Lawyer Gingham I made away with a paper of settlements—me and father; and, as I hope to be saved, Tom Cooper, there never was a bigger lie! I'd a had the law of him for them identical words, and cast him for more than he's worth; only Lawyer Gingham never goes into nothing for me since money grew scarce in Gylingden; and I can't change my lawyer, I owe him such a hatful of money. But he did, he swore he'd hang me yet for it. He said it in them identical words—he'd never rest till he *hanged* me for it, and I think it was, like enough, something about *that,* the old master was troubled; but it's enough to drive a man mad. I *can't* bring it to mind—I can't remember a word he said, only he threatened awful, and looked—Lord 'a mercy on us!—frightful bad."

"There's no need he should. May the Lord a-mercy on him!" said the old butler.

"No, of course; and you're not to tell a soul, Cooper—not a living soul, mind, that I said he looked bad, nor nothing about it."

"God forbid!" said old Cooper, shaking his head. "But I was thinking, sir, it might ha' been about the slight that's bin so long put on him by having no stone over him, and never a scratch o' a chisel to say who he is."

"Ay! Well, I didn't think o' that. Put on your hat, old Cooper, and come down wi' me; for I'll look after that, at any rate."

There is a bye-path leading by a turnstile to the park, and thence to the picturesque old burying-place, which lies in a nook by the roadside, embowered in ancient trees. It was a fine autumnal sunset, and melancholy lights and long shadows spread their peculiar effects over the landscape as "Handsome Charlie" and the old butler made their way slowly toward the place where Handsome Charlie was himself to lie at last.

"Which of the dogs made that howling all last night?" asked the Squire, when they had got on a little way.

" 'Twas a strange dog, Master Charlie, in front of the house; ours was all in the yard—a white dog wi' a black head, he looked to be, and he was smelling round them mounting-steps the old master, God be wi' him! set up, the time his knee was bad. When the tyke got up a' top of them, howlin' up at the windows, I'd a liked to shy something at him."

"Hullo! Is that like him?" said the Squire, stopping short, and pointing with his stick at a dirty-white dog, with a large black head, which was scampering round them in a wide circle, half crouching with that air of uncertainty and deprecation which dogs so well know how to assume.

He whistled the dog up. He was a large, half-starved bull-dog.

"That fellow has made a long journey—thin as a whipping-post, and stained all over, and his claws worn to the stumps," said the Squire, musingly. "He isn't a bad dog, Cooper. My father liked a good bull-dog, and knew a cur from a good 'un."

The dog was looking up into the Squire's face with the peculiar grim visage of his kind, and the Squire was thinking irreverently how strong a likeness it presented to the character of his father's fierce pug features when he was clutching his horsewhip and swearing at a keeper.

"If I did right I'd shoot him. He'll worry the cattle, and kill our dogs," said the Squire. "Hey, Cooper? I'll tell the keeper to look after him. That fellow could pull down a sheep, and he shan't live on my mutton."

But the dog was not to be shaken off. He looked wistfully after the Squire, and after they had got a little way on, he followed timidly.

It was vain trying to drive him off. The dog ran round them in wide circles, like the infernal dog in "Faust"; only he left no track of thin flame behind him. These manoeuvres were executed with a sort of beseeching air, which flattered and touched the object of this odd preference. So he called him up again, patted him, and then and there in a manner adopted him.

The dog now followed their steps dutifully, as if he had belonged to Handsome Charlie all his days. Cooper unlocked the little iron door, and the dog walked in close behind their heels, and followed them as they visited the roofless chapel.

The Marstons were lying under the floor of this little building in rows. There is not a vault. Each has his distinct grave enclosed in a lining of masonry. Each is surmounted by a stone kist, on the upper flag of which is enclosed his epitaph, except that of poor old Squire Toby. Over him was nothing but the grass and the line of masonry which indicate the site of the kist, whenever his family should afford him one like the rest.

"Well, it does look shabby. It's the elder brother's business; but if he won't, I'll see to it myself, and I'll take care, old boy, to cut sharp and deep in it, that the elder son having refused to lend a hand the stone was put there by the younger."

They strolled round this little burial ground. The sun was now below the horizon, and the red metallic glow from the clouds, still illuminated by the departed sun, mingled luridity with the twilight. When Charlie peeped again into the little chapel, he saw the ugly dog stretched upon Squire Toby's grave, looking at least twice his natural length, and performing such antics as made the young Squire stare. If you have ever seen a cat stretched on the floor, with a bunch of Valerian, straining, writhing, rubbing its jaws in long-drawn caresses, and in the absorption of a sensual ecstasy, you have seen a phenomenon resembling that which Handsome Charlie witnessed on looking in.

The head of the brute looked so large, its body long and thin, and its joints so ungainly and dislocated, that the Squire, with old Cooper beside him, looked on with a feeling of disgust and astonishment, which, in a moment or two more, brought the Squire's stick down upon him with a couple of heavy thumps. The beast awakened from his ecstasy, sprang to the head of the grave, and there on a sudden, thick and bandy as before, confronted the Squire, who stood at its foot, with a terrible grin, and eyes that glared with the peculiar green of canine fury.

The next moment the dog was crouching abjectly at the Squire's feet.

"Well, he's a rum 'un!" said old Cooper, looking hard at him.

"I like him," said the Squire.

"I don't," said Cooper.

"But he shan't come in here again," said the Squire.

"I shouldn't wonder if he was a witch," said old Cooper, who remembered more tales of witchcraft than are now current in that part of the world.

"He's a good dog," said the Squire, dreamily. "I remember the time I'd a given a handful for him—but I'll never be good for nothing again. Come along."

And he stooped down and patted him. So up jumped the dog and looked up in his face, as if watching for some sign, ever so slight, which he might obey.

Cooper did not like a bone under that dog's skin. He could not imagine what his master saw to admire in him. He kept him all night in the gun-room, and the dog accompanied him in his halting rambles about the place. The fonder his master grew of him, the less did Cooper and the other servants like him.

"He hasn't a point of a good dog about him," Cooper would growl. "I think Master

Charlie be blind. And old Captain (an old red parrot, who sat chained to a perch in the oak parlour, and conversed with himself, and nibbled at his claws and bit his perch all day), —old Captain, the only living thing, except one or two of us, and the Squire himself, that remembers the old master, the minute he saw the dog, screeched as if he was struck, shakin' his feathers out quite wild, and drops down, poor old soul, a-hangin' by his foot, in a fit."

But there is no accounting for fancies, and the Squire was one of those dogged persons who persist more obstinately in their whims the more they are opposed. But Charles Marston's health suffered by his lameness. The transition from habitual and violent exercise to such a life as his privation now consigned him to, was never made without a risk to health; and a host of dyspeptic annoyances, the existence of which he had never dreamed of before, now beset him in sad earnest. Among these was the now not unfrequent troubling of his sleep with dreams and nightmares. In these his canine favourite invariably had a part and was generally a central, and sometimes a solitary figure. In these visions the dog seemed to stretch himself up the side of the Squire's bed, and in dilated proportions to sit at his feet, with a horrible likeness to the pug features of old Squire Toby, with tricks of wagging his head and throwing up his chin; and then he would talk to him about Scroope, and tell him "all wasn't straight," and that he "must make it up wi' Scroope," that he, the old Squire, had "served him an ill turn," that "time was nigh up," and that "fair was fair,' and he was "troubled where he was, about Scroope."

Then in his dream this semi-human brute would approach his face to his, crawling and crouching up his body, heavy as lead, till the face of the beast was laid on his, with the same odious caresses and stretchings and writhings which he had seen over the old Squire's grave. Then Charlie would wake up with a gasp and a howl, and start upright in the bed, bathed in a cold moisture, and fancy he saw something white sliding off the foot of the bed. Sometimes he thought it might be the curtain with white lining that slipped down, or the coverlet disturbed by his uneasy turnings; but he always fancied, at such moments, that he saw something white sliding hastily off the bed; and always when he had been visited by such dreams the dog next morning was more than usually caressing and servile, as if to obliterate, by a more than ordinary welcome, the sentiment of disgust which the horror of the night had left behind it.

The doctor half-satisfied the Squire that there was nothing in these dreams, which, in one shape or another, invariably attended forms of indigestion such as he was suffering from.

For a while, as if to corroborate this theory, the dog ceased altogether to figure in them. But at last there came a vision in which, more unpleasantly than before, he did resume his old place.

In his nightmare the room seemed all but dark; he heard what he knew to be the dog walking from the door round his bed slowly, to the side from which he always had come upon it. A portion of the room was uncarpeted, and he said he distinctly heard the peculiar tread of a dog, in which the faint clatter of the claws is audible. It was a light stealthy step, but at every tread the whole room shook heavily; he felt something place itself at the foot of his bed, and saw a pair of green eyes staring at him in the dark, from which he could not remove his own. Then he heard, as he thought, the old Squire Toby say—"The eleventh hour be passed, Charlie, and ye've done nothing—you and I 'a done Scroope a wrong!" and then came a good deal more, and then—"The time's nigh up, it's going to strike." And with a long low growl, the thing began to creep up upon his feet; the growl continued, and he saw the reflection of the up-turned green eyes upon the bed-clothes, as it began slowly to stretch itself up his body towards his face. With a loud scream, he waked. The light, which of late the Squire was accustomed to have in his bed-room, had accidentally gone out. He was afraid to get up, or even to look about the room for some time; so sure did he feel of seeing the green eyes in the dark fixed on him from some corner. He had hardly recovered from his first agony which nightmare leaves behind it, and was beginning to collect his thoughts, when he heard the clock strike twelve. And he bethought him of the words "the eleventh hour be passed—time's nigh up—it's going to strike!" and he almost feared that he would hear the voice reopening the subject.

Next morning the Squire came down looking ill.

"Do you know a room, old Cooper," said he, "they used to call King Herod's Chamber?"

"Ay, sir; the story of King Herod was on the walls o't when I was a boy."

"There's a closet off it—is there?"

"I can't be sure o' that; but 'tisn't worth your looking at, now; the hangings was rotten, and took off the walls, before you was born; and there's nou't there but some old broken things and lumber. I seed them put there myself by poor Twinks; he was blind of an eye, and footman afterwards. You'll remember Twinks? He died here, about the time o' the great snow. There was a deal o' work to bury him, poor fellow!"

"Get the key, old Cooper; I'll look at the room," said the Squire.

"And what the devil can you want to look at it for?" said Cooper, with the old-world privilege of a rustic butler.

"And what the devil's that to you? But I don't mind if I tell you. I don't want that dog in the gun-room, and I'll put him somewhere else; and I don't care if I put him there."

"A bull-dog in a bedroom! Oons, sir! the folks 'ill say you're clean mad!"

"Well, let them; get you the key, and let us look at the room."

"You'd shoot him if you did right, Master Charlie. You never heard what a noise he kept up all last night in the gun-room, walking to and fro growling like a tiger in a show; and, say what you like, the dog's not worth his feed; he hasn't a point of a dog; he's a bad dog."

"I know a dog better than you—and he's a good dog!" said the Squire, testily.

"If you was a judge of a dog you'd hang that 'un," said Cooper.

"I'm not going to hang him, so there's an end. Go you, and get the key; and don't be talking, mind, when you go down. I may change my mind."

Now this freak of visiting King Herod's room had, in truth, a totally different object from that pretended by the Squire. The voice in his nightmare had uttered a particular direction, which haunted him, and would give him no peace until he had tested it. So far from liking that dog to-day, he was beginning to regard it with a horrible suspicion; and if old Cooper had not stirred his obstinate temper by seeming to dictate, I dare say he would have got rid of that inmate effectually before evening.

Up to the third storey, long disused, he and old Cooper mounted. At the end of a dusty gallery, the room lay. The old tapestry, from which the spacious chamber had taken its name, had long given place to modern paper, and this was mildewed, and in some places hanging from the walls. A thick mantle of dust lay over the floor. Some broken chairs and boards, thick with dust, lay, along with other lumber, piled together at one end of the room.

They entered the closet, which was quite empty. The Squire looked round, and you could hardly have said whether he was relieved or disappointed.

"No furniture here," said the Squire, and looked through the dusty window. "Did you say anything to me lately—I don't mean this morning—about this room, or the closet—or anything—I forget—"

"Lor' bless you! Not I. I han't been thinkin' o' this room this forty year."

"Is there any sort of old furniture called a *buffet*—do you remember?" asked the Squire.

"A buffet? why, yes—to be sure—there was a buffet, sure enough, in this closet, now you bring it to mind," said Cooper. "But it's papered over."

"And what is it?"

"A little cupboard in the wall," answered the old man.

"Ho—I see—and there's such a thing here, is there, under the paper? Show me whereabouts it was."

"Well—I think it was somewhere about here," answered he, rapping his knuckles along the wall opposite the window. "Ay, there it is," he added, as the hollow sound of a wooden door was returned to his knock.

The Squire pulled the loose paper from the wall, and disclosed the doors of a small press, about two feet square, fixed in the wall.

"The very thing for my buckles and pistols, and the rest of my gimcracks," said the Squire. "Come away, we'll leave the dog where he is. Have you the key of that little press?"

No, he had not. The old master had emptied and locked it up, and desired that it should be papered over, and that was the history of it.

Down came the Squire, and took a strong turn-screw from his gun-case; and quietly reascended to King Herod's room, and with little trouble, forced the door of the small press in the closet wall. There were in it some letters and cancelled leases, and also a parchment deed which he took to the window and read with much agitation. It was a supplemental deed executed about a fortnight after the others, and previously to his father's marriage, placing Gylingden under strict settlement to the elder son, in what is called "tail male." Handsome Charlie, in his fraternal litigation, had acquired a smattering of technical knowledge, and he perfectly well knew that the effect of this would be not only to transfer the house and lands to his brother Scroope, but to leave him at the mercy of that exasperated brother, who might recover from him personally every guinea he had ever received by way of rent, from the date of his father's death.

It was a dismal, clouded day, with something threatening in its aspect, and the darkness, where he stood, was made deeper by the top of one of the huge old trees overhanging the window.

In a state of awful confusion he attempted to think over his position. He placed the deed in his pocket, and nearly made up his mind to destroy it. A short time ago he would not have hesitated for a moment under such circumstances; but now his health and his nerves were shattered, and he was under a supernatural alarm which the strange discovery of his deed had powerfully confirmed.

In this state of profound agitation he heard a sniffing at the closet-door, and then an impatient scratch and a long low growl. He screwed his courage up, and, not knowing what to expect, threw the door open and saw the dog, not in his dream-shape, but wriggling with joy, and crouching and fawning with eager submission; and then wandering about the closet, the brute growled awfully into the corners of it, and seemed in an unappeasable agitation.

Then the dog returned and fawned and crouched again at his feet.

After the first moment was over, the sensations of abhorrence and fear began to subside, and he almost reproached himself for requiting the affection of this poor friendless brute with the antipathy which he had really done nothing to earn.

The dog pattered after him down the stairs. Oddly enough, the sight of this animal, after the first revulsion, reassured him; in his eyes, so attached, so good-natured, and palpably so mere a dog.

By the hour of evening the Squire had resolved on a middle course; he would not inform his brother of his discovery, nor yet would he destroy the deed. He would never marry. He was past that time. He would leave a letter, explaining the discovery of the deed, addressed to the only surviving trustee—who had probably forgotten everything about it—and having seen out his own tenure, he would provide that all should be set right after his death. Was not that fair? At all events it quite satisfied what he called his conscience, and he thought it a devilish good compromise for his brother; and he went out, towards sunset, to take his usual walk.

Returning in the darkening twilight, the dog, as usual attending him, began to grow frisky and wild, at first scampering round him in great circles, as before, nearly at the top of his speed, his great head between his paws as he raced. Gradually more excited grew the pace and narrower his circuit, louder and fiercer his continuous growl, and the Squire stopped and grasped his stick hard, for the lurid eyes and grin of the brute threatened an attack. Turning round and round as the excited brute encircled him, and striking vainly at him with his stick, he grew at last so tired that he almost despaired of keeping him longer at bay; when on a sudden the dog stopped short and crawled up to his feet wriggling and crouching submissively.

Nothing could be more apologetic and abject; and when the Squire dealt him two heavy thumps with his stick, the dog whimpered only, and writhed and licked his feet. The Squire sat down on a prostrate tree; and his dumb companion, recovering his wonted spirits immediately, began to sniff and nuzzle among the roots. The Squire felt in his breast-pocket for the deed—it was safe; and again he pondered, in this loneliest of spots, on the question whether he should preserve it for restoration after his death to his brother, or destroy it forthwith. He began rather to lean toward the latter solution, when the long low growl of the dog not far off startled him.

He was sitting in a melancholy grove of old trees, that slants gently westward. Exactly the same odd effect of light I have before described—a faint red glow reflected downward from the upper sky, after the sun had set, now gave to the growing darkness a lurid uncertainty. This grove, which lies in a gentle hollow, owing to its circumscribed horizon on all but one side, has a peculiar character of loneliness.

He got up and peeped over a sort of barrier, accidentally formed of the trunks of felled trees laid one over the other, and saw the dog straining up the other side of it, and hideously stretched out, his ugly head looking in consequence twice the natural size. His dream was coming over him again. And now between the trunks the brute's ungainly head was thrust, and the long neck came straining through, and the body, twining after it like a huge white lizard; and as it came striving and twisting through, it growled and glared as if it would devour him.

As swiftly as his lameness would allow, the Squire hurried from this solitary spot towards the house. What thoughts exactly passed through his mind as he did so, I am sure he could not have told. But when the dog came up with him it seemed appeased, and even in high good humor, and no longer resembled the brute that haunted his dreams.

That night, near ten o'clock, the Squire, a good deal agitated, sent for the keeper, and told him that he believed the dog was mad, and that he must shoot him. He might shoot the dog in the gunroom, where he was—a grain of shot or two in the wainscot did not matter, and the dog must not have a chance of getting out.

The Squire gave the gamekeeper his double-barrelled gun, loaded with heavy shot. He did not go with him beyond the hall. He placed his hand on the keeper's arm; the keeper said his hand trembled, and that he looked "as white as curds."

"Listen a bit!" said the Squire under his breath.

They heard the dog in a state of high excitement in the room—growling ominously, jumping on the window-stool and down again, and running round the room.

"You'll need to be sharp, mind—don't give him a chance—slip in edgeways, d'ye see? and give him both barrels!"

"Not the first mad dog I've knocked over, sir," said the man, looking very serious as he cocked the gun.

As the keeper opened the door, the dog had sprung into the empty grate. He said he "never see sich a stark, staring devil." The beast made a twist round, as if, he thought, to jump up the chimney—"but that wasn't to be done at no price,"—and he made a yell—not like a dog—like a man caught in a mill-crank, and before he could spring, the keeper fired one barrel into him. The dog leaped towards him, and rolled over, receiving the second barrel in his head, as he lay snorting at the keeper's feet!

"I never seed the like; I never heard a screech like that!" said the keeper, recoiling. "It makes a fellow feel queer."

"Quite dead?" asked the Squire.

"Not a stir in him, sir," said the man, pulling him along the floor by the neck.

"Throw him outside the hall-door now," said the Squire; "and mind you pitch him outside the gate to-night—old Cooper says he's a witch," and the pale Squire smiled, "so he shan't lie in Gylingden."

Never was man more relieved than the Squire, and he slept better for a week after this than he had done for many weeks before.

It behooves us all to act promptly on our good resolutions. There is a determined gravitation towards evil, which, if left to itself, will bear down first intentions. If at one moment of superstitious fear, the Squire had made up his mind to a great sacrifice, and resolved in the matter of that deed so strangely recovered, to act honestly by his brother, that resolution very soon gave place to the compromise with fraud, which so conveniently postponed the restitution to the period when further enjoyment on his part was impossible. Then came more tidings of Scroope's violent and minatory language, with always the same burthen—that he would leave no stone unturned to show that there had existed a deed which Charles had either secreted or destroyed, and that he would never rest till he had hanged him.

This of course was wild talk. At first it had only enraged him; but, with his recent guilty knowledge and suppression, had come fear. His danger was the existence of the deed, and little by little he brought himself to a resolution to destroy it. There were many falterings and recoils before he could bring himself to commit this crime. At length, however, he did it, and got rid of the custody of that which at any time might become the instrument of disgrace and ruin. There was relief in this, but also the new and terrible sense of actual guilt.

He had got pretty well rid of his supernatural qualms. It was a different kind of trouble that agitated him now.

But this night, he imagined, he was awakened by a violent shaking of his bed. He could see, in the very imperfect light, two figures at the foot of it, holding each a bedpost. One of these he half-fancied was his brother Scroope, but the other was the old Squire—of that he was sure—and he fancied that they had shaken him up from his sleep. Squire Toby was talking as Charlie wakened, and he heard him say:

"Put out of our own house by you! It won't hold for long. We'll come in together, friendly, and stay. Forewarned, wi' yer eyes open, ye did it; and now Scroope 'll hang you! We'll hang you together! Look at me, you devil's limb."

And the old Squire tremblingly stretched his face, torn with shot and bloody, and growing every moment more and more into the likeness of the dog, and began to stretch himself out and climb the bed over the foot-board, and he saw the figure at the other side, little more than a black shadow, begin also to scale the bed; and there was instantly a dreadful confusion and uproar in the room, and such a grabbling and laughing; he could not catch the words; but, with a scream he woke, and found himself standing on the floor. The phantoms and the clamour were gone, but a crash and ringing of fragments was in his ears. The great china bowl, from which for generations the Marstons of Gylingden had been baptized, had fallen from the mantlepiece, and was smashed on the hearth-stone.

"I've bin dreamin' all night about Mr. Scroope, and I wouldn't wonder, old Cooper, if he was dead," said the Squire, when he came down in the morning.

"God forbid! I was adreamed about him, too, sir; I dreamed he was dammin' and sinkin' about a hole was burnt in his coat, and the old master, God be wi' him! said—quite plain— I'd 'a swore 'twas himself—'Cooper, get up, ye d——d land-loupin' thief, and lend a hand to hang him—for he's a daft cur, and no dog o' mine.' 'Twas the dog shot over night, I do suppose, as was runnin' in my old head. I thought old master gied me a punch wi' his knuckles, and says I, wakenin' up, 'At yer service, sir'; and for a while I couldn't get it out o' my head, master was in the room still."

Letters from town soon convinced the Squire that his brother Scroope, so far from being dead, was particularly active; and Charlie's attorney wrote to say, in serious alarm, that he had heard, accidentally, that he intended setting up a case, of a supplementary deed of settlement, of which he had secondary evidence, which would give him Gylingden. And at this menace Handsome Charlie snapped his fingers, and wrote courageously to his attorney; abiding what might follow with, however, a secret foreboding.

Scroope threatened loudly now, and swore after his bitter fashion, and reiterated his old promise of hanging that cheat at last. In the midst of these menaces and preparations, however, a sudden peace proclaimed itself: Scroope died, without time even to make provisions for a posthumous attack upon his brother. It was one of those cases of disease of the heart in which death is as sudden as a bullet.

Charlie's exultation was undisguised. It was shocking. Not, of course, altogether malignant. For there was the expansion consequent on the removal of a secret fear. There was also the comic piece of luck, that only the day before Scroope had destroyed his old will, which left to a stranger every farthing he possessed, intending in a day or two to execute another to the same person, charged with the express condition of prosecuting the suit against Charlie.

The result was, that all his possessions went unconditionally to his brother Charles as his heir. Here were grounds for abundance of savage elation. But there was also the deep-seated hatred of half a life of mutual and persistent aggression and revilings; and Handsome Charlie was capable of nursing a grudge, and enjoying a revenge with his whole heart.

He would gladly have prevented his brother's being buried in the old Gylingden chapel, where he wished to lie; but his lawyers doubted his power, and he was not quite proof against the scandal which would attend his turning back the funeral, which would, he knew, be attended by some of the country gentry and others, with an hereditary regard for the Marstons.

But he warned his servants that not one of them were to attend it; promising, with oaths and curses not to be disregarded, that any one of them who did so, should find the door shut in his face on his return.

I don't think, with the exception of old Cooper, that the servants cared for this prohibition, except as it baulked a curiosity always strong in the solitude of the country. Cooper was very much vexed that the eldest son of the old Squire should be buried in the old family chapel, and no sign of decent respect from Gylingden Hall. He asked his master, whether he would not, at least, have some wine and refreshments in the oak parlour, in case any of the country gentlemen who paid this respect to the old family should come up to the house? But the Squire only swore at him, told him to mind his own business, and ordered him to say, if such a thing happened, that he was out, and no preparations made, and, in fact to send them away as they came. Cooper expostulated stoutly, and the Squire grew angrier; and after a tempestuous scene, took his hat and stick and walked out, just as the funeral descending the valley from the direction of the "Old Angel Inn" came in sight.

Old Cooper prowled about disconsolately, and counted the carriages as well as he could from the gate. When the funeral was over, and they began to drive away, he returned to the hall, the door of which lay open, and as usual deserted. Before he reached it quite, a mourning coach drove up, and two gentlemen in black cloaks, and crapes to their hats, got out, and without looking to the right or the left, went up the steps into the house. Cooper followed them slowly. The carriage had, he supposed, gone round to the yard, for, when he reached the door, it was no longer there.

So he followed the two mourners into the house. In the hall he found a fellow-servant, who said he had seen two gentlemen, in black cloaks, pass through the hall, and go up the stairs without removing their hats, or asking leave of anyone. This was very odd, old Cooper thought, and a great liberty; so upstairs he went to make them out.

But he could not find them then, nor ever. And from that hour the house was troubled.

In a little time there was not one of the servants who had not something to tell. Steps and voices followed them sometimes in the passages, and tittering whispers, always minatory, scared them at corners of the galleries, or from dark recesses; so that they would return panic-striken to be rebuked by thin Mrs. Beckett, who looked on such stories as worse than idle. But Mrs. Beckett herself, a short time after, took a very different view of the matter.

She had herself begun to hear these voices, and with this formidable aggravation, that they came always when she was at her prayers, which she had been punctual in saying all her life, and utterly interrupted them. She was scared at such moments by dropping words and sentences, which grew, as she persisted, into threats and blasphemies.

These voices were not always in the room. They called, as she fancied, through the walls, very thick in that old house, from the neighbouring apartments, sometimes on one side, sometimes on the other; sometimes they seemed to holloa from distant lobbies, and came muffled, but threateningly, through the long panelled passages. As they approached they grew furious, as if several voices were speaking together. Whenever, as I said, this worthy woman applied herself to her devotions, these horrible sentences came hurrying towards the door, and, in panic, she would start from her knees, and all then would subside except the thumping of her heart against her stays, and the dreadful tremors of her nerves.

What these voices said, Mrs. Beckett never could quite remember one minute after they had ceased speaking; one sentence chased another away; gibe and menace and impious denunciation, each hideously articulate, were lost as soon as heard. And this added to the effect of these terrifying mockeries and invectives, that she could not, by any effort, retain their exact import, although their horrible character remained vividly present in her mind.

For a long time the Squire seemed to be the only person in the house absolutely unconscious of these annoyances. Mrs. Beckett had twice made up her mind within the week to leave. A prudent woman, however, who has been comfortable for more than twenty years in a place, thinks oftener than twice before she leaves it. She and old Cooper were the only servants in the house who remembered the good old housekeeping in Squire Toby's day. The others were few, and such as could hardly be accounted regular servants. Meg Dobbs, who acted as housemaid, would not sleep in the house, but walked home in trepidation, to her father's, at the gatehouse, under the escort of her little brother, every night. Old Mrs. Beckett, who was high and mighty with the make-shift servants of fallen Gylingden, let herself down all at once, and made Mrs. Kymes and the kitchen-maid move their beds into her large and faded room, and there, very frankly, shared her nightly terrors with them.

Old Cooper was testy and captious about these stories. He was already uncomfortable enough by reason of the entrance of the two muffled figures into the house, about which there could be no mistake. His own eyes had seen them. He refused to credit the stories of the women, and affected to think that the two mourners might have left the house and driven away, on finding no one to receive them.

Old Cooper was summoned at night to the oak parlour, where the Squire was smoking.

"I say, Cooper," said the Squire, looking pale and angry, "what for ha' you been frightenin' they crazy women wi' your plaguy stories? d——me, if you see ghosts here it's no place for you, and it's time you should pack. I won't be left without servants. Here has been old Beckett wi' the cook and the kitchenmaid, as white as pipe clay, all in a row, to tell me I must have a parson to sleep among them, and preach down the devil! Upon my soul, you're a wise old body, filling their heads wi' maggots! and Meg goes down to the lodge every night, afeared to lie in the house—all your doing wi' your old wives stories,—ye withered old Tom o' Bedlam!"

"I'm not to blame, Master Charles. 'Tisn't along o' no stories o' mine, for I'm never done telling 'em it's all vanity and vapours. Mrs. Beckett 'ill tell you that, and there's been many a wry word betwixt us on the head o't. Whate'er I may *think*," said old Cooper, significantly, and looking askance, with the sternness of fear in the Squire's face.

The Squire averted his eyes, and muttered angrily to himself, and turned away to knock the ashes out of his pipe on the hob, and then turning suddenly round upon Cooper again, he spoke, with a pale face, but not quite so angrily as before.

"I know you're no fool, old Cooper, when you like. Suppose there was such a thing as a ghost here, don't you see, it ain't to them snipe-headed women it 'id go to tell its story. What ails you, man, that you should think ought about it, but just what *I* think? You had a good headpiece o' yer own once, Cooper, don't be you clappin' a goosecap over it, as my poor father used to say; d——it, old boy, you mustn't let 'em be fools, settin' one another wild wi' their blether, and makin' the folks talk what they shouldn't, about Gylingden and the family. I don't think ye'd like that, old Cooper, I'm sure ye wouldn't. The women has gone out o' the kitchen, make up a bit o' fire, and get your pipe. I'll go to you, when I finish this one, and we'll smoke a bit together, and a glass o' brandy and water."

Down went the old butler, not altogether unused to such condescensions in that disorderly and lonely household; and let not those who can choose their company, be too hard on the Squire who couldn't.

When he got things tidy, as he said, he sat down in that big old kitchen, with his feet on the fender, the kitchen candle burning in a great brass candlestick, which stood on the deal table at his elbow, with the brandy bottle and tumblers beside it, and Cooper's pipe also in readiness. And these preparations completed, the old butler, who had remembered other generations and better times, fell into rumination, and so, gradually, into a deep sleep.

Old Cooper was half awakened by some one laughing low, near his head. He was dreaming of old times in the Hall, and fancied one of "the young gentlemen" going to play him a trick, and he mumbled something in his sleep, from which he was awakened by a stern deep voice, saying, "You wern't at the funeral; I might take your life, I'll take your ear." At the same moment, the side of his head received a violent push, and he started to his feet. The fire had gone down, and he was chilled. The candle was expiring in the socket, and threw on the white wall long shadows, that danced up and down from the ceiling to the ground, and their black outlines he fancied resembled the two men in cloaks, whom he remembered with a profound horror.

He took the candle, with all the haste he could, getting along the passage, on whose walls the same dance of black shadows was continued, very anxious to reach his room before the light should go out. He was startled half out of his wits by the sudden clang of his master's bell, close over his head, ringing furiously.

"Ha, ha! There it goes—yes, sure enough," said Cooper, reassuring himself with the sound of his own voice, as he hastened on, hearing more and more distinct every moment the same furious ringing. "He's fell asleep, like me; that's it, and his lights is out, I lay you fifty—"

When he turned the handle of the door of the oak parlour, the Squire wildly called, "Who's *there?*" in the tone of a man who expects a robber.

"It's me, old Cooper, all right, Master Charlie, you didn't come to the kitchen after all, sir."

"I'm very bad, Cooper; I don't know how I've been. Did you meet anything?" asked the Squire.

"No," said Cooper.

They stared on one another.

"Come here—stay here! Don't you leave me! Look round the room, and say is all right; and gie us your hand, old Cooper, for I must hold it." The Squire's was damp and cold, and trembled very much, It was not very far from day-break now.

After a time he spoke again: "I 'a done many a thing I shouldn't; I'm not fit to go, and wi' God's blessin' I'll look to it—why shouldn't I? I'm as lame as old Billy—I'll never be able to do any good no more, and I'll give over drinking, and marry, as I ought to 'a done long ago— none o' yer fine ladies, but a good homely wench; there's Farmer Crump's youngest daughter, a good lass, and discreet. What for shouldn't I take her? She'd take care o' me and wouldn't bring a head full o' romances here, and mantua-makers' trumpery, and I'll talk with the parson, and I'll do what's fair wi' everyone; and mind, I said I'm sorry for many a thing I 'a done."

A wild cold dawn had by this time broken. The Squire, Cooper said, looked "awful bad," as he got his hat and stick, and sallied out for a walk, instead of going to his bed, as Cooper besought him, looking so wild and distracted, that it was plain his object was simply to escape from the house. It was twelve o'clock when the Squire walked into the kitchen, where he was sure of finding some of the servants, looking as if ten years had passed over him since yesterday. He pulled a stool by the fire, without speaking a word, and sat down. Cooper had sent to Applebury for the doctor, who had just arrived, but the Squire would not go to him. "If he wants to see me, he may come here," he muttered as often as Cooper urged him. So the doctor did come, charily enough, and found the Squire very much worse than he had expected.

The Squire resisted the order to get to his bed. But the doctor insisted under a threat of death, at which his patient quailed.

"Well, I'll do what you say—only this—you must let old Cooper and Dick Keeper stay wi' me. I mustn't be left alone, and they must keep awake o' nights; and stay a while, do *you*. When I get round a bit, I'll go and live in a town. It's dull livin' here, now that I can't do nou't as I used, and I'll live a better life, mind ye; ye heard me say that, and I don't care who laughs, and I'll talk wi' the parson. I like 'em to laugh, hang 'em, it's a sign I'm doin' right, at last."

The doctor sent a couple of nurses from the County Hospital, not choosing to trust his patient to the management he had selected, and he went down himself to Gylingden to meet them in the evening. Old Cooper was ordered to occupy the dressing-room, and sit up at night, which satisfied the Squire, who was in a strangely excited state, very low, and threatened, the doctor said, with fever.

The clergyman came, an old, gentle, "book-learned" man, and talked and prayed with him late that evening. After he had gone the Squire called the nurses to his bedside, and said:

"There's a fellow sometimes comes; you'll never mind him. He looks in at the door and beckons,—a thin, hump-backed chap in mourning, wi' black gloves on; ye'll know him by his lean face, as brown as the wainscot: don't ye mind his smilin'. You don't go out to him, nor ask him in; he won't say nout; and if he grows anger'd and looks awry at ye, don't ye be afeared, for he can't hurt ye, and he'll grow tired waitin', and go away; and for God's sake mind ye don't ask him in, nor go out after him!''

The nurses put their heads together when this was over, and held afterwards a whispering conference with old Cooper. "Law bless ye!—no, there's no madman in the house," he protested; "not a soul but what ye saw,—it's just a trifle o' the fever in his head—no more.''

The Squire grew worse as the night wore on. He was heavy and delirious, talking of all sorts of things—of wine, and dogs, and lawyers; and then he began to talk, as it were, to his brother Scroope. As he did so Mrs. Oliver, the nurse, who was sitting up alone with him, heard, as she thought, a hand softly laid on the door-handle outside, and a stealthy attempt to turn it. "Lord bless us! who's there?" she cried, and her heart jumped into her mouth, as she thought of the hump-backed man in black, who was to put in his head smiling and beckoning—"Mr. Cooper! sir! are you there?" she cried. "Come here, Mr. Cooper, please—do, sir, quick!''

Old Cooper, called up from his doze by the fire, stumbled in from the dressing-room, and Mrs. Oliver seized him tightly as he emerged.

"The man with the hump has been atryin' the door, Mr. Cooper, as sure as I am here.'' The Squire was moaning and mumbling in his fever, understanding nothing, as she spoke. "No, no! Mrs. Oliver, ma'am, it's impossible, for there's no sich man in the house: what is Master Charlie sayin'?''

"He's saying *Scroope* every minute, whatever he means by that, and—and—hisht!— listen—there's the handle again,'' and, with a loud scream, she added—"Look at his head and neck in the door!'' and in her tremour she strained old Cooper in an agonizing embrace.

The candle was flaring, and there was a wavering shadow at the door that looked like the head of a man with a long neck, and a longish sharp nose, peeping in and drawing back.

"Don't be a d——fool, ma'am!'' cried Cooper, very white, and shaking her with all his might. "It's only the candle, I tell you—nothing in life but that. Don't you see?'' and he raised the light; "and I'm sure there was no one at the door, and I'll try, if you let me go.''

The other nurse was asleep on the sofa, and Mrs. Oliver called her up in a panic, for company, as old Cooper opened the door.

There was no one near it, but at the angle of the gallery was a shadow resembling that which he had seen in the room. He raised the candle a little, and it seemed to beckon with a long hand as the head drew back. "Shadow from the candle!'' exclaimed Cooper aloud, resolved not to yield to Mrs. Oliver's panic; and candle in hand, he walked to the corner. There was nothing. He could not forbear peeping down the long gallery from this point, and as he moved the light, he saw precisely the same sort of shadow, a little further down, and as he advanced the same withdrawal, and beckon. "Gammon!'' said he; "it is nout but the candle.'' And on he went, growing half angry and half frightened at the persistency with which this ugly shadow—a literal shadow he was sure it was—presented itself. As he drew near the point where it now appeared, it seemed to collect itself, and nearly dissolve in the central panel of an old carved cabinet which he was now approaching.

In the centre panel of this is a sort of boss carved into a wolf's head. The light fell oddly upon this, and the fugitive shadow seemed to be breaking up, and re-arranging itself as oddly. The eye-ball gleamed with a point of reflected light, which glittered also upon the grinning mouth, and he saw the long, sharp nose of Scroope Marston, and his fierce eye looking at him, he thought, with a steadfast meaning.

Old Cooper stood gazing upon this sight, unable to move, till he saw the face, and the figure that belonged to it, begin gradually to emerge from the wood. At the same time he heard voices approaching rapidly up a side gallery, and Cooper, with a loud "Lord a-mercy on us!" turned and ran back again, pursued by a sound that seemed to shake the old house like a mighty gust of wind.

Into his master's room burst old Cooper, half wild with fear, and clapped the door and turned the key in a twinkling, looking as if he had been pursued by murderers.

"Did you hear it?" whispered Cooper, now standing near the dressing-room door. They all listened, but not a sound from without disturbed the utter stillness of night. "God bless us! I doubt it's my old head that's gone crazy!" exclaimed Cooper.

He would tell them nothing but that he was himself "an old fool," to be frightened by their talk, and that "the rattle of a window, or the dropping o' a pin" was enough to scare him now; and so he helped himself through the night with brandy, and sat up talking by his master's fire.

The Squire recovered slowly from his brain fever, but not perfectly. A very little thing, the doctor said, would suffice to upset him. He was not yet sufficiently strong to remove for change of scene and air, which were necessary for his complete restoration.

Cooper slept in the dressing-room, and was now his only nightly attendant. The ways of the invalid were odd: he liked, half sitting up in his bed, to smoke his churchwarden o' nights, and made old Cooper smoke, for company, at the fire-side. As the Squire and his humble friend indulged in it, smoking is a taciturn pleasure, and it was not until the Master of Gylingden had finished his third pipe that he essayed conversation, and when he did, the subject was not such as Cooper would have chosen.

"I say, old Cooper, look in my face, and don't be afeared to speak out," said the Squire, looking at him with a steady, cunning smile; "you know all this time, as well as I do, who's in the house. You needn't deny—hey?—Scroope and my father?"

"Don't you be talking like that, Charlie," said old Cooper, rather sternly and frightened, after a long silence; still looking in his face, which did not change.

"What's the good of shammin', Cooper? Scroope's took the hearin' o' yer right ear—you know he did. He's looking angry. He's nigh took my life wi' this fever. But he's not done wi' me yet, and he looks awful wicked. Ye saw him—ye know ye did."

Cooper was awfully frightened, and the odd smile on the Squire's lips frightened him still more. He dropped his pipe, and stood gazing in silence at his master, and feeling as if he were in a dream.

"If ye think so, ye should not be smiling like that," said Cooper, grimly.

"I'm tired, Cooper, and it's as well to smile as t'other thing; so I'll even smile while I can. You know what they mean to do wi' me. That's all I wanted to say. Now, lad, go on wi' yer pipe—I'm goin' asleep."

So the Squire turned over in his bed, and lay down serenely, with his head on the pillow. Old Cooper looked at him, and glanced at the door, and then half-filled his tumbler with brandy, and drank it off, and felt better, and got to his bed in the dressing-room.

In the dead of night he was suddenly awakened by the Squire, who was standing, in his dressing-gown and slippers, by his bed.

"I've brought you a bit o' a present. I got the rents o' Hazelden yesterday, and ye'll keep that for yourself—it's a fifty—and give t'other to Nelly Carwell to-morrow; I'll sleep the sounder; and I saw Scroope since; he's not such a bad 'un after all, old fellow! He's got a crape over his face—for I told him I couldn't bear it; and I'd do many a thing for him now. I never could stand shilly-shally. Good-night, old Cooper!"

And the Squire laid his trembling hand kindly on the old man's shoulder, and returned to his own room.

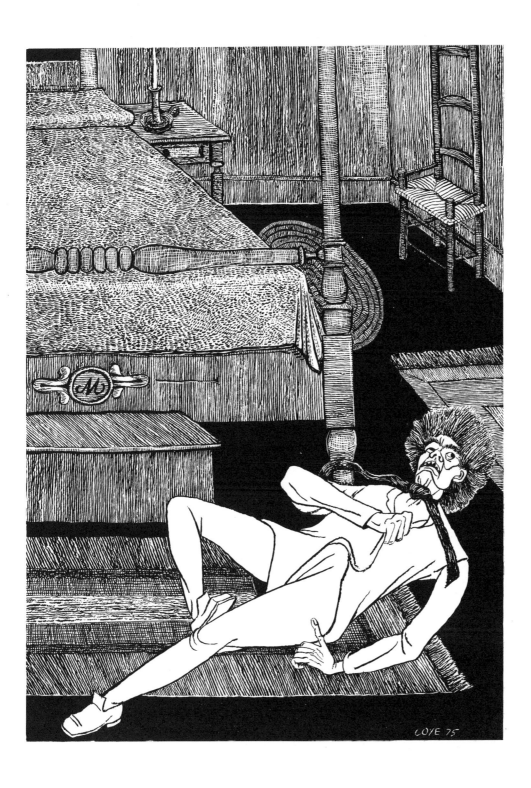

"I don't half like how he is. Doctor don't come half often enough. I don't like that queer smile o' his, and his hand was as cold as death. I hope in God his brain's not a-turnin'!" With these reflections, Cooper turned to the pleasanter subject of his present, and at last fell asleep.

In the morning, when he went into the Squire's room, the Squire had left his bed. "Never mind; he'll come back, like a bad shillin'," thought old Cooper, preparing the room as usual. But he did not return. Then began an uneasiness, succeeded by a panic, when it began to be plain that the Squire was not in the house. What had become of him? None of his clothes, but his dressing-gown and slippers were missing. Had he left the house, in his present sickly state, in that garb? and, if so, could he be in his right senses; and was there a chance of his surviving a cold, damp night, so passed, in the open air?

Tom Edwards was up to the house, and told them, that, walking a mile or so that morning, at four o'clock—there being no moon—along with Farmer Nokes, who was driving his cart to market, in the dark, three men walked, in front of the horse, not twenty yards before them, all the way from near Gylingden Lodge to the burial ground, the gate of which was opened for them from within, and the three men entered, and the gate was shut. Tom Edwards thought they were gone in to make preparations for a funeral of some member of the Marston family. But the occurrence seemed to Cooper, who knew there was no such thing, horribly ominous.

He now commenced a careful search, and at last bethought him of the lonely upper storey, and King Herod's chamber. He saw nothing changed there, but the closet door was shut, and, dark as was the morning, something, like a large white knot sticking out over the door, caught his eye.

The door resisted his efforts to open it for a time; some great weight forced it down against the floor; at length, however, it did yield a little, and a heavy crash, shaking the whole floor, and sending an echo flying through all the silent corridors, with a sound like receding laughter, half stunned him.

When he pushed open the door, his master was lying dead upon the floor. His cravat was drawn halter-wise tight round his throat, and had done its work well. The body was cold, and had been long dead.

In due course the coroner held his inquest, and the jury pronounced, "that the deceased, Charles Marston, had died by his own hand, in a state of temporary insanity." But old Cooper had his own opinion about the Squire's death, though his lips were sealed, and he never spoke about it. He went and lived for the residue of his days in York, where there are still people who remember him, a taciturn and surly old man, who attended church regularly, and also drank a little, and was known to have saved some money.

# F. Marion Crawford

Francis Marion Crawford (1854–1909), whose name is virtually unknown today, was once among the most popular and respected authors working in the English language. During a comparatively short career, he wrote forty-four novels in addition to several works of nonfiction. If his work is forgotten, it is because it is too sentimental and romantic for modern taste; if he is remembered at all, it is for a handful of grim and incisive horror tales. Written at various points throughout his life, these were finally collected into the volume *Wandering Ghosts,* which was published in England under the title *Uncanny Tales.*

Crawford was born in Italy, the son of expatriate American parents, and educated in the United States and abroad. He contemplated a career as a professor of Sanskrit and went to India to study the language. While there, he began to write some newspaper articles, and in 1879 he was offered the editorship of the *Indian Herald.* Two years later he was in New York, doing some more articles and still trying to decide on a career. His uncle urged him to write some of his Indian experiences in fictional form; the result was his first novel, *Mr. Isaacs* (1882). It was very successful, and Crawford's future was determined.

A lover of luxury, Crawford tended to live beyond his means. He purchased an elegant estate in Italy and worked furiously to keep his income high. The current critical consensus is that he neglected his considerable talent in order to write faster and make more money. In fact, he burned himself out physically as well as artistically; the exhaustion caused by a profitable series of lecture tours is said to have contributed to his death.

Only two of his novels have supernatural overtones. *The Witch of Prague* (1891) is subtitled "A Fantastic Tale." Its principal motif is hypnotism, and in it there are some attempts to prolong life artificially; however, the book is not considered one of Crawford's better efforts. Superior, if less sinister, is *Khaled* (1891), about an Arabian genie who takes human form with the promise that he will gain a soul if he can win human love.

When his reputation was still in the making, Crawford accepted an offer to have his work appear in an anthology of new stories, *The Broken Shaft* (1886). His motives were to get some quick cash and to be included in a book with some of the most prominent authors of the era. He dictated his story in the evening, after working all day on a novel. The result was "The Upper Berth," still considered one of the finest terror tales ever written. It has been called one of the few classics in the field by commentators as diverse as Edith Wharton and H. P. Lovecraft. The story represented a new style in the supernatural, summed up in its last line. Crawford helped inaugurate a tradition of tangible terrors, supplanting those sinister spirits that were content to keep their distance.

*Wandering Ghosts* contains only seven stories, but it had a tremendous influence on other writers, not only because of its own merits, but because Crawford's work had such a wide circulation. The other important stories include "The Dead Smile," "The Screaming Skull," and "For the Blood Is the Life," but there can be little doubt that "The Upper Berth" is Crawford's masterpiece, a clammy chronicle that has done more than anything else to keep its author's name alive.

# THE UPPER BERTH

# F. Marion Crawford

## 1

Somebody asked for the cigars. We had talked long, and the conversation was beginning to languish; the tobacco smoke had got into the heavy curtains, the wine had got into those brains which were liable to become heavy, and it was already perfectly evident that, unless somebody did something to rouse our oppressed spirits, the meeting would soon come to its natural conclusion, and we, the guests, would speedily go home to bed, and most certainly to sleep. No one had said anything very remarkable; it may be that no one had anything very remarkable to say. Jones had given us every particular of his last hunting adventure in Yorkshire. Mr. Tompkins, of Boston, had explained at elaborate length those working principles, by the due and careful maintenance of which the Atchison, Topeka, and Santa Fe Railroad not only extended its territory, increased its departmental influence, and transported live stock without starving them to death before the day of actual delivery, but, also, had for years succeeded in deceiving those passengers who bought its tickets into the fallacious belief that the corporation aforesaid was really able to transport human life without destroying it. Signor Tombola had endeavored to persuade us, by arguments which we took no trouble to oppose, that the unity of his country in no way resembled the average modern torpedo, carefully planned, constructed with all the skill of the greatest European arsenals, but, when constructed, destined to be directed by feeble hands into a region where it must undoubtedly explode, unseen, unfeared, and unheard, into the illimitable wastes of political chaos.

It is unnecessary to go into further details. The conversation had assumed proportions which would have bored Prometheus on his rock, which would have driven Tantalus to distraction, and which would have impelled Ixion to seek relaxation in the simple but instructive dialogues of Herr Ollendorff, rather than submit to the greater evil of listening to our talk. We had sat at table for hours; we were bored, we were tired, and nobody showed signs of moving.

Somebody called for cigars. We all instinctively looked towards the speaker. Brisbane was a man of five-and-thirty years of age, and remarkable for those gifts which chiefly attract the attention of men. He was a strong man. The external proportions of his figure presented nothing extraordinary to the common eye, though his size was above the average. He was a little over six feet in height, and moderately broad in the shoulder; he did not appear to be stout, but, on the other hand, he was certainly not thin; his small head was supported by a strong and sinewy neck; his broad, muscular hands appeared to possess a peculiar skill in breaking walnuts without the assistance of the ordinary cracker, and, seeing him in profile, one could not help remarking the extraordinary breadth of his sleeves, and the unusual thickness of his chest. He was one of those men who are commonly spoken of among men as deceptive; that is to say, that though he looked exceedingly strong he was in reality very much stronger than he looked. Of his features I need say little. His head is small, his hair is thin, his eyes are blue, his nose is large, he has a small moustache, and a square jaw. Everybody knows Brisbane, and when he asked for a cigar everybody looked at him.

"It is a very singular thing," said Brisbane.

Everybody stopped talking. Brisbane's voice was not loud, but possessed a peculiar quality of penetrating general conversation, and cutting it like a knife. Everybody listened. Brisbane, perceiving that he had attracted their general attention, lit his cigar with great equanimity.

"It is very singular," he continued, "that thing about ghosts. People are always asking whether anybody has seen a ghost. I have."

"Bosh! What, you? You don't mean to say so, Brisbane? Well, for a man of his intelligence!"

A chorus of exclamations greeted Brisbane's remarkable statement. Everybody called for cigars, and Stubbs, the butler, suddenly appeared from the depths of nowhere with a fresh bottle of dry champagne. The situation was saved; Brisbane was going to tell a story.

I am an old sailor, said Brisbane, and as I have to cross the Atlantic pretty often, I have my favourites. Most men have their favourites. I have seen a man wait in a Broadway bar for three-quarters of an hour for a particular car which he liked. I believe the bar-keeper made at least one-third of his living by that man's preference. I have a habit of waiting for certain ships when I am obliged to cross that duck-pond. It may be a prejudice, but I was never cheated out of a good passage but once in my life. I remember it very well; it was a warm morning in June, and the Custom House officials, who were hanging about waiting for a steamer already on her way up from Quarantine, presented a peculiarly hazy and thoughtful appearance. I had not much luggage—I never have. I mingled with the crowd of passengers, porters, and officious individuals in blue coats and brass buttons, who seem to spring up like mushrooms from the deck of a moored steamer to obtrude their unnecessary services upon the independent passenger. I have often noticed with a certain interest the spontaneous evolution of these fellows. They are not there when you arrive; five minutes after the pilot has called "Go ahead!" they, or at least their blue coats and brass buttons, have disappeared from deck and gangway as completely as though they had been consigned to that locker which tradition unanimously ascribes to Davy Jones. But, at the moment of starting, they are there, clean shaved, blue coated, and ravenous for fees. I hastened on board. The *Kamtschatka* was one of my favourite ships. I say was, because she emphatically no longer is. I cannot conceive of any inducement which could entice me to make another voyage in her. Yes, I know what you are going to say. She is uncommonly clean in the run aft, she has enough bluffing off in the bows to keep her dry, and the lower berths are most of them double. She has a lot of advantages, but I won't cross in her again. Excuse the digression. I got on board. I hailed a steward, whose red nose and redder whiskers were equally familiar to me.

"One hundred and five, lower berth," said I, in the business-like tone peculiar to men who think no more of crossing the Atlantic than taking a whisky cocktail at downtown Delmonico's.

The steward took my portmanteau, great-coat, and rug. I shall never forget the expression of his face. Not that he turned pale. It is maintained by the most eminent divines that even miracles cannot change the course of nature. I have no hesitation in saying that he did not turn pale; but, from his expression, I judged that he was either about to shed tears, to sneeze, or to drop my portmanteau. As the latter contained two bottles of particularly fine old sherry presented to me for my voyage by my old friend Snigginson van Pickyns, I felt extremely nervous. But the steward did none of these things.

"Well, I'm d——d!" said he in a low voice, and led the way.

I supposed my Hermes, as he led me to the lower regions, had had a little grog, but I said nothing, and followed him. One hundred and five was on the port side, well aft. There was nothing remarkable about the state-room. The lower berth, like most of those upon the *Kamtschatka,* was double. There was plenty of room; there was the usual washing apparatus, calculated to convey an idea of luxury to the mind of a North American Indian; there were the usual inefficient racks of brown wood, in which it is more easy to hang a large-sized umbrella than the common tooth-brush of commerce. Upon the uninviting mattresses were carefully folded together those blankets which a great modern humorist has aptly compared to cold buckwheat cakes. The question of towels was left entirely to the imagination. The glass decanters were filled with a transparent liquid faintly tinged with brown, but from which an odour less faint, but not more pleasing, ascended to the nostrils, like a far-off sea-sick reminiscence of oily machinery. Sad-coloured curtains half closed the upper berth. The hazy June daylight shed a faint illumination upon the desolate little scene. Ugh! how I hate that stateroom!

The steward deposited my traps and looked at me, as though he wanted to get away — probably in search of more passengers and more fees. It is always a good plan to start in favour with those functionaries, and I accordingly gave him certain coins there and then.

"I'll try to make yer comfortable all I can," he remarked, as he put the coins in his pocket. Nevertheless, there was a doubtful intonation in his voice which surprised me. Possibly his scale of fees had gone up, and he was not satisfied; but on the whole I was inclined to think that, as he himself would have expressed it, he was "the better for a glass." I was wrong, however, and did the man injustice.

## 2

Nothing especially worthy of mention occurred during that day. We left the pier punctually, and it was very pleasant to be fairly under way, for the weather was warm and sultry, and the motion of the steamer produced a refreshing breeze. Everybody knows what the first day at sea is like. People pace the decks and stare at each other, and occasionally meet acquaintances whom they did not know to be on board. There is the usual uncertainty as to whether the food will be good, bad, or indifferent, until the first two meals have put the matter beyond a doubt; there is the usual uncertainty about the weather, until the ship is fairly off Fire Island. The tables are crowded at first, and then suddenly thinned. Pale-faced people spring from their seats and precipitate themselves towards the door, and each old sailor breathes more freely as his sea-sick neighbour rushes from his side, leaving him plenty of elbow-room and an unlimited command over the mustard.

One passage across the Atlantic is very much like another, and we who cross very often do not make the voyage for the sake of novelty. Whales and icebergs are indeed always objects of interest, but, after all, one whale is very much like another whale, and one rarely sees an iceberg at close quarters. To the majority of us the most delightful moment of the day on board an ocean steamer is when we have taken our last turn on deck, have smoked our last cigar, and having succeeded in tiring ourselves, feel at liberty to turn in with a clear conscience. On that first night of the voyage I felt particularly lazy, and went to bed in 105 rather earlier than I usually do. As I turned in, I was amazed to see that I was to have a companion. A portmanteau, very like my own, lay in the opposite corner, and in the upper berth had been deposited a neatly folded rug, with a stick and umbrella. I had hoped to be alone, and I was disappointed; but I wondered who my room-mate was to be, and I determined to have a look at him.

Before I had been long in bed he entered. He was, as far as I could see, a very tall man, very thin, very pale, with sandy hair and whiskers and colourless grey eyes. He had about him, I thought, an air of rather dubious fashion; the sort of man you might see in Wall Street, without being able precisely to say what he was doing there—the sort of man who frequents the Café Anglais, who always seems to be alone and who drinks champagne; you might meet him on a race-course, but he would never appear to be doing anything there either. A little overdressed—a little odd. There are three or four of his kind on every ocean steamer. I made up my mind that I did not care to make his acquaintance, and I went to sleep saying to myself that I would study his habits in order to avoid him. If he rose early, I would rise late; if he went to bed late, I would go to bed early. I did not care to know him. If you once know people of that kind they are always turning up. Poor fellow! I need not have taken the trouble to come to so many decisions about him, for I never saw him again after that first night in 105.

I was sleeping soundly when I was suddenly waked by a loud noise. To judge from the sound, my room-mate must have sprung with a single leap from the upper berth to the floor. I heard him fumbling with the latch and bolt of the door, which opened almost immediately, and then I heard his footsteps as he ran at full speed down the passage, leaving the door open behind him. The ship was rolling a little, and I expected to hear him stumble or fall, but he ran as though he were running for his life. The door swung on its hinges with the motion of the vessel, and the sound annoyed me. I got up and shut it, and groped my way back to my berth in the darkness. I went to sleep again; but I have no idea how long I slept.

When I awoke it was still quite dark, but I felt a disagreeable sensation of cold, and it seemed to me that the air was damp. You know the peculiar smell of a cabin which has been wet with sea-water. I covered myself up as well as I could and dozed off again, framing complaints to be made the next day, and selecting the most powerful epithets in the language. I could hear my room-mate turn over in the upper berth. He had probably returned while I was asleep. Once I thought I heard him groan, and I argued that he was sea-sick. That is particularly unpleasant when one is below. Nevertheless I dozed off and slept till early daylight.

The ship was rolling heavily, much more than on the previous evening, and the grey light which came in through the porthole changed in tint with every movement according as the angle of the vessel's side turned the glass seawards or skywards. It was very cold—unaccountably so for the month of June. I turned my head and looked at the porthole, and saw to my surprise that it was wide open and hooked back. I believe I swore audibly. Then I got up and shut it. As I turned back I glanced at the upper berth. The curtains were drawn close together; my companion had probably felt cold as well as I. It struck me that I had slept enough. The stateroom was uncomfortable, though, strange to say, I could not smell the dampness which had annoyed me in the night. My room-mate was still asleep—excellent opportunity for avoiding him, so I dressed at once and went on deck. The day was warm and cloudy, with an oily smell on the water. It was seven o'clock as I came out—much later than I had imagined. I came across the doctor, who was taking his first sniff of the morning air. He was a young man from the West of Ireland—a tremendous fellow, with black hair and blue eyes, already inclined to be stout; he had a happy-go-lucky, healthy look about him which was rather attractive.

"Fine morning," I remarked, by way of introduction.

"Well," said he, eyeing me with an air of ready interest, "it's a fine morning and it's not a fine morning. I don't think it's much of a morning."

"Well, no—it is not so very fine," said I.

"It's just what I call fuggly weather," replied the doctor.

"It was very cold last night, I thought," I remarked. "However, when I looked about, I found that the porthole was wide open. I had not noticed it when I went to bed. And the state-room was damp, too."

"Damp!" said he. "Whereabouts are you?"

"One hundred and five——"

To my surprise the doctor started visibly, and stared at me.

"What is the matter?" I asked.

"Oh—nothing," he answered; "only everybody has complained of that state-room for the last three trips."

"I shall complain, too," I said. "It has certainly not been properly aired. It is a shame!"

"I don't believe it can be helped," answered the doctor. "I believe there is something— well, it is not my business to frighten passengers."

"You need not be afraid of frightening me," I replied. "I can stand any amount of damp. If I should get a bad cold I will come to you."

I offered the doctor a cigar, which he took and examined very critically.

"It is not so much the damp," he remarked. "However, I dare say you will get on very well. Have you a room-mate?"

"Yes; a deuce of a fellow, who bolts out in the middle of the night, and leaves the door open."

Again the doctor glanced curiously at me. Then he lit the cigar and looked grave.

"Did he come back?" he asked presently.

"Yes. I was asleep, but I waked up, and heard him moving. Then I felt cold and went to sleep again. This morning I found the porthole open."

"Look here," said the doctor quietly, "I don't care much for this ship. I don't care a rap for her reputation. I tell you what I will do. I have a good-sized place up here. I will share it with you, though I don't know you from Adam."

I was very much surprised at the proposition. I could not imagine why he should take such a sudden interest in my welfare. However, his manner as he spoke of the ship was peculiar.

"You are very good, doctor," I said. "But, really, I believe even now the cabin could be aired, or cleaned out, or something. Why do you not care for the ship?"

"We are not superstitious in our profession, sir," replied the doctor, "but the sea makes people so. I don't want to prejudice you, and I don't want to frighten you, but if you will take my advice you will move in here. I would as soon see you overboard," he added earnestly, "as know that you or any other man was to sleep in 105."

"Good gracious! Why?" I asked.

"Just because on the last three trips the people who have slept there actually have gone overboard," he answered gravely.

The intelligence was startling and exceedingly unpleasant, I confess. I looked hard at the doctor to see whether he was making game of me, but he looked perfectly serious. I thanked him warmly for his offer, but told him I intended to be the exception to the rule by which everyone who slept in that particular state-room went overboard. He did not say much, but looked as grave as ever, and hinted that, before we got across, I should probably reconsider his proposal. In the course of time we went to breakfast, at which only an inconsiderable number of passengers assembled. I noticed that one or two of the officers who breakfasted with us looked grave. After breakfast I went into my state-room in order to get a book. The curtains of the upper berth were still closely drawn. Not a word was to be heard. My room-mate was probably still asleep.

As I came out I met the steward whose business it was to look after me. He whispered that the captain wanted to see me, and then scuttled away down the passage as if very anxious to avoid any questions. I went toward the captain's cabin, and found him waiting for me.

"Sir," said he, "I want to ask a favour of you."

I answered that I would do anything to oblige him.

"Your room-mate has disappeared," he said. "He is known to have turned in early last night. Did you notice anything extraordinary in his manner?"

The question coming, as it did, in exact confirmation of the fears the doctor had expressed half an hour earlier, staggered me.

"You don't mean to say he has gone overboard?" I asked.

"I fear he has," answered the captain.

"This is the most extraordinary thing ——" I began.

"Why?" he asked.

"He is the fourth, then?" I explained. In answer to another question from the captain, I explained, without mentioning the doctor, that I had heard the story concerning 105. He seemed very much annoyed at hearing that I knew of it. I told him what had occurred in the night.

"What you say," he replied, "coincides almost exactly with what was told me by the room-mates of two of the other three. They bolt out of bed and run down the passage. Two of them were seen to go overboard by the watch; we stopped and lowered boats, but they were not found. Nobody, however, saw or heard the man who was lost last night—if he is really lost. The steward, who is a superstitious fellow, perhaps, and expected something to go wrong, went to look for him this morning, and found his berth empty, but his clothes lying about, just as he had left them. The steward was the only man on board who knew him by sight, and he has been searching everywhere for him. He has disappeared! Now, sir, I want to beg you not to mention the circumstance to any of the passengers; I don't want the ship to get a bad name, and nothing hangs about an ocean-goer like stories of suicides. You shall have your choice of any one of the officers' cabins you like, including my own, for the rest of the passage. Is that a fair bargain?"

"Very," said I; "and I am much obliged to you. But since I am alone, and have the state-room to myself, I would rather not move. If the steward will take out that unfortunate man's things, I would as lief stay where I am. I will not say anything about the matter, and I think I can promise you that I will not follow my room-mate."

The captain tried to dissuade me from my intention, but I preferred having a state-room alone to being the chum of any officer on board. I do not know whether I acted foolishly, but if I had taken his advice I should have had nothing more to tell. There would have remained the disagreeable coincidence of several suicides occurring among men who had slept in the same cabin, but that would have been all.

That was not the end of the matter, however, by any means. I obstinately made up my mind that I would not be disturbed by such tales, and I even went so far as to argue the question with the captain. There was something wrong about the state-room, I said. It was rather damp. The porthole had been left open last night. My room-mate might have been ill when he came on board, and he might have become delirious after he went to bed. He might even now be hiding somewhere on board, and might be found later. The place ought to be aired and the fastening of the port looked to. If the captain would give me leave, I would see that what I thought necessary was done immediately.

"Of course you have a right to stay where you are if you please," he replied, rather petulantly; "but I wish you would turn out and let me lock the place up, and be done with it."

I did not see it in the same light, and left the captain, after promising to be silent concerning the disappearance of my companion. The latter had had no acquaintances on board, and was not missed in the course of the day. Towards evening I met the doctor again, and he asked me whether I had changed my mind. I told him I had not.

"Then you will before long," he said, very gravely.

## 3

We played whist in the evening, and I went to bed late. I will confess now that I felt a disagreeable sensation when I entered my state-room. I could not help thinking of the tall man I had seen on the previous night, who was now dead, drowned, tossed about in the long swell, two or three hundred miles astern. His face rose very distinctly before me as I undressed, and I even went so far as to draw back the curtains of the upper berth, as though to persuade myself that he was actually gone. I also bolted the door of the state-room. Suddenly I became aware that the porthole was open, and fastened back. This was more than I could stand. I hastily threw on my dressing-gown and went in search of Robert, the steward of my passage. I was very angry, I remember, and when I found him I dragged him roughly to the door of 105, and pushed him towards the open porthole.

"What the deuce do you mean, you scoundrel, by leaving that port open every night? Don't you know it is against the regulations? Don't you know that if the ship heeled and the water began to come in, ten men could not shut it? I will report you to the captain, you blackguard, for endangering the ship!"

I was exceedingly wroth. The man trembled and turned pale, and then began to shut the round glass plate with the heavy brass fittings.

"Why don't you answer me?" I said roughly.

"If you please sir," faltered Robert, "there's nobody on board as can keep this 'ere port shut at night. You can try it yourself, sir. I ain't a-going to stop hany longer on board o' this vessel, sir; I ain't, indeed. But if I was you, sir, I'd just clear out and go and sleep with the surgeon, or something, I would. Look 'ere, sir, is that fastened what you may call securely, or not, sir? Try it, sir, see if it will move a hinch."

I tried the port, and found it perfectly tight.

"Well, sir," continued Robert triumphantly, "I wager my reputation as a A-1 steward that in 'arf an hour it will be open again; fastened back, too, sir, that's the horful thing— fastened back!"

I examined the great screw and the looped nut that ran on it.

"If I find it open in the night, Robert, I will give you a sovereign. It is not possible. You may go."

"Soverin' did you say, sir? Very good, sir. Thank ye, sir. Good night, sir. Pleasant reepose, sir, and all manner of hinchantin' dreams, sir."

Robert scuttled away, delighted at being released. Of course, I thought he was trying to account for his negligence by a silly story, intended to frighten me, and I disbelieved him. The consequence was that he got his sovereign, and I spent a very peculiarly unpleasant night.

I went to bed, and five minutes after I had rolled myself up in my blankets the inexorable Robert extinguished the light that burned steadily behind the ground-glass pane near the door. I lay quite still in the dark trying to go to sleep, but I soon found that impossible. It had been some satisfaction to be angry with the steward, and the diversion had banished that unpleasant sensation I had at first experienced when I thought of the drowned man who had been my chum; but I was no longer sleepy, and I lay awake for some time, occasionally glancing at the porthole, which I could just see from where I lay, and which, in the darkness, looked like a faintly luminous soup-plate suspended in blackness. I believe I must have lain there for an hour, and, as I remember, I was just dozing into sleep when I was roused by a draught of cold air, and by distinctly feeling the spray of the sea blown upon my face. I started to my feet, and not having allowed in the dark for the motion of the ship, I was instantly thrown violently across the state-room upon the couch which was placed beneath the porthole. I recovered myself immediately, however, and climbed upon my knees. The porthole was again wide open and fastened back!

Now these things are facts. I was wide awake when I got up, and I should certainly have been waked by the fall had I still been dozing. Moreover, I bruised my elbows and knees badly, and the bruises were there on the following morning to testify to the fact, if I myself had doubted it. The porthole was wide open and fastened back—a thing so unaccountable that I remember very well feeling astonishment rather than fear when I discovered it. I at once closed the plate again, and screwed down the loop nut with all my strength. It was very dark in the state-room. I reflected that the port had certainly been opened within an hour after Robert had at first shut it in my presence, and I determined to watch it, and see whether it would open again. Those brass fittings are very heavy and by no means easy to move; I could not believe that the clump had been turned by the shaking of the screw. I stood peering out through the thick glass at the alternate white and grey streaks of the sea that foamed beneath the ship's side. I must have remained there a quarter of an hour.

Suddenly, as I stood, I distinctly heard something moving behind me in one of the berths, and a moment afterwards, just as I turned instinctively to look—though I could, of course, see nothing in the darkness—I heard a very faint groan. I sprang across the state-room, and tore the curtains of the upper berth aside, thrusting in my hands to discover if there were any one there. There was someone.

I remember that the sensation as I put my hands forward was as though I were plunging them into the air of a damp cellar, and from behind the curtains came a gust of wind that smelled horribly of stagnant sea-water. I laid hold of something that had the shape of a man's arm, but was smooth, and wet, and icy cold. But suddenly, as I pulled, the creature sprang violently forward against me, a clammy, oozy mass, as it seemed to me, heavy and wet, yet endowed with a sort of supernatural strength. I reeled across the state-room, and in an instant the door opened and the thing rushed out. I had not had time to be frightened, and quickly recovering myself, I sprang through the door and gave chase at the top of my speed, but I was too late. Ten yards before me I could see—I am sure I saw it—a dark shadow moving in the dimly lighted passage, quickly as the shadow of a fast horse thrown before a dog-cart by the lamp on a dark night. But in a moment it had disappeared, and I found myself holding on to the polished rail that ran along the bulkhead where the passage turned towards the companion. My hair stood on end, and the cold perspiration rolled down my face. I am not ashamed of it in the least: I was very badly frightened.

Still I doubted my senses, and pulled myself together. It was absurd, I thought. The Welsh rarebit I had eaten had disagreed with me. I had been in a nightmare. I made my way back to my state-room, and entered it with an effort. The whole place smelled of stagnant sea-water, as it had when I had waked on the previous evening. It required my utmost strength to go in, and grope among my things for a box of wax lights. As I lighted a railway reading lantern which I always carry in case I want to read after the lamps are out, I perceived that the porthole was again open, and a sort of creeping horror began to take possession of me which I never felt before, nor wish to feel again. But I got a light and proceeded to examine the upper berth, expecting to find it drenched with sea-water.

But I was disappointed. The bed had been slept in, and the smell of the sea was strong; but the bedding was as dry as a bone. I fancied that Robert had not had the courage to make the bed after the accident of the previous night—it had all been a hideous dream. I drew the curtains back as far as I could and examined the place very carefully. It was perfectly dry. But the porthole was open again. With a sort of dull bewilderment of horror I closed it and screwed it down, and thrusting my heavy stick through the brass loop, wrenched it with all my might, till the thick metal began to bend under the pressure. Then I hooked my reading lantern into the red velvet at the head of the couch, and sat down to recover my senses if I could. I sat there all night, unable to think of rest—hardly able to think at all. But the porthole remained closed, and I did not believe it would now open again without the application of a considerable force.

The morning dawned at last, and I dressed myself slowly, thinking over all that had happened in the night. It was a beautiful day and I went on deck, glad to get out into the early, pure sunshine, and to smell the breeze from the blue water, so different from the noisome, stagnant odour of my state-room. Instinctively I turned aft, towards the surgeon's cabin. There he stood, with a pipe in his mouth, taking his morning airing precisely as on the preceding day.

"Good morning," said he quietly, but looking at me with evident curiosity.

"Doctor, you were quite right," said I. "There is something wrong about that place."

"I thought you would change your mind," he answered, rather triumphantly. "You have had a bad night, eh? Shall I make you a pick-me-up? I have a capital recipe."

"No, thanks," I cried. "But I would like to tell you what happened."

I then tried to explain as clearly as possible precisely what had occurred, not omitting to state that I had been scared as I had never been scared in my whole life before. I dwelt particularly on the phenomenon of the porthole, which was a fact to which I could testify, even if the rest had been an illusion. I had closed it twice in the night, and the second time I had actually bent the brass in wrenching it with my stick. I believe I insisted a good deal on this point.

"You seem to think I am likely to doubt the story." said the doctor, smiling at the detailed account of the state of the porthole. "I do not doubt it in the least. I renew my invitation to you. Bring your traps here, and take half my cabin."

"Come and take half of mine for one night," I said. "Help me to get at the bottom of this thing."

"You will get to the bottom of something else if you try," answered the doctor.

"What?" I asked.

"The bottom of the sea. I am going to leave this ship. It is not canny."

"Then you will not help me to find out——"

"Not I," said the doctor quickly. "It is my business to keep my wits about me—not to go fiddling about with ghosts and things."

"Do you really believe it is a ghost?" I enquired, rather contemptuously. But as I spoke I remembered very well the horrible sensation of the supernatural which had got possession of me during the night. The doctor turned sharply on me.

"Have you any reasonable explanation of these things to offer?" he asked. "No; you have not. Well, you say you will find an explanation. I say that you won't, sir, simply because there is not any."

"But, my dear sir," I retorted, "do you, a man of science, mean to tell me that such things cannot be explained?"

"I do," he answered stoutly. "And, if they could, I would not be concerned in the explanation."

I did not care to spend another night alone in the stateroom, and yet I was obstinately determined to get at the root of the disturbances. I do not believe there are many men who would have slept there alone, after passing two such nights. But I made up my mind to try it, if I could not get any one to share a watch with me. The doctor was evidently not inclined for such an experiment. He said he was a surgeon, and that in case any accident occurred on board he must be always in readiness. He could not afford to have his nerves unsettled. Perhaps he was quite right, but I am inclined to think that his precaution was prompted by his inclination. On enquiry, he informed me that there was no one on board who would be likely to join me in my investigations, and after a little more conversation I left him. A little later I met the captain, and told him my story. I said that, if no one would spend the night with me, I would ask leave to have the light burning all night, and would try it alone.

"Look here," said he, "I will tell you what I will do. I will share your watch myself, and we will see what happens. It is my belief that we can find out between us. There may be some fellow skulking on board, who steals a passage by frightening the passengers. It is just possible that there may be something queer in the carpentering of that berth."

I suggested taking the ship's carpenter below and examining the place; but I was overjoyed at the captain's offer to spend the night with me. He accordingly sent for the workman and ordered him to do anything I required. We went below at once. I had all the bedding cleared out of the upper berth, and we examined the place thoroughly to see if there was a board loose anywhere, or a panel which could be opened or pushed aside. We tried the planks everywhere, tapped the flooring, unscrewed the fittings of the lower berth and took it to pieces—in short, there was not a square inch of the state-room which was not searched and tested. Everything was in perfect order, and we put everything back in its place. As we were finishing our work, Robert came to the door and looked in.

"Well, sir—find anything, sir?" he asked, with a ghastly grin.

"You were right about the porthole, Robert," I said, and I gave him the promised sovereign. The carpenter did his work silently and skilfully, following my directions. When he had done he spoke.

"I'm just a plain man, sir," he said. "But it's my belief you had better just turn out your things, and let me run half a dozen four-inch screws through the door of this cabin. There's no good never came o' this cabin yet, sir, and that's all about it. There's been four lives lost out o' here to my own remembrance, and that in four trips. Better give it up, sir—better give it up!"

"I will try it for one night more," I said.

"Better give it up, sir—better give it up! It's a precious bad job," repeated the workman, putting his tools in his bag and leaving the cabin.

But my spirits had risen considerably at the prospect of having the captain's company, and I made up my mind not to be prevented from going to the end of the strange business. I abstained from Welsh rarebits and grog that evening, and did not even join in the customary game of whist. I wanted to be quite sure of my nerves, and my vanity made me anxious to make a good figure in the captain's eyes.

**4**

The captain was one of those splendidly tough and cheerful specimens of seafaring humanity whose combined courage, hardihood, and calmness in difficulty leads them naturally into high positions of trust. He was not the man to be led away by an idle tale, and the mere fact that he was willing to join me in the investigation was proof that he thought there was something seriously wrong, which could not be accounted for on ordinary theories, nor laughed down as a common superstition. To some extent, too, his reputation was at stake, as well as the reputation of the ship. It is no light thing to lose passengers overboard, and he knew it.

About ten o'clock that evening, as I was smoking a last cigar, he came up to me, and drew me aside from the beat of the other passengers who were patrolling the deck in the warm darkness.

"This is a serious matter, Mr. Brisbane," he said. "We must make up our minds either way—to be disappointed or to have a pretty rough time of it. You see I cannot afford to laugh at the affair, and I will ask you to sign your name to a statement of whatever occurs. If nothing happens to-night we will try it again to-morrow and next day. Are you ready?"

So we went below, and entered the state-room. As we went in I could see Robert the steward, who stood a little further down the passage, watching us, with his usual grin, as though certain that something dreadful was about to happen. The captain closed the door behind us and bolted it.

"Supposing we put your portmanteau before the door," he suggested. "One of us can sit on it. Nothing can get out then. Is the port screwed down?"

I found it as I had left it in the morning. Indeed, without using a lever, as I had done, no one could have opened it. I drew back the curtains of the upper berth so that I could see well into it. By the captain's advice I lighted my reading lantern, and placed it so that it shone upon the white sheets above. He insisted upon sitting on the portmanteau, declaring that he wished to be able to swear that he had sat before the door.

Then he requested me to search the state-room thoroughly, an operation very soon accomplished, as it consisted merely in looking beneath the lower berth and under the couch below the porthole. The spaces were quite empty.

"It is impossible for any human being to get in," I said, "or for any human being to open the port."

"Very good," said the captain calmly. "If we see anything now, it must be either imagination or something supernatural."

I sat down on the edge of the lower berth.

"The first time it happened," said the captain, crossing his legs and leaning back against the door, "was in March. The passenger who slept here, in the upper berth, turned out to have been a lunatic—at all events, he was known to have been a little touched, and he had taken his passage without the knowledge of his friends. He rushed out in the middle of the night and threw himself overboard, before the officer who had the watch could stop him. We stopped and lowered a boat; it was a quiet night, just before that heavy weather came on; but we could not find him. Of course, his suicide was afterwards accounted for on the ground of his insanity."

"I suppose that often happens?" I remarked, rather absently.

"Not often—no," said the captain; "never before in my experience, though I have heard of it happening on board of other ships. Well, as I was saying, that occurred in March. On the very next trip——What are you looking at?" he asked, stopping suddenly in his narration.

I believe I gave no answer. My eyes were riveted upon the porthole. It seemed to me that the brass loop-nut was beginning to turn very slowly upon the screw—so slowly, however, that I was not sure it moved at all. I watched it intently, fixing its position in my mind, and trying to ascertain whether it changed. Seeing where I was looking, the captain looked, too.

"It moves!" he exclaimed, in a tone of conviction. "No, it does not," he added, after a minute.

"If it were the jarring of the screw," said I, "it would have opened during the day; but I found it this evening jammed tight as I left it this morning."

I rose and tried the nut. It was certainly loosened, for by an effort I could move it with my hands.

"The queer thing," said the captain, "is that the second man who was lost is supposed to have got through that very port. We had a terrible time over it. It was in the middle of the night, and the weather was very heavy; there was an alarm that one of the ports was open and the sea running in. I came below and found everything flooded, the water pouring in every time she rolled, and the whole port swinging from the top bolts—not the porthole in the middle. Well, we managed to shut it, but the water did some damage. Ever since that the place smells of sea-water from time to time. We supposed the passenger had thrown himself out, though the Lord only knows how he did it. The steward kept telling me that he cannot keep anything shut here. Upon my word—I can smell it now, cannot you?" he enquired, sniffing the air suspiciously.

"Yes—distinctly," I said, and I shuddered as that same odour of stagnant sea-water grew stronger in the cabin. "Now, to smell like this, the place must be damp," I continued, "and yet when I examined it with the carpenter this morning everything was perfectly dry. It is most extraordinary—hallo!"

My reading lantern, which had been placed in the upper berth, was suddenly extinguished. There was still a good deal of light from the pane of ground glass near the door, behind which loomed the regulation lamp. The ship rolled heavily, and the curtain of the upper berth swung far out into the state-room and back again. I rose quickly from my seat on the edge of the bed, and the captain at the same moment started to his feet with a loud cry of surprise. I had turned with the intention of taking down the lantern to examine it, when I heard his exclamation, and immediately afterwards his call for help. I sprang towards him. He was wrestling with all his might with the brass loop of the port. It seemed to turn against his hands in spite of all his efforts. I caught up my cane, a heavy oak stick I always used to carry, and thrust it through the ring and bore on it with all my strength. But the strong wood snapped suddenly and I fell upon the couch. When I rose again the port was wide open, and the captain was standing with his back against the door, pale to the lips.

"There is something in that berth!" he cried, in a strange voice, his eyes almost starting from his head. "Hold the door, while I look—it shall not escape us, whatever it is!"

But instead of taking his place, I sprang upon the lower bed, and seized something which lay in the upper berth.

It was something ghostly, horrible beyond words, and it moved in my grip. It was like the body of a man long drowned, and yet it moved, and had the strength of ten men living; but I gripped it with all my might—the slippery, oozy, horrible thing—the dead white eyes seemed to stare at me out of the dusk; the putrid odour of rank sea-water was about it, and its shiny hair hung in foul wet curls over its dead face. I wrestled with the dead thing; it thrust itself upon me and forced me back and nearly broke my arms; it wound its corpse's arms about my neck, the living death, and overpowered me, so that I, at last, cried aloud and fell, and left my hold.

As I fell the thing sprang across me, and seemed to throw itself upon the captain. When I last saw him on his feet his face was white and his lips set. It seemed to me that he struck a violent blow at the dead being, and then he, too, fell forward upon his face, with an inarticulate cry of horror.

The thing paused an instant, seeming to hover over his prostrate body, and I could have screamed again for very fright, but I had no voice left. The thing vanished suddenly, and it seemed to my disturbed senses that it made its exit through the open port, though how that was possible, considering the smallness of the aperture, is more than any one can tell. I lay a

long time upon the floor, and the captain lay beside me. At last I partially recovered my senses and moved, and instantly I knew that my arm was broken—the small bone of the left forearm near the wrist.

I got upon my feet somehow, and with my remaining hand I tried to raise the captain. He groaned and moved, and at last came to himself. He was not hurt, but he seemed badly stunned.

Well, do you want to hear any more? There is nothing more. That is the end of my story. The carpenter carried out his scheme of running half a dozen four-inch screws through the door of 105; and if ever you take a passage in the *Kamtschatka,* you may ask for a berth in that state-room. You will be told that it is engaged—yes—it is engaged by that dead thing.

I finished the trip in the surgeon's cabin. He doctored my broken arm, and advised me not to "fiddle about with ghosts and things" any more. The captain was very silent, and never sailed again in that ship, though it is still running. And I will not sail in her either. It was a very disagreeable experience, and I was very badly frightened, which is a thing I do not like. That is all. That is how I saw a ghost—if it were a ghost. It was dead, anyhow.

# M. R. James

Montague Rhodes James (1862–1936) is often considered the greatest master of the ghost story in English, at least by those who view the ghost story as only one of the distinct divisions of the terror tale. He was a serious scholar whose fiction was a hobby, and the majority of his works have titles like *Verses in the Windows of Canterbury Cathedral* (1902) and *The Lost Apocrypha of the New Testament* (1920). His supernatural stories were originally designed to be read aloud to groups of university friends during Christmas celebrations, despite what might be perceived as the incongruity in juxtaposing horrors and holidays.

James was especially influenced by J. Sheridan Le Fanu and helped to retrieve many of his tales from oblivion by collecting and editing the stories in *Madam Crowl's Ghost and Other Tales of Mystery* (1923). In his turn, James influenced several later authors, particularly H. Russell Wakefield.

James is a traditionalist in many aspects of his work. He refined old techniques rather than devising new ones, and his style and subjects remained consistent for decades. Yet his stories are so effective that they have stayed in print continuously for decades. Part of their charm lies in the fact that they were composed for listening rather than reading; for all their careful construction, they are part of the oral tradition that many authorities describe as the origin of the ghostly tale.

He claimed to have no theories of his own on the subject:

Often I have been asked to formulate my views about ghost stories, and tales of the marvellous, the mysterious, the supernatural. Never have I been able to find out whether I had any views that could be formulated. The truth is, I suspect, that the genre is too small and special to bear the imposition of far-reaching principles.

He did offer a sort of formula, though:

Let us be introduced to the actors in a placid way; let us see them going about their ordinary business, undisturbed by forebodings, pleased with their surroundings; and into this calm environment let the ominous thing put out its head, unobtrusively at first, and then more insistently, until it holds the stage.

Among his more famous tales are "Count Magnus," "The Mezzotint," "The Ash-Tree," "An Episode of Cathedral History," and "Casting the Runes." His collections include *Ghost Stories of an Antiquary* (1904), *More Ghost Stories* (1911), *A Thin Ghost and Others* (1919), and *A Warning to the Curious* (1925). James was an authority on certain aspects of English history, and many of his stories display his special knowledge.

61

"Lost Hearts" is unusual for James in that it is actually set in the past and yet draws on even more ancient ideas than those contemporary with its setting. Some of the lore introduced is authentic, but the writer confessed that "as for the fragments of ostensible erudition which are scattered about my pages, hardly anything in them is not pure invention." Still, the principal purpose of the esoteric details here is to provide a setting for the figures of spirits seeking revenge. This theme of poetic justice is comparatively rare in stories by James, who usually preferred to present creatures of more or less motiveless malignancy.

"Lost Hearts" is one of his first pair of ghost stories, read at Cambridge University in 1893. It was published the next year in the *Pall Mall Magazine*.

# LOST HEARTS

## M. R. James

It was, as far as I can ascertain, in September of the year 1811 that a post-chaise drew up before the door of Aswarby Hall, in the heart of Lincolnshire. The little boy who was the only passenger in the chaise, and who jumped out as soon as it had stopped, looked about him with the keenest curiosity during the short interval that elapsed between the ringing of the bell and the opening of the hall door. He saw a tall, square, red-brick house, built in the reign of Anne; a stone-pillared porch had been added in the purer classical style of 1790; the windows of the house were many, tall and narrow, with small panes and thick white woodwork. A pediment, pierced with a round window, crowned the front. There were wings to right and left, connected by curious glazed galleries, supported by colonnades, with the central block. These wings plainly contained the stables and offices of the house. Each was surmounted by an ornamental cupola with a gilded vane.

An evening light shone on the building, making the window-panes glow like so many fires. Away from the Hall in front stretched a flat park studded with oaks and fringed with firs, which stood out against the sky. The clock in the church-tower, buried in trees on the edge of the park, only its golden weathercock catching the light, was striking six, and the sound came gently beating down the wind. It was altogether a pleasant impression, though tinged with the sort of melancholy appropriate to an evening in early autumn, that was conveyed to the mind of the boy who was standing in the porch waiting for the door to open to him.

The post-chaise had brought him from Warwickshire, where, some six months before, he had been left an orphan. Now, owing to the generous offer of his elderly cousin, Mr. Abney, he had come to live at Aswarby. The offer was unexpected, because all who knew anything of Mr. Abney looked upon him as a somewhat austere recluse, into whose steadygoing household the advent of a small boy would import a new and, it seemed, incongruous element. The truth is that very little was known of Mr. Abney's pursuits or temper. The Professor of Greek at Cambridge had been heard to say that no one knew more of the religious beliefs of the later pagans than did the owner of Aswarby. Certainly his library contained all the then available books bearing on the Mysteries, the Orphic poems, the worship of Mithras, and the Neo-Platonists. In the marble-paved hall stood a fine group of Mithras slaying a bull, which had been imported from the Levant at great expense by the owner. He had contributed a description of it to the *Gentleman's Magazine,* and he had written a remarkable series of articles in the *Critical Museum* on the superstitions of the Romans of the Lower Empire. He was looked upon, in fine, as a man wrapped up in his books, and it was a matter of great surprise among his neighbours that he should even have heard of his orphan cousin, Stephen Elliott, much more that he should have volunteered to make him an inmate of Aswarby Hall.

Whatever may have been expected by his neighbours, it is certain that Mr. Abney—the tall, the thin, the austere—seemed inclined to give his young cousin a kindly reception. The moment the front door was opened he darted out of his study, rubbing his hands with delight.

"How are you, my boy?—how are you? How old are you?" said he—"that is, you are not too much tired, I hope, by your journey to eat your supper?"

"No, thank you, sir," said Master Elliott; "I am pretty well."

"That's a good lad," said Mr. Abney. "And how old are you, my boy?"

It seemed a little odd that he should have asked the question twice in the first two minutes of their acquaintance.

"I'm twelve years old next birthday, sir," said Stephen.

"And when is your birthday, my dear boy? Eleventh of September, eh? That's well—that's very well. Nearly a year hence, isn't it? I like—ha, ha!—I like to get these things down in my book. Sure it's twelve? Certain?"

"Yes, quite sure, sir."

"Well, well! Take him to Mrs. Bunch's room, Parkes, and let him have his tea—supper—whatever it is."

"Yes, sir," answered the staid Mr. Parkes; and conducted Stephen to the lower regions.

Mrs. Bunch was the most comfortable and human person whom Stephen had as yet met in Aswarby. She made him completely at home; they were great friends in a quarter of an hour: and great friends they remained. Mrs. Bunch had been born in the neighbourhood some fifty-five years before the date of Stephen's arrival, and her residence at the Hall was of twenty years' standing. Consequently, if anyone knew the ins and outs of the house and the district, Mrs. Bunch knew them; and she was by no means disinclined to communicate her information.

Certainly there were plenty of things about the Hall and the Hall gardens which Stephen, who was of an adventurous and inquiring turn, was anxious to have explained to him. "Who built the temple at the end of the laurel walk? Who was the old man whose picture hung on the staircase, sitting at a table, with a skull under his hand?" These and many similar points were cleared up by the resources of Mrs. Bunch's powerful intellect. There were others, however, of which the explanations furnished were less satisfactory.

One November evening Stephen was sitting by the fire in the housekeeper's room reflecting on his surroundings.

"Is Mr. Abney a good man, and will he go to heaven?" he suddenly asked, with the peculiar confidence which children possess in the ability of their elders to settle these questions, the decision of which is believed to be reserved for other tribunals.

"Good?—bless the child!" said Mrs. Bunch. "Master's as kind a soul as ever I see! Didn't I never tell you of the little boy as he took in out of the street, as you may say, this seven years back? and the little girl, two years after I first come here?"

"No. Do tell me all about them, Mrs. Bunch—now this minute!"

"Well," said Mrs. Bunch, "the little girl I don't seem to recollect so much about. I know master brought her back with him from his walk one day, and give orders to Mrs. Ellis, as was housekeeper then, as she should be took every care with. And the pore child hadn't no one belonging to her—she told me so her own self—and here she lived with us a matter of three weeks it might be; and then, whether she were somethink of a gipsy in her blood or what not, but one morning she out of her bed afore any of us had opened a eye, and neither track nor yet trace of her have I set eyes on since. Master was wonderful put about, and had all the ponds dragged; but it's my belief she was had away by them gipsies, for there was singing round the house for as much as an hour the night she went, and Parkes, he declare as he heard them a-calling in the woods all that afternoon. Dear, dear! a hodd child she was, so silent in her ways and all, but I was wonderful taken up with her, so domesticated she was— surprising."

"And what about the little boy?" said Stephen.

"Ah, that pore boy!" sighed Mrs. Bunch. "He were a foreigner—Jevanny he called hisself—and he come a-tweaking his 'urdy-gurdy round and about the drive one winter day, and master 'ad him in that minute, and ast all about where he came from, and how old he was, and how he made his way, and where was his relatives, and all as kind as heart could wish. But it went the same way with him. They're a hunruly lot, them foreign nations, I do suppose, and he was off one fine morning just the same as the girl. Why he went and what he done was our question for as much as a year after; for he never took his 'urdy-gurdy, and there it lays on the shelf."

The remainder of the evening was spent by Stephen in miscellaneous cross-examination of Mrs. Bunch and in efforts to extract a tune from the hurdy-gurdy.

That night he had a curious dream. At the end of the passage at the top of the house, in which his bedroom was situated, there was an old disused bathroom. It was kept locked, but the upper half of the door was glazed, and, since the muslin curtains which used to hang there had long been gone, you could look in and see the lead-lined bath affixed to the wall on the right hand, with its head towards the window.

On the night of which I am speaking, Stephen Elliott found himself, as he thought, looking through the glazed door. The moon was shining through the window, and he was gazing at a figure which lay in the bath.

His description of what he saw reminds me of what I once beheld myself in the famous vaults of St. Michan's Church in Dublin, which possess the horrid property of preserving corpses from decay for centuries. A figure inexpressibly thin and pathetic, of a dusty leaden colour, enveloped in a shroud-like garment, the thin lips crooked into a faint and dreadful smile, the hands pressed tightly over the region of the heart.

As he looked upon it, a distant, almost inaudible moan seemed to issue from its lips, and the arms began to stir. The terror of the sight forced Stephen backwards, and he awoke to the fact that he was indeed standing on the cold boarded floor of the passage in the full light of the moon. With a courage which I do not think can be common among boys of his age, he went to the door of the bathroom to ascertain if the figure of his dream was really there. It was not, and he went back to bed.

Mrs. Bunch was much impressed next morning by his story, and went so far as to replace the muslin curtain over the glazed door of the bathroom. Mr. Abney, moreover, to whom he confided his experiences at breakfast, was greatly interested, and made notes of the matter in what he called "his book."

The spring equinox was approaching, as Mr. Abney frequently reminded his cousin, adding that this had been always considered by the ancients to be a critical time for the young: that Stephen would do well to take care of himself, and to shut his bedroom window at night; and that Censorinus had some valuable remarks on the subject. Two incidents that occurred about this time made an impression upon Stephen's mind.

The first was after an unusually uneasy and oppressed night that he had passed—though he could not recall any particular dream that he had had.

The following evening Mrs. Bunch was occupying herself in mending his nightgown.

"Gracious me, Master Stephen!" she broke forth rather irritably, "how do you manage to tear your nightdress all to flinders this way? Look here, sir, what trouble you do give to poor servants that have to darn and mend after you!"

There was indeed a most destructive and apparently wanton series of slits or scorings in the garment, which would undoubtedly require a skilful needle to make good. They were confined to the left side of the chest—long, parallel slits, about six inches in length, some of them not quite piercing the texture of the linen. Stephen could only express his entire ignorance of their origin: he was sure they were not there the night before.

"But," he said, "Mrs. Bunch, they are just the same as the scratches on the outside of my bedroom door; and I'm sure I never had anything to do with making *them*."

Mrs. Bunch gazed at him open-mouthed, then snatched up a candle, departed hastily from the room, and was heard making her way upstairs. In a few minutes she came down.

"Well," she said, "Master Stephen, it's a funny thing to me how them marks and scratches can 'a' come there—too high up for any cat or dog to 'ave made 'em, much less a rat: for all the world like a Chinaman's finger-nails, as my uncle in the tea-trade used to tell us of when we was girls together. I wouldn't say nothing to master, not if I was you, Master Stephen, my dear; and just turn the key of the door when you go to your bed."

"I always do, Mrs. Bunch, as soon as I've said my prayers."

"Ah, that's a good child: always say your prayers, and then no one can't hurt you."

Herewith Mrs. Bunch addressed herself to mending the injured nightgown, with intervals of meditation, until bed-time. This was on a Friday night in March, 1812.

On the following evening the usual duet of Stephen and Mrs. Bunch was augmented by the sudden arrival of Mr. Parkes, the butler, who as a rule kept himself rather *to* himself in his own pantry. He did not see that Stephen was there: he was, moreover, flustered, and less slow of speech than was his wont.

"Master may get up his own wine, if he likes, of an evening," was his first remark. "Either I do it in the daytime or not at all, Mrs. Bunch. I don't know what it may be: very like it's the rats, or the wind got into the cellars; but I'm not so young as I was, and I can't go through with it as I have done."

"Well, Mr. Parkes, you know it is a surprising place for the rats, is the Hall."

"I'm not denying that, Mrs. Bunch; and, to be sure, many a time I've heard the tale from the men in the shipyards about the rat that could speak. I never laid no confidence in that before; but to-night, if I'd demeaned myself to lay my ear to the door of the further bin, I could pretty much have heard what they was saying."

"Oh, there, Mr. Parkes, I've no patience with your fancies! Rats talking in the wine-cellar indeed!"

"Well, Mrs. Bunch, I've no wish to argue with you: all I say is, if you choose to go to the far bin, and lay your ear to the door, you may prove my words this minute."

"What nonsense you do talk, Mr. Parkes—not fit for children to listen to! Why, you'll be frightening Master Stephen there out of his wits."

"What! Master Stephen?" said Parkes, awaking to the consciousness of the boy's presence. "Master Stephen knows well enough when I'm a-playing a joke with you, Mrs. Bunch."

In fact, Master Stephen knew much too well to suppose that Mr. Parkes had in the first instance intended a joke. He was interested, not altogether pleasantly, in the situation; but all his questions were unsuccessful in inducing the butler to give any more detailed account of his experiences in the wine-cellar.

We have now arrived at March 24, 1812. It was a day of curious experiences for Stephen: a windy, noisy day, which filled the house and the gardens with a restless impression. As Stephen stood by the fence of the grounds, and looked out into the park, he felt as if an endless procession of unseen people were sweeping past him on the wind, borne on resistlessly and aimlessly, vainly striving to stop themselves, to catch at something that might arrest their flight and bring them once again into contact with the living world of which they had formed a part. After luncheon that day Mr. Abney said:

"Stephen, my boy, do you think you could manage to come to me to-night as late as eleven o'clock in my study? I shall be busy until that time, and I wish to show you something connected with your future life which it is most important that you should know. You are not to mention this matter to Mrs. Bunch nor to anyone else in the house; and you had better go to your room at the usual time,"

Here was a new excitement added to life: Stephen eagerly grasped at the opportunity of sitting up till eleven o'clock. He looked in at the library door on his way upstairs that evening, and saw a brazier, which he had often noticed in the corner of the room, moved out before the fire; an old silver-gilt cup stood on the table, filled with red wine, and some written sheets of paper lay near it. Mr. Abney was sprinkling some incense on the brazier from a round silver box as Stephen passed, but did not seem to notice his step.

The wind had fallen, and there was a still night and a full moon. At about ten o'clock Stephen was standing at the open window of his bedroom, looking out over the country. Still as the night was, the mysterious population of the distant moonlit woods was not yet lulled to rest. From time to time strange cries as of lost and despairing wanderers sounded from across the mere. They might be the notes of owls or water-birds, yet they did not quite resemble either sound. Were not they coming nearer? Now they sounded from the nearer side of the water, and in a few moments they seemed to be floating about among the shrubberies. Then they ceased; but just as Stephen was thinking of shutting the window and resuming his reading of *Robinson Crusoe,* he caught sight of two figures standing on the gravelled terrace that ran along the garden side of the Hall—the figures of a boy and girl, as it seemed; they stood side by side, looking up at the windows. Something in the form of the girl recalled irresistibly his dream of the figure in the bath. The boy inspired him with more acute fear.

Whilst the girl stood still, half smiling, with her hands clasped over her heart, the boy, a thin shape, with black hair and ragged clothing, raised his arms in the air with an appearance of menace and of unappeasable hunger and longing. The moon shone upon his almost transparent hands, and Stephen saw that the nails were fearfully long and that the light shone through them. As he stood with his arms thus raised, he disclosed a terrifying spectacle. On the left side of his chest there opened a black and gaping rent; and there fell upon Stephen's brain, rather than upon his ear, the impression of one of those hungry and desolate cries that he had heard resounding over the woods of Aswarby all that evening. In another moment this dreadful pair had moved swiftly and noiselessly over the dry gravel, and he saw them no more.

Inexpressibly frightened as he was, he determined to take his candle and go down to Mr. Abney's study, for the hour appointed for their meeting was near at hand. The study or library opened out of the front hall on one side, and Stephen, urged on by his terrors, did not take long in getting there. To effect an entrance was not so easy. The door was not locked, he felt sure, for the key was on the outside of it as usual. His repeated knocks produced no answer. Mr. Abney was engaged: he was speaking. What! why did he try to cry out? and why was the cry choked in his throat? Had he, too, seen the mysterious children? But now everything was quiet, and the door yielded to Stephen's terrified and frantic pushing.

On the table in Mr. Abney's study certain papers were found which explained the situation to Stephen Elliott when he was of an age to understand them. The most important sentences were as follows:

"It was a belief very strongly and generally held by the ancients—of whose wisdom in these matters I have had such experience as induces me to place confidence in their assertions—that by enacting certain processes, which to us moderns have something of a barbaric complexion, a very remarkable enlightenment of the spiritual faculties in man may be attained: that, for example, by absorbing the personalities of a certain number of his fellow-creatures, an individual may gain a complete ascendancy over those orders of spiritual beings which control the elemental forces of our universe.

"It is recorded of Simon Magus that he was able to fly in the air, to become invisible, or to assume any form he pleased, by the agency of the soul of a boy whom, to use the libellous phrase employed by the author of the *Clementine Recognitions*, he had 'murdered.' I find it set down, moreover, with considerable detail in the writings of Hermes Trismegistus, that similar happy results may be produced by the absorption of the hearts of not less than three human beings below the age of twenty-one years. To the testing of the truth of this receipt I have devoted the greater part of the last twenty years, selecting as the *corpora vilia* of my experiment such persons as could conveniently be removed without occasioning a sensible gap in society. The first step I effected by the removal of one Phoebe Stanley, a girl of gipsy extraction, on March 24, 1792. The second, by the removal of a wandering Italian lad, named Giovanni Paoli, on the night of March 23, 1805. The final 'victim'—to employ a word repugnant in the highest degree to my feelings—must be my cousin, Stephen Elliott. His day must be this March 24, 1812.

"The best means of effecting the required absorption is to remove the heart from the *living* subject, to reduce it to ashes, and to mingle them with about a pint of some red wine, preferably port. The remains of the first two subjects, at least, it will be well to conceal: a disused bathroom or wine-cellar will be found convenient for such a purpose. Some annoyance may be experienced from the psychic portion of the subjects, which popular language dignifies with the name of ghosts. But the man of philosophic temperament—to whom alone the experiment is appropriate—will be little prone to attach importance to the feeble efforts of these beings to wreak their vengeance on him. I contemplate with the liveliest satisfaction the enlarged and emancipated existence which the experiment, if successful, will confer on me; not only placing me beyond the reach of human justice (so-called), but eliminating to a great extent the prospect of death itself."

Mr. Abney was found in his chair, his head thrown back; his face stamped with an expression of rage, fright, and mortal pain. In his left side was a terrible lacerated wound, exposing the heart. There was no blood on his hands, and a long knife that lay on the table was perfectly clean. A savage wild-cat might have inflicted the injuries. The window of the study was open, and it was the opinion of the coroner that Mr. Abney had met his death by the agency of some wild creature. But Stephen Elliott's study of the papers I have quoted led him to a very different conclusion.

# Arthur Machen

Arthur Machen (1863–1947) is one of the major British authors of supernatural stories. Born Arthur Jones, he left his home in the Welsh countryside to seek a literary career in London. He had great difficulty for several years and felt he was inhabiting "rather a goblin's castle than a city of delights." His outsider's view of the mysterious metropolis later provided material for some of his best terror tales.

A series of small legacies supported him during the last decade of the nineteenth century, enabling him to produce some of his most famous stories, including "The Great God Pan," "The Inmost Light," "The White People," "The Red Hand," and two novels, *The Hill of Dreams* and *The Three Impostors*. He felt that his ability to produce horrors had been exhausted, but he continued to create them sporadically in subsequent decades, concluding with *The Green Round* in 1933.

His first publication in this vein, "The Great God Pan," made a minor sensation when it appeared in 1894, and the critic for the *Westminster Review* kindly warned Machen that continued brooding on such matters would probably drive him mad. Nevertheless he persevered, and in 1895 *The Three Impostors* appeared, representing Machen's hopes for "a certain originality of experiment in the tale of terror." This novel, which contains much of his best work, includes a number of short stories, told by members of an evil cult who are determined to distract a pair of amateur investigators. It was less immediately successful than its predecessor; Machen claimed that the reviews implied "that I was something of a pretentious ass and that my horrors were all humbug; and for some obscure reason, which I cannot undertake to explain, these notices cheered me on immensely in my new work."

Machen is a strange mass of contradictions. He is generally regarded as something of a mystic, and his autobiography recounts several of his weird experiences, yet it also displays a certain contempt for attempts to explain or control the uncanny. This attitude is all the more improbable in view of the fact that Machen was a member of The Order of the Golden Dawn, a society devoted to the study of such matters. It is possible that Machen was deliberately clouding the issue, since he received his indoctrination under a pledge of secrecy. His standard theme of ancient evil has obscured the fact that his stories are often close to science fiction, involving medical experiments that lead to revolting regressions. And his character Mr. Dyson, who appears unobtrusively in several stories, is one of the earliest examples of the occult detective.

Dyson is in fact the hero of *The Three Impostors*, which once included a werewolf story, although Machen destroyed it before publication and replaced it with the famous "Novel of the Black Seal." The central portion of the book, however, is the "History of the Young Man with Spectacles." This elusive figure, pursued throughout the book by various villains, leaves this narrative behind him, thus providing Dyson with a key to his queries. It is a powerful piece, delineating the slow steps that seduce a scholar into sin.

After its publication, Machen had a strange experience:

I was once talking to a dark young man, of quiet and retiring aspect, who wore glasses—he and I had met at a place where we had to be blindfolded before we could see the light—and he told me a queer tale of the manner in which his life was in daily jeopardy. He described the doings of a fiend in human form, a man well known to be an expert in Black Magic, a man who hung up naked women in cupboards by hooks which pierced the flesh of their arms. This monster—I may say that there is such a person, though I can by no means go bail for the actuality of any of the misdeeds charged against him—had, for some reason which I do not recollect, taken a dislike to my dark young friend. In consequence, so I was assured, he had hired a gang in Lambeth, who were grievously to maim or preferably to slaughter the dark young man. . . . It was only when I got home that it dawned upon me that I had been listening to the Young Man in Spectacles, and that he came straight out of *The Three Impostors.*

# HISTORY OF THE YOUNG MAN WITH SPECTACLES

## Arthur Machen

From the filthy and obscure lodging, situated, I verily believe, in one of the foulest slums of Clerkenwell, I indite this history of a life which, daily threatened, cannot last very much longer. Every day—nay, every hour, I know too well my enemies are drawing their nets closer about me; even now I am condemned to be a close prisoner in my squalid room, and I know that when I go out I shall go to my destruction. This history, if it chance to fall into good hands, may, perhaps, be of service in warning young men of the dangers and pitfalls that most surely must accompany any deviation from the ways of rectitude.

My name is Joseph Walters. When I came of age I found myself in possession of a small but sufficient income, and I determined that I would devote my life to scholarship. I do not mean the scholarship of these days; I had no intention of associating myself with men whose lives are spent in the unspeakably degrading occupation of 'editing' classics, befouling the fair margins of the fairest books with idle and superfluous annotation, and doing their utmost to give a lasting disgust of all that is beautiful. An abbey church turned to the base use of a stable or bakehouse is a sorry sight; but more pitiable still is a masterpiece spluttered over with the commentator's pen, and his hideous mark 'cf.'

For my part, I chose the glorious career of scholar in its ancient sense; I longed to possess encyclopaedic learning, to grow old amongst books, to distil day by day, and year after year, the inmost sweetness of all worthy writings. I was not rich enough to collect a library, and I was therefore forced to betake myself to the reading-room of the British Museum.

O dim, far-lifted, and mighty dome, Mecca of many minds, mausoleum of many hopes, sad house where all desires fail! For there men enter in with hearts uplifted, and dreaming minds, seeing in those exalted stairs a ladder to fame, in that pompous portico the gate of knowledge, and going in, find but vain vanity, and all but in vain. There, when the long streets are ringing, is silence, there eternal twilight, and the odour of heaviness. But there the blood flows thin and cold, and the brain burns adust; there is the hunt of shadows, and the chase of embattled phantoms; a striving against ghosts, and a war that has no victory. O dome, tomb of the quick! surely in thy galleries, where no reverberant voice can call, sighs whisper ever, and mutterings of dead hopes; and there men's souls mount like moths towards the flame, and fall scorched and blackened beneath thee, O dim, far-lifted, and mighty dome!

Bitterly do I now regret the day when I took my place at a desk for the first time, and began my studies. I had not been an habitué of the place for many months, when I became acquainted with a serene and benevolent gentleman, a man somewhat past middle age, who nearly always occupied a desk next to mine. In the reading-room it takes little to make an acquaintance—a casual offer of assistance, a hint as to the search in the catalogue, and the ordinary politeness of men who constantly sit near each other; it was thus I came to know the man calling himself Dr. Lipsius. By degrees I grew to look for his presence, and to miss him when he was away, as was sometimes the case, and so a friendship sprang up between us. His immense range of learning was placed freely at my service; he would often astonish me by the way in which he would sketch out in a few minutes the bibliography of a given subject, and before long I had confided to him my ambitions.

'Ah,' he said, 'you should have been a German. I was like that myself when I was a boy. It is a wonderful resolve, an infinite career. I will know all things; yes, it is a device indeed. But it means this—a life of labour without end, and a desire unsatisfied at last. The scholar has to die, and die saying, "I know very little!" '

Gradually, by speeches such as these, Lipsius seduced me: he would praise the career, and at the same time hint that it was as hopeless as the search for the philosopher's stone, and so by artful suggestions, insinuated with infinite address, he by degrees succeeded in undermining all my principles. 'After all,' he used to say, 'the greatest of all sciences, the key to all knowledge, is the science and art of pleasure. Rabelais was perhaps the greatest of all the encyclopaedic scholars; and he, as you know, wrote the most remarkable book that has ever been written. And what does he teach men in this book? Surely the joy of living. I need not remind you of the words, suppressed in most of the editions, the key of all the Rabelaisian mythology, of all the enigmas of his grand philosophy, *Vivez joyeux*. There you have all his learning; his work is the institutes of pleasure as the fine art; the finest art there is; the art of all arts. Rabelais had all science, but he had all life too. And we have gone a long way since his time. You are enlightened, I think; you do not consider all the petty rules and bylaws that a corrupt society has made for its own selfish convenience as the immutable decrees of the Eternal.'

Such were the doctrines that he preached; and it was by such insidious arguments, line upon line, here a little and there a little, that he at last succeeded in making me a man at war with the whole social system. I used to long for some opportunity to break the chains and to live a free life, to be my own rule and measure. I viewed existence with the eyes of a pagan, and Lipsius understood to perfection the art of stimulating the natural inclinations of a young man hitherto a hermit. As I gazed up at the great dome I saw it flushed with the flames and colours of a world of enticement unknown to me, my imagination played me a thousand wanton tricks, and the forbidden drew me as surely as a loadstone draws on iron. At last my resolution was taken, and I boldly asked Lipsius to be my guide.

He told me to leave the Museum at my usual hour, half-past four, to walk slowly along the northern pavement of Great Russell Street, and to wait at the corner of the street till I was addressed, and then to obey in all things the instructions of the person who came up to me. I carried out these directions, and stood at the corner looking about me anxiously, my heart beating fast, and my breath coming in gasps. I waited there for some time, and had begun to fear I had been made the object of a joke, when I suddenly became conscious of a gentleman who was looking at me with evident amusement from the opposite pavement of Tottenham Court Road. He came over, and raising his hat, politely begged me to follow him, and I did so without a word, wondering where we were going, and what was to happen. I was taken to a house of quiet and respectable aspect in a street lying to the north of Oxford Street, and my guide rang the bell. A servant showed us into a large room, quietly furnished, on the ground floor. We sat there in silence for some time, and I noticed that the furniture, though unpretending, was extremely valuable. There were large oak presses, two bookcases of extreme elegance, and in one corner a carved chest which must have been mediaeval. Presently Dr. Lipsius came in and welcomed me with his usual manner, and after some desultory conversation my guide left the room. Then an elderly man dropped in and began talking to Lipsius, and from their conversation I understood that my friend was a dealer in antiques; they spoke of the Hittite seal, and of the prospects of further discoveries, and later, when two or three more persons joined us, there was an argument as to the possibility of a systematic exploration of the pre-Celtic monuments of England. I was, in fact, present at an archaeological reception of an informal kind; and at nine o'clock, when the antiquaries were gone, I stared at Lipsius in a manner that showed I was puzzled, and sought an explanation.

'Now,' he said, 'we will go upstairs.'

As we passed up the stairs, Lipsius lighting the way with a hand-lamp, I heard the sound of a jarring lock and bolts and bars shot on at the front door. My guide drew back a baize door and we went down a passage, and I began to hear odd sounds, a noise of curious mirth; then he pushed me through a second door, and my initiation began. I cannot write down what I witnessed that night; I cannot bear to recall what went on in those secret rooms fast shuttered and curtained so that no light should escape into the quiet street; they gave me red wine to drink, and a woman told me as I sipped it that it was wine of the Red Jar that Avallaunius had made. Another asked me how I liked the wine of the Fauns, and I heard a dozen fantastic names, while the stuff boiled in my veins, and stirred, I think, something that had slept within me from the moment I was born. It seemed as if my self-consciousness deserted me; I was no longer a thinking agent, but at once subject and object; I mingled in the horrible sport, and watched the mystery of the Greek groves and fountains enacted before me, saw the reeling dance and heard the music calling as I sat beside my mate, and yet I was outside it all, and viewed my own part an idle spectator. Thus with strange rites they made me drink the cup, and when I woke up in the morning I was one of them, and had sworn to be faithful. At first I was shown the enticing side of things; I was bidden enjoy myself and care for nothing but pleasure, and Lipsius himself indicated to me as the acutest enjoyment the spectacle of the terrors of the unfortunate persons who were from time to time decoyed into the evil house. But after a time it was pointed out to me that I must take my share in the work, and so I found myself compelled to be in my turn a seducer; and thus it is on my conscience that I have led many to the depths of the pit.

One day Lipsius summoned me to his private room, and told me that he had a difficult task to give me. He unlocked a drawer and gave me a sheet of type-written paper, and bade me read it.

It was without place, or date, or signature, and ran as follows: —

Mr. James Headley, F.S.A. will receive from his agent in Armenia, on the 12th inst., a unique coin, the gold Tiberius. It bears on the reverse a faun with the legend VICTORIA. It is believed that this coin is of immense value. Mr. Headley will come up to town to show the coin to his friend, Professor Memys, of Chenies Street, Oxford Street, on some date between the 13th and the 18th.

Dr. Lipsius chuckled at my face of blank surprise when I laid down this singular communication.

'You will have a good chance of showing your discretion,' he said. 'This is not a common case; it requires great management and infinite tact. I am sure I wish I had a Panurge in my service, but we will see what you can do.'

'But is it not a joke?' I asked him. 'How can you know—or rather, how can this correspondent of yours know—that a coin has been despatched from Armenia to Mr. Headley? And how is it possible to fix the period in which Mr. Headley will take it into his head to come up to town? It seems to me a lot guesswork.'

'My dear Mr. Walters,' he replied, 'we do not deal in guesswork here. It would bore you if I went into all these little details, the cogs and wheels, if I may say so, which move the machine. Don't you think it is much more amusing to sit in front of the house and be astonished than to be behind the scenes and see the mechanism? Better tremble at the thunder, believe me, than see the man rolling the cannon-ball. But, after all, you needn't bother about the how and why; you have your share to do. Of course I shall give you full instructions, but a great deal depends on the way the thing is carried out. I have often heard very young men maintain that style is everything in literature, and I can assure you that the same maxim holds good in our far more delicate profession. With us style is absolutely everything, and that is why we have friends like yourself.'

I went away in some perturbation: he had no doubt designedly left everything in mystery, and I did not know what part I should have to play. Though I had assisted at scenes of hideous revelry, I was not yet dead to all echo of human feeling, and I trembled lest I should receive the order to be Mr. Headley's executioner.

A week later, it was on the sixteenth of the month, Dr. Lipsius made me a sign to come into his room.

'It is for to-night,' he began. 'Please to attend carefully to what I am going to say, Mr. Walters, and on peril of your life, for it is a dangerous matter,—on peril of your life, I say, follow these instructions to the letter. You understand? Well, to-night at about half-past seven, you will stroll quietly up the Hampstead Road till you come to Vincent Street. Turn down here and walk along, taking the third turning to your right, which is Lambert Terrace. Then follow the terrace, cross the road, and go along Hertford Street, and so into Lillington Square. The second turning you will come to in the square is called Sheen Street; but in reality it is more a passage between blank walls than a street. Whatever you do, take care to be at the corner of this street at eight o'clock precisely. You will walk along it, and just at the bend where you lose sight of the square you will find an old gentleman with white beard and whiskers. He will in all probability be abusing a cabman for having brought him to Sheen Street instead of Chenies Street. You will go up to him quietly and offer your services; he will tell you where he wants to go, and you will be so courteous as to offer to show him the way. I may say that Professor Memys moved into Chenies Street a month ago; thus Mr. Headley has never been to see him there, and, moreover, he is very shortsighted, and knows little of the topography of London. Indeed, he has quite lived the life of a learned hermit at Audley Hall.

'Well, need I say more to a man of your intelligence? You will bring him to this house, he will ring the bell, and a servant in quiet livery will let him in. Then your work will be done, and I am sure done well. You will leave Mr. Headley at the door, and simply continue your walk, and I shall hope to see you the next day. I really don't think there is anything more I can tell you.'

These minute instructions I took care to carry out to the letter. I confess that I walked up the Tottenham Court Road by no means blindly, but with an uneasy sense that I was coming to a decisive point in my life. The noise and rumour of the crowded pavements were to me but dumb show; I revolved again and again in ceaseless iteration the task that had been laid on me, and I questioned myself as to the possible results. As I got near the point of turning, I asked myself whether danger were not about my steps; the cold thought struck me that I was suspected and observed, and every chance foot-passenger who gave me a second glance seemed to me an officer of police. My time was running out, the sky had darkened, and I hesitated, half resolved to go no farther, but to abandon Lipsius and his friends for ever. I had almost determined to take this course, when the conviction suddenly came to me that the whole thing was a gigantic joke, a fabrication of rank improbability. Who could have procured the information about the Armenian agent? I asked myself. By what means could Lipsius have known the particular day and the very train that Mr. Headley was to take? how engage him to enter one special cab amongst the dozens waiting at Paddington? I vowed it a mere Milesian tale, and went forward merrily, turned down Vincent Street, and threaded out the route that Lipsius had so carefully impressed upon me. The various streets he had named were all places of silence and an oppressive cheap gentility; it was dark, and I felt alone in the musty squares and crescents, where people pattered by at intervals, and the shadows were growing blacker. I entered Sheen Street, and found it as Lipsius had said, more a passage than a street; it was a byway, on one side a low wall and neglected gardens, and grim backs of a line of houses, and on the other a timber-yard. I turned the corner, and lost sight of the square, and then, to my astonishment, I saw the scene of which I had been told. A hansom cab had come to a stop beside the pavement, and an old man, carrying a handbag, was fiercely abusing the cabman, who sat on his perch the image of bewilderment.

'Yes, but I'm sure you said Sheen Street, and that's where I brought you,' I heard him saying as I came up, and the old gentleman boiled in a fury, and threatened police and suits at law.

The sight gave me a shock, and in an instant I resolved to go through with it. I strolled on, and without noticing the cabman, lifted my hat politely to old Mr. Headley.

'Pardon me, sir,' I said, 'but is there any difficulty? I see you are a traveller; perhaps the cabman has made a mistake. Can I direct you?'

The old fellow turned to me, and I noticed that he snarled and showed his teeth like an ill-tempered cur as he spoke.

'This drunken fool has brought me here,' he said. 'I told him to drive to Chenies Street, and he brings me to this infernal place. I won't pay him a farthing, and I meant to have given him a handsome sum. I am going to call for the police and give him in charge.'

At this threat the cabman seemed to take alarm; he glanced round, as if to make sure that no policeman was in sight, and drove off grumbling loudly, and Mr. Headley grinned savagely with satisfaction at having saved his fare, and put back one and sixpence into his pocket, the 'handsome sum' the cabman had lost.

'My dear sir,' I said, 'I am afraid this piece of stupidity has annoyed you a great deal. It is a long way to Chenies Street, and you will have some difficulty in finding the place unless you know London pretty well.'

'I know it very little,' he replied. 'I never come up except on important business, and I've never been to Chenies Street in my life.'

'Really? I should be happy to show you the way. I have been for a stroll, and it will not at all inconvenience me to take you to your destination.'

'I want to go to Professor Memys, at Number 15. It's most annoying to me; I'm short-sighted, and I can never make out the numbers on the doors.'

'This way if you please,' I said, and we set out.

I did not find Mr. Headley an agreeable man; indeed, he grumbled the whole way. He informed me of his name, and I took care to say, 'The well-known antiquary?' and thenceforth I was compelled to listen to the history of his complicated squabbles with publishers, who treated him, as he said, disgracefully; the man was a chapter in the Irritability of Authors. He told me that he had been on the point of making the fortune of several firms, but had been compelled to abandon the design owing to their rank ingratitude. Besides these ancient histories of wrong, and the more recent misadventure of the cabman, he had another grievous complaint to make. As he came along in the train, he had been sharpening a pencil, and the sudden jolt of the engine as it drew up at a station had driven the penknife against his face, inflicting a small triangular wound just on the cheek-bone, which he showed me. He denounced the railway company, heaped imprecations on the head of the driver, and talked of claiming damages. Thus he grumbled all the way, not noticing in the least where he was going; and so unamiable did his conduct appear to me, that I began to enjoy the trick I was playing on him.

Nevertheless, my heart beat a little faster as we turned into the street where Lipsius was waiting. A thousand accidents, I thought, might happen; some chance might bring one of Headley's friends to meet us; perhaps, though he knew not Chenies Street, he might know the street where I was taking him; in spite of his short sight, he might possibly make out the number, or, in a sudden fit of suspicion, he might make an inquiry of the policeman at the corner. Thus every step upon the pavement, as we drew nearer to the goal, was to me a pang and a terror, and every approaching passenger carried a certain threat of danger. I gulped down my excitement with an effort, and made shift to say pretty quietly —

'Number 15, I think you said? That is the third house from this. If you will allow me, I will leave you now; I have been delayed a little, and my way lies on the other side of Tottenham Court Road.'

He snarled out some kind of thanks, and I turned my back and walked swiftly in the opposite direction. A minute or two later I looked round and saw Mr. Headley standing on the doorstep, and then the door opened and he went in. For my part, I gave a sigh of relief; I hastened to get away from the neighbourhood, and endeavoured to enjoy myself in merry company.

The whole of the next day I kept away from Lipsius. I felt anxious, but I did not know what had happened, or what was happening, and a reasonable regard for my own safety told me that I should do well to remain quietly at home. My curiosity, however, to learn the end of the odd drama in which I had played a part stung me to the quick, and late in the evening I made up my mind to see how events had turned out. Lipsius nodded when I came in, and asked if I could give him five minutes' talk. We went to his room, and he began to walk up and down, while I sat waiting for him to speak.

'My dear Mr. Walters,' he said at length, 'I congratulate you warmly; your work was done in the most thorough and artistic manner. You will go far. Look.'

He went to his escritoire and pressed a secret spring; a drawer flew out, and he laid something on the table. It was a gold coin; I took it up and examined it eagerly, and read the legend about the figure of the faun.

'Victoria,' I said, smiling.

'Yes; it was a great capture, which we owe to you. I had great difficulty in persuading Mr. Headley that a little mistake had been made; that was how I put it. He was very disagreeable, and indeed ungentlemanly, about it; didn't he strike you as a very cross old man?'

I held the coin, admiring the choice and rare design, clear cut as if from the mint; and I thought the fine gold glowed and burnt like a lamp.

'And what finally became of Mr. Headley?' I said at last.

Lipsius smiled, and shrugged his shoulders.

'What on earth does it matter?' he said. 'He might be here, or there, or anywhere; but what possible consequence could it be? Besides,your question rather surprises me; you are an intelligent man, Mr. Walters. Just think it over, and I'm sure you won't repeat the question.'

'My dear sir,' I said, 'I hardly think you are treating me fairly. You have paid me some handsome compliments on my share in the capture, and I naturally wish to know how the matter ended. From what I saw of Mr. Headley I should think you must have had some difficulty with him.'

He gave me no answer for the moment, but began again to walk up and down the room, apparently absorbed in thought.

'Well,' he said at last, 'I suppose there is something in what you say. We are certainly indebted to you. I have said that I have a high opinion of your intelligence, Mr. Walters. Just look here, will you?'

He opened a door communicating with another room, and pointed.

There was a great box lying on the floor, a queer, coffin-shaped thing. I looked at it, and saw it was a mummy case, like those in the British Museum, vividly painted in the brilliant Egyptian colours, with I knew not what proclamation of dignity or hopes of life immortal. The mummy swathed about in the robes of death was lying within, and the face had been uncovered.

'You are going to send this away?' I said, forgetting the question I had put.

'Yes; I have an order from a local museum. Look a little more closely, Mr. Walters.'

Puzzled by his manner, I peered into the face, while he held the lamp. The flesh was black with the passing of the centuries; but as I looked I saw upon the right cheek bone a small triangular scar, and the secret of the mummy flashed upon me: I was looking at the dead body of the man whom I had decoyed into that house.

There was no thought or design of action in my mind. I held the accursed coin in my hand, burning me with a foretaste of hell, and I fled as I would have fled from pestilence and death, and dashed into the street in blind horror, not knowing where I went. I felt the gold coin grasped in my clenched fist, and throwing it away, I knew not where, I ran on and on through by-streets and dark ways, till at last I issued out into a crowded thoroughfare and checked myself. Then as consciousness returned I realized my instant peril, and understood what would happen if I fell into the hands of Lipsius. I knew that I had put forth my finger to thwart a relentless mechanism rather than a man. My recent adventure with the unfortunate Mr. Headley had taught me that Lipsius had agents in all quarters; and I foresaw that if I fell into his hands, he would remain true to his doctrine of style, and cause me to die a death of some horrible and ingenious torture. I bent my whole mind to the task of outwitting him and his emissaries, three of whom I knew to have proved their ability for tracking down persons who for various reasons preferred to remain obscure. These servants of Lipsius were two men and a woman, and the woman was incomparably the most subtle and the most deadly. Yet I considered that I too had some portion of craft, and I took my resolve. Since then I have matched myself day by day and hour by hour against the ingenuity of Lipsius and his myrmidons. For a time I was successful; though they beat furiously after me in the covert of London, I remained *perdu*, and watched with some amusement their frantic efforts to recover the scent lost in two or three minutes. Every lure and wile was put forth to entice me from my hiding-place; I was informed by the medium of the public prints that what I had taken had been recovered, and meetings were proposed in which I might hope to gain a great deal without the slightest risk. I laughed at their endeavours, and began a little to despise the organization I had so dreaded, and ventured more abroad. Not once or twice, but several

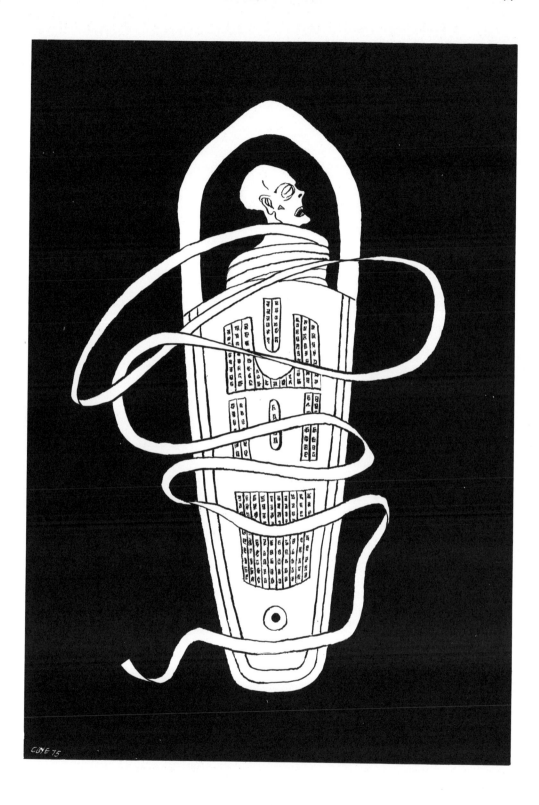

times, I recognized the two men who were charged with my capture, and I succeeded in eluding them at close quarters; and a little too hastily I decided that I had nothing to dread, and that my craft was greater than theirs. But in the meanwhile, while I congratulated myself on my cunning, the third of Lipsius's emissaries was weaving her nets; and in an evil hour I paid a visit to an old friend, a literary man named Russell, who lived in a quiet street in Bayswater. The woman, as I found out too late, a day or two ago occupied rooms in the same house, and I was followed and tracked down. Too late, as I have said I recognized that I had made a fatal mistake, and that I was besieged. Sooner or later I shall find myself in the power of an enemy without pity; and so surely as I leave this house I shall go to receive doom. I hardly dare to guess how it will at last fall upon me; my imagination, always a vivid one, paints to me appalling pictures of the unspeakable torture which I shall probably endure; and I know that I shall die with Lipsius standing near and gloating over the refinements of my suffering and my shame.

Hours, nay minutes, have become precious to me. I sometimes pause in the midst of anticipating my tortures, to wonder whether even now I cannot hit upon some supreme stroke, some design of infinite subtlety, to free myself from the toils. But I find that the faculty of combination has left me; I am as the scholar in the old myth, deserted by the power which has helped me hitherto. I do not know when the supreme moment will come, but sooner or later it is inevitable; before long I shall receive sentence, and from the sentence to execution will not be long.

# Robert W. Chambers

Robert William Chambers (1865–1933) is now remembered almost exclusively as a master of the macabre, despite the fact that his weird writings constitute a minute fraction of his published work. By the beginning of the twentieth century, he had established a glib, vacant writing style that brought him riches and renown, although his numerous novels of adventure and romance were despised by contemporary critics and have now been consigned to oblivion.

What has survived is his early work, composed before Chambers embarked on his career of calculated commercialism. Most significant is the 1895 collection of short stories, *The King in Yellow.* The title is also the title of a book described in the stories, a printed play so grotesque and evil that it drives readers mad. Chambers may have named the book for *The Yellow Book,* the scandalous English publication that had included the work of decadent artists like Aubrey Beardsley and Oscar Wilde. The parallel is not entirely inappropriate, since Chambers had been an art student in Paris, and many of his tales, like "The Yellow Sign," describe the bohemian life of unconventional creators.

The device of a dangerously wicked book was just one of the legacies that Chambers left to later authors; a more important legacy was the suggestion that the foundations of human existence are shaky, and that unseen powers, different from those described in traditional mythology, are in control of the universe. Although these ideas are presented only by implication, it is impossible to read any of these tales, which include "The Repairer of Reputations" and "In the Court of the Dragon," without inferring more than is directly described.

Chambers owes some of his inspiration and terminology to an unusual Ambrose Bierce story, "An Inhabitant of Carcosa," but he originated more than he appropriated. His work was a major influence on H. P. Lovecraft and, through him, on dozens of other writers. Although he is most frequently discussed as the author of a single uncanny book, Chambers made other excursions into this realm, including stories in *The Maker of Moons* (1896) and *The Mystery of Choice* (1897), and the late novel *The Slayer of Souls* (1920). His most famous character, although not usually associated with his originator, is Mr. Keene, hero of *The Tracer of Lost Persons* (1906), who was featured after the author's death in a popular series of radio and television plays.

"The Yellow Sign" is generally acknowledged to be the best of the tales in *The King in Yellow.* It is not without its flaws, particularly in the introduction of the romantic sentimentality that was to corrupt the bulk of Chambers's subsequent publications. Still, this is largely the fault of the era in which it was composed. And there is a contrast to this Victorian

79

vapidness in certain discreet references to depravity, to say nothing of the fact that the heroine spends most of the story in the nude, which must have scandalized at least some readers of the day. "The Yellow Sign" is a deceptive story that seems at first to concern itself with such traditional topics as dreams and death and only gradually and tantalizingly dropping hints that its horrors represent something more ghastly and grandiose. Despite the occasionally inflated rhetoric, there is a powerful pattern submerged beneath the sometimes purple prose, and it is this for which Chambers is remembered.

---

# THE YELLOW SIGN

---

# Robert W. Chambers

## 1. BEING THE CONTENTS OF AN UNSIGNED LETTER SENT TO THE AUTHOR

There are so many things which are impossible to explain! Why should certain chords in music make me think of the brown and golden tints of autumn foliage? Why should the Mass of Sainte Cécile send my thoughts wandering among caverns whose walls blaze with ragged masses of virgin silver? What was it in the roar and turmoil of Broadway at six o'clock that flashed before my eyes the picture of a still Breton forest where sunlight filtered through spring foliage and Sylvia bent, half curiously, half tenderly, over a small green lizard, murmuring: "To think that this also is a little ward of God!"

When I first saw the watchman his back was toward me. I looked at him indifferently until he went into the church. I paid no more attention to him than I had to any other man who lounged through Washington Square that morning, and when I shut my window and turned back into my studio I had forgotten him. Late in the afternoon, the day being warm, I raised the window again and leaned out to get a sniff of air. A man was standing in the courtyard of the church, and I noticed him again with as little interest as I had that morning. I looked across the square to where the fountain was playing and then, with my mind filled with vague impressions of trees, asphalt drives, and the moving groups of nursemaids and holiday-makers, I started to walk back to my easel. As I turned, my listless glance included the man below in the churchyard. His face was toward me now, and with a perfectly involuntary movement I bent to see it. At the same moment he raised his head and looked at me. Instantly I thought of a coffin-worm. Whatever it was about the man that repelled me I did not know, but the impression of a plump white grave-worm was so intense and nauseating that I must have shown it in my expression, for he turned his puffy face away with a movement which made me think of a disturbed grub in a chestnut.

I went back to my easel and motioned the model to resume her pose. After working awhile I was satisfied that I was spoiling what I had done as rapidly as possible, and I took up a palette knife and scraped the color out again. The flesh tones were sallow and unhealthy, and I did not understand how I could have painted such sickly color into a study which before that had glowed with healthy tones.

I looked at Tessie. She had not changed, and the clear flush of health dyed her neck and cheeks as I frowned.

"Is it something I've done?" she said.

"No,—I've made a mess of this arm, and for the life of me I can't see how I came to paint such mud as that into the canvas," I replied.

"Don't I pose well?" she insisted.

"Of course, perfectly."

"Then it's not my fault?"

"No. It's my own."

"I'm very sorry," she said.

I told her she could rest while I applied rag and turpentine to the plague spot on my canvas, and she went off to smoke a cigarette and look over the illustrations in the *Courier Français.*

I did not know whether it was something in the turpentine or a defect in the canvas, but the more I scrubbed the more that gangrene seemed to spread. I worked like a beaver to get it out, and yet the disease appeared to creep from limb to limb of the study before me. Alarmed I strove to arrest it, but now the color on the breast changed and the whole figure seemed to absorb the infection as a sponge soaks up water. Vigorously I plied palette knife, turpentine, and scraper, thinking all the time what a séance I should hold with Duval who had sold me the canvas; but soon I noticed that it was not the canvas which was defective nor yet the colors of Edward. "It must be the turpentine," I thought angrily, "or else my eyes have become so blurred and confused by the afternoon light that I can't see straight." I called Tessie, the model. She came and leaned over my chair blowing rings of smoke into the air.

"What *have* you been doing to it?" she exclaimed.

"Nothing," I growled, "it must be this turpentine!"

"What a horrible color it is now," she continued. "Do you think my flesh resembles green cheese?"

"No, I don't," I said angrily, "did you ever know me to paint like that before?"

"No, indeed!"

"Well, then!"

"It must be the turpentine, or something," she admitted.

She slipped on a Japanese robe and walked to the window. I scraped and rubbed until I was tired and finally picked up my brushes and hurled them through the canvas with a forcible expression, the tone alone of which reached Tessie's ears.

Nevertheless she promptly began: "That's it! Swear and act silly and ruin your brushes! You have been three weeks on that study, and now look! What's the good of ripping the canvas? What creatures artists are!"

I felt about as much ashamed as I usually did after such an outbreak, and I turned the ruined canvas to the wall. Tessie helped me clean my brushes, and then danced away to dress. From the screen she regaled me with bits of advice concerning whole or partial loss of temper, until, thinking, perhaps, I had been tormented sufficiently, she came out to implore me to button her waist where she could not reach it on the shoulder.

"Everything went wrong from the time you came back from the window and talked about that horrid-looking man you saw in the churchyard," she announced.

"Yes, he probably bewitched the picture," I said, yawning. I looked at my watch.

"It's after six, I know," said Tessie, adjusting her hat before the mirror.

"Yes," I replied, "I didn't mean to keep you so long." I leaned out of the window but recoiled with disgust, for the young man with the pasty face stood below in the churchyard. Tessie saw my gesture of disapproval and leaned from the window.

"Is that the man you don't like?" she whispered.

I nodded.

"I can't see his face, but he does look fat and soft. Someway or other," she continued, turning to look at me, "he reminds me of a dream,—an awful dream I once had. Or," she mused, looking down at her shapely shoes, "was it a dream after all?"

"How should I know?" I smiled.

Tessie smiled in reply.

"You were in it," she said, "so perhaps you might know something about it."

"Tessie! Tessie!" I protested, "don't you dare flatter by saying you dream about me!"

"But I did," she insisted; "shall I tell you about it?"

"Go ahead," I replied, lighting a cigarette.

Tessie leaned back on the open window-sill and began very seriously.

"One night last winter I was lying in bed thinking about nothing at all in particular. I had been posing for you and I was tired out, yet it seemed impossible for me to sleep. I heard the bells in the city ring ten, eleven, and midnight. I must have fallen asleep about midnight because I don't remember hearing the bells after that. It seemed to me that I had scarcely closed my eyes when I dreamed that something impelled me to go to the window. I rose, and raising the sash, leaned out. Twenty-fifth Street was deserted as far as I could see. I began to be afraid; everything outside seemed so—so black and uncomfortable. Then the sound of wheels in the distance came to my ears, and it seemed to me as though that was what I must wait for. Very slowly the wheels approached, and, finally, I could make out a vehicle moving along the street. It came nearer and nearer, and when it passed beneath my window I saw it was a hearse. Then, as I trembled with fear, the driver turned and looked straight at me. When I awoke I was standing by the open window shivering with cold, but the black-plumed hearse and the driver were gone. I dreamed this dream again in March last, and again awoke beside the open window. Last night the dream came again. You remember how it was raining; when I awoke, standing at the open window, my night-dress was soaked."

"But where did I come into the dream?" I asked.

"You—you were in the coffin; but you were not dead."

"In the coffin?"

"Yes."

"How did you know? Could you see me?"

"No; I only knew you were there."

"Had you been eating Welsh rarebits, or lobster salad?" I began laughing, but the girl interrupted me with a frightened cry.

"Hello! What's up?" I said, as she shrank into the embrasure by the window.

"The—the man below in the churchyard;—he drove the hearse."

"Nonsense," I said, but Tessie's eyes were wide with terror. I went to the window and looked out. The man was gone. "Come, Tessie," I urged, "don't be foolish. You have posed too long; you are nervous."

"Do you think I could forget that face?" she murmured. "Three times I saw the hearse pass below my window, and every time the driver turned and looked up at me. Oh, his face was so white and—and soft? It looked dead—it looked as if it had been dead a long time."

I induced the girl to sit down and swallow a glass of Marsala. Then I sat down beside her, and tried to give her some advice.

"Look here, Tessie," I said, "you go to the country for a week or two, and you'll have no more dreams about hearses. You pose all day, and when night comes your nerves are upset. You can't keep this up. Then again, instead of going to bed when your day's work is done, you run off to picnics at Sulzer's Park, or go to the Eldorado or Coney Island, and when you come down here next morning you are fagged out. There was no real hearse. That was a soft-shell crab dream."

She smiled faintly.

"What about the man in the churchyard?"

"Oh, he's only an ordinary unhealthy, everyday creature."

"As true as my name is Tessie Reardon, I swear to you, Mr. Scott, that the face of the man below in the churchyard is the face of the man who drove the hearse!"

"What of it?" I said. "It's an honest trade."

"Then you think I *did* see the hearse?"

"Oh," I said, diplomatically, "if you really did, it might not be unlikely that the man below drove it. There is nothing in that."

Tessie rose, unrolled her scented handkerchief, and taking a bit of gum from a knot in the hem, placed it in her mouth. Then drawing on her gloves she offered me her hand, with a frank, "Good-night, Mr. Scott," and walked out.

**2**

The next morning, Thomas, the bellboy, brought me the *Herald* and a bit of news. The church next door had been sold. I thanked Heaven for it, not that being a Catholic I had any repugnance for the congregation next door, but because my nerves were shattered by a blatant exhorter, whose every word echoed through the aisle of the church as if it had been my own rooms, and who insisted on his r's with a nasal persistence which revolted my every instinct. Then, too, there was a fiend in human shape, an organist, who reeled off some of the grand old hymns with an interpretation of his own, and I longed for the blood of a creature who could play the doxology with an amendment of minor chords which one hears only in a quartet of very young undergraduates. I believe the minister was a good man, but when he bellowed: "And the Lorrrrd said unto Moses, the Lorrrd is a man of war; the Lorrrd is his name. My wrath shall wax hot and I will kill you with the sworrrd!" I wondered how many centuries of purgatory it would take to atone for such a sin.

"Who bought the property?" I asked Thomas.

"Nobody that I knows, sir. They do say the gent wot owns this 'ere 'Amilton flats was lookin' at it. 'E might be a bildin' more studios."

I walked to the window. The young man with the unhealthy face stood by the churchyard gate, and at the mere sight of him the same overwhelming repugnance took possession of me.

"By the way, Thomas," I said, "who is that fellow down there?"

Thomas sniffed. "That there worm, sir? 'E's night-watchman of the church, sir. 'E maikes me tired a-sittin' out all night on them steps and lookin' at you insultin' like. I'd a punched 'is 'ed, sir—beg pardon, sir—"

"Go on, Thomas."

"One night a comin' 'ome with 'Arry, the other English boy, I sees 'im a sittin' there on them steps. We 'ad Molly and Jen with us, sir, the two girls on the tray service, an' 'e looks so insultin' at us that I up and sez: 'Wat you looking hat, you fat slug?'—beg pardon, sir, but that's 'ow I sez, sir. Then 'e don't say nothin' and I sez: 'Come out and I'll punch that puddin' 'ed.' Then I hopens the gate an' goes in, but 'e don't say nothin', only looks insultin' like. Then I 'its 'im one, but, ugh! 'is 'ed was that cold and mushy it ud sicken you to touch 'im."

"What did he do then?" I asked, curiously.

"'Im? Nawthin'."

"And you, Thomas?"

The young fellow flushed with embarrassment and smiled uneasily.

"Mr. Scott, sir, I ain't no coward an' I can't make it out at all why I run. I was in the 5th Lawncers, sir, bugler at Tel-el-Kebir, an' was shot by the wells."

"You don't mean to say you ran away?"

"Yes, sir; I run."

"Why?"

"That's just what I want to know, sir. I grabbed Molly an' run, an' the rest was as frightened as I."

"But what were they frightened at?"

Thomas refused to answer for a while, but now my curiosity was aroused about the repulsive young man below and I pressed him. Three years' sojourn in America had not only modified Thomas' cockney dialect but had given him the American's fear of ridicule.

"You won't believe me, Mr. Scott, sir?"

"Yes, I will."

"You will lawf at me, sir?"

"Nonsense!"

He hesitated. "Well, sir, it's God's truth that when I 'it 'im 'e grabbed me wrists, sir, and when I twisted 'is soft, mushy fist one of 'is fingers come off in me 'and."

The utter loathing and horror of Thomas' face must have been reflected in my own for he added:

"It's orful, an' now when I see 'im I just go away. 'E maikes me hill."

When Thomas had gone I went to the window. The man stood beside the church-railing with both hands on the gate, but I hastily retreated to my easel again, sickened and horrified, for I saw that the middle finger of his right hand was missing.

At nine o'clock Tessie appeared and vanished behind the screen with a merry "Good-morning, Mr. Scott." When she had reappeared and taken her pose upon the model-stand I started a new canvas much to her delight. She remained silent as long as I was on the drawing, but as soon as the scrape of the charcoal ceased and I took up my fixative she began to chatter.

"Oh, I had such a lovely time last night. We went to Tony Pastor's."

"Who are 'we'?" I demanded.

"Oh, Maggie, you know, Mr. Whyte's model, and Pinkie McCormick—we call her Pinkie because she's got that beautiful red hair you artists like so much—and Lizzie Burke."

I sent a shower of spray from the fixative over the canvas, and said: "Well, go on."

"We saw Kelly and Baby Barnes the skirt-dancer and—and all the rest. I made a mash."

"Then you have gone back on me, Tessie?"

She laughed and shook her head.

"He's Lizzie Burke's brother, Ed. He's a perfect gen'l'man."

I felt constrained to give her some parental advice concerning mashing, which she took with a bright smile.

"Oh, I can take care of a strange mash," she said, examining her chewing gum, "but Ed is different. Lizzie is my best friend."

Then she related how Ed had come back from the stocking mill in Lowell, Massachusetts, to find her and Lizzie grown up, and what an accomplished young man he was, and how he thought nothing of squandering half a dollar for ice-cream and oysters to celebrate his entry as clerk into the woollen department of Macy's. Before she finished I began to paint, and she resumed the pose, smiling and chattering like a sparrow. By noon I had the study fairly well rubbed in and Tessie came to look at it.

"That's better," she said.

I thought so too, and ate my lunch with a satisfied feeling that all was going well. Tessie spread her lunch on a drawing table opposite me and we drank our claret from the same bottle and lighted our cigarettes from the same match. I was very much attached to Tessie. I had watched her shoot up into a slender but exquisitely formed woman from a frail, awkward

child. She had posed for me during the last three years, and among all my models she was my favorite. It would have troubled me very much indeed had she become "tough" or "fly," as the phrase goes, but I never noticed any deterioration of her manner, and felt at heart that she was all right. She and I never discussed morals at all, and I had no intention of doing so, partly because I had none myself, and partly because I knew she would do what she liked in spite of me. Still I did hope she would steer clear of complications, because I wished her well, and then also I had a selfish desire to retain the best model I had. I knew that mashing, as she termed it, had no significance with girls like Tessie, and that such things in America did not resemble in the least the same things in Paris. Yet, having lived with my eyes open, I also knew that somebody would take Tessie away some day, in one manner or another, and though I professed to myself that marriage was nonsense, I sincerely hoped that, in this case, there would be a priest at the end of the vista. I am a Catholic. When I listen to high mass, when I sign myself, I feel that everything, including myself, is more cheerful, and when I confess, it does me good. A man who lives as much alone as I do, must confess to somebody. Then, again, Sylvia was Catholic, and it was reason enough for me. But I was speaking of Tessie, which is very different. Tessie also was Catholic and much more devout than I, so, taking it all in all, I had little fear for my pretty model until she should fall in love. But *then* I knew that fate alone would decide her future for her, and I prayed inwardly that fate would keep her away from men like me and throw into her path nothing but Ed Burkes and Jimmy McCormicks, bless her sweet face!

Tessie sat blowing rings of smoke up to the ceiling and tinkling the ice in her tumbler.

"Do you know, Kid, that I also had a dream last night?" I observed. I sometimes called her "the Kid."

"Not about that man," she laughed.

"Exactly. A dream similar to yours, only much worse."

It was foolish and thoughtless of me to say this, but you know how little tact the average painter has.

"I must have fallen asleep about 10 o'clock," I continued, "and after awhile I dreamt that I awoke. So plainly did I hear the midnight bells, the wind in the tree-branches, and the whistle of steamers from the bay, that even now I can scarcely believe I was not awake. I seemed to be lying in a box which had a glass cover. Dimly I saw the street lamps as I passed, for I must tell you, Tessie, the box in which I reclined appeared to lie in a cushioned wagon which jolted me over a stony pavement. After a while I became impatient and tried to move but the box was too narrow. My hands were crossed on my breast so I could not raise them to help myself. I listened and then tried to call. My voice was gone. I could hear the trample of the horses attached to the wagon and even the breathing of the driver. Then another sound broke upon my ears like the raising of a window sash. I managed to turn my head a little, and found I could look, not only through the glass cover of my box, but also through the glass panes in the side of the covered vehicle. I saw houses, empty and silent, with neither light nor life about any of them excepting one. In that house a window was open on the first floor and a figure all in white stood looking down into the street. It was you."

Tessie had turned her face away from me and leaned on the table with her elbow.

"I could see your face," I resumed, "and it seemed to me to be very sorrowful. Then we passed on and turned into a narrow black lane. Presently the horses stopped. I waited and waited, closing my eyes with fear and impatience, but all was silent as the grave. After what seemed to me hours, I began to feel uncomfortable. A sense that somebody was close to me made me unclose my eyes. Then I saw the white face of the hearse-driver looking at me through the coffin-lid—"

A sob from Tessie interrupted me. She was trembling like a leaf. I saw I had made an ass of myself and attempted to repair the damage.

"Why, Tess," I said, "I only told you this to show you what influence your story might have on another person's dreams. You don't suppose I really lay in a coffin, do you? What are you trembling for? Don't you see that your dream and my unreasonable dislike for that inoffensive watchman of the church simply set my brain working as soon as I fell asleep?"

She laid her head between her arms and sobbed as if her heart would break. What a precious triple donkey I had made of myself! But I was about to break my record. I went over and put my arm about her.

"Tessie dear, forgive me," I said; "I had no business to frighten you with such nonsense. You are too sensible a girl, too good a Catholic to believe in dreams."

Her hand tightened on mine and her head fell back upon my shoulder, but she still trembled and I petted her and comforted her.

"Come, Tess, open your eyes and smile."

Her eyes opened with a slow languid movement and met mine, but their expression was so queer that I hastened to reassure her again.

"It's all humbug, Tessie, you surely are not afraid that any harm will come to you because of that."

"No," she said, but her scarlet lips quivered.

"Then what's the matter? Are you afraid?"

"Yes. Not for myself."

"For me, then?" I demanded gayly.

"For you," she murmured in a voice almost inaudible, "I—I care for you."

At first I started to laugh, but when I understood her, a shock passed through me and I sat like one turned to stone. This was the crowning bit of idiocy I had committed. During the moment which elapsed between her reply and my answer I thought of a thousand responses to that innocent confession. I could pass it by with a laugh, I could misunderstand her and reassure her as to my health, I could simply point out that it was impossible she could love me. But my reply was quicker than my thoughts, and I might think and think now when it was too late, for I had kissed her on the mouth.

That evening I took my usual walk in Washington Park, pondering over the occurrences of the day. I was thoroughly committed. There was no back out now, and I stared the future straight in the face. I was not good, not even scrupulous, but I had no idea of deceiving either myself or Tessie. The one passion of my life lay buried in the sunlit forests of Brittany. Was it buried forever? Hope cried "No!" For three years I had been listening to the voice of Hope, and for three years I had waited for a footstep on my threshold. Had Sylvia forgotten? "No!" cried Hope.

I said that I was not good. That is true, but still I was not exactly a comic opera villain. I had led an easy-going reckless life, taking what invited me of pleasure, deploring and sometimes bitterly regretting consequences. In one thing alone, except my painting, was I serious, and that was something which lay hidden if not lost in the Breton forests.

It was too late now for me to regret what had occurred during the day. Whatever it had been, pity, a sudden tenderness for sorrow, or the more brutal instinct of gratified vanity, it was all the same now, and unless I wished to bruise an innocent heart my path lay marked before me. The fire and strength, the depth of passion of a love which I had never even suspected, with all my imagined experience in the world, left me no alternative but to respond or send her away. Whether because I am so cowardly about giving pain to others, or whether it was that I have little of the gloomy Puritan in me, I do not know, but I shrank from disclaiming responsibility for that thoughtless kiss, and in fact had no time to do so before the gates of her heart opened and the flood poured forth. Others who habitually do their duty and find a sullen satisfaction in making themselves and everybody else unhappy, might have withstood it. I did not. I dared not. After the storm had abated I did tell her that she might better have loved Ed Burke and worn a plain gold ring, but she would not hear of it, and I thought perhaps that as long as she had decided to love somebody she could not marry, it had better be me. I, at least, could treat her with an intelligent affection, and whenever she became tired of her infatuation she could go none the worse for it. For I was decided on that point although I knew how hard it would be. I remembered the usual termination of Platonic liaisons and thought how disgusted I had been whenever I heard of one. I knew I was undertaking a great deal for so unscrupulous a man as I was, and I dreaded the future, but never for one moment did I doubt that she was safe with me. Had it been anybody but Tessie I should not have bothered my head about scruples. For it did not occur to me to sacrifice Tessie as I would have sacrificed a woman of the world. I looked the future squarely in the face and saw the several probable endings to the affair. She would either tire of the whole thing, or become so unhappy that I should have either to marry her or go away. If I married her we would be unhappy. I with a wife unsuited to me, and she with a husband unsuitable for any woman. For my past life could scarcely entitle me to marry. If I went away she might either fall ill, recover, and marry some Eddie Burke, or she might recklessly or deliberately go and do something foolish. On the other hand if she tired of me, then her whole life would be before her with beautiful vistas of Eddie Burkes and marriage rings and twins and Harlem flats and Heaven knows what. As I strolled along through the trees by the Washington Arch, I decided that she should find a substantial friend in me anyway and the future could take care of itself. Then I went into the house and put on my evening dress for the little faintly perfumed note on my dresser said, "Have a cab at the stage door at eleven," and the note was signed "Edith Carmichel, Metropolitan Theater, June 19th, 189—."

I took supper that night, or rather we took supper, Miss Carmichel and I, at Solari's and the dawn was just beginning to gild the cross on the Memorial Church as I entered Washington Square after leaving Edith at the Brunswick. There was not a soul in the park as I passed among the trees and took the walk which leads from the Garibaldi statue to the Hamilton Apartment House, but as I passed the churchyard I saw a figure sitting on the stone steps. In spite of myself a chill crept over me at the sight of the white puffy face, and I hastened to pass. Then he said something which might have been addressed to me or might merely have been a mutter to himself, but a sudden furious anger flamed up within me that such a creature should address me. For an instant I felt like wheeling about and smashing my stick over his head, but I walked on, and entering the Hamilton went to my apartment. For some time I tossed about the bed trying to get the sound of his voice out of my ears, but could not. It filled my head, that muttering sound, like thick oily smoke from a fat-rendering vat or an odor of noisome decay. And as I lay and tossed about, the voice in my ears seemed more distinct, and I began to understand the words he had muttered. They came to me slowly as if I had forgotten them, and at last I could make some sense out of the sounds. It was this:

"Have you found the Yellow Sign?"

"Have you found the Yellow Sign?"

"Have you found the Yellow Sign?"

I was furious. What did he mean by that? Then with a curse upon him and his I rolled over and went to sleep, but when I awoke later I looked pale and haggard, for I had dreamed the dream of the night before and it troubled me more than I cared to think.

I dressed and went down into my studio. Tessie sat by the window, but as I came in she rose and put both arms around my neck for an innocent kiss. She looked so sweet and dainty that I kissed her again and then sat down before the easel.

"Hello! Where's the study I began yesterday?" I asked.

Tessie looked conscious, but did not answer. I began to hunt among the piles of canvases, saying, "Hurry up, Tess, and get ready; we must take advantage of the morning light."

When at last I gave up the search among the other canvases and turned to look around the room for the missing study I noticed Tessie standing by the screen with her clothes still on.

"What's the matter," I asked, "don't you feel well?"

"Yes."

"Then hurry."

"Do you want me to pose as—as I have always posed?"

Then I understood. Here was a new complication. I had lost, of course, the best nude model I had ever seen. I looked at Tessie. Her face was scarlet. Alas! Alas! We had eaten of the tree of knowledge, and Eden and native innocence were dreams of the past—I mean for her.

I suppose she noticed the disappointment on my face, for she said: "I will pose if you wish. The study is behind the screen here where I put it."

"No," I said, "we will begin something new;" and I went into my wardrobe and picked out a Moorish costume which fairly blazed with tinsel. It was a genuine costume, and Tessie retired to the screen with it enchanted. When she came forth again I was astonished. Her long black hair was bound above her forehead with a circlet of turquoises, and the ends curled about her glittering girdle. Her feet were encased in the embroidered pointed slippers and the skirt of her costume, curiously wrought with arabesques in silver, fell to her ankles. The deep metallic blue vest embroidered with silver and the short Mauresque jacket spangled and sewn with turquoises became her wonderfully. She came up to me and held up her face smiling. I slipped my hand into my pocket and drawing out a gold chain with a cross attached, dropped it over her head.

"It's yours, Tessie."

"Mine?" she faltered.

"Yours. Now go and pose." Then with a radiant smile she ran behind the screen and presently reappeared with a little box on which was written my name.

"I had intended to give it to you when I went home to-night," she said, "but I can't wait now."

I opened the box. On the pink cotton inside lay a clasp of black onyx, on which was inlaid a curious symbol or letter in gold. It was neither Arabic nor Chinese, nor as I found afterwards did it belong to any human script.

"It's all I had to give you for a keepsake," she said, timidly.

I was annoyed, but I told her how much I should prize it, and promised to wear it always. She fastened it on my coat beneath the lapel.

"How foolish, Tess, to go and buy me such a beautiful thing as this," I said.

"I did not buy it," she laughed.

"Where did you get it?"

Then she told me how she had found it one day while coming from the Aquarium in the Battery, how she had advertised it and watched the papers, but at last gave up all hopes of finding the owner.

"That was last winter," she said, "the very day I had the first horrid dream about the hearse."

I remembered my dream of the previous night but said nothing, and presently my charcoal was flying over a new canvas, and Tessie stood motionless on the model-stand.

## 3

The day following was a disastrous one for me. While moving a framed canvas from one easel to another my foot slipped on the polished floor and I fell heavily on both wrists. They were so badly sprained that it was useless to attempt to hold a brush, and I was obliged to wander about the studio, glaring at unfinished drawings and sketches until despair seized me and I sat down to smoke and twiddle my thumbs with rage. The rain blew against the windows and rattled on the roof of the church, driving me into a nervous fit with its interminable patter. Tessie sat sewing by the window, and every now and then raised her head and looked at me with such innocent compassion that I began to feel ashamed of my irritation and looked about for something to occupy me. I had read all the papers and all the books in the library, but for the sake of something to do I went to the bookcases and shoved them open with my elbow. I knew every volume by its color and examined them all, passing slowly around the library and whistling to keep up my spirits. I was turning to go into the dining-room when my eye fell upon a book bound in yellow, standing in a corner of the top shelf of the last bookcase. I did not remember it and from the floor could not decipher the pale lettering on the back, so I went to the smoking-room and called Tessie. She came in from the studio and climbed up to reach the book.

"What is it?" I asked.

" 'The King in Yellow.' "

I was dumfounded. Who had placed it there? How came it in my rooms? I had long ago decided that I should never open that book, and nothing on earth could have persuaded me to buy it. Fearful lest curiosity might tempt me to open it, I had never even looked at it in bookstores. If I ever had had any curiosity to read it, the awful tragedy of young Castaigne, whom I knew, prevented me from exploring its wicked pages. I had always refused to listen to any description of it, and indeed, nobody ever ventured to discuss the second part aloud, so I had absolutely no knowledge of what those leaves might reveal. I stared at the poisonous yellow binding as I would at a snake.

"Don't touch it, Tessie," I said; "come down."

Of course my admonition was enough to arouse her curiosity, and before I could prevent it she took the book and, laughing, danced away into the studio with it. I called to her but she slipped away with a tormenting smile at my helpless hands, and I followed her with some impatience.

"Tessie!" I cried, entering the library, "listen, I am serious. Put that book away. I do not wish you to open it!" The library was empty. I went into both drawing-rooms, then into the bedrooms, laundry, kitchen, and finally returned to the library and began a systematic search. She had hidden herself so well that it was half an hour later when I discovered her crouching white and silent by the latticed window in the store-room above. At the first glance I saw she had been punished for her foolishness. "The King in Yellow" lay at her feet, but the book was open at the second part. I looked at Tessie and saw it was too late. She had opened "The King in Yellow." Then I took her by the hand and led her into the studio. She seemed dazed, and when I told her to lie down on the sofa she obeyed me without a word. After a while she closed her eyes and her breathing became regular and deep, but I could not determine whether or not she slept. For a long while I sat silently beside her, but she neither stirred nor spoke, and at last I rose and entering the unused store-room took the yellow book in my least injured hand. It seemed heavy as lead, but I carried it into the studio again, and sitting down on the rug beside the sofa, opened it and read it through from beginning to end.

When, faint with the excess of my emotions, I dropped the volume and leaned wearily back against the sofa, Tessie opened her eyes and looked at me.

We had been speaking for some time in a dull monotonous strain before I realized that we were discussing "The King in Yellow." Oh the sin of writing such words,—words which are clear as crystal, limpid and musical as bubbling springs, words which sparkle and glow like the poisoned diamonds of the Medicis! Oh the wickedness, the hopeless damnation of a soul who could fascinate and paralyze human creatures with such words,—words understood by the ignorant and wise alike, words which are more precious than jewels, more soothing than Heavenly music, more awful than death itself.

We talked on, unmindful of the gathering shadows, and she was begging me to throw away the clasp of black onyx quaintly inlaid with what we now knew to be the Yellow Sign. I never shall know why I refused, though even at this hour, here in my bedroom as I write this confession, I should be glad to know *what* it was that prevented me from tearing the Yellow Sign from my breast and casting it into the fire. I am sure I wished to do so, but Tessie pleaded with me in vain. Night fell and the hours dragged on, but still we murmured to each other of the King and the Pallid Mask, and midnight sounded from the misty spires in the fog-wrapped city. We spoke of Hastur and of Cassilda, while outside the fog rolled against the blank window-panes as the cloud waves roll and break on the shores of Hali.

The house was very silent now and not a sound from the misty streets broke the silence. Tessie lay among the cushions, her face a gray blot in the gloom, but her hands were clasped in mine and I knew that she knew and read my thoughts as I read hers, for we had understood the mystery of the Hyades and the Phantom of Truth was laid. Then as we answered each other, swiftly, silently, thought on thought, the shadows stirred in the gloom about us, and far in the distant streets we heard a sound. Nearer and nearer it came, the dull crunching of wheels, nearer and yet nearer, and now, outside before the door it ceased, and I dragged myself to the window and saw a black-plumed hearse. The gate below opened and shut, and I crept shaking to my door and bolted it, but I knew no bolts, no locks, could keep that creature out who was coming for the Yellow Sign. And now I heard him moving very softly along the hall. Now he was at the door, and the bolts rotted at his touch. Now he had entered. With eyes starting from my head I peered into the darkness, but when he came into the room I did not see him. It was only when I felt him envelop me in his cold soft grasp that I cried out and struggled with deadly fury, but my hands were useless and he tore the onyx clasp from my coat and struck me full in the face. Then, as I fell, I heard Tessie's soft cry and her spirit fled to God, and even while falling I longed to follow her, for I knew that the King in Yellow had opened his tattered mantle and there was only Christ to cry to now.

I could tell more, but I cannot see what help it will be to the world. As for me I am past human help or hope. As I lie here, writing, careless even whether or not I die before I finish, I can see the doctor gathering up his powders and phials with a vague gesture to the good priest beside me, which I understand.

They will be very curious to know the tragedy—they of the outside world who write books and print millions of newspapers, but I shall write no more, and the father confessor will seal my last words with the seal of sanctity when his holy office is done. They of the outside world may send their creatures into wrecked homes and death-smitten firesides, and their newspapers will batten on blood and tears, but with me their spies must halt before the confessional. They know that Tessie is dead and that I am dying. They know how the people in the house, aroused by an infernal scream, rushed into my room and found one living and two dead, but they do not know what I shall tell them now; they do not know that the doctor said as he pointed to a horrible decomposed heap on the floor—the livid corpse of the watchman from the church: "I have no theory, no explanation. That man must have been dead for months!"

I think I am dying. I wish the priest would—

# H. G. Wells

Herbert George Wells (1886–1946) is, of course, the father of science fiction in the English language. What is perhaps more remarkable is that even though the best part of a century has passed since his most popular works in the field were published, his stories and novels in this genre have rarely been equaled in imagination or literary merit. During the later and longer period of his career, Wells wrote dozens of volumes of realistic fiction, history, sociology, and prophecy; yet his comparatively few books of fantastic fiction are the ones that are still eagerly appreciated by countless readers and writers.

The most renowned of his novels, which Wells called "scientific romances," are *The Time Machine* (1895), *The Island of Dr. Moreau* (1896), *The Invisible Man* (1897), and *The War of the Worlds* (1898). Each was eventually made into a vivid and memorable motion picture, which has proved to be an important factor in their apparent immortality. James Whale's brilliant 1933 film *The Invisible Man,* with a fine performance by Claude Rains and spectacular special effects by John P. Fulton, gave birth to a pair of sequels and several thematically related productions; the story later became the basis for two separate television series, the most recent starring David McCallum. *The War of the Worlds* made its greatest sensation as a radio broadcast by Orson Welles and The Mercury Theater on Hallowe'en eve in 1938.

An important factor in the success of these novels, one that the film versions have emphasized, is that they are not only science fiction but immensely powerful horror stories as well. *The War of the Worlds* is particularly noteworthy as the first important example of what has become a standard plot: the invasion of this planet by beings from another. And *The Time Machine* inaugurated another new branch of speculative stories. Both of these novels were skillfully filmed by producer George Pal.

Most of the fantasies of H. G. Wells were written during the first decade of his literary career, and his works of science fiction are so familiar that many readers are unaware of the supernatural stories he produced during the same period. In addition to such supernatural novels as *The Wonderful Visit* (1895) and *The Sea Lady* (1902), Wells wrote such short stories of the uncanny and the horrifying as "The Cone," "Pollock and the Porroh Man," "The Story of the Late Mr. Elvesham," "The Stolen Body," "The Door in the Wall," and "The Man Who Could Work Miracles." Wells claimed to see little difference between his scientific and his supernatural fantasies, since he expected them in any case to be only as believable as "a good, gripping dream."

Wells even wrote a pair of excellent ghost stories, proving himself a master of that most traditional branch of fantastic fiction. One is "The Inexperienced Ghost," a predominantly humorous piece that ends on an unexpectedly grim and ironic note. The other is "The Red Room," which appeared in the 1897 collection *The Plattner Story and Others*. Sometimes reprinted as "The Ghost of Fear," it appears here under its original and more evocative title. Using the stock situation of the visitor who dares to spend the night in a haunted chamber, Wells achieves remarkable results, renovating such venerable clichés as the ancient servant and the guttering candle. It is little wonder that to critics at the turn of the century Wells was best known as a specialist in tales of terror.

# THE RED ROOM

# H. G. Wells

"I can assure you," said I, "that it will take a very tangible ghost to frighten me." And I stood up before the fire with my glass in my hand.

"It is your own choosing," said the man with the withered arm, and glanced at me askance.

"Eight-and-twenty years," said I, "I have lived, and never a ghost have I seen as yet."

The old woman sat staring hard into the fire, her pale eyes wide open. "Ay," she broke in, "and eight-and-twenty years you have lived, and never seen the likes of this house, I reckon. There's a many things to see, when one's still but eight-and-twenty." She swayed her head slowly from side to side. "A many things to see and sorrow for."

I half suspected these old people were trying to enhance the spectral terrors of their house by this droning insistence. I put down my empty glass on the table, and, looking about the room, caught a glimpse of myself, abbreviated and broadened to an impossible sturdiness, in the queer old mirror beside the china cupboard. "Well," I said, "if I see anything to-night, I shall be so much the wiser. For I come to the business with an open mind."

"It's your own choosing," said the man with the withered arm once more.

I heard the faint sound of a stick and a shambling step on the flags in the passage outside. The door creaked on its hinges as a second old man entered, more bent, more wrinkled, more aged even than the first. He supported himself by the help of a crutch, his eyes were covered by a shade, and his lower lip, half averted, hung pale and pink from his decaying yellow teeth. He made straight for an armchair on the opposite side of the table, sat down clumsily, and began to cough. The man with the withered hand gave the newcomer a short glance of positive dislike; the old woman took no notice of his arrival, but remained with her eyes fixed steadily on the fire.

"I said—it's your own choosing," said the man with the withered hand, when the coughing had ceased for a while.

"It's my own choosing," I answered.

The man with the shade became aware of my presence for the first time, and threw his head back for a moment, and sidewise, to see me. I caught a momentary glimpse of his eyes, small and bright and inflamed. Then he began to cough and splutter again.

"Why don't you drink?" said the man with the withered arm, pushing the beer toward him. The man with the shade poured out a glassful with a shaking hand, that splashed half as much again on the deal table. A monstrous shadow of him crouched upon the wall, and mocked his action as he poured and drank. I must confess I had scarcely expected these grotesque custodians. There is, to my mind, something inhuman in senility, something crouching and atavistic; the human qualities seem to drop from old people insensibly day by day. The three of them made me feel uncomfortable with their gaunt silences, their bent carriage, their evident unfriendliness to me and to one another. And that night, perhaps, I was in the mood for uncomfortable impressions. I resolved to get away from their vague foreshadowings of the evil things upstairs.

"If," said I, "you will show me to this haunted room of yours, I will make myself comfortable there."

The old man with the cough jerked his head back so suddenly that it startled me, and shot another glance of his red eyes at me from out of the darkness under the shade, but no one answered me. I waited a minute, glancing from one to the other. The old woman stared like a dead body, glaring into the fire with the lack-luster eyes.

"If," I said, a little louder, "if you will show me to this haunted room of yours, I will relieve you from the task of entertaining me."

"There's a candle on the slab outside the door," said the man with the withered hand, looking at my feet as he addressed me. "But if you go to the Red Room tonight——"

"This night of all nights!" said the old woman, softly.

"—You go alone."

"Very well," I answered shortly, "and which way do I go?"

"You go along the passage for a bit," said he, nodding his head on his shoulder at the door, "until you come to a spiral staircase; and on the second landing is a door covered with green baize. Go through that, and down the long corridor to the end, and the Red Room is on your left up the steps."

"Have I got that right?" I said, and repeated his directions.

He corrected me in one particular.

"And you are really going?" said the man with the shade, looking at me again for the third time with that queer, unnatural tilting of the face.

"This night of all nights!" whispered the old woman.

"It is what I came for," I said, and moved toward the door. As I did so, the old man with the shade rose and staggered round the table, so as to be closer to the others and to the fire. At the door I turned and looked at them, and saw they were all close together, dark against the firelight, staring at me over their shoulders, with an intent expression on their ancient faces.

"Good-night," I said, setting the door open.

"It's your own choosing," said the man with the withered arm.

I left the door wide open until the candle was well alight, and then I shut them in, and walked down the chilly, echoing passage.

I must confess that the oddness of these three old pensioners in whose charge her ladyship had left the castle, and the deep-toned, old-fashioned furniture of the housekeeper's room, in which they forgathered, had affected me curiously in spite of my effort to keep myself at a matter-of-fact phase. They seemed to belong to another age, an older age, an age when things spiritual were indeed to be feared, when common sense was uncommon, an age when omens and witches were credible, and ghosts beyond denying. Their very existence, thought I, is spectral; the cut of their clothing, fashions born in dead brains; the ornaments and conveniences in the room about them even are ghostly—the thoughts of vanished men, which still haunt rather than participate in the world of to-day. And the passage I was in, long and shadowy, with a film of moisture glistening on the wall, was as gaunt and cold as a thing that is dead and rigid. But with an effort I sent such thoughts to the right-about. The long, drafty

subterranean passage was chilly and dusty, and my candle flared and made the shadows cower and quiver. The echoes rang up and down the spiral staircase, and a shadow came sweeping up after me, and another fled before me into the darkness overhead. I came to the wide landing and stopped there for a moment listening to a rustling that I fancied I heard creeping behind me, and then, satisfied of the absolute silence, pushed open the unwilling baize-covered door and stood in the silent corridor.

The effect was scarcely what I expected, for the moonlight, coming in by the great window on the grand staircase, picked out everything in vivid black shadow or reticulated silvery illumination. Everything seemed in its proper position; the house might have been deserted on the yesterday instead of twelve months ago. There were candles in the sockets of the sconces, and whatever dust had gathered on the carpets or upon the polished flooring was distributed so evenly as to be invisible in my candlelight. A waiting stillness was over everything. I was about to advance, and stopped abruptly. A bronze group stood upon the landing hidden from me by a corner of the wall; but its shadow fell with marvelous distinctness upon the white paneling, and gave me the impression of some one crouching to waylay me. The thing jumped upon my attention suddenly. I stood rigid for half a moment, perhaps. Then, with my hand in the pocket that held the revolver, I advanced, only to discover a Ganymede and Eagle, glistening in the moonlight. That incident for a time restored my nerve, and a dim porcelain Chinaman on a buhl table, whose head rocked as I passed, scarcely startled me.

The door of the Red Room and the steps up to it were in a shadowy corner. I moved my candle from side to side in order to see clearly the nature of the recess in which I stood, before opening the door. Here it was, thought I, that my predecessor was found, and the memory of that story gave me a sudden twinge of apprehension. I glanced over my shoulder at the black Ganymede in the moonlight, and opened the door of the Red Room rather hastily, with my face half turned to the pallid silence of the corridor.

I entered, closed the door behind me at once, turned the key I found in the lock within, and stood with the candle held aloft surveying the scene of my vigil, the great Red Room of Lorraine Castle, in which the young Duke had died; or rather in which he had begun his dying, for he had opened the door and fallen headlong down the steps I had just ascended. That had been the end of his vigil, of his gallant attempt to conquer the ghostly tradition of the place, and never, I thought, had apoplexy better served the ends of superstition. There were other and older stories that clung to the room, back to the half-incredible beginning of it all, the tale of a timid wife and the tragic end that came to her husband's jest of frightening her. And looking round that huge shadowy room with its black window bays, its recesses and alcoves, its dusty brown-red hangings and dark gigantic furniture, one could well understand the legends that had sprouted in its black corners, its germinating darknesses. My candle was a little tongue of light in the vastness of the chamber; its rays failed to pierce to the opposite end of the room, and left an ocean of dull red mystery and suggestion, sentinel shadows and watching darknesses beyond its island of light. And the stillness of desolation brooded over it all.

I must confess some impalpable quality of that ancient room disturbed me. I tried to fight the feeling down. I resolved to make a systematic examination of the place, and so, by leaving nothing to the imagination, dispel the fanciful suggestions of the obscurity before they obtained a hold upon me. After satisfying myself of the fastening of the door, I began to walk round the room, peering round each article of furniture, tucking up the valances of the bed and opening its curtains wide. In one place there was a distinct echo to my footsteps, the noises I made seemed so little that they enhanced rather than broke the silence of the place. I pulled up the blinds and examined the fastenings of the several windows. Attracted by the fall of a particle of dust, I leaned forward and looked up the blackness of the wide chimney. Then, trying to preserve my scientific attitude of mind, I walked round and began tapping the oak paneling for any secret opening, but I desisted before reaching the alcove. I saw my face in a mirror—white.

There were two big mirrors in the room, each with a pair of sconces bearing candles, and on the mantelshelf, too, were candles in china candlesticks. All these I lit one after the other. The fire was laid—an unexpected consideration from the old housekeeper—and I lit it, to keep down any disposition to shiver, and when it was burning well I stood round with my back to it and regarded the room again. I had pulled up a chintz-covered armchair and a table to form a kind of barricade before me. On this lay my revolver, ready to hand. My precise examination had done me a little good, but I still found the remoter darkness of the place and its perfect stillness too stimulating for the imagination. The echoing of the stir and crackling of the fire was no sort of comfort to me. The shadow in the alcove at the end of the room began to display that undefinable quality of a presence, that odd suggestion of a lurking living thing that comes so easily in silence and solitude. And to reassure myself, I walked with a candle into it and satisfied myself that there was nothing tangible there. I stood that candle upon the floor of the alcove and left it in that position.

By this time I was in a state of considerable nervous tension, although to my reason there was no adequate cause for my condition. My mind, however, was perfectly clear. I postulated quite unreservedly that nothing supernatural could happen, and to pass the time I began stringing some rhymes together, Ingoldsby fashion, concerning the original legend of the place. A few I spoke aloud, but the echoes were not pleasant. For the same reason I also abandoned, after a time, a conversation with myself upon the impossibility of ghosts and haunting. My mind reverted to the three old and distorted people downstairs, and I tried to keep it upon that topic.

The somber reds and grays of the room troubled me; even with its seven candles the place was merely dim. The light in the alcove flaring in a draft, and the fire flickering, kept the shadows and penumbra perpetually shifting and stirring in a noiseless flighty dance. Casting about for a remedy, I recalled the wax candles I had seen in the corridor, and, with a slight effort, carrying a candle and leaving the door open, I walked out into the moonlight, and presently returned with as many as ten. These I put in the various knick-knacks of china with which the room was sparsely adorned, and lit and placed them where the shadows had lain deepest, some on the floor, some in the window recesses, arranging and rearranging them until at last my seventeen candles were so placed that not an inch of the room but had the direct light of at least one of them. It occurred to me that when the ghost came I could warn him not to trip over them. The room was now quite brightly illuminated. There was something very cheering and reassuring in these little silent streaming flames, and to notice their steady diminution of length offered me an occupation and gave me a reassuring sense of the passage of time.

Even with that, however, the brooding expectation of the vigil weighed heavily enough upon me. I stood watching the minute hand of my watch creep towards midnight.

Then something happened in the alcove. I did not see the candle go out, I simply turned and saw that the darkness was there, as one might start and see the unexpected presence of a stranger. The black shadow had sprung back to its place. "By Jove," said I aloud, recovering from my surprise, "that draft's a strong one"; and taking the matchbox from the table, I walked across the room in a leisurely manner to relight the corner again. My first match would not strike, and as I succeeded with the second, something seemed to blink on the wall before me. I turned my head involuntarily and saw that the two candles on the little table by the fireplace were extinguished. I rose at once to my feet.

"Odd," I said. "Did I do that myself in a flash of absent-mindedness?"

I walked back, relit one, and as I did so I saw the candle in the right sconce of one of the mirrors wink and go right out, and almost immediately its companion followed it. The flames vanished as if the wick had been suddenly nipped between a finger and thumb, leaving the wick neither glowing nor smoking, but black. While I stood gaping the candle at the foot of the bed went out, and the shadows seemed to take another step toward me.

"This won't do!" said I, and first one and then another candle on the mantelshelf followed.

"What's up?" I cried, with a queer high note getting into my voice somehow. At that the candle on the corner of the wardrobe went out, and the one I had relit in the alcove followed.

"Steady on!" I said, "those candles are wanted," speaking with a half-hysterical face-tiousness, and scratching away at a match the while, "for the mantel candlesticks." My hands trembled so much that twice I missed the rough paper of the matchbox. As the mantel emerged from darkness again, two candles in the remoter end of the room were eclipsed. But with the same match I also relit the larger mirror candles, and those on the floor near the doorway, so that for the moment I seemed to gain on the extinctions. But then in a noiseless volley there vanished four lights at once in different corners of the room, and I struck another match in quivering haste, and stood hesitating whither to take it.

As I stood undecided, an invisible hand seemed to sweep out the two candles on the table. With a cry of terror I dashed at the alcove, then into the corner and then into the window, relighting three as two more vanished by the fireplace, and then, perceiving a better way, I dropped matches on the iron-bound deedbox in the corner, and caught up the bedroom candlestick. With this I avoided the delay of striking matches, but for all that the steady process of extinction went on, and the shadows I feared and fought against returned, and crept in upon me, first a step gained on this side of me, then on that. I was now almost frantic with the horror of the coming darkness, and my self-possession deserted me. I leaped panting from candle to candle in a vain struggle against that remorseless advance.

I bruised myself in the thigh against a table, I sent a chair headlong, I stumbled and fell and whisked the cloth from the table in my fall. My candle rolled away from me and I snatched another as I rose. Abruptly this was blown out as I swung it off the table by the wind of my sudden movement, and immediately the two remaining candles followed. But there was light still in the room, a red light, that streamed across the ceiling and staved off the shadows from me. The fire! Of course I could still thrust my candle between the bars and relight it!

I turned to where the flames were still dancing between the glowing coals and splashing red reflections upon the furniture; made two steps toward the grate, and incontinently the flames dwindled and vanished, the glow vanished, the reflections rushed together and disap-peared, and as I thrust the candle between the bars darkness closed upon me like the shutting of an eye, wrapped about me in a stifling embrace, sealed my vision, and crushed the last vestiges of self-possession from my brain. And it was not only palpable darkness, but in-tolerable terror. The candle fell from my hands. I flung out my arms in a vain effort to thrust that ponderous blackness away from me, and lifting up my voice, screamed with all my might, once, twice, thrice. Then I think I must have staggered to my feet. I know I thought suddenly of the moonlit corridor, and with my head bowed and my arms over my face, made a stumbling run for the door.

But I had forgotten the exact position of the door, and I struck myself heavily against the corner of the bed. I staggered back, turned, and was either struck or struck myself against some other bulky furnishing. I have a vague memory of battering myself thus to and fro in the darkness, of a heavy blow at last upon my forehead, of a horrible sensation of falling that lasted an age, of my last frantic effort to keep my footing, and then I remember no more.

I opened my eyes in daylight. My head was roughly bandaged, and the man with the withered hand was watching my face. I looked about me trying to remember what had happened, and for a space I could not recollect. I rolled my eyes into the corner and saw the old woman, no longer abstracted, no longer terrible, pouring out some drops of medicine from a little blue phial into a glass. "Where am I?" I said. "I seem to remember you, and yet I can not remember who you are."

They told me then, and I heard of the haunted Red Room as one who hears a tale. "We found you at dawn," said he, "and there was blood on your forehead and lips."

I wondered that I had ever disliked him. The three of them in the daylight seemed commonplace old folk enough. The man with the green shade had his head bent as one who sleeps.

It was very slowly I recovered the memory of my experience. "You believe now," said the old man with the withered hand, "that the room is haunted?" He spoke no longer as one who greets an intruder, but as one who condoles with a friend.

"Yes," said I, "the room is haunted."

"And you have seen it. And we who have been here all our lives have never set eyes upon it. Because we have never dared. Tell us, is it truly the old earl who——"

"No," said I, "it is not."

"I told you so," said the old lady, with the glass in her hand. "It is his poor young countess who was frightened——"

"It is not," I said. "There is neither ghost of earl nor ghost of countess in that room; there is no ghost there at all, but worse, far worse, something impalpable——"

"Well?" they said.

"The worst of all the things that haunt poor mortal men," said I; "and that is, in all its nakedness—'Fear!' Fear that will not have light nor sound, that will not bear with reason, that deafens and darkens and overwhelms. It followed me through the corridor, it fought against me in the room——"

I stopped abruptly. There was an interval of silence. My hand went up to my bandages. "The candles went out one after another, and I fled——"

Then the man with the shade lifted his face sideways to see me and spoke.

"That is it," said he. "I knew that was it. A Power of Darkness. To put such a curse upon a home! It lurks there always. You can feel it even in the daytime, even of a bright summer's day, in the hangings, in the curtains, keeping behind you however you face about. In the dusk it creeps into the corridor and follows you, so that you dare not turn. It is even as you say. Fear itself is in that room. Black Fear . . . And there it will be . . . so long as this house of sin endures."

# Ambrose Bierce

Ambrose Gwinnett Bierce (1842–1914?) is an important figure in American literature, one who has not received the attention he deserves. His reputation has been hurt by the monotony of his tone, which is uniformly grim, and, paradoxically, by the fact that he is too versatile to be classified, since he is an expert in the apparently diverse fields of humor and horror. He also fused these two moods in several of his most remarkable tales, producing not just parodies of standard terror tales, but stories that really are funny and frightening at the same time.

Bierce was once considered second only to Poe as an American master of the macabre, but he has been thrown into a shadow by the recent rise in the reputation of H. P. Lovecraft, who shares with Poe both feverish intensity and fantastic imagery. Bierce really represents a separate tradition, one which his work defined. His cruel, cynical, and detached attitude is unique; only John Collier and Robert Bloch can be compared to him as purveyors of gallows humor.

Bierce was the son of a poor farmer, whose many children all had names beginning with the letter "A." He spent some time as a printer's apprentice, then a year in military school, and he enlisted as a drummer boy in the Ninth Indiana Infantry at the outbreak of the Civil War. He emerged from this conflict with an officer's rank. He also received a serious wound in the head, and he often claimed, presumably in jest, that he was never the same afterward. Soon afterward, he moved to San Francisco, where he became involved in newspaper work. He first achieved notoriety as a political cartoonist, and was soon renowned for his efforts in what he called "journalism, a thing so low that it cannot be mentioned in the same breath with literature." His first short story, "The Haunted Valley," was published in 1871.

He then spent several years in London, where his work was published under the pseudonym "Dod Grile." His health finally forced him to return to the American West; he had a serious respiratory condition, said to be the result of sleeping throughout a cold night on a marble slab in a cemetery. Upon his return, Bierce began an association with William Randolph Hearst's *San Francisco Examiner,* and he was soon established as the central figure of the area's literary community.

Bierce's most important comic works are *The Devil's Dictionary* and *Fantastic Fables.* Most of his better stories are in *Can Such Things Be?* (1893) and *In the Midst of Life* (1892), also known as *Tales of Soldiers and Civilians.* Among his finest tales are "The Damned Thing," "The Death of Halpin Frayser," "An Occurrence at Owl Creek Bridge," and "My Favorite Murder." The early editions of *Can Such Things Be?* contain a number of good stories that are not usually reprinted today; they are purportedly documentary accounts, and they appear under the headings "The Ways of Ghosts," "Soldier Folk," and "Some Haunted Houses."

In late 1913, Bierce traveled to war-torn Mexico, because, he said, "I like the fighting; I want to see it." There he disappeared without a trace. In one of his last letters he wrote: "If you hear of my being stood up against a Mexican stone wall and shot to rags, please know that I think that a pretty good way to depart this life. It beats old age, disease, or falling down the cellar stairs. To be a Gringo in Mexico—ah, that is euthanasia!"

"Oil of Dog" was first published in book form in the eighth volume of Bierce's *Collected Works* (1912). Presumably, it saw periodical publication previously, but no record of this remains. It is perhaps his most outrageous tale, treating calculatedly offensive material with exquisite irony and understatement. Attacking such sacred cows as medicine, motherhood, religion, democracy, and free enterprise, this little story is a masterpiece of malice and morbidity.

# OIL OF DOG

## Ambrose Bierce

My name is Boffer Bings. I was born of honest parents in one of the humbler walks of life, my father being a manufacturer of dog-oil and my mother having a small studio in the shadow of the village church, where she disposed of unwelcome babes. In my boyhood I was trained to habits of industry; I not only assisted my father in procuring dogs for his vats, but was frequently employed by my mother to carry away the débris of her work in the studio. In performance of this duty I sometimes had need of all my natural intelligence for all the law officers of the vicinity were opposed to my mother's business. They were not elected on an opposition ticket, and the matter had never been made a political issue; it just happened so. My father's business of making dog-oil was, naturally, less unpopular, though the owners of missing dogs sometimes regarded him with suspicion, which was reflected, to some extent, upon me. My father had, as silent partners, all the physicians of the town, who seldom wrote a prescription which did not contain what they were pleased to designate as *Ol. can.* It is really the most valuable medicine ever discovered. But most persons are unwilling to make personal sacrifices for the afflicted, and it was evident that many of the fattest dogs in town had been forbidden to play with me—a fact which pained my young sensibilities, and at one time came near driving me to become a pirate.

Looking back upon those days, I cannot but regret, at times, that by indirectly bringing my beloved parents to their death I was the author of misfortunes profoundly affecting my future.

One evening while passing my father's oil factory with the body of a foundling from my mother's studio I saw a constable who seemed to be closely watching my movements. Young as I was, I had learned that a constable's acts, of whatever apparent character, are prompted by the most reprehensible motives, and I avoided him by dodging into the oilery by a side door which happened to stand ajar. I locked it at once and was alone with my dead. My father had retired for the night. The only light in the place came from the furnace, which glowed a deep, rich crimson under one of the vats, casting ruddy reflections on the walls. Within the cauldron the oil still rolled in indolent ebullition, occasionally pushing to the surface a piece of dog. Seating myself to wait for the constable to go away, I held the naked body of the foundling in my lap and tenderly stroked its short, silken hair. Ah, how beautiful it was! Even at that early age I was passionately fond of children, and as I looked upon this cherub I could almost find it in my heart to wish that the small, red wound upon its breast— the work of my dear mother—had not been mortal.

It had been my custom to throw the babes into the river which nature had thoughtfully provided for the purpose, but that night I did not dare to leave the oilery for fear of the constable. "After all," I said to myself, "it cannot greatly matter if I put it into this cauldron. My father will never know the bones from those of a puppy, and the few deaths which may result from administering another kind of oil for the incomparable *ol. can.* are not important in a population which increases so rapidly." In short, I took the first step in crime and brought myself untold sorrow by casting the babe into the cauldron.

The next day, somewhat to my surprise, my father, rubbing his hands with satisfaction, informed me and my mother that he had obtained the finest quality of oil that was ever seen; that the physicians to whom he had shown samples had so pronounced it. He added that he had no knowledge as to how the result was obtained; the dogs had been treated in all respects as usual, and were of an ordinary breed. I deemed it my duty to explain—which I did, though palsied would have been my tongue if I could have foreseen the consequences. Bewailing their previous ignorance of the advantages of combining their industries, my parents at once took measures to repair the error. My mother removed her studio to a wing of the factory building and my duties in connection with the business ceased; I was no longer required to dispose of the bodies of the small superfluous, and there was no need of alluring dogs to their doom, for my father discarded them altogether, though they still had an honorable place in the name of the oil. So suddenly thrown into idleness, I might naturally have been expected to become vicious and dissolute, but I did not. The holy influence of my dear mother was ever about me to protect me from the temptations which beset youth, and my father was a deacon in a church. Alas, that through my fault these estimable persons should have come to so bad an end!

Finding a double profit in her business, my mother now devoted herself to it with a new assiduity. She removed not only superfluous and unwelcome babes to order, but went out into the highways and byways, gathering in children of a larger growth, and even such adults as she could entice to the oilery. My father, too, enamored of the superior quality of oil produced, purveyed for his vats with diligence and zeal. The conversion of their neighbors into dog-oil became, in short, the one passion of their lives—an absorbing and overwhelming greed took possession of their souls and served them in place of a hope in Heaven—by which, also, they were inspired.

So enterprising had they now become that a public meeting was held and resolutions passed severely censuring them. It was intimated by the chairman that any further raids upon the population would be met in a spirit of hostility. My poor parents left the meeting broken-hearted, desperate and, I believe, not altogether sane. Anyhow, I deemed it prudent not to enter the oilery with them that night, but slept outside in a stable.

At about midnight some mysterious impulse caused me to rise and peer through a window into the furnace-room, where I knew my father now slept. The fires were burning as brightly as if the following day's harvest had been expected to be abundant. One of the large cauldrons was slowly "walloping" with a mysterious appearance to self-restraint, as if it bided its time to put forth its full energy. My father was not in bed; he had risen in his nightclothes and was preparing a noose in a strong cord. From the looks which he cast at the door

of my mother's bedroom I knew too well the purpose that he had in mind. Speechless and motionless with terror, I could do nothing in prevention or warning. Suddenly the door of my mother's apartment was opened, noiselessly, and the two confronted each other, both apparently surprised. The lady, also, was in her nightclothes, and she held in her right hand the tool of her trade, a long, narrow-bladed dagger.

She, too, had been unable to deny herself the last profit which the unfriendly action of the citizens and my absence had left her. For one instant they looked into each other's blazing eyes and then sprang together with indescribable fury. Round and round the room they struggled, the man cursing, the woman shrieking, both fighting like demons—she to strike him with the dagger, he to strangle her with his great bare hands. I know not how long I had the unhappiness to observe this disagreeable instance of domestic infelicity, but at last, after a more than usually vigorous struggle, the combatants suddenly moved apart.

My father's breast and my mother's weapon showed evidences of contact. For another instant they glared at each other in the most unamiable way; then my poor, wounded father, feeling the hand of death upon him, leaped forward, unmindful of resistance, grasped my dear mother in his arms, dragged her to the side of the boiling cauldron, collected all his failing energies, and sprang in with her! In a moment, both had disappeared and were adding their oil to that of the committee of citizens who had called the day before with an invitation to the public meeting.

Convinced that these unhappy events closed to me every avenue to an honorable career in that town, I removed to the famous city of Otumwee, where these memoirs are written with a heart full of remorse for a heedless act entailing so dismal a commercial disaster.

# Algernon Blackwood

Algernon Blackwood (1869–1951) is, among all authors of supernatural stories, the one whose tales convey the strongest sense of conviction. He possessed, or at least believed he possessed, certain psychic or mystical abilities and claimed that "to write a ghost-story I must first feel ghostly, a condition not to be artificially induced."

Along with Arthur Machen and other writers, Blackwood was a member of the esoteric Order of the Golden Dawn, an organization offering indoctrination into occult teachings. This, however, was not his first exposure to such concepts. His parents were rigidly religious, and he wrote that throughout childhood he was "always afraid of hell." The chance appearance of a book on Yoga opened his mind to different possibilities, and he embarked on studies relating to the potential inherent in less dogmatic spiritual teachings. A fellow student, a Hindu, taught Blackwood meditation and later became the model for the author's most popular creation, Dr. John Silence, who investigates uncanny phenomena. Blackwood continued his quest for arcane knowledge and years later said that "the belief in extension of consciousness to some $n$th degree, with its correlative of greater powers and faculties, have not only remained with me, but have justified themselves."

Blackwood's success as a writer came late in life. His first book, *The Empty House,* was not published until 1906; and his greatest fame came in his last years, when he was known throughout England for reading his stories on radio and television. As a young man, he spent years in North America. He lost his inheritance in Canada, through bad investments in an inn and a ranch, then became a part-time reporter for the *New York Sun.* Newspaper work gave him his first writing experience, and his jobs as a crime reporter inspired some of his stories, most notably "Max Hensig."

Blackwood's major tales include "The Wendigo," "The Listener," "An Episode in a Lodging House," "A Psychical Invasion," "Ancient Sorceries," "The Glamour of the Snow," and "The Damned." In addition to numerous collections of short stories, Blackwood produced several novels, usually treating some less menacing manifestation of the uncanny. In fact, he somewhat regretted the fact that he was identified with terror. "I have been called the 'Ghost Man,' " he wrote, "so when I broadcast it must preferably be a ghost story of some sort. My real interest here, however, lay always and still lies in the question of a possible *extension of human faculty* and the suggestion that the Man in the Street possesses strange powers which never manifest normally."

Blackwood found great inspiration in nature, both personally and professionally. His own travels down the Danube led to the story "The Willows," published in his 1907 collection

*The Listener.* It is a long story, with a perfectly controlled atmosphere and constantly mounting suspense. It also has a remarkable theme, but what is most remarkable about "The Willows" is the high esteem in which it is held. Critics and creators of frightening fiction make diverse demands on the genre, and controversy rages over the merits of various styles and subjects, yet almost every commentator agrees that this tale is one of the very finest in the field.

# THE WILLOWS

## Algernon Blackwood

### 1

After leaving Vienna, and long before you come to Buda-Pesth, the Danube enters a region of singular loneliness and desolation, where its waters spread away on all sides regardless of a main channel, and the country becomes a swamp for miles upon miles, covered by a vast sea of low willow-bushes. On the big maps this deserted area is painted in a fluffy blue, growing fainter in colour as it leaves the banks, and across it may be seen in large straggling letters the word *Sümpfe,* meaning marshes.

In high flood this great acreage of sand, shingle-beds, and willow-grown islands is almost topped by the water, but in normal seasons the bushes bend and rustle in the free winds, showing their silver leaves to the sunshine in an ever-moving plain of bewildering beauty. These willows never attain to the dignity of trees; they have no rigid trunks; they remain humble bushes, with rounded tops and soft outline, swaying on slender stems that answer to the least pressure of the wind; supple as grasses, and so continually shifting that they somehow give the impression that the entire plain is moving and *alive.* For the wind sends waves rising and falling over the whole surface, waves of leaves instead of waves of water, green swells like the sea, too, until the branches turn and lift, and then silvery white as their under-side turns to the sun.

Happy to slip beyond the control of stern banks, the Danube here wanders about at will among the intricate network of channels intersecting the islands everywhere with broad avenues down which the waters pour with a shouting sound; making whirlpools, eddies, and foaming rapids; tearing at the sandy banks; carrying away masses of shore and willow-clumps; and forming new islands innumerable which shift daily in size and shape and possess at best an impermanent life, since the flood-time obliterates their very existence.

Properly speaking, this fascinating part of the river's life begins soon after leaving Pressburg, and we, in our Canadian canoe, with gipsy tent and frying-pan on board, reached it on the crest of a rising flood about mid-July. That very same morning, when the sky was reddening before sunrise, we had slipped swiftly through still-sleeping Vienna, leaving it a couple of hours later a mere patch of smoke against the blue hills of the Wienerwald on the horizon; we had breakfasted below Fischeramend under a grove of birch trees roaring in the wind; and had then swept up on the tearing current past Orth, Hainburg, Petronell (the old Roman Carnuntum of Marcus Aurelius), and so under the frowning heights of Theben on a spur of the Carpathians, where the March steals in quietly from the left and the frontier is crossed between Austria and Hungary.

Racing along at twelve kilometres an hour soon took us well into Hungary, and the muddy waters—sure sign of flood—sent us aground on many a shingle-bed, and twisted us like a cork in many a sudden belching whirlpool before the towers of Pressburg (Hungarian, Poszóny) showed against the sky; and then the canoe, leaping like a spirited horse, flew at top speed under the grey walls, negotiated safely the sunken chain of the Fliegende Brücke ferry, turned the corner sharply to the left, and plunged on yellow foam into the wilderness of islands, sand-banks, and swamp-land beyond—the land of the willows.

The change came suddenly, as when a series of bioscope pictures snaps down on the streets of a town and shifts without warning into the scenery of lake and forest. We entered the land of desolation on wings, and in less than half an hour there was neither boat nor fishing-hut nor red roof, nor any single sign of human habitation and civilisation within sight. The sense of remoteness from the world of human-kind, the utter isolation, the fascination of this singular world of willows, winds, and waters, instantly laid its spell upon us both, so that we allowed laughingly to one another that we ought by rights to have held some special kind of passport to admit us, and that we had, somewhat audaciously, come without asking leave into a separate little kingdom of wonder and magic—a kingdom that was reserved for the use of others who had a right to it, with everywhere unwritten warnings to trespassers for those who had the imagination to discover them.

Though still early in the afternoon, the ceaseless buffetings of a most tempestuous wind made us feel weary, and we at once began casting about for a suitable camping-ground for the night. But the bewildering character of the islands made landing difficult; the swirling flood carried us inshore and then swept us out again; the willow branches tore our hands as we seized them to stop the canoe, and we pulled many a yard of sandy bank into the water before at length we shot with a great sideways blow from the wind into a backwater and managed to beach the bows in a cloud of spray. Then we lay panting and laughing after our exertions on hot yellow sand, sheltered from the wind, and in the full blaze of a scorching sun, a cloudless blue sky above, and an immense army of dancing, shouting willow bushes, closing in from all sides, shining with spray and clapping their thousand little hands as though to applaud the success of our efforts.

"What a river!" I said to my companion, thinking of all the way we had travelled from the source in the Black Forest, and how we had often been obliged to wade and push in the upper shallows at the beginning of June.

"Won't stand much nonsense now, will it?" he said, pulling the canoe a little farther into safety up the sand, and then composing himself for a nap.

I lay by his side, happy and peaceful in the bath of the elements—water, wind, sand, and the great fire of the sun—thinking of the long journey that lay behind us, and of the great stretch before us to the Black Sea, and how lucky I was to have such a delightful and charming travelling companion as my friend, the Swede.

We had made many similar journeys together, but the Danube, more than any other river I knew, impressed us from the very beginning with its *aliveness*. From its tiny bubbling entry into the world among the pinewood gardens of Donaueschingen, until this moment when it began to play the great river-game of losing itself among the deserted swamps, unobserved, unrestrained, it had seemed to us like following the growth of some living creature. Sleepy at first, but later developing violent desires as it became conscious of its deep soul, it rolled, like some huge fluid being, through all the countries we had passed, holding our little craft on its mighty shoulders, playing roughly with us sometimes, yet always friendly and well-meaning, till at length we had come inevitably to regard it as a Great Personage.

How, indeed, could it be otherwise, since it told us so much of its secret life? At night we heard it singing to the moon as we lay in our tent, uttering that odd sibilant note peculiar to itself and said to be caused by the rapid tearing of the pebbles along its bed, so great is its hurrying speed. We knew, too, the voice of its gurgling whirlpools, suddenly bubbling up on a surface previously quite calm; the roar of its shallows and swift rapids; its constant steady thundering below all mere surface sounds; and that ceaseless tearing of its icy waters at the banks. How it stood up and shouted when the rains fell flat upon its face! And how its laughter roared out when the wind blew upstream and tried to stop its growing speed! We knew all its sounds and voices, its tumblings and foamings, its unnecessary splashing against the bridges; that self-conscious chatter when there were hills to look on; the affected dignity of its speech when it passed through the little towns, far too important to laugh; and all these faint, sweet whisperings when the sun caught it fairly in some slow curve and poured down upon it till the steam rose.

It was full of tricks, too, in its early life before the great world knew it. There were places in the upper reaches among the Swabian forests, when yet the first whispers of its destiny had not reached it, where it elected to disappear through holes in the ground, to appear again on the other side of the porous limestone hills and start a new river with another name; leaving, too, so little water in its own bed that we had to climb out and wade and push the canoe through miles of shallows!

And a chief pleasure, in those early days of its irresponsible youth, was to lie low, like Brer Fox, just before the little turbulent tributaries came to join it from the Alps, and to refuse to acknowledge them when in, but to run for miles side by side, the dividing line well marked, the very levels different, the Danube utterly declining to recognise the newcomer. Below Passau, however, it gave up this particular trick, for there the Inn comes in with a thundering power impossible to ignore, and so pushes and incommodes the parent river that there is hardly room for them in the long twisting gorge that follows, and the Danube is shoved this way and that against the cliffs, and forced to hurry itself with great waves and much dashing to and fro in order to get through in time. And during the fight our canoe slipped down from its shoulder to its breast, and had the time of its life among the struggling waves. But the Inn taught the old river a lesson, and after Passau it no longer pretended to ignore new arrivals.

This was many days back, of course, and since then we had come to know other aspects of the great creature, and across the Bavarian wheat plain of Straubing she wandered so slowly under the blazing June sun that we could well imagine only the surface inches were water, while below there moved, concealed as by a silken mantle, a whole army of Undines, passing silently and unseen down to the sea, and very leisurely too, lest they be discovered.

Much, too, we forgave her because of her friendliness to the birds and animals that haunted the shores. Cormorants lined the banks in lonely places in rows like short black palings; grey crows crowded the shingle beds; storks stood fishing in the vistas of shallower water that opened up between the islands, and hawks, swans, and marsh birds of all sorts filled the air with glinting wings and singing, petulant cries. It was impossible to feel annoyed with the river's vagaries after seeing a deer leap with a splash into the water at sunrise and swim past the bows of the canoe; and often we saw fawns peering at us from the underbrush, or looked straight into the brown eyes of a stag as we charged full tilt round a corner and entered another reach of the river. Foxes, too, everywhere haunted the banks, tripping daintily among the driftwood and disappearing so suddenly that it was impossible to see how they managed it.

But now, after leaving Pressburg, everything changed a little, and the Danube became more serious. It ceased trifling. It was half-way to the Black Sea, within scenting distance almost of other, stranger countries where no tricks would be permitted or understood. It became suddenly grown-up, and claimed our respect and even awe. It broke out into three arms, for one thing, that only met again a hundred kilometres farther down, and for a canoe there were no indications which one was intended to be followed.

"If you take a side channel," said the Hungarian officer we met in the Pressburg shop while buying provisions, "you may find yourselves, when the flood subsides, forty miles from anywhere, high and dry, and you may easily starve. I warn you not to continue. The river, too, is still rising, and this wind will increase."

The rising river did not alarm us in the least, but the matter of being left high and dry by a sudden subsidence of the waters might be serious, and we had consequently laid in an extra stock of provisions. For the rest, the officer's prophecy held true, and the wind, blowing down a perfectly clear sky, increased steadily till it reached the dignity of a westerly gale.

It was earlier than usual when we camped, for the sun was a good hour or two from the horizon, and leaving my friend still asleep on the hot sand, I wandered about in desultory examination of our hotel. The island, I found, was less than an acre in extent, a mere sandy bank standing some two or three feet above the level of the river. The far end, pointing into the sunset, was covered with flying spray which the tremendous wind drove off the crests of the broken waves. It was triangular in shape, with the apex upstream.

I stood there for several minutes, watching the impetuous crimson flood bearing down with a shouting roar, dashing in waves against the bank as though to sweep it bodily away, and then swirling by in two foaming streams on either side. The ground seemed to shake with the shock and rush, while the furious movement of the willow bushes as the wind poured over them increased the curious illusion that the island itself actually moved. Above, for a mile or two, I could see the great river descending upon me: it was like looking up the slope of a sliding hill, white with foam, and leaping up everywhere to show itself to the sun.

The rest of the island was too thickly grown with willows to make walking pleasant, but I made the tour, nevertheless. From the lower end the light, of course, changed, and the river looked dark and angry. Only the backs of the flying waves were visible, streaked with foam, and pushed forcibly by the great puffs of wind that fell upon them from behind. For a short mile it was visible, pouring in and out among the islands, and then disappearing with a huge sweep into the willows, which closed about it like a herd of monstrous antediluvian creatures crowding down to drink. They made me think of gigantic sponge-like growths that sucked the river up into themselves. They caused it to vanish from sight. They herded there together in such overpowering numbers.

Altogether it was an impressive scene, with its utter loneliness, its bizarre suggestion; and as I gazed, long and curiously, a singular emotion began to stir somewhere in the depths of me. Midway in my delight of the wild beauty, there crept, unbidden and unexplained, a curious feeling of disquietude, almost of alarm.

A rising river, perhaps, always suggests something of the ominous: many of the little islands I saw before me would probably have been swept away by the morning; this resistless, thundering flood of water touched the sense of awe. Yet I was aware that my uneasiness lay deeper far than the emotions of awe and wonder. It was not that I felt. Nor had it directly to do with the power of the driving wind—this shouting hurricane that might almost carry up a few acres of willows into the air and scatter them like so much chaff over the landscape. The wind was simply enjoying itself, for nothing rose out of the flat landscape to stop it, and I was conscious of sharing its great game with a kind of pleasurable excitement. Yet this novel emotion had nothing to do with the wind. Indeed, so vague was the sense of distress I experienced, that it was impossible to trace it to its source and deal with it accordingly, though I was aware somehow that it had to do with my realisation of our utter insignificance before this unrestrained power of the elements about me. The huge-grown river had something to do with it too—a vague, unpleasant idea that we had somehow trifled with these great elemental forces in whose power we lay helpless every hour of the day and night. For here, indeed, they were gigantically at play together, and the sight appealed to the imagination.

But my emotion, so far as I could understand it, seemed to attach itself more particularly to the willow bushes, to these acres and acres of willows, crowding so thickly growing there, swarming everywhere the eye could reach, pressing upon the river as though to suffocate it, standing in dense array mile after mile beneath the sky, watching, waiting, listening. And, apart quite from the elements, the willows connected themselves subtly with my malaise, attacking the mind insidiously somehow by reason of their vast numbers, and contriving in some way or other to represent to the imagination a new and mighty power, a power, moreover, not altogether friendly to us.

Great revelations of nature, of course, never fail to impress in one way or another, and I was no stranger to moods of the kind. Mountains overawe and oceans terrify, while the mystery of great forests exercises a spell peculiarly its own. But all these, at one point or another, somewhere link on intimately with human life and human experience. They stir comprehensible, even if alarming, emotions. They tend on the whole to exalt.

With this multitude of willows, however, it was something far different, I felt. Some essence emanated from them that besieged the heart. A sense of awe awakened, true, but of awe touched somewhere by a vague terror. Their serried ranks, growing everywhere darker about me as the shadows deepened, moving furiously yet softly in the wind, woke in me the curious and unwelcome suggestion that we had trespassed here upon the borders of an alien world, a world where we were intruders, a world where we were not wanted or invited to remain—where we ran grave risks perhaps!

The feeling, however, though it refused to yield its meaning entirely to analysis, did not at the time trouble me by passing into menace. Yet it never left me quite, even during the very practical business of putting up the tent in a hurricane of wind and building a fire for the stew-pot. It remained, just enough to bother and perplex, and to rob a most delightful camping-ground of a good portion of its charm. To my companion, however, I said nothing, for he was a man I considered devoid of imagination. In the first place, I could never have explained to him what I meant, and in the second, he would have laughed stupidly at me if I had.

There was a slight depression in the centre of the island, and here we pitched the tent. The surrounding willows broke the wind a bit.

"A poor camp," observed the imperturbable Swede when at last the tent stood upright; "no stones and precious little firewood. I'm for moving on early to-morrow—eh? This sand won't hold anything."

But the experience of a collapsing tent at midnight had taught us many devices, and we made the cosy gipsy house as safe as possible, and then set about collecting a store of wood to last till bedtime. Willow bushes drop no branches, and driftwood was our only source of supply. We hunted the shores pretty thoroughly. Everywhere the banks were crumbling as the rising flood tore at them and carried away great portions with a splash and a gurgle.

"The island's much smaller than when we landed," said the accurate Swede. "It won't last long at this rate. We'd better drag the canoe close to the tent, and be ready to start at a moment's notice. I shall sleep in my clothes."

He was a little distance off, climbing along the bank, and I heard his rather jolly laugh as he spoke.

"By Jove!" I heard him call, a moment later, and turned to see what had caused his exclamation. But for the moment he was hidden by the willows, and I could not find him.

"What in the world's this?" I heard him cry again, and this time his voice had become serious.

I ran up quickly and joined him on the bank. He was looking over the river, pointing at something in the water.

"Good Heavens, it's a man's body!" he cried excitedly. "Look!"

A black thing, turning over and over in the foaming waves, swept rapidly past. It kept disappearing and coming up to the surface again. It was about twenty feet from the shore, and just as it was opposite to where we stood it lurched round and looked straight at us. We saw its eyes reflecting the sunset, and gleaming an odd yellow as the body turned over. Then it gave a swift, gulping plunge, and dived out of sight in a flash.

"An otter, by gad!" we exclaimed in the same breath, laughing.

It *was* an otter, alive, and out on the hunt; yet it had looked exactly like the body of a drowned man turning helplessly in the current. Far below it came to the surface once again, and we saw its black skin, wet and shining in the sunlight.

Then, too, just as we turned back, our arms full of driftwood, another thing happened to recall us to the river bank. This time it really was a man, and what was more, a man in a boat. Now a small boat on the Danube was an unusual sight at any time, but here in this deserted region, and at flood time, it was so unexpected as to constitute a real event. We stood and stared.

Whether it was due to the slanting sunlight, or the refraction from the wonderfully illuminated water, I cannot say, but, whatever the cause, I found it difficult to focus my sight properly upon the flying apparition. It seemed, however, to be a man standing upright in a sort of flat-bottomed boat, steering with a long oar, and being carried down the opposite shore at a tremendous pace. He apparently was looking across in our direction, but the distance was too great and the light too uncertain for us to make out very plainly what he was about. It seemed to me that he was gesticulating and making signs at us. His voice came across the water to us, shouting something furiously, but the wind drowned it so that no single word was audible. There was something curious about the whole appearance—man, boat, signs, voice—that made an impression on me out of all proportion to its cause.

"He's crossing himself!" I cried. "Look, he's making the sign of the Cross!"

"I believe you're right," the Swede said, shading his eyes with his hand and watching the man out of sight. He seemed to be gone in a moment, melting away down there into the sea of willows where the sun caught them in the bend of the river and turned them into a great crimson wall of beauty. Mist, too, had begun to rise, so that the air was hazy.

"But what in the world is he doing at nightfall on this flooded river?" I said, half to myself. "Where is he going at such a time, and what did he mean by his signs and shouting? D'you think he wished to warn us about something?"

"He saw our smoke, and thought we were spirits probably," laughed my companion. "These Hungarians believe in all sorts of rubbish: you remember the shopwoman at Pressburg warning us that no one ever landed here because it belonged to some sort of beings outside man's world! I suppose they believe in fairies and elementals, possibly demons too. That peasant in the boat saw people on the islands for the first time in his life," he added, after a slight pause, "and it scared him, that's all."

The Swede's tone of voice was not convincing, and his manner lacked something that was usually there. I noted the change instantly while he talked, though without being able to label it precisely.

"If they had enough imagination," I laughed loudly—I remember trying to make as much *noise* as I could—"they might well people a place like this with the old gods of antiquity. The Romans must have haunted all this region more or less with their shrines and sacred groves and elemental deities."

The subject dropped and we returned to our stewpot, for my friend was not given to imaginative conversation as a rule. Moreover, just then I remember feeling distinctly glad that he was not imaginative; his stolid, practical nature suddenly seemed to me welcome and comforting. It was an admirable temperament, I felt: he could steer down rapids like a red Indian, shoot dangerous bridges and whirlpools better than any white man I ever saw in a canoe. He was a grand fellow for an adventurous trip, a tower of strength when untoward things happened. I looked at his strong face and light curly hair as he staggered along under his pile of driftwood (twice the size of mine!), and I experienced the feeling of relief. Yes, I was distinctly glad just then that the Swede was—what he was, and that he never made remarks that suggested more than they said.

"The river's still rising, though," he added, as if following some thoughts of his own, and dropping his load with a gasp. "This island will be under water in two days if it goes on."

"I wish the *wind* would go down," I said. "I don't care a fig for the river."

The flood, indeed, had no terrors for us; we could get off at ten minutes' notice, and the more water the better we liked it. It meant an increasing current and the obliteration of the treacherous shingle-beds that so often threatened to tear the bottom out of our canoe.

Contrary to our expectations, the wind did not go down with the sun. It seemed to increase with the darkness, howling overhead and shaking the willows round us like straws. Curious sounds accompanied it sometimes, like the explosion of heavy guns, and it fell upon the water and the island in great flat blows of immense power. It made me think of the sounds a planet must make, could we only hear it, driving along through space.

But the sky kept wholly clear of clouds, and soon after supper the full moon rose up in the east and covered the river and the plain of shouting willows with a light like the day.

We lay on the sandy patch beside the fire, smoking, listening to the noises of the night round us, and talking happily of the journey we had already made, and of our plans ahead. The map lay spread in the door of the tent, but the high wind made it hard to study, and presently we lowered the curtain and extinguished the lantern. The firelight was enough to smoke and see each other's faces by, and the sparks flew about overhead like fireworks. A few yards beyond, the river gurgled and hissed, and from time to time a heavy splash announced the falling away of further portions of the bank.

Our talk, I noticed, had to do with the far-away scenes and incidents of our first camps in the Black Forest, or of other subjects altogether remote from the present setting, for neither of us spoke of the actual moment more than was necessary—almost as though we had agreed tacitly to avoid discussion of the camp and its incidents. Neither the otter nor the boatman, for instance, received the honour of a single mention, though ordinarily these would have furnished discussion for the greater part of the evening. They were, of course, distinct events in such a place.

The scarcity of the wood made it a business to keep the fire going, for the wind, that drove the smoke in our faces wherever we sat, helped at the same time to make a forced draught. We took it in turn to make foraging expeditions into the darkness, and the quantity the Swede brought back always made me feel that he took an absurdly long time finding it; for the fact was I did not care much about being left alone, and yet it always seemed to be my turn to grub about among the bushes or scramble along the slippery banks in the moonlight. The long day's battle with wind and water—such wind and such water!—had tired us both, and an early bed was the obvious programme. Yet neither of us made the move for the tent. We lay there, tending the fire, talking in desultory fashion, peering about us into the dense willow bushes, and listening to the thunder of wind and river. The loneliness of the place had entered our very bones, and silence seemed natural, for after a bit the sound of our voices became a trifle unreal and forced; whispering would have been the fitting mode of communication, I felt, and the human voice, always rather absurd amid the roar of the elements, now carried with it something almost illegitimate. It was like talking out loud in church, or in some place where it was not lawful, perhaps not quite *safe*, to be overheard.

The eeriness of this lonely island, set among a million willows, swept by a hurricane, and surrounded by hurrying deep waters, touched us both, I fancy. Untrodden by man, almost unknown to man, it lay there beneath the moon, remote from human influence, on the frontier of another world, an alien world, a world tenanted by willows only and the souls of willows. And we, in our rashness, had dared to invade it, even to make use of it! Something more than the power of its mystery stirred in me as I lay on the sand, feet to fire, and peered up through the leaves at the stars, For the last time I rose to get firewood.

"When this has burnt up," I said firmly, "I shall turn in," and my companion watched me lazily as I moved off into the surrounding shadows.

For an unimaginative man I thought he seemed unusually receptive that night, unusually open to suggestion of things other than sensory. He too was touched by the beauty and loneliness of the place. I was not altogether pleased, I remember, to recognise this slight change in him, and instead of immediately collecting sticks, I made my way to the far point of the island where the moonlight on plain and river could be seen to better advantage. The desire to be alone had come suddenly upon me; my former dread returned in force; there was a vague feeling in me I wished to face and probe to the bottom.

When I reached the point of sand jutting out among the waves, the spell of the place descended upon me with a positive shock. No mere "scenery" could have produced such an effect. There was something more here, something to alarm.

I gazed across the waste of wild waters; I watched the whispering willows; I heard the ceaseless beating of the tireless wind; and, one and all, each in its own way, stirred in me this sensation of a strange distress. But the *willows* especially: for ever they went on chattering and talking among themselves, laughing a little, shrilly crying out, sometimes sighing—but what it was they made so much to-do about belonged to the secret life of the great plain they inhabited. And it was utterly alien to the world I knew, or to that of the wild yet kindly elements. They made me think of a host of beings from another plane of life, another evolution altogether, perhaps, all discussing a mystery known only to themselves. I watched them moving busily together, oddly shaking their big bushy heads, twirling their myriad leaves even when there was no wind. They moved of their own will as though alive, and they touched, by some incalculable method, my own keen sense of the *horrible*.

There they stood in the moonlight, like a vast army surrounding our camp, shaking their innumerable silver spears defiantly, formed all ready for an attack.

The psychology of places, for some imaginations at least, is very vivid; for the wanderer, especially, camps have their "note" either of welcome or rejection. At first it may not always be apparent, because the busy preparations of tent and cooking prevent, but with the first pause—after supper usually—it comes and announces itself. And the note of this willow-camp now became unmistakably plain to me: we were interlopers, trespassers; we were not welcomed. The sense of unfamiliarity grew upon me as I stood there watching. We touched the frontier of a region where our presence was resented. For a night's lodging we might perhaps be tolerated; but for a prolonged and inquisitive stay—No! by all the gods of the trees and the wilderness, no! We were the first human influences upon this island, and we were not wanted. *The willows were against us.*

Strange thoughts like these, bizarre fancies, born I know not whence, found lodgment in my mind as I stood listening. What, I thought, if, after all, these crouching willows proved to be alive; if suddenly they should rise up, like a swarm of living creatures, marshalled by the gods whose territory we had invaded, sweep towards us off the vast swamps, booming overhead in the night—and then *settle down!* As I looked it was so easy to imagine they actually moved, crept nearer, retreated a little, huddled together in masses, hostile, waiting for the great wind that should finally start them a-running. I could have sworn their aspect changed a little, and their ranks deepened and pressed more closely together.

The melancholy shrill cry of a night-bird sounded overhead, and suddenly I nearly lost my balance as the piece of bank I stood upon fell with a great splash into the river, undermined by the flood. I stepped back just in time, and went on hunting for firewood again, half laughing at the odd fancies that crowded so thickly into my mind and cast their spell upon me. I recalled the Swede's remark about moving on the next day, and I was just thinking that I fully agreed with him, when I turned with a start and saw the subject of my thoughts standing immediately in front of me. He was quite close. The roar of the elements had covered his approach.

"You've been gone so long," he shouted above the wind, "I thought something must have happened to you."

But there was that in his tone, and a certain look in his face as well, that conveyed to me more than his actual words, and in a flash I understood the real reason for his coming. It was because the spell of the place had entered his soul too, and he did not like being alone.

"River still rising," he cried, pointing to the flood in the moonlight, "and the wind's simply awful."

He always said the same things, but it was the cry for companionship that gave the real importance to his words.

"Lucky," I cried back, "our tent's in the hollow. I think it'll hold all right." I added something about the difficulty of finding wood, in order to explain my absence, but the wind caught my words and flung them across the river, so that he did not hear, but just looked at me through the branches, nodding his head.

"Lucky if we get away without disaster!" he shouted, or words to that effect; and I remember feeling half-angry with him for putting the thought into words, for it was exactly what I felt myself. There was disaster impending somewhere, and the sense of presentiment lay unpleasantly upon me.

We went back to the fire and made a final blaze, poking it up with our feet. We took a last look round. But for the wind the heat would have been unpleasant. I put this thought into words, and I remember my friend's reply struck me oddly: that he would rather have the heat, the ordinary July weather, than this "diabolical wind."

Everything was snug for the night; the canoe lying turned over beside the tent, with both yellow paddles beneath her; the provision sack hanging from a willow-stem, and the washed-up dishes removed to a safe distance from the fire, all ready for the morning meal.

We smothered the embers of the fire with sand, and then turned in. The flap of the tent door was up, and I saw the branches and the stars and the white moonlight. The shaking willows and the heavy buffetings of the wind against our taut little house were the last things I remembered as sleep came down and covered all with its soft and delicious forgetfulness.

## 2

Suddenly I found myself lying awake, peering from my sandy mattress through the door of the tent. I looked at my watch pinned against the canvas, and saw by the bright moonlight that it was past twelve o'clock—the threshold of a new day—and I had therefore slept a couple of hours. The Swede was asleep still beside me; the wind howled as before; something plucked at my heart and made me feel afraid. There was a sense of disturbance in my immediate neighbourhood.

I sat up quickly and looked out. The trees were swaying violently to and fro as the gusts smote them, but our little bit of green canvas lay snugly safe in the hollow, for the wind passed over it without meeting enough resistance to make it vicious. The feeling of disquietude did not pass, however, and I crawled quietly out of the tent to see if our belongings were safe. I moved carefully so as not to waken my companion. A curious excitement was on me.

I was half-way out, kneeling on all fours, when my eye first took in that the tops of the bushes opposite, with their moving tracery of leaves, made shapes against the sky. I sat back on my haunches and stared. It was incredible, surely, but there, opposite and slightly above me, were shapes of some indeterminate sort among the willows, and as the branches swayed in the wind they seemed to group themselves about these shapes, forming a series of monstrous outlines that shifted rapidly beneath the moon. Close, about fifty feet in front of me, I saw these things.

My first instinct was to waken my companion, that he too might see them, but something made me hesitate—the sudden realisation, probably, that I should not welcome corroboration; and meanwhile I crouched there staring in amazement with smarting eyes. I was wide awake. I remember saying to myself that I was *not* dreaming.

They first became properly visible, these huge figures, just within the tops of the bushes— immense, bronze-coloured, moving, and wholly independent of the swaying of the branches. I saw them plainly and noted, now I came to examine them more calmly, that they were very much larger than human, and indeed that something in their appearance proclaimed them to be *not human* at all. Certainly they were not merely the moving tracery of the branches against the moonlight. They shifted independently. They rose upwards in a continuous stream from earth to sky, vanishing utterly as soon as they reached the dark of the sky. They were interlaced one with another, making a great column, and I saw their limbs and huge bodies melting in and out of each other, forming this serpentine line that bent and swayed and twisted spirally with the contortions of the wind-tossed trees. They were nude, fluid shapes, passing up the bushes, *within* the leaves almost—rising up in a living column into the heavens. Their faces I never could see. Unceasingly they poured upwards, swaying in great bending curves, with a hue of dull bronze upon their skins.

I stared, trying to force every atom of vision from my eyes. For a long time I thought they *must* every moment disappear and resolve themselves into the movements of the branches and prove to be an optical illusion. I searched everywhere for a proof of reality, when all the while I understood quite well that the standard of reality had changed. For the longer I looked the more certain I became that these figures were real and living, though perhaps not according to the standards that the camera and the biologist would insist upon.

Far from feeling fear, I was possessed with a sense of awe and wonder such as I have never known. I seemed to be gazing at the personified elemental forces of this haunted and primeval region. Our intrusion had stirred the powers of the place into activity. It was we who were the cause of the disturbance, and my brain filled to bursting with stories and legends of the spirits and deities of places that have been acknowledged and worshipped by men in all ages of the world's history. But, before I could arrive at any possible explanation, something impelled me to go farther out, and I crept forward on to the sand and stood upright. I felt the ground still warm under my bare feet; the wind tore at my hair and face; and the sound of the river burst upon my ears with a sudden roar. These things, I knew, were real, and proved that my senses were acting normally. Yet the figures still rose from earth to heaven, silent, majestically, in a great spiral of grace and strength that overwhelmed me at length with a genuine deep emotion of worship. I felt that I must fall down and worship— absolutely worship.

Perhaps in another minute I might have done so, when a gust of wind swept against me with such force that it blew me sideways, and I nearly stumbled and fell. It seemed to shake the dream violently out of me. At least it gave me another point of view somehow. The figures still remained, still ascended into heaven from the heart of the night, but my reason at last began to assert itself. It must be a subjective experience, I argued—none the less real for that, but still subjective. The moonlight and the branches combined to work out these pictures upon the mirror of my imagination, and for some reason I projected them outwards and made them appear objective. I knew this must be the case, of course. I was the subject of a vivid and interesting hallucination. I took courage, and began to move forward across the open patches of sand. By Jove, though, was it all hallucination? Was it merely subjective? Did not my reason argue in the old futile way from the little standard of the known?

I only know that great column of figures ascended darkly into the sky for what seemed a very long period of time, and with a very complete measure of reality as most men are accustomed to gauge reality. Then suddenly they were gone!

And, once they were gone and the immediate wonder of their great presence had passed, fear came down upon me with a cold rush. The esoteric meaning of this lonely and haunted region suddenly flamed up within me, and I began to tremble dreadfully. I took a quick look round—a look of horror that came near to panic—calculating vainly ways of escape; and then, realising how helpless I was to achieve anything really effective, I crept back silently into the tent and lay down again upon my sandy mattress, first lowering the door-curtain to shut out the sight of the willows in the moonlight, and then burying my head as deeply as possibly beneath the blankets to deaden the sound of the terrifying wind.

## 3

As though further to convince me that I had not been dreaming, I remember that it was a long time before I fell again into a troubled and restless sleep; and even then only the upper crust of me slept, and underneath there was something that never quite lost consciousness, but lay alert and on the watch.

But this second time I jumped up with a genuine start of terror. It was neither the wind nor the river that woke me, but the slow approach of something that caused the sleeping portion of me to grow smaller and smaller till at last it vanished altogether, and I found myself sitting bolt upright—listening.

Outside there was a sound of multitudinous little patterings. They had been coming, I was aware, for a long time, and in my sleep they had first become audible. I sat there nervously wide awake as though I had not slept at all. It seemed to me that my breathing came with difficulty, and that there was a great weight upon the surface of my body. In spite of the hot night, I felt clammy with cold and shivered. Something surely was pressing steadily against the sides of the tent and weighing down upon it from above. Was it the body of the wind? Was this the pattering rain, the dripping of the leaves? The spray blown from the river by the wind and gathering in big drops? I thought quickly of a dozen things.

Then suddenly the explanation leaped into my mind: a bough from the poplar, the only large tree on the island, had fallen with the wind. Still half-caught by the other branches, it would fall with the next gust and crush us, and meanwhile its leaves brushed and tapped upon the tight canvas surface of the tent. I raised the loose flap and rushed out, calling to the Swede to follow.

But when I got out and stood upright I saw that the tent was free. There was no hanging bough; there was no rain or spray; nothing approached.

A cold, grey light filtered down through the bushes and lay on the faintly gleaming sand. Stars still crowded the sky directly overhead, and the wind howled magnificently, but the fire no longer gave out any glow, and I saw the east reddening in streaks through the trees. Several hours must have passed since I stood there before watching the ascending figures, and the memory of it now came back to me horribly, like an evil dream. Oh, how tired it made me feel, that ceaseless raging wind! Yet, though the deep lassitude of a sleepless night was on me, my nerves were tingling with the activity of an equally tireless apprehension, and all idea of repose was out of the question. The river I saw had risen further. Its thunder filled the air, and a fine spray made itself felt through my thin sleeping shirt.

Yet nowhere did I discover the slightest evidences of anything to cause alarm. This deep, prolonged disturbance in my heart remained wholly unaccounted for.

My companion had not stirred when I called him, and there was no need to waken him now. I looked about me carefully, noting everything: the turned-over canoe; the yellow paddles—two of them, I'm certain; the provision sack and the extra lantern hanging together from the tree; and, crowding everywhere about me, enveloping all, the willows, those endless, shaking willows. A bird uttered its morning cry, and a string of duck passed with whirring flight overhead in the twilight. The sand whirled, dry and stinging, about my bare feet in the wind.

I walked round the tent and then went out a little way into the bush, so that I could see across the river to the farther landscape, and the same profound yet indefinable emotion of distress seized upon me again as I saw the interminable sea of bushes stretching to the horizon, looking ghostly and unreal in the wan light of dawn. I walked softly here and there, still puzzling over that odd sound of infinite pattering, and of that pressure upon the tent that had wakened me. It *must* have been the wind, I reflected—the wind beating upon the loose, hot sand, driving the dry particles smartly against the taut canvas—the wind dropping heavily upon our fragile roof.

Yet all the time my nervousness and malaise increased appreciably.

I crossed over to the farther shore and noted how the coastline had altered in the night, and what masses of sand the river had torn away. I dipped my hands and feet into the cool current, and bathed my forehead. Already there was a glow of sunrise in the sky and the exquisite freshness of coming day. On my way back I passed purposely beneath the very bushes where I had seen the column of figures rising into the air, and midway among the clumps I suddenly found myself overtaken by a sense of vast terror. From the shadows a large figure went swiftly by. Someone passed me, as sure as ever man did. . . .

It was a great staggering blow from the wind that helped me forward again, and once out in the more open space, the sense of terror diminished strangely. The winds were about and walking, I remember saying to myself; for the winds often move like great presences under the trees. And altogether the fear that hovered about me was such an unknown and immense kind of fear, so unlike anything I had ever felt before, that it woke a sense of awe and wonder in me that did much to counteract its worst effects; and when I reached a high point in the middle of the island from which I could see the wide stretch of river, crimson in the sunrise, the whole magical beauty of it all was so overpowering that a sort of wild yearning woke in me and almost brought a cry up into the throat.

But this cry found no expression, for as my eyes wandered from the plain beyond to the island round me and noted our little tent half-hidden among the willows, a dreadful discovery leaped out at me, compared to which my terror of the walking winds seemed as nothing at all.

For a change, I thought, had somehow come about in the arrangement of the landscape. It was not that my point of vantage gave me a different view but that an alteration had apparently been effected in the relation of the tent to the willows, and of the willows to the tent. Surely the bushes now crowded much closer—unnecessarily, unpleasantly close. *They had moved nearer.*

Creeping with silent feet over the shifting sands, drawing imperceptibly nearer by soft, unhurried movements, the willows had come closer during the night. But had the wind

moved them, or had they moved of themselves? I recalled the sound of infinite small patterings and the pressure upon the tent and upon my own heart that caused me to wake in terror.
I swayed for a moment in the wind like a tree, finding it hard to keep my upright position on
the sandy hillock. There was a suggestion here of personal agency, of deliberate intention, of
aggressive hostility, and it terrified me into a sort of rigidity.

Then the reaction followed quickly. The idea was so bizarre, so absurd, that I felt inclined
to laugh. But the laughter came no more readily than the cry, for the knowledge that my
mind was so receptive to such dangerous imaginings brought the additional terror that it was
through our minds and not through our physical bodies that the attack would come, and was
coming.

The wind buffeted me about, and, very quickly it seemed, the sun came up over the horizon, for it was after four o'clock, and I must have stood on that little pinnacle of sand longer
than I knew, afraid to come down at close quarters with the willows. I returned quietly,
creepily, to the tent, first taking another exhaustive look round and—yes, I confess it—making a few measurements. I paced out on the warm sand the distances between the willows
and the tent, making a note of the shortest distance particularly.

I crawled stealthily into my blankets. My companion, to all appearances, still slept
soundly, and I was glad that this was so. Provided my experiences were not corroborated, I
could find strength somehow to deny them, perhaps. With the daylight I could persuade
myself that it was all a subjective hallucination, a fantasy of the night, a projection of the excited imagination.

Nothing further came to disturb me, and I fell asleep almost at once, utterly exhausted, yet
still in dread of hearing again that weird sound of multitudinous pattering, or of feeling the
pressure upon my heart that had made it difficult to breathe.


## 4

The sun was high in the heavens when my companion woke me from a heavy sleep and announced that the porridge was cooked and there was just time to bathe. The grateful smell of
frizzling bacon entered the tent door.

"River still rising," he said, "and several islands out in midstream have disappeared
altogether. Our own island's much smaller."

"Any wood left?" I asked sleepily.

"The wood and the island will finish to-morrow in a dead heat," he laughed, "but there's
enough to last us till then."

I plunged in from the point of the island, which had indeed altered a lot in size and shape
during the night, and was swept down in a moment to the landing-place opposite the tent.
The water was icy, and the banks flew by like the country from an express train. Bathing
under such conditions was an exhilarating operation, and the terror of the night seemed
cleansed out of me by a process of evaporation in the brain. The sun was blazing hot; not a
cloud showed itself anywhere; the wind, however, had not abated one little jot.

Quite suddenly then the implied meaning of the Swede's words flashed across me, showing
that he no longer wished to leave post-haste, and had changed his mind. "Enough to last till
to-morrow"—he assumed we should stay on the island another night. It struck me as odd.
The night before he was so positive the other way. How had the change come about?

Great crumblings of the banks occurred at breakfast, with heavy splashings and clouds of
spray which the wind brought into our frying-pan, and my fellow-traveller talked incessantly
about the difficulty the Vienna-Pesth steamers must have to find the channel in flood. But the
state of his mind interested and impressed me far more than the state of the river or the diffi-

culties of the steamers. He had changed somehow since the evening before. His manner was different—a trifle excited, a trifle shy, with a sort of suspicion about his voice and gestures. I hardly know how to describe it now in cold blood, but at the time I remember being quite certain of one thing, viz., that he had become frightened!

He ate very little breakfast, and for once omitted to smoke his pipe. He had the map spread open beside him, and kept studying its markings.

"We'd better get off sharp in an hour," I said presently, feeling for an opening that must bring him indirectly to a partial confession at any rate. And his answer puzzled me uncomfortably: "Rather! If they'll let us."

"Who'll let us? The elements?" I asked quickly, with affected indifference.

"The powers of this awful place, whoever they are," he replied, keeping his eyes on the map. "The gods are here, if they are anywhere at all in the world."

"The elements are always the true immortals," I replied, laughing as naturally as I could manage, yet knowing quite well that my face reflected my true feelings when he looked up gravely at me and spoke across the smoke:

"We shall be fortunate if we get away without further disaster."

This was exactly what I had dreaded, and I screwed myself up to the point of the direct question. It was like agreeing to allow the dentist to extract the tooth; it *had* to come anyhow in the long run, and the rest was all pretence.

"Further disaster! Why, what's happened?"

"For one thing—the steering paddle's gone," he said quietly.

"The steering paddle gone!" I repeated, greatly excited, for this was our rudder, and the Danube in flood without a rudder was suicide. "But what . . ."

"And there's a tear in the bottom of the canoe," he added, with a genuine little tremor in his voice.

I continued staring at him, able only to repeat the words in his face somewhat foolishly. There, in the heat of the sun, and on this burning sand, I was aware of a freezing atmosphere descending round us. I got up to follow him, for he merely nodded his head gravely and led the way towards the tent a few yards on the other side of the fireplace. The canoe still lay there as I had last seen her in the night, ribs uppermost, the paddles, or rather, *the* paddle, on the sand beside her.

"There's only one," he said, stooping to pick it up. "And here's the rent in the baseboard."

It was on the tip of my tongue to tell him that I had clearly noticed *two* paddles a few hours before, but a second impulse made me think better of it, and I said nothing. I approached to see.

There was a long, finely-made tear in the bottom of the canoe where a little slither of wood had been neatly taken clean out; it looked as if the tooth of a sharp rock or snag had eaten down her length, and investigation showed that the hole went through. Had we launched out in her without observing it we must inevitably have foundered. At first the water would have made the wood swell so as to close the hole, but once out in midstream the water must have poured in, and the canoe, never more than two inches above the surface, would have filled and sunk very rapidly.

"There, you see, an attempt to prepare a victim for the sacrifice," I heard him saying, more to himself than to me, "two victims rather," he added as he bent over and ran his fingers along the slit.

I began to whistle—a thing I always do unconsciously when utterly nonplussed—and purposely paid no attention to his words. I was determined to consider them foolish.

"It wasn't there last night," he said presently, straightening up from his examination and looking anywhere but at me.

"We must have scratched her in landing, of course," I stopped whistling to say. "The stones are very sharp. . . ."

I stopped abruptly, for at that moment he turned round and met my eye squarely. I knew just as well as he did how impossible my explanation was. There were no stones, to begin with.

"And then there's this to explain too," he added quietly, handing me the paddle and pointing to the blade.

A new and curious emotion spread freezingly over me as I took and examined it. The blade was scraped down all over, beautifully scraped, as though someone had sand-papered it with care, making it so thin that the first vigorous stroke must have snapped it off at the elbow.

"One of us walked in his sleep and did this thing," I said feebly, "or—or it has been filed by the constant stream of sand particles blown against it by the wind, perhaps."

"Ah," said the Swede, turning away, laughing a little, "you can explain everything!"

"The same wind that caught the steering paddle and flung it so near the bank that it fell in with the next lump that crumbled," I called out after him, absolutely determined to find an explanation for everything he showed me.

"I see," he shouted back, turning his head to look at me before disappearing among the willow bushes.

Once alone with these perplexing evidences of personal agency, I think my first thought took the form of "One of us must have done this thing, and it certainly was not I." But my second thought decided how impossible it was to suppose, under all the circumstances, that either of us had done it. That my companion, the trusted friend of a dozen similar expeditions, could have knowingly had a hand in it, was a suggestion not to be entertained for a moment. Equally absurd seemed the explanation that this imperturbable and densely practical nature had suddenly become insane and was busied with insane purposes.

Yet the fact remained that what disturbed me most, and kept my fear actively alive even in this blaze of sunshine and wild beauty, was the clear certainty that some curious alteration had come about in his *mind*—that he was nervous, timid, suspicious, aware of goings on he did not speak about, watching a series of secret and hitherto unmentionable events—waiting, in a word, for a climax that he expected, and, I thought, expected very soon. This grew up in my mind intuitively—I hardly knew how.

I made a hurried examination of the tent and its surroundings, but the measurements of the night remained the same. There were deep hollows formed in the sand, I now noticed for the first time, basin-shaped and of various depths and sizes, varying from that of a tea-cup to a large bowl. The wind, no doubt, was responsible for these miniature craters, just as it was for lifting the paddle and tossing it towards the water. The rent in the canoe was the only thing that seemed quite inexplicable; and, after all, it *was* conceivable that a sharp point had caught it when we landed. The examination I made of the shore did not assist this theory, but all the same I clung to it with that diminishing portion of my intelligence which I called my "reason." An explanation of some kind was an absolute necessity, just as some working explanation of the universe is necessary—however absurd—to the happiness of every individual who seeks to do his duty in the world and face the problems of life. The simile seemed to me at the time an exact parallel.

I at once set the pitch melting, and presently the Swede joined me at the work, though under the best conditions in the world the canoe could not be safe for travelling till the following day. I drew his attention casually to the hollows in the sand.

"Yes," he said, "I know. They're all over the island. But *you* can explain them, no doubt!"

"Wind, of course," I answered without hesitation. "Have you never watched those little whirlwinds in the street that twist and twirl everything into a circle? This sand's loose enough to yield, that's all."

He made no reply, and we worked on in silence for a bit. I watched him surreptitiously all the time, and I had an idea he was watching me. He seemed, too, to be always listening attentively to something I could not hear, or perhaps for something that he expected to hear, for he kept turning about and staring into the bushes, and up into the sky, and out across the water where it was visible through the openings among the willows. Sometimes he even put his hand to his ear and held it there for several minutes. He said nothing to me, however, about it, and I asked no questions. And meanwhile, as he mended that torn canoe with the skill and address of a Red Indian, I was glad to notice his absorption in the work, for there was a vague dread in my heart that he would speak of the changed aspect of the willows. And, if he had noticed *that,* my imagination could no longer be held a sufficient explanation of it.

At length, after a long pause, he began to talk.

"Queer thing," he added in a hurried sort of voice, as though he wanted to say something and get it over. "Queer thing, I mean, about that otter last night."

I had expected something so totally different that he caught me with surprise, and I looked up sharply.

"Shows how lonely this place is. Otters are awfully shy things. . . ."

"I don't mean that, of course," he interrupted. "I mean—do you think—did you think it really *was* an otter?"

"What else, in the name of Heaven, what else?"

"You know, I saw it before you did, and at first it seemed—so *much* bigger than an otter."

"The sunset as you looked upstream magnified it, or something," I replied.

He looked at me absently a moment, as though his mind were busy with other thoughts.

"It had such extraordinary yellow eyes," he went on half to himself.

"That was the sun too," I laughed, a trifle boisterously. "I suppose you'll wonder next if that fellow in the boat . . ."

I suddenly decided not to finish the sentence. He was in the act again of listening, turning his head to the wind, and something in the expression of his face made me halt. The subject dropped, and we went on with our caulking. Apparently he had not noticed my unfinished sentence. Five minutes later, however, he looked at me across the canoe, the smoking pitch in his hand, his face exceedingly grave.

"I *did* rather wonder, if you want to know," he said slowly, "what that thing in the boat was. I remember thinking at the time it was not a man. The whole business seemed to rise quite suddenly out of the water."

I laughed again boisterously in his face, but this time there was impatience, and a strain of anger too, in my feeling.

"Look here now," I cried, "this place is quite queer enough without going out of our way to imagine things! That boat was an ordinary boat, and the man in it was an ordinary man, and they were both going downstream as fast as they could lick. And that otter *was* an otter, so don't let's play the fool about it!"

He looked steadily at me with the same grave expression. He was not in the least annoyed. I took courage from his silence.

"And, for Heaven's sake," I went on, "don't keep pretending you hear things, because it only gives me the jumps, and there's nothing to hear but the river and this cursed old thundering wind."

"You *fool!*" he answered in a low, shocked voice, "you utter fool. That's just the way all victims talk. As if you didn't understand just as well as I do!" he sneered with scorn in his voice, and a sort of resignation. "The best thing you can do is to keep quiet and try to hold your mind as firm as possible. This feeble attempt at self-deception only makes the truth harder when you're forced to meet it."

My little effort was over, and I found nothing more to say, for I knew quite well his words were true, and that *I* was the fool, not *he*. Up to a certain stage in the adventure he kept ahead of me easily, and I think I felt annoyed to be out of it, to be thus proved less psychic, less sensitive than himself to these extraordinary happenings, and half-ignorant all the time of what was going on under my very nose. *He knew* from the very beginning, apparently. But at the moment I wholly missed the point of his words about the necessity of there being a victim, and that we ourselves were destined to satisfy the want. I dropped all pretence thenceforward, but thenceforward likewise my fear increased steadily to the climax.

"But you're quite right about one thing," he added, before the subject passed, "and that is that we're wiser not to talk about it, or even to think about it, because what one *thinks* finds expression in words, and what one *says,* happens."

That afternoon, while the canoe dried and hardened, we spent trying to fish, testing the leak, collecting wood, and watching the enormous flood of rising water. Masses of driftwood swept near our shores sometimes, and we fished for them with long willow branches. The island grew perceptibly smaller as the banks were torn away with great gulps and splashes. The weather kept brilliantly fine till about four o'clock, and then for the first time for three days the wind showed signs of abating. Clouds began to gather in the southwest, spreading thence slowly over the sky.

This lessening of the wind came as a great relief, for the incessant roaring, banging, and thundering had irritated our nerves. Yet the silence that came about five o'clock with its sudden cessation was in a manner quite as oppressive. The booming of the river had everything its own way then: it filled the air with deep murmurs, more musical than the wind noises, but infinitely more monotonous. The wind held many notes, rising, falling, always beating out some sort of great elemental tune; whereas the river's song lay between three notes at most—dull pedal notes, that held a lugubrious quality foreign to the wind, and somehow seemed to me, in my then nervous state, to sound wonderfully well the music of doom.

It was extraordinary, too, how the withdrawal suddenly of bright sunlight took everything out of the landscape that made for cheerfulness; and since this particular landscape had already managed to convey the suggestion of something sinister, the change, of course, was all the more unwelcome and noticeable. For me, I know, the darkening outlook became distinctly more alarming, and I found myself more than once calculating how soon after sunset the full moon would get up in the east, and whether the gathering clouds would greatly interfere with her lighting of the little island.

With this general hush of the wind—though it still indulged in occasional brief gusts—the river seemed to me to grow blacker, the willows to stand more densely together. The latter, too, kept up a sort of independent movement of their own, rustling among themselves when no wind stirred, and shaking oddly from the roots upwards. When common objects in this way become charged with the suggestion of horror, they stimulate the imagination far more than things of unusual appearance; and these bushes, crowding huddled about us, assumed for me in the darkness a bizarre *grotesquerie* of appearance that lent to them somehow the aspect of purposeful and living creatures. Their very ordinariness, I felt, masked what was malignant and hostile to us. The forces of the region drew nearer with the coming of night. They were focusing upon our island, and more particularly upon ourselves. For thus, somehow, in the terms of the imagination, did my really indescribable sensations in this extraordinary place present themselves.

I had slept a good deal in the early afternoon, and had thus recovered somewhat from the exhaustion of a disturbed night, but this only served apparently to render me more susceptible than before to the obsessing spell of the haunting. I fought against it, laughing at my feelings as absurd and childish, with very obvious physiological explanations, yet, in spite of every effort, they gained in strength upon me so that I dreaded the night as a child lost in a forest must dread the approach of darkness.

The canoe we had carefully covered with a waterproof sheet during the day, and the one remaining paddle had been securely tied by the Swede to the base of a tree, lest the wind should rob us of that too. From five o'clock onwards I busied myself with the stew-pot and preparations for dinner, it being my turn to cook that night. We had potatoes, onions, bits of bacon fat to add flavour, and a general thick residue from former stews at the bottom of the pot; with black bread broken up into it the result was most excellent, and it was followed by a stew of plums with sugar and a brew of strong tea with dried milk. A good pile of wood lay close at hand, and the absence of wind made my duties easy. My companion sat lazily watching me, dividing his attentions between cleaning his pipe and giving useless advice—an admitted privilege of the off-duty man. He had been very quiet all the afternoon, engaged in re-caulking the canoe, strengthening the tent ropes, and fishing for driftwood while I slept. No more talk about undesirable things had passed between us, and I think his only remarks had to do with the gradual destruction of the island, which he declared was now fully a third smaller than when we first landed.

The pot had just begun to bubble when I heard his voice calling to me from the bank, where he had wandered away without my noticing. I ran up.

"Come and listen," he said, "and see what you make of it." He held his hand cupwise to his ear, as so often before.

"*Now* do you hear anything?" he asked, watching me curiously.

We stood there, listening attentively together. At first I heard only the deep note of the water and the hissings rising from its turbulent surface. The willows, for once, were motionless and silent. Then a sound began to reach my ears faintly, a peculiar sound—something like the humming of a distant gong. It seemed to come across to us in the darkness from the waste of swamps and willows opposite. It was repeated at regular intervals, but it was certainly neither the sound of a bell nor the hooting of a distant steamer. I can liken it to nothing so much as to the sound of an immense gong, suspended far up in the sky, repeating incessantly its muffled metallic note, soft and musical, as it was repeatedly struck. My heart quickened as I listened.

"I've heard it all day," said my companion. "While you slept this afternoon it came all round the island. I hunted it down, but could never get near enough to see—to localise it correctly. Sometimes it was overhead, and sometimes it seemed under the water. Once or twice, too, I could have sworn it was not outside at all, but *within myself*—you know—the way a sound in the fourth dimension is supposed to come."

I was too much puzzled to pay much attention to his words. I listened carefully, striving to associate it with any known familiar sound I could think of, but without success. It changed in direction, too, coming nearer, and then sinking utterly away into remote distance. I cannot say that it was ominous in quality, because to me it seemed distinctly musical, yet I must admit it set going a distressing feeling that made me wish I had never heard it.

"The wind blowing in those sand-funnels," I said, determined to find an explanation, "or the bushes rubbing together after the storm perhaps."

"It comes off the whole swamp," my friend answered. "It comes from everywhere at once." He ignored my explanations. "It comes from the willow bushes somehow. . . ."

"But now the wind has dropped," I objected. "The willows can hardly make a noise by themselves, can they?"

His answer frightened me, first because I had dreaded it, and, secondly, because I knew intuitively it was true.

"It is *because* the wind has dropped we now hear it. It was drowned before. It is the cry, I believe, of the  . . ."

I dashed back to my fire, warned by a sound of bubbling that the stew was in danger, but determined at the same time to escape from further conversation. I was resolute, if possible, to avoid the exchanging of views. I dreaded, too, that he would begin about the gods, or the elemental forces, or something else disquieting, and I wanted to keep myself well in hand for what might happen later. There was another night to be faced before we escaped from this distressing place, and there was no knowing yet what it might bring forth.

"Come and cut up bread for the pot," I called to him, vigorously stirring the appetising mixture. That stew-pot held sanity for us both, and the thought made me laugh.

He came over slowly and took the provision sack from the tree, fumbling in its mysterious depths, and then emptying the entire contents upon the ground-sheet at his feet.

"Hurry up!" I cried; "it's boiling."

The Swede burst out into a roar of laughter that startled me. It was forced laughter, not artificial exactly, but mirthless.

"There's nothing here!" he shouted, holding his sides.

"Bread, I mean."

"It's gone. There is no bread. They've taken it!"

I dropped the long spoon and ran up. Everything the sack had contained lay upon the groundsheet, but there was no loaf.

The whole dead weight of my growing fear fell upon me and shook me. Then I burst out laughing too. It was the only thing to do: and the sound of my own laughter also made me understand his. The strain of physical pressure caused it—this explosion of unnatural laughter in both of us; it was an effort of repressed forces to seek relief; it was a temporary safety valve. And with both of us it ceased quite suddenly.

"How criminally stupid of me!" I cried, still determined to be consistent and find an explanation. "I clean forgot to buy a loaf at Pressburg. That chattering woman put everything out of my head, and I must have left it lying on the counter or  . . ."

"The oatmeal, too, is much less than it was this morning," the Swede interrupted.

Why in the world need he draw attention to it? I thought angrily.

"There's enough for tomorrow," I said, stirring vigorously, "and we can get lots more at Komorn or Gran. In twenty-four hours we shall be miles from here."

"I hope so—to God," he muttered, putting the things back into the sack, "unless we're claimed first as victims for the sacrifice," he added with a foolish laugh. He dragged the sack into the tent, for safety's sake, I suppose, and I heard him mumbling on to himself, but so indistinctly that it seemed quite natural for me to ignore his words.

Our meal was beyond question a gloomy one, and we ate it almost in silence, avoiding one another's eyes, and keeping the fire bright. Then we washed up and prepared for the night, and, once smoking, our minds unoccupied with any definite duties, the apprehension I had felt all day long became more and more acute. It was not then active fear, I think, but the very vagueness of its origin distressed me far more than if I had been able to ticket and face it squarely. The curious sound I have likened to the note of a gong became now almost incessant, and filled the stillness of the night with a faint, continuous ringing rather than a series of distinct notes. At one time it was behind and at another time in front of us. Sometimes I fancied it came from the bushes on our left, and then again from the clumps on our right. More often it hovered directly overhead like the whirring of wings. It was really everywhere at once, behind, in front, at our sides and over our heads, completely surrounding us. The sound really defies description. But nothing within my knowledge is like that ceaseless muffled humming rising off the deserted world of swamps and willows.

We sat smoking in comparative silence, the strain growing every minute greater. The worst feature of the situation seemed to me that we did not know what to expect, and could therefore make no sort of preparation by way of defence. We could anticipate nothing. My explanations made in the sunshine, moreover, now came to haunt me with their foolish and wholly unsatisfactory nature, and it was more and more clear to us that some kind of plain talk with my companion was inevitable, whether I liked it or not. After all, we had to spend the night together, and to sleep in the same tent side by side. I saw that I could not get along much longer without the support of his mind, and for that, of course, plain talk was imperative. As long as possible, however, I postponed this little climax, and tried to ignore or laugh at the occasional sentences he flung into the emptiness.

Some of these sentences, moreover, were confoundedly disquieting to me, coming as they did to corroborate much that I felt myself: corroboration, too—which made it so much more convincing—from a totally different point of view. He composed such curious sentences, and hurled them at me in such an inconsequential sort of way, as though his main line of thought was secret to himself, and these fragments were the bits he found it impossible to digest. He got rid of them by uttering them. Speech relieved him. It was like being sick.

"There are things about us, I'm sure, that make for disorder, disintegration, destruction, *our* destruction," he said once, while the fire blazed between us. "We've strayed out of a safe line somewhere."

And another time, when the gong sounds had come nearer, ringing much louder than before, and directly over our heads, he said, as though talking to himself:

"I don't think a phonograph would show any record of that. The sound doesn't come to me by the ears at all. The vibrations reach me in another manner altogether, and seem to be within me, which is precisely how a fourth-dimensional sound might be supposed to make itself heard."

I purposely made no reply to this, but I sat up a little closer to the fire and peered about me into the darkness. The clouds were massed all over the sky and no trace of moonlight came through. Very still, too, everything was, so that the river and the frogs had things all their own way.

"It has that about it," he went on, "which is utterly out of common experience. It is *unknown*. Only one thing describes it really: it is a non-human sound; I mean a sound outside humanity."

Having rid himself of this indigestible morsel, he lay quiet for a time; but he had so admirably expressed my own feeling that it was a relief to have the thought out, and to have confined it by the limitation of words from dangerous wandering to and fro in the mind.

The solitude of that Danube camping-place, can I ever forget it? The feeling of being utterly alone on an empty planet! My thoughts ran incessantly upon cities and the haunts of men. I would have given my soul, as the saying is, for the "feel" of those Bavarian villages we had passed through by the score; for the normal, human commonplaces: peasants drinking beer, tables beneath the trees, hot sunshine, and a ruined castle on the rocks behind the red-roofed church. Even the tourists would have been welcome.

Yet what I felt of dread was no ordinary ghostly fear. It was infinitely greater, stranger, and seemed to arise from some dim ancestral sense of terror more profoundly disturbing than anything I had known or dreamed of. We had "strayed," as the Swede put it, into some region or some set of conditions where the risks were great, yet unintelligible to us; where the frontiers of some unknown world lay close about us. It was a spot held by the dwellers in some outer space, a sort of peep-hole whence they could spy upon the earth, themselves unseen, a point where the veil between had worn a little thin. As the final result of too long a sojourn here, we should be carried over the border and deprived of what we called "our lives," yet by mental, not physical, processes. In that sense, as he said, we should be the victims of our adventure—a sacrifice.

It took us in different fashion, each according to the measure of his sensitiveness and powers of resistance. I translated it vaguely into a personification of the mightily disturbed elements, investing them with the horror of a deliberate and malefic purpose, resentful of our audacious intrusion into their breeding-place; whereas my friend threw it into the unoriginal form at first of a trespass on some ancient shrine, some place where the old gods still held sway, where the emotional forces of former worshippers still clung, and the ancestral portion of him yielded to the old pagan spell.

At any rate, here was a place unpolluted by men, kept clean by the winds from coarsening human influences, a place where spiritual agencies were within reach and aggressive. Never, before or since, have I been so attacked by indescribable suggestions of a "beyond region," of another scheme of life, another evolution not parallel to the human. And in the end our minds would succumb under the weight of the awful spell, and we should be drawn across the frontier into *their* world.

Small things testified to this amazing influence of the place, and now in the silence round the fire they allowed themselves to be noted by the mind. The very atmosphere had proved itself a magnifying medium to distort every indication: the otter rolling in the current, the hurrying boatman making signs, the shifting willows, one and all had been robbed of its natural character, and revealed in something of its other aspect—as it existed across the border in that other region. And this changed aspect I felt was new not merely to me, but to the race. The whole experience whose verge we touched was unknown to humanity at all. It was a new order of experience, and in the true sense of the word *unearthly*.

"It's the deliberate, calculating purpose that reduces one's courage to zero," the Swede said suddenly, as if he had been actually following my thoughts. "Otherwise imagination might count for much. But the paddle, the canoe, the lessening food . . ."

"Haven't I explained all that once?" I interrupted viciously.

"You have," he answered dryly; "you have indeed."

He made other remarks too, as usual, about what he called the "plain determination to provide a victim"; but, having now arranged my thoughts better, I recognised that this was simply the cry of his frightened soul against the knowledge that he was being attacked in a vital part, and that he would be somehow taken or destroyed. The situation called for a courage and calmness of reasoning that neither of us could compass, and I have never before been so clearly conscious of two persons in me—the one that explained everything, and the other that laughed at such foolish explanations, yet was horribly afraid.

Meanwhile, in the pitchy night the fire died down and the wood pile grew small. Neither of us moved to replenish the stock, and the darkness consequently came up very close to our faces. A few feet beyond the circle of firelight it was inky black. Occasionally a stray puff of wind set the willows shivering about us, but apart from this not very welcome sound a deep and depressing silence reigned, broken only by the gurgling of the river and the humming in the air overhead.

We both missed, I think, the shouting company of the winds.

At length, at a moment when a stray puff prolonged itself as though the wind were about to rise again, I reached the point for me of saturation, the point where it was absolutely necessary to find relief in plain speech, or else to betray myself by some hysterical extravagance that must have been far worse in its effect upon both of us. I kicked the fire into a blaze, and turned to my companion abruptly. He looked up with a start.

"I can't disguise it any longer," I said; "I don't like this place, and the darkness, and the noises, and the awful feelings I get. There's something here that beats me utterly. I'm in a blue funk, and that's the plain truth. If the other shore was—different, I swear I'd be inclined to swim for it!"

The Swede's face turned very white beneath the deep tan of sun and wind. He stared straight at me and answered quietly, but his voice betrayed his huge excitement by its unnatural calmness. For the moment, at any rate, he was the strong man of the two. He was more phlegmatic, for one thing.

"It's not a physical condition we can escape from by running away," he replied, in the tone of a doctor diagnosing some grave disease; "we must sit tight and wait. There are forces close here that could kill a herd of elephants in a second as easily as you or I could squash a fly. Our only chance is to keep perfectly still. Our insignificance perhaps may save us."

I put a dozen questions into my expression of face, but found no words. It was precisely like listening to an accurate description of a disease whose symptoms had puzzled me.

"I mean that so far, although aware of our disturbing presence, they have not *found* us— not 'located' us, as the Americans say," he went on. "They're blundering about like men hunting for a leak of gas. The paddle and canoe and provisions prove that. I think they *feel* us, but cannot actually see us. We must keep our minds quiet—it's our minds they feel. We must control our thoughts, or it's all up with us."

"Death you mean?" I stammered, icy with the horror of his suggestion.

"Worse—by far," he said. "Death, according to one's belief, means either annihilation or release from the limitations of the senses, but it involves no change of character. *You* don't suddenly alter just because the body's gone. But this means a radical alteration, a complete change, a horrible loss of oneself by substitution—far worse than death, and not even annihilation. We happen to have camped in a spot where their region touches ours, where the veil between has worn thin"—horrors! he was using my very own phrase, my actual words—"so that they are aware of our being in their neighbourhood."

"But *who* are aware?" I asked.

I forgot the shaking of the willows in the windless calm, the humming overhead, everything except that I was waiting for an answer that I dreaded more than I can possibly explain.

He lowered his voice at once to reply, leaning forward a little over the fire, an indefinable change in his face that made me avoid his eyes and look down upon the ground.

"All my life," he said, "I have been strangely, vividly conscious of another region—not far removed from our own world in one sense, yet wholly different in kind—where great things go on unceasingly, where immense and terrible personalities hurry by, intent on vast purposes compared to which earthly affairs, the rise and fall of nations, the destinies of empires, the fate of armies and continents, are all as dust in the balance; vast purposes, I mean, that deal directly with the soul, and not indirectly with mere expressions of the soul. . . ."

"I suggest just now . . ." I began, seeking to stop him, feeling as though I was face to face with a madman. But he instantly overbore me with his torrent that *had* to come.

"You think," he said, "it is the spirits of the elements, and I thought perhaps it was the old gods. But I tell you now it is—*neither*. These would be comprehensible entities, for they have relations with men, depending upon them for worship or sacrifice, whereas these beings who are now about us have absolutely nothing to do with mankind, and it is mere chance that their space happens just at this spot to touch our own."

The mere conception, which his words somehow made so convincing, as I listened to them there in the dark stillness of that lonely island, set me shaking a little all over. I found it impossible to control my movements.

"And what do you propose?" I began again.

"A sacrifice, a victim, might save us by distracting them until we could get away," he went on, "just as the wolves stop to devour the dogs and give the sleigh another start. But—I see no chance of any other victim now."

I stared blankly at him. The gleam in his eyes was dreadful. Presently he continued.

"It's the willows, of course. The willows *mask* the others, but the others are feeling about for us. If we let our minds betray our fear, we're lost, lost utterly." He looked at me with an expression so calm, so determined, so sincere, that I no longer had any doubts as to his sanity. He was as sane as any man ever was. "If we can hold out through the night," he added, "we may get off in the daylight unnoticed, or rather, *undiscovered*."

"But you really think a sacrifice would . . ."

That gong-like humming came down very close over our heads as I spoke, but it was my friend's scared face that really stopped my mouth.

"Hush!" he whispered, holding up his hand. "Do not mention them more than you can help. Do not refer to them *by name*. To name is to reveal: it is the inevitable clue, and our only hope lies in ignoring them, in order that they may ignore us."

"Even in thought?" He was extraordinarily agitated.

"Especially in thought. Our thoughts make spirals in their world. We must keep them *out of our minds* at all costs if possible."

I raked the fire together to prevent the darkness having everything its own way. I never longed for the sun as I longed for it then in the awful blackness of that summer night.

"Were you awake all last night?" he went on suddenly.

"I slept badly a little after dawn," I replied evasively, trying to follow his instructions, which I knew instinctively were true, "but the wind, of course. . . ."

"I know. But the wind won't account for all the noises."

"Then you heard it too?"

"The multiplying countless little footsteps I heard," he said, adding, after a moment's hesitation, "and that other sound. . . ."

"You mean above the tent, and the pressing down upon us of something tremendous, gigantic?"

He nodded significantly.

"It was like the beginning of a sort of inner suffocation?" I said.

"Partly, yes. It seemed to me that the weight of the atmosphere had been altered—had increased enormously, so that we should be crushed."

"And *that*," I went on, determined to have it all out, pointing upwards where the gong-like note hummed ceaselessly, rising and falling like wind. "What do you make of that?"

"It's *their* sound," he whispered gravely. "It's the sound of their world, the humming in their region. The division here is so thin that it leaks through somehow. But, if you listen carefully, you'll find it's not above so much as around us. It's in the willows. It's the willows themselves humming, because here the willows have been made symbols of the forces that are against us."

I could not follow exactly what he meant by this, yet the thought and idea in my mind were beyond question the thought and idea in his. I realised what he realised, only with less power of analysis than his. It was on the tip of my tongue to tell him at last about my hallucination of the ascending figures and the moving bushes, when he suddenly thrust his face again close into mine across the firelight and began to speak in a very earnest whisper. He amazed me by his calmness and pluck, his apparent control of the situation. This man I had for years deemed unimaginative, stolid!

"Now listen," he said. "The only thing for us to do is to go on as though nothing had happened, follow our usual habits, go to bed, and so forth; pretend we feel nothing and notice nothing. It is a question wholly of the mind, and the less we think about them the better our chance of escape. Above all, don't *think*, for what you think happens!"

"All right," I managed to reply, simply breathless with his words and the strangeness of it all; "all right, I'll try, but tell me one thing more first. Tell me what you make of those hollows in the ground all about us, those sand-funnels?"

"No!" he cried, forgetting to whisper in his excitement. "I dare not, simply dare not, put the thought into words. If you have not guessed, I am glad. Don't try to. *They* have put it into my mind; try your hardest to prevent their putting it into yours."

He sank his voice again to a whisper before he finished, and I did not press him to explain. There was already just about as much horror in me as I could hold. The conversation came to an end, and we smoked our pipes busily in silence.

Then something happened, something unimportant apparently, as the way is when the nerves are in a very great state of tension, and this small thing for a brief space gave me an entirely different point of view. I chanced to look down at my sand-shoe—the sort we used for the canoe—and something to do with the hole at the toe suddenly recalled to me the London shop where I had bought them, the difficulty the man had in fitting me, and other details of the uninteresting but practical operation. At once, in its train, followed a wholesome view of the modern sceptical world I was accustomed to move in at home. I thought of roast beef and ale, motorcars, policemen, brass bands, and a dozen other things that proclaimed the soul of ordinariness or utility. The effect was immediate and astonishing even to myself. Psychologically, I suppose, it was simply a sudden and violent reaction after the strain of living in an atmosphere of things that to the normal consciousness must seem impossible and incredible. But, whatever the cause, it momentarily lifted the spell from my heart, and left me for the short space of a minute feeling free and utterly unafraid. I looked up at my friend opposite.

"You damned old pagan!" I cried, laughing aloud in his face. "You imaginative idiot! You superstitious idolator! You . . ."

I stopped in the middle, seized anew by the old horror. I tried to smother the sound of my voice as something sacrilegious. The Swede, of course, heard it too—that strange cry overhead in the darkness—and that sudden drop in the air as though something had come nearer.

He turned ashen white under the tan. He stood bolt upright in front of the fire, stiff as a rod, staring at me.

"After that," he said in a sort of helpless, frantic way, "we must go! We can't stay now; we must strike camp this very instant and go on—down the river."

He was talking, I saw, quite wildly, his words dictated by abject terror—the terror he had resisted so long, but which had caught him at last.

"In the dark?" I exclaimed, shaking with fear after my hysterical outburst, but still realising our position better than he did. "Sheer madness! The river's in flood, and we've only got a single paddle. Besides, we only go deeper into their country! There's nothing ahead for fifty miles but willows, willows, willows!"

He sat down again in a state of semi-collapse. The positions, by one of those kaleidoscopic changes nature loves, were suddenly reversed, and the control of our forces passed over into my hands. His mind at last had reached the point where it was beginning to weaken.

"What on earth possessed you to do such a thing?" he whispered, with the awe of genuine terror in his voice and face.

I crossed round to his side of the fire. I took both his hands in mine, kneeling down beside him and looking straight into his frightened eyes.

"We'll make one more blaze," I said firmly, "and then turn in for the night. At sunrise we'll be off full speed for Komorn. Now, pull yourself together a bit, and remember your own advice about *not thinking fear*!"

He said no more, and I saw that he would agree and obey. In some measure, too, it was a sort of relief to get up and make an excursion into the darkness for more wood. We kept close together, almost touching, groping among the bushes and along the bank. The humming overhead never ceased, but seemed to me to grow louder as we increased our distance from the fire. It was shivery work!

We were grubbing away in the middle of a thickish clump of willows where some drift-wood from a former flood had caught high among the branches, when my body was seized in a grip that made me half drop upon the sand. It was the Swede. He had fallen against me, and was clutching me for support. I heard his breath coming and going in short gasps.

"Look! By my soul!" he whispered, and for the first time in my experience I knew what it was to hear tears of terror in a human voice. He was pointing to the fire, some fifty feet away. I followed the direction of his finger, and I swear my heart missed a beat.

There, in front of the dim glow, *something was moving.*

I saw it through a veil that hung before my eyes like the gauze drop-curtain used at the back of a theatre—hazily a little. It was neither a human figure nor an animal. To me it gave the strange impression of being as large as several animals grouped together, like horses, two or three, moving slowly. The Swede, too, got a similar result, though expressing it differently, for he thought it was shaped and sized like a clump of willow bushes, rounded at the top, and moving all over upon its surface—"coiling upon itself like smoke," he said afterwards.

"I watched it settle downwards through the bushes," he sobbed at me. "Look, by God! It's coming this way! Oh, oh!"—he gave a kind of whistling cry. *"They've found us."*

I gave one terrified glance, which just enabled me to see that the shadowy form was swinging towards us through the bushes, and then I collapsed backwards with a crash into the branches. These failed, of course, to support my weight, so that with the Swede on the top of me we fell in a struggling heap upon the sand. I really hardly knew what was happening. I was conscious only of a sort of enveloping sensation of icy fear that plucked the nerves out of their fleshly covering, twisted them this way and that, and replaced them quivering. My eyes were tightly shut; something in my throat choked me; a feeling that my consciousness was expanding, extending out into space, swiftly gave way to another feeling that I was losing it altogether, and about to die.

An acute spasm of pain passed through me, and I was aware that the Swede had hold of me in such a way that he hurt me abominably. It was the way he caught at me in falling.

But it was this pain, he declared afterwards, that saved me: it caused me to *forget them* and think of something else at the very instant when they were about to find me. It concealed my mind from them at the moment of discovery, yet just in time to evade their terrible seizing of me. He himself, he says, actually swooned at the same moment, and that was what saved him.

I only know that at a later time, how long or short is impossible to say, I found myself scrambling up out of the slippery network of willow branches, and saw my companion standing in front of me holding out a hand to assist me. I stared at him in a dazed way, rubbing the arm he had twisted for me. Nothing came to me to say, somehow.

"I lost consciousness for a moment or two," I heard him say. "That's what saved me. It made me stop thinking about them."

"You nearly broke my arm in two," I said, uttering my only connected thought at the moment. A numbness came over me.

"That's what saved *you!*" he replied. "Between us, we've managed to set them off on a false tack somewhere. The humming has ceased. It's gone—for the moment at any rate!"

A wave of hysterical laughter seized me again, and this time spread to my friend too—great healing gusts of shaking laughter that brought a tremendous sense of relief in their train. We made our way back to the fire and put the wood on so that it blazed at once. Then we saw that the tent had fallen over and lay in a tangled heap upon the ground.

We picked it up, and during the process tripped more than once and caught our feet in sand.

"It's those sand-funnels," exclaimed the Swede, when the tent was up again and the firelight lit up the ground for several yards about us. "And look at the size of them!"

All around the tent and about the fireplace where we had seen the moving shadows there were deep funnel-shaped hollows in the sand, exactly similar to the ones we had already found all over the island, only far bigger and deeper, beautifully formed and wide enough in some instances to admit the whole of my foot and leg.

Neither of us said a word. We both knew that sleep was the safest thing we could do, and to bed we went accordingly without further delay, having first thrown sand on the fire and taken the provision sack and the paddle inside the tent with us. The canoe, too, we propped in such a way at the end of the tent that our feet touched it, and the least motion would disturb and wake us.

In case of emergency, too, we again went to bed in our clothes, ready for a sudden start.

# 5

It was my firm intention to lie awake all night and watch, but the exhaustion of nerves and body decreed otherwise, and sleep after a while came over me with a welcome blanket of oblivion. The fact that my companion also slept quickened its approach. At first he fidgeted and constantly sat up, asking me if I "heard this" or "heard that." He tossed about on his cork mattress, and said the tent was moving and the river had risen over the point of the island; but each time I went out to look I returned with the report that all was well, and finally he grew calmer and lay still. Then at length his breathing became regular and I heard unmistakable sounds of snoring—the first and only time in my life when snoring has been a welcome and calming influence.

This, I remember, was the last thought in my mind before dozing off.

A difficulty in breathing woke me, and I found the blanket over my face. But something else besides the blanket was pressing upon me, and my first thought was that my companion had rolled off his mattress on to my own in his sleep. I called to him and sat up, and at the same moment it came to me that the tent was *surrounded*. That sound of multitudinous soft pattering was again audible outside, filling the night with horror.

I called again to him, louder than before. He did not answer, but I missed the sound of his snoring, and also noticed that the flap of the tent door was down. This was the unpardonable sin. I crawled out in the darkness to hook it back securely, and it was then for the first time I realised positively that the Swede was not there. He had gone.

I dashed out in a mad run, seized by a dreadful agitation, and the moment I was out I plunged into a sort of torrent of humming that surrounded me completely and came out of every quarter of the heavens at once. It was that same familiar humming—gone mad! A swarm of great invisible bees might have been about me in the air. The sound seemed to thicken the very atmosphere, and I felt that my lungs worked with difficulty.

But my friend was in danger, and I could not hesitate.

The dawn was just about to break, and a faint whitish light spread upwards over the clouds from a thin strip of clear horizon. No wind stirred. I could just make out the bushes and river beyond, and the pale sandy patches. In my excitement I ran frantically to and fro about the island, calling him by name, shouting at the top of my voice the first words that came into my head. But the willows smothered my voice, and the humming muffled it, so that the sound only travelled a few feet round me. I plunged among the bushes, tripping head-long, tumbling over roots, and scraping my face as I tore this way and that among the pre-venting branches.

Then, quite unexpectedly, I came out upon the island's point and saw a dark figure out-lined between the water and the sky. It was the Swede. And already he had one foot in the river! A moment more and he would have taken the plunge.

I threw myself upon him, flinging my arms about his waist and dragging him shorewards with all my strength. Of course he struggled furiously, making a noise all the time just like that cursed humming, and using the most outlandish phrases in his anger about "going *in-side* to Them," and "taking the way of the water and the wind," and God only knows what more besides, that I tried in vain to recall afterwards, but which turned me sick with horror and amazement as I listened. But in the end I managed to get him into the comparative safety of the tent, and flung him breathless and cursing upon the mattress, where I held him until the fit had passed.

I think the suddenness with which it all went and he grew calm, coinciding as it did with the equally abrupt cessation of the humming and pattering outside—I think this was almost the strangest part of the whole business perhaps. For he just opened his eyes and turned his tired face up to me so that the dawn threw a pale light upon it through the doorway, and said, for all the world just like a frightened child:

"My life, old man—it's my life I owe you. But it's all over now anyhow. They've found a victim in our place!"

Then he dropped back upon his blankets and went to sleep literally under my eyes. He simply collapsed, and began to snore again as healthily as though nothing had happened and he had never tried to offer his own life as a sacrifice by drowning. And when the sunlight woke him three hours later—hours of ceaseless vigil for me—it became so clear to me that he remembered absolutely nothing of what he had attempted to do, that I deemed it wise to hold my peace and ask no dangerous questions.

He woke naturally and easily, as I have said, when the sun was already high in a windless hot sky, and he at once got up and set about the preparation of the fire for breakfast. I followed him anxiously at bathing, but he did not attempt to plunge in, merely dipping his head and making some remark about the extra coldness of the water.

"River's falling at last," he said, "and I'm glad of it."

"The humming has stopped too," I said.

He looked up at me quietly with his normal expression. Evidently he remembered every-thing except his own attempt at suicide.

"Everything has stopped," he said, "because . . ."

He hesitated. But I knew some reference to that remark he had made just before he fainted was in his mind, and I was determined to know it.

"Because 'They've found another victim'?" I said, forcing a little laugh.

"Exactly," he answered, "exactly! I feel as positive of it as though—as though—I feel quite safe again, I mean," he finished.

He began to look curiously about him. The sunlight lay in hot patches on the sand. There was no wind. The willows were motionless. He slowly rose to feet.

"Come," he said; "I think if we look, we shall find it."

He started off on a run, and I followed him. He kept to the banks, poking with a stick among the sandy bays and caves and little back-waters, myself always close on his heels.

"Ah!" he exclaimed presently, "ah!"

The tone of his voice somehow brought back to me a vivid sense of the horror of the last twenty-four hours, and I hurried up to join him. He was pointing with his stick at a large

black object that lay half in the water and half on the sand. It appeared to be caught by some twisted willow roots so that the river could not sweep it away. A few hours before the spot must have been under water.

"See," he said quietly, "the victim that made our escape possible!"

And when I peered across his shoulder I saw that his stick rested on the body of a man. He turned it over. It was the corpse of a peasant, and the face was hidden in the sand. Clearly the man had been drowned but a few hours before, and his body must have been swept down upon our island somewhere about the hour of the dawn—*at the very time the fit had passed.*

"We must give it a decent burial, you know."

"I suppose so," I replied. I shuddered a little in spite of myself, for there was something about the appearance of that poor drowned man that turned me cold.

The Swede glanced up sharply at me, an undecipherable expression on his face, and began clambering down the bank. I followed him more leisurely. The current, I noticed, had torn away much of the clothing from the body, so that the neck and part of the chest lay bare.

Half-way down the bank my companion suddenly stopped and held up his hand in warning; but either my foot slipped, or I had gained too much momentum to bring myself quickly to a halt, for I bumped into him and sent him forward with a sort of leap to save himself. We tumbled together on to the hard sand so that our feet splashed into the water. And, before anything could be done, we had collided a little heavily against the corpse.

The Swede uttered a sharp cry. And I sprang back as if I had been shot.

At the moment we touched the body there rose from its surface the loud sound of humming—the sound of several hummings—which passed with a vast commotion as of winged things in the air about us and disappeared upwards into the sky, growing fainter and fainter till they finally ceased in the distance. It was exactly as though we had disturbed some living yet invisible creatures at work.

My companion clutched me, and I think I clutched him, but before either of us had time properly to recover from the unexpected shock, we saw that a movement of the current was turning the corpse round so that it became released from the grip of the willow roots. A moment later it had turned completely over, the dead face uppermost, staring at the sky. It lay on the edge of the main stream. In another moment it would be swept away.

The Swede started to save it, shouting again something I did not catch about a "proper burial"—and then abruptly dropped upon his knees on the sand and covered his eyes with his hands. I was beside him in an instant.

I saw what he had seen.

For just as the body swung round to the current the face and the exposed chest turned full towards us, and showed plainly how the skin and flesh were indented with small hollows, beautifully formed, and exactly similar in shape and kind to the sand-funnels that we had found all over the island.

"Their mark!" I heard my companion mutter under his breath. "Their awful mark!"

And when I turned my eyes again from his ghastly face to the river, the current had done its work, and the body had been swept away into midstream and was already beyond our reach and almost out of sight, turning over and over on the waves like an otter.

# William Hope Hodgson

William Hope Hodgson (1875–1918) is unique among authors of uncanny tales. His writing alone entitles him to some special distinction; yet he is most unusual because, while the typical writer of weird stories leads a sedentary and contemplative life, Hodgson was primarily a man of action.

Hodgson spent eight years at sea, under the brutal conditions prevalent at the time, and the result was that he conceived a horror of the vast waters, which later supplied him with some of his best story material. Sam Moskowitz, the literary historian and anthologist who has researched the details of Hodgson's life, has called him "probably the greatest writer of horror at sea who ever lived." Although the topic has produced some impressive tales by other hands, there is little reason to argue with this assessment.

Although Hodgson's career as a sailor brought him a medal for heroism, his early literary work included numerous attacks on life at sea. His first publications, though, concerned themselves with muscular development. He had built himself up into an impressive specimen of manhood, primarily to preserve himself from the beatings that were all too common a part of life aboard ship. When he left the sea, he opened "W. H. Hodgson's School of Physical Culture" in Blackburn, England. He was also an expert amateur photographer, and many of his articles were illustrated with his own pictures. He fought bravely in World War I and was killed by a shell in France.

From this apparently unlikely source emerged some of the most imaginative English fiction of the last century. Two of Hodgson's novels, *The House on the Borderland* (1908) and *The Night Land* (1912), are powerful science fantasies portraying awesome glimpses of infinity and eternity, and they have had a profound effect on later writers. More traditional are the adventures of an occult detective collected in the volume *Carnacki, the Ghost-Finder* (1910). The best and most bizarre of these are "The Hog" and "The Whistling Room."

Hodgson's sinister sea stories include the two novels *The Boats of the Glen Carrig* (1907) and *The Ghost Pirates* (1909), as well as numerous shorter tales. The first of these was "A Tropical Horror" (1905), concerning a sea serpent that wipes out a ship's crew. Among the best is "The Derelict," a variation on the theme of Hodgson's most renowned short story, "The Voice in the Night." Although recent investigations and explorations have made some of his descriptions of uncharted waters seem slightly implausible, the central device of "The Voice in the Night" retains an air of believability. And by adding a note of tragedy to his terrors, Hodgson has, despite his sentimentality, succeeded in creating a morbid yet moving narrative that is a masterpiece of the macabre.

137

# THE VOICE IN THE NIGHT

## William Hope Hodgson

It was a dark, starless night. We were becalmed in the Northern Pacific. Our exact position I do not know; for the sun had been hidden during the course of a weary, breathless week, by a thin haze which had seemed to float above us, about the height of our mastheads, at whiles descending and shrouding the surrounding sea.

With there being no wind, we had steadied the tiller, and I was the only man on deck. The crew, consisting of two men and a boy, were sleeping forward in their den; while Will—my friend, and the master of our little craft—was aft in his bunk on the port side of the little cabin.

Suddenly, from out of the surrounding darkness, there came a hail: —

"Schooner, ahoy!"

The cry was so unexpected that I gave no immediate answer, because of my surprise.

It came again—a voice curiously throaty and inhuman, calling from somewhere upon the dark sea away on our port broadside: —

"Schooner, ahoy!"

"Hullo!" I sung out, having gathered my wits somewhat. "What are you? What do you want?"

"You need not be afraid," answered the queer voice, having probably noticed some trace of confusion in my tone. "I am only an old—man."

The pause sounded oddly; but it was only afterwards that it came back to me with any significance.

"Why don't you come alongside, then?" I queried somewhat snappishly; for I liked not his hinting at my having been a trifle shaken.

"I—I—can't. It wouldn't be safe. I——" The voice broke off, and there was silence.

"What do you mean?" I asked, growing more and more astonished. "Why not safe? Where are you?"

I listened for a moment; but there came no answer. And then, a sudden indefinite suspicion, of I knew not what, coming to me, I stepped swiftly to the binnacle, and took out the lighted lamp. At the same time, I knocked on the deck with my heel to waken Will. Then I was back at the side, throwing the yellow funnel of light out into the silent immensity beyond our rail. As I did so, I heard a slight, muffled cry, and then the sound of a splash, as though some one had dipped oars abruptly. Yet I cannot say that I saw anything with certainty; save, it seemed to me, that with the first flash of the light, there had been something upon the waters, where now there was nothing.

"Hullo, there!" I called. "What foolery is this!"

But there came only the indistinct sounds of a boat being pulled away into the night.

Then I heard Will's voice, from the direction of the after scuttle: —

"What's up, George?"

"Come here, Will!" I said.

"What is it?" he asked, coming across the deck.

I told him the queer thing which had happened. He put several questions; then, after a moment's silence, he raised his hands to his lips, and hailed: —

"Boat, ahoy!"

From a long distance away, there came back to us a faint reply, and my companion repeated his call. Presently, after a short period of silence, there grew on our hearing the muffled sound of oars; at which Will hailed again.

This time there was a reply: —

"Put away the light."

"I'm damned if I will," I muttered; but Will told me to do as the voice bade, and I shoved it down under the bulwarks.

"Come nearer," he said, and the oar-strokes continued. Then, when apparently some half-dozen fathoms distant, they again ceased.

"Come alongside," exclaimed Will. "There's nothing to be frightened of aboard here!"

"Promise that you will not show the light?"

"What's to do with you," I burst out, "that you're so infernally afraid of the light?"

"Because——" began the voice, and stopped short.

"Because what?" I asked, quickly.

Will put his hand on my shoulder.

"Shut up a minute, old man," he said, in a low voice. "Let me tackle him."

He leant more over the rail.

"See here, Mister," he said, "this is a pretty queer business, you coming upon us like this, right out in the middle of the blessed Pacific. How are we to know what sort of a hanky-panky trick you're up to? You say there's only one of you. How are we to know, unless we get a squint at you—eh? What's your objection to the light, anyway?"

As he finished, I heard the noise of the oars again, and then the voice came; but now from a greater distance, and sounding extremely hopeless and pathetic.

"I am sorry—sorry! I would not have troubled you, only I am hungry, and—so is she."

The voice died away, and the sound of the oars, dipping irregularly, was borne to us.

"Stop!" sung out Will. "I don't want to drive you away. Come back! We'll keep the light hidden, if you don't like it."

He turned to me: —

"It's a damned queer rig, this; but I think there's nothing to be afraid of?"

There was a question in his tone, and I replied.

"No, I think the poor devil's been wrecked around here, and gone crazy."

The sound of the oars drew nearer.

"Shove that lamp back in the binnacle," said Will; then he leaned over the rail, and listened. I replaced the lamp, and came back to his side. The dipping of the oars ceased some dozen yards distant.

"Won't you come alongside now?" asked Will in an even voice. "I have had the lamp put back in the binnacle."

"I—I cannot," replied the voice. "I dare not come nearer. I dare not even pay you for the—the provisions."

"That's all right," said Will, and hesitated. "Your're welcome to as much grub as you can take——" Again he hesitated.

"You are very good," exclaimed the voice. "May God, Who understands everything, reward you——" It broke off huskily.

"The—the lady?" said Will, abruptly. "Is she——"

"I have left her behind upon the island," came the voice.

"What island?" I cut in.

"I know not its name," returned the voice. "I would to God——!" it began, and checked itself as suddenly.

"Could we not send a boat for her?" asked Will at this point.

"No!" said the voice, with extraordinary emphasis. "My God! No!" There was a moment's pause; then it added, in a tone which seemed a merited reproach: —

"It was because of our want I ventured—Because her agony tortured me."

"I am a forgetful brute," exclaimed Will. "Just wait a minute, whoever you are, and I will bring you up something at once."

In a couple of minutes he was back again, and his arms were full of various edibles. He paused at the rail.

"Can't you come alongside for them?" he asked.

"No—I *dare not,*" replied the voice, and it seemed to me that in its tone I detected a note of stifled craving—as though the owner hushed a mortal desire. It came to me then in a flash, that the poor old creature out there in the darkness, was *suffering* for actual need of that which Will held in his arms; and yet, because of some unintelligible dread, refraining from dashing to the side of our little schooner, and receiving it. And with the lightning-like conviction, there came the knowledge that the Invisible was not mad; but sanely facing some intolerable horror.

"Damn it, Will!" I said, full of many feelings, over which predominated a vast sympathy. "Get a box. We must float off the stuff to him in it."

This we did—propelling it away from the vessel, out into the darkness, by means of a boathook. In a minute, a slight cry from the Invisible came to us, and we knew that he had secured the box.

A little later, he called out a farewell to us, and so heartful a blessing, that I am sure we were the better for it. Then, without more ado, we heard the ply of oars across the darkness.

"Pretty soon off," remarked Will, with perhaps just a little sense of injury.

"Wait," I replied. "I think somehow he'll come back. He must have been badly needing that food."

"And the lady," said Will. For a moment he was silent; then he continued: —

"It's the queerest thing ever I've tumbled across, since I've been fishing."

"Yes," I said, and fell to pondering.

And so the time slipped away—an hour, another, and still Will stayed with me; for the queer adventure had knocked all desire for sleep out of him.

The third hour was three parts through, when we heard again the sound of oars across the silent ocean.

"Listen!" said Will, a low note of excitement in his voice.

"He's coming, just as I thought," I muttered.

The dipping of the oars grew nearer, and I noted that the strokes were firmer and longer. The food had been needed.

They came to a stop a little distance off the broadside; and the queer voice came again to us through the darkness: —

"Schooner, ahoy!"

"That you?" asked Will.

"Yes," replied the voice, "I left you suddenly; but—but there was great need."

"The—lady is grateful now on earth. She will be more grateful soon in—in heaven."

Will began to make some reply, in a puzzled voice; but became confused, and broke off short. I said nothing. I was wondering at the curious pauses, and, apart from my wonder, I was full of a great sympathy.

The voice continued: —

"We—she and I, have talked, as we shared the result of God's tenderness and yours——"

Will interposed; but without coherence.

"I beg of you not to—to belittle your deed of Christian charity this night," said the voice. "Be sure that it has not escaped His notice."

It stopped, and there a full minute's silence. Then it came again: —

"We have spoken together upon that which—which has befallen us. We had thought to go out, without telling any, of the terror which has come into our——lives. She is with me in believing that to-night's happenings are under a special ruling, and that it is God's wish that we should tell to you all that we have suffered since—since——"

"Yes?" said Will, softly.

"Since the sinking of the 'Albatross.' "

"Ah!" I exclaimed, involuntarily. "She left Newcastle for 'Frisco some six months ago, and hasn't been heard of since."

"Yes," answered the voice. "But some few degrees to the North of the line she was caught in a terrible storm, and dismasted. When the day came, it was found that she was leaking badly, and, presently, it falling to a calm, the sailors took to the boats, leaving—leaving a young lady—my fiancee—and myself upon the wreck.

"We were below, gathering together a few of our belongings, when they left. They were entirely callous, through fear, and when we came up upon the decks, we saw them only as small shapes afar off upon the horizon. Yet we did not despair, but set to work and constructed a small raft. Upon this we put such few matters as it would hold, including a quantity of water and some ship's biscuit. Then, the vessel being very deep in the water, we got ourselves on to the raft, and pushed off.

"It was later, when I observed that we seemed to be in the way of some tide or current, which bore us from the ship at an angle; so that in the course of three hours, by my watch, her hull became invisible to our sight, her broken masts remaining in view for a somewhat longer period. Then, towards evening, it grew misty, and so through the night. The next day we were still encompassed by the mist, the weather remaining quiet.

"For four days, we drifted through this strange haze, until, on the evening of the fourth day, there grew upon our ears the murmur of breakers at a distance. Gradually it became plainer, and, somewhat after midnight, it appeared to sound upon either hand at no very great space. The raft was raised upon a swell several times, and then we were in smooth water, and the noise of the breakers was behind.

"When the morning came, we found that we were in a sort of great lagoon; but of this we noticed little at the time; for close before us, through the enshrouding mist, loomed the hull of a large sailing-vessel. With one accord, we fell upon our knees and thanked God; for we thought that here was an end to our perils. We had much to learn.

"The raft drew near to the ship, and we shouted on them, to take us aboard; but none answered. Presently, the raft touched against the side of the vessel, and, seeing a rope hanging downwards, I seized it and began to climb. Yet I had much ado to make my way up, because of a kind of grey, lichenous fungus, which had seized upon the rope, and which blotched the side of the ship, lividly.

"I reached the rail, and clambered over it, on to the deck. Here, I saw that the decks were covered, in great patches, with the grey masses, some of them rising into nodules several feet in height; but at the time, I thought less of this matter than of the possibility of there being people aboard the ship. I shouted; but none answered. Then I went to the door below the poop deck. I opened it, and peered in. There was a great smell of staleness, so that I knew in a moment that nothing living was within, and with the knowledge, I shut the door quickly; for I felt suddenly lonely.

"I went back to the side, where I had scrambled up. My—my sweetheart was still sitting quietly upon the raft. Seeing me look down, she called up to know whether there were any aboard of the ship. I replied that the vessel had the appearance of having been long deserted; but that if she would wait a little, I would see whether there was anything in the shape of a ladder, by which she could ascend to the deck. Then we would make a search through the vessel together. A little later, on the opposite side of the decks, I found a rope side-ladder. This I carried across, and a minute afterwards, she was beside me.

"Together, we explored the cabins and apartments in the afterpart of the ship; but nowhere was there any sign of life. Here and there, within the cabins themselves, we came across odd patches of that queer fungus; but this, as my sweetheart said, could be cleansed away.

"In the end, having assured ourselves that the after portion of the vessel was empty, we picked our ways to the bows, between the ugly grey nodules of that strange growth; and here we made a further search, which told us that there was indeed none aboard but ourselves.

"This being now beyond any doubt, we returned to the stern of the ship, and proceeded to make ourselves as comfortable as possible. Together, we cleared out and cleaned two of the cabins; and, after that, I made examination whether there was anything eatable in the ship. This I soon found was so, and thanked God in my heart for His goodness. In addition to this, I discovered the whereabouts of the freshwater pump, and having fixed it, I found the water drinkable, though somewhat unpleasant to the taste.

"For several days, we stayed aboard the ship, without attempting to get to the shore. We were busily engaged in making the place habitable. Yet even thus early, we became aware that our lot was even less to be desired than might have been imagined; for though, as a first step, we scraped away the old patches of growth that studded the floors and walls of the cabins and saloon, yet they returned almost to their original size within the space of twenty-four hours, which not only discouraged us, but gave us a feeling of vague unease.

"Still, we would not admit ourselves beaten, so set to work afresh, and not only scraped away the fungus, but soaked the places where it had been with carbolic, a can-full of which I had found in the pantry. Yet, by the end of the week, the growth had returned in full strength, and, in addition, it had spread to other places, as though our touching it had allowed germs from it to travel elsewhere.

"On the seventh morning, my sweetheart woke to find a small patch of it growing on her pillow, close to her face. At that, she came to me, so soon as she could get her garments upon her. I was in the galley at the time, lighting the fire for breakfast.

" 'Come here, John,' she said, and led me aft. When I saw the thing upon her pillow, I shuddered, and then and there we agreed to go right out of the ship, and see whether we could not fare to make ourselves more comfortable ashore.

"Hurriedly, we gathered together our few belongings, and even among these, I found that the fungus had been at work; for one of her shawls had a little lump of it growing near one edge. I threw the whole thing over the side, without saying anything to her.

"The raft was still alongside; but it was too clumsy to guide, and I lowered down a small boat that hung across the stern, and in this we made our way to the shore. Yet, as we drew near to it, I became gradually aware that here the vile fungus, which had driven us from the ship, was growing riot. In places it rose into horrible, fantastic mounds, which seemed almost to quiver, as with a quiet life, when the wind blew across them. Here and there, it took on the forms of vast fingers, and in others it just spread out flat and smooth and treacherous. Odd places, it appeared as grotesque stunted trees, seeming extraordinarily kinked and gnarled—— The whole quaking vilely at times.

"At first, it seemed to us that there was no single portion of the surrounding shore which was not hidden beneath the masses of the hideous lichen; yet, in this, I found we were mistaken; for somewhat later, coasting along the shore at a little distance, we descried a smooth white patch of what appeared to be fine sand, and there we landed. It was not sand. What it was, I do not know. All that I have observed, is that upon it, the fungus will not grow; while everywhere else, save where the sand-like earth wanders oddly, path-wise, amid the grey desolation of the lichen, there is nothing but that loathsome greyness.

"It is difficult to make you understand how cheered we were to find one place that was absolutely free from the growth, and here we deposited our belongings. Then we went back to the ship for such things as it seemed to us we should need. Among other matters, I managed to bring ashore with me one of the ship's sails, with which I constructed two small tents, which, though exceedingly roughshaped, served the purposes for which they were intended. In these, we lived and stored our various necessities, and thus for a matter of some four weeks, all went smoothly and without particular unhappiness. Indeed, I may say with much of happiness——for—for we were together.

"It was on the thumb of her right hand, that the growth first showed. It was only a small circular spot, much like a little grey mole. My God! how the fear leapt to my heart when she showed me the place. We cleansed it, between us, washing it with carbolic and water. In the morning of the following day, she showed her hand to me again. The grey warty thing had returned. For a little while, we looked at one another in silence. Then, still wordless, we started again to remove it. In the midst of the operation, she spoke suddenly.

" 'What's that on the side of your face, Dear?' Her voice was sharp with anxiety. I put my hand up to feel.

" 'There! Under the hair by your ear.—A little to the front a bit.' My finger rested upon the place, and then I knew.

" 'Let us get your thumb done first,' I said. And she submitted, only because she was afraid to touch me until it was cleansed. I finished washing and disinfecting her thumb, and then she turned to my face. After it was finished, we sat together and talked awhile of many things; for there had come into our lives sudden, very terrible thoughts. We were, all at once, afraid of something worse than death. We spoke of loading the boat with provisions and water, and making our way out on to the sea; yet we were helpless, for many causes, and—and the growth had attacked us already. We decided to stay. God would do with us what was His will. We would wait.

"A month, two months, three months passed, and the places grew somewhat, and there had come others. Yet we fought so strenuously with the fear, that its headway was but slow, comparatively speaking.

"Occasionally, we ventured off to the ship for such stores as we needed. There, we found that the fungus grew persistently. One of the nodules on the maindeck became soon as high as my head.

"We had now given up all thought or hope of leaving the island. We had realised that it would be unallowable to go among healthy humans, with the thing from which we were suffering.

"With this determination and knowledge in our minds, we knew that we should have to husband our food and water; for we did not know, at that time, but that we should possibly live for many years.

"This reminds me that I have told you that I am an old man. Judged by years this is not so. But—but——"

He broke off; then continued somewhat abruptly: —

"As I was saying, we knew that we should have to use care in the matter of food. But we had no idea then how little food there was left, of which to take care. It was a week later, that I made the discovery that all the other bread tanks—which I had supposed full—were empty, and that (beyond odd tins of vegetables and meat, and some other matters) we had nothing on which to depend, but the bread in the tank which I had already opened.

"After learning this, I bestirred myself to do what I could, and set to work at fishing in the lagoon; but with no success. At this, I was somewhat inclined to feel desperate, until the thought came to me to try outside the lagoon, in the open sea.

"Here, at times, I caught odd fish; but, so infrequently, that they proved of but little help in keeping us from the hunger which threatened. It seemed to me that our deaths were likely to come by hunger, and not by the growth of the thing which had seized upon our bodies.

"We were in this state of mind when the fourth month wore out. Then I made a very horrible discovery. One morning, a little before midday, I came off from the ship, with a portion of the biscuits which were left. In the mouth of her tent, I saw my sweetheart sitting, eating something.

" 'What is it, my Dear?' I called out as I leapt ashore. Yet, on hearing my voice, she seemed confused, and, turning, slyly threw something towards the edge of the little clearing. It fell short, and, a vague suspicion having arisen within me, I walked across and picked it up. It was a piece of the grey fungus.

"As I went to her, with it in my hand, she turned deadly pale; then a rose red.

"I felt strangely dazed and frightened.

" 'My Dear! My Dear!' I said, and could say no more. Yet, at my words, she broke down and cried bitterly. Gradually, as she calmed, I got from her the news that she had tried it the preceding day, and—and liked it. I got her to promise on her knees not to touch it again, however great our hunger. After she had promised, she told me that the desire for it had come suddenly, and that, until the moment of desire, she had experienced nothing towards it, but the most extreme repulsion.

"Later in the day, feeling strangely restless, and much shaken with the thing which I had discovered, I made my way along one of the twisted paths—formed by the white, sand-like substance—which led among the fungoid growth. I had, once before, ventured along there; but not to any great distance. This time, being involved in perplexing thought, I went much further than hitherto.

"Suddenly, I was called to myself, by a queer hoarse sound on my left. Turning quickly, I saw that there was movement among an extraordinarily shaped mass of fungus, close to my elbow. It was swaying uneasily, as though it possessed life of its own. Abruptly, as I stared, the thought came to me that the thing had a grotesque resemblance to the figure of a distorted human creature. Even as the fancy flashed into my brain, there was a slight, sickening noise of tearing, and I saw that one of the branch-like arms was detaching itself from the surrounding grey masses and coming towards me. The head of the thing—a shapeless grey ball, inclined in my direction. I stood stupidly, and the vile arm brushed across my face. I gave out a frightened cry, and ran back a few paces. There was a sweetish taste upon my lips, where the thing had touched me. I licked them, and was immediately filled with an inhuman desire. I turned and seized a mass of the fungus. Then more, and—more. I was insatiable. In the midst of the devouring, the remembrance of the morning's discovery swept into my amazed brain. It was sent by God. I dashed the fragment I held to the ground. Then, utterly wretched and feeling a dreadul guiltiness, I made my way back to the little encampment.

"I think she knew, by some marvellous intuition which love must have given, so soon as she set eyes on me. Her quiet sympathy made it easier for me, and I told her of my sudden weakness; yet omitted to mention the extraordinary thing which had gone before. I desired to spare her all unnecessary terror.

"But, for myself, I had added an intolerable knowledge, to breed an incessant terror in my brain; for I doubted not but that I had seen the end of one of those men who had come to the island in the ship in the lagoon; and in that monstrous ending, I had seen our own.

"Thereafter, we kept from the abominable food, though the desire for it had entered into our blood. Yet, our drear punishment was upon us; for, day by day, with monstrous rapidity, the fungoid growth took hold of our poor bodies. Nothing we could do would check it materially, and so—and so—we who had been human, became—Well, it matters less each day. Only—only we had been man and maid!

"And day by day, the fight is more dreadful, to withstand the hunger-lust for the terrible lichen.

"A week ago we ate the last of the biscuit, and since that time I have caught three fish. I was out here fishing to-night, when your schooner drifted upon me out of the mist. I hailed you. You know the rest, and may God, out of His great heart, bless you for your goodness to a—a couple of poor outcast souls."

There was the dip of an oar—another. Then the voice came again, and for the last time, sounding through the slight surrounding mist, ghostly and mournful.

"God bless you! Good-bye!"

"Good-bye," we shouted together, hoarsely, our hearts full of many emotions.

I glanced about me. I became aware that the dawn was upon us.

The sun flung a stray beam across the hidden sea; pierced the mist dully, and lit up the receding boat with a gloomy fire. Indistinctly, I saw something nodding between the oars. I thought of a sponge—a great, grey nodding sponge——The oars continued to ply. They were grey—as was the boat—and my eyes searched a moment vainly for the conjunction of hand and oar. My gaze flashed back to the—head. It nodded forward as the oars went backward for the stroke. Then the oars were dipped, the boat shot out of the patch of light, and the—the thing went nodding into the mist.

# W. F. Harvey

William Fryer Harvey (1885–1937) was educated in England as a doctor, but the circumstances of his life prevented him from practicing medicine very frequently. His own health gave him considerable difficulty and, after receiving his degree, he embarked on a trip around the world in search of a suitable climate. Dr. Harvey, a Quaker, became a naval surgeon in World War I. He was decorated for life-saving as the result of an action that unfortunately also served to shorten his own life. He performed an emergency amputation on an officer trapped in a flooded engine room, and the fumes Harvey inhaled injured his lungs, leaving him a permanent invalid.

His illnesses did at least allow him ample opportunity for writing; he produced a novel, a book for children, several studies of Quaker life, and three volumes of supernatural stories: *Midnight House* (1910), *The Beast with Five Fingers* (1928), and *Moods and Tenses* (1933). The best pieces from these books were gathered into the posthumous volume *Midnight Tales* (1946).

Harvey's most famous tale is certainly "The Beast with Five Fingers," the gripping account of a dead man's severed hand that acquires a life of its own. Although many critics have offered Freudian interpretations for the origin and effect of this powerful piece, it seems likely that the story may have been inspired by the author's harrowing wartime experience, when he was forced to remove a man's arm and nearly lost his own life in the process. In any case, the story has led to numerous imitations. However, it seems to have no immediate antecedent, although J. Sheridan Le Fanu's novel *The House by the Churchyard* (1863) contains an episode in which a hand haunts a house. Le Fanu emphasizes, however, that it is not "a hand separated from a body, but only a hand so manifested and introduced that its owner was always, by some crafty accident, hidden from view." Harvey's story is especially renowned because it was adapted into a Warner Brothers film, starring Peter Lorre and directed by Robert Florey; this is especially remarkable as the last major Hollywood horror movie made during the cycle of classics that had begun in 1931.

The majority of Harvey's stories, however, deal with less tangible terrors. Perhaps because of his medical background, he was particularly concerned with psychological studies in which it is difficult to determine whether the manifestations involve the uncanny or just insanity. Several of his tales, including "Miss Cornelius," involve variations on the theme of what has been called "psychic vampirism," in which a malevolent character is able to weaken or destroy others without engaging in overtly antagonistic behavior.

"August Heat," published in 1910, is a clever and compact tale that is perhaps the best fictional treatment on the subject of premonition; it also suggests the disturbing mental phenomenon known as "déjà vu." It is most impressive in its air of plausibility and loses nothing by ending just short of its inevitable climax. In fact, Harvey's technique provides a model for the treatment of a story in which the narrator is about to meet a sticky end. And he devised a new sort of horrible atmosphere, one in which the traditional cold and clammy climate is replaced by an oppressive and sickening heat.

# AUGUST HEAT

## W. F. Harvey

PHENISTONE ROAD, CLAPHAM,

*August 20th, 190-*. I have had what I believe to be the most remarkable day in my life, and while the events are still fresh in my mind, I wish to put them down on paper as clearly as possible.

Let me say at the outset that my name is James Clarence Withencroft.

I am forty years old, in perfect health, never having known a day's illness.

By profession I am an artist, not a very successful one, but I earn enough money by my black-and-white work to satisfy my necessary wants.

My only near relative, a sister, died five years ago, so that I am independent.

I breakfasted this morning at nine, and after glancing through the morning paper I lighted my pipe and proceeded to let my mind wander in the hope that I might chance upon some subject for my pencil.

The room, though door and windows were open, was oppressively hot, and I had just made up my mind that the coolest and most comfortable place in the neighbourhood would be the deep end of the public swimming bath, when the idea came.

I began to draw. So intent was I on my work that I left my lunch untouched, only stopping work when the clock of St. Jude's struck four.

The final result, for a hurried sketch, was, I felt sure, the best thing I had done.

It showed a criminal in the dock immediately after the judge had pronounced sentence. The man was fat —enormously fat. The flesh hung in rolls about his chin; it creased his huge, stumpy neck. He was clean shaven (perhaps I should say a few days before he must have been clean shaven) and almost bald. He stood in the dock, his short, clumsy fingers clasping the rail, looking straight in front of him. The feeling that his expression conveyed was not so much one of horror as of utter, absolute collapse.

There seemed nothing in the man strong enough to sustain that mountain of flesh.

I rolled up the sketch, and without quite knowing why, placed it in my pocket. Then with the rare sense of happiness which the knowledge of a good thing well done gives, I left the house.

I believe that I set out with the idea of calling upon Trenton, for I remember walking along Lytton Street and turning to the right along Gilchrist Road at the bottom of the hill where the men were at work on the new tram lines.

From there onwards I have only the vaguest recollections of where I went. The one thing of which I was fully conscious was the awful heat, that came up from the dusty asphalt pave-

ment as an almost palpable wave. I longed for the thunder promised by the great banks of copper-coloured cloud that hung low over the western sky.

I must have walked five or six miles, when a small boy roused me from my reverie by asking the time.

It was twenty minutes to seven.

When he left me I began to take stock of my bearings. I found myself standing before a gate that led into a yard bordered by a strip of thirsty earth, where there were flowers, purple stock and scarlet geranium. Above the entrance was a board with the inscription—

CHS. ATKINSON            MONUMENTAL MASON
WORKER IN ENGLISH AND ITALIAN MARBLES

From the yard itself came a cheery whistle, the noise of hammer blows, and the cold sound of steel meeting stone.

A sudden impulse made me enter.

A man was sitting with his back towards me, busy at work on a slab of curiously veined marble. He turned round as he heard my steps and I stopped short.

It was the man I had been drawing, whose portrait lay in my pocket.

He sat there, huge and elephantine, the sweat pouring from his scalp, which he wiped with a red silk handkerchief. But though the face was the same, the expression was absolutely different.

He greeted me smiling, as if we were old friends, and shook my hand.

I apologised for my intrusion.

"Everything is hot and glary outside," I said. "This seems an oasis in the wilderness."

"I don't know about the oasis," he replied, "but it certainly is hot, as hot as hell. Take a seat, sir!"

He pointed to the end of the gravestone on which he was at work, and I sat down.

"That's a beautiful piece of stone you've got hold of," I said.

He shook his head. "In a way it is," he answered; "the surface here is as fine as anything you could wish, but there's a big flaw at the back, though I don't expect you'd ever notice it. I could never make really a good job of a bit of marble like that. It would be all right in the summer like this; it wouldn't mind the blasted heat. But wait till the winter comes. There's nothing quite like frost to find out the weak points in stone."

"Then what's it for?" I asked.

The man burst out laughing.

"You'd hardly believe me if I was to tell you it's for an exhibition, but it's the truth. Artists have exhibitions: so do grocers and butchers; we have them too. All the latest little things in headstones, you know."

He went on to talk of marbles, which sort best withstood wind and rain, and which were easiest to work; then of his garden and a new sort of carnation he had bought. At the end of every other minute he would drop his tools, wipe his shining head, and curse the heat.

I said little, for I felt uneasy. There was something unnatural, uncanny, in meeting this man.

I tried at first to persuade myself that I had seen him before, that his face, unknown to me, had found a place in some out-of-the-way corner of my memory, but I knew that I was practicing little more than a plausible piece of self-deception.

Mr. Atkinson finished his work, spat on the ground, and got up with a sigh of relief.

"There! what do you think of that?" he said, with an air of evident pride.

The inscription which I read for the first time was this—


SACRED TO THE MEMORY
OF
JAMES CLARENCE WITHENCROFT.
BORN JAN. 18TH, 1860.
HE PASSED AWAY VERY SUDDENLY
ON AUGUST 20TH, 190-
*"In the midst of life we are in death."*


For some time I sat in silence. Then a cold shudder ran down my spine. I asked him where he had seen the name.

"Oh, I didn't see it anywhere,'" replied Mr. Atkinson. "I wanted some name, and I put down the first that came into my head. Why do you want to know?"

"It's a strange coincidence, but it happens to be mine."

He gave a long, low whistle.

"And the dates?"

"I can only answer for one of them, and that's correct."

"It's a rum go!" he said.

But he knew less than I did. I told him of my morning's work. I took the sketch from my pocket and showed it to him. As he looked, the expression of his face altered until it became more and more like that of the man I had drawn.

"And it was only the day before yesterday," he said, "that I told Maria there were no such things as ghosts!"

Neither of us had seen a ghost, but I knew what he meant.

"You probably heard my name," I said.

"And you must have seen me somewhere and have forgotten it! Were you at Clacton-on-Sea last July?"

I had never been to Clacton in my life. We were silent for some time. We were both looking at the same thing, the two dates on the gravestone, and one was right.

"Come inside and have some supper," said Mr. Atkinson.

His wife is a cheerful little woman, with the flaky red cheeks of the country-bred. Her husband introduced me as a friend of his who was an artist. The result was unfortunate, for after the sardines and watercress had been removed, she brought me out a Doré Bible, and I had to sit and express my admiration for nearly half an hour.

I went outside, and found Atkinson sitting on the gravestone smoking.

We resumed the conversation at the point we had left off.

"You must excuse my asking," I said, "but do you know of anything you've done for which you could be put on trial?"

He shook his head.

"I'm not a bankrupt, the business is prosperous enough. Three years ago I gave turkeys to some of the guardians at Christmas, but that's all I can think of. And they were small ones, too," he added as an afterthought.

He got up, fetched a can from the porch, and began to water the flowers. "Twice a day regular in the hot weather," he said, "and then the heat sometimes gets the better of the delicate ones. And ferns, good Lord! they could never stand it. Where do you live?"

I told him my address. It would take an hour's quick walk to get back home.

"It's like this," he said. "We'll look at the matter straight. If you go back home to-night, you take your chance of accidents. A cart may run over you, and there's always banana skins and orange peel, to say nothing of falling ladders."

He spoke of the improbable with an intense seriousness that would have been laughable six hours before. But I did not laugh.

"The best thing we can do," he continued, "is for you to stay here till twelve o'clock. We'll go upstairs and smoke; it may be cooler inside."

To my surprise I agreed.

We are sitting in a long, low room beneath the eaves. Atkinson has sent his wife to bed. He himself is busy sharpening some tools at a little oilstone, smoking one of my cigars the while.

The air seems charged with thunder. I am writing this at a shaky table before the open window. The leg is cracked, and Atkinson, who seems a handy man with his tools, is going to mend it as soon as he has finished putting an edge on his chisel.

It is after eleven now. I shall be gone in less than an hour.

But the heat is stifling.

It is enough to send a man mad.

# Lord Dunsany

Edward John Moreton Drax Plunkett (1878–1957), eighteenth Baron Dunsany, has a remarkable style and an imagination so vivid that he was able to create his own mythology. Several commentators have called him the finest fantasy writer of the twentieth century.

Dunsany's life and his work make a strange contrast. He was an Irish nobleman, a soldier, a sportsman, and a prominent figure in the highest society. He said that "all the people who knew me knew me as something else, and I was not regarded as being a writer at all." Yet his interior life belied his apparently worldly character, and he began to write strange stories about uncanny universes. "There was something in those tales, coming so suddenly and so fervently and from no source that I knew of, which seemed like inspiration to me; so that I came to have a reverence for my work, and to think it far more important than myself."

The first of his books was *The Gods of Pegana* (1905), one of several devoted to the description of a cosmos concocted out of whole cloth. *Time and the Gods* (1906) continued in the same vein; about this book he wrote: "I invented heavens and earths, and kings and peoples and customs, just as I needed them; but I did not feel in the least as though I were inventing, but rather as though I wrote the history of lands that I had known in forgotten wanderings."

Dunsany also wrote a number of short plays, the first of them at the urging of the great Irish poet William Butler Yeats. Among these, the author's favorite was *The Gods of the Mountain,* about a band of thieves who impersonate ancient idols and are dreadfully punished for their blasphemy. Dunsany's short drama *The Queen's Enemies* seems to have inspired the first published work by the American playwright Tennessee Williams, a short story called "The Vengeance of Nitocris."

What principally inspired other writers in Dunsany's work, however, was not his plots, or his style, or even the fabulous worlds he invented. Instead, what proved most influential was the very idea of imagining new myths and elaborating them in successive stories, until they became as coherent and compelling as authentic ancient lore. Among the writers who adopted this approach, apparently because of Dunsany's example, are H. P. Lovecraft, Clark Ashton Smith, and Robert E. Howard, three of the most important contributors to the American magazine *Weird Tales*. Dunsany's best stories in this vein include "How Nuth Would Have Practised His Art upon the Gnoles," "The Distressing Tale of Thangobrind the Jeweller, and of the Doom That Befell Him," and "The Hoard of the Gibbelins."

These tales, which he described as written "as though I were an inhabitant of a different planet," gave way to others having a closer connection with the real world. The first in the new vein was "The Highwayman," based on a drawing by Dunsany's illustrator and active collaborator S. H. Sime. The more recent stories are less astounding, but more accessible to the average audience. Some of the most entertaining are those in which Dunsany said he had "put many lands and adventures that I had seen into the mouth of a drink-cadging old man called Jorkens, with a reputation at his club of being by far its greatest liar." These stories filled five books among Dunsany's dozens. He is also noteworthy for the gruesome detective story "Two Bottles of Relish," often included in lists of the finest mysteries ever written.

"The Exiles' Club," from Dunsany's 1916 collection *Tales of Wonder,* combines his two approaches. It is set in a recognizable London, but it draws its power from glimpses of exotic lands and legends. This juxtaposition of the known and the unknown creates Lord Dunsany's most awesome effects.

# THE EXILES' CLUB

# Lord Dunsany

It was an evening party; and something someone had said to me had started me talking about a subject that to me is full of fascination, the subject of old religions, forsaken gods. The truth (for all religions have some of it), the wisdom, the beauty, of the religions of countries to which I travel have not the same appeal for me; for one only notices in them their tyranny and intolerance and the abject servitude that they claim from thought; but when a dynasty has been dethroned in heaven and goes forgotten and outcast even among men, one's eyes no longer dazzled by its power find something very wistful in the faces of fallen gods suppliant to be remembered, something almost tearfully beautiful, like a long warm summer twilight fading gently away after some day memorable in the story of earthly wars. Between what Zeus, for instance, has been once and the half-remembered tale he is to-day there lies a space so great that there is no change of fortune known to man whereby we may measure the height down which he has fallen. And it is the same with many another god at whom once the ages trembled and the twentieth century treats as an old wives' tale. The fortitude that such a fall demands is surely more than human.

Some such things as these I was saying, and being upon a subject that much attracts me I possibly spoke too loudly. Certainly I was not aware that standing close behind me was no less a person than the ex-King of Eritivaria, the thirty islands of the East, or I would have moderated my voice and moved away a little to give him more room. I was not aware of his presence until his satellite, one who had fallen with him into exile but still revolved about him, told me that his master desired to know me: and so to my surprise I was presented, though neither of them even knew my name. And that was how I came to be invited by the ex-King to dine at his club.

At the time I could only account for his wishing to know me by supposing that he found in his own exiled condition some likeness to the fallen fortunes of the gods of whom I talked unwitting of his presence; but now I know that it was not of himself he was thinking when he asked me to dine at that club.

The club would have been the most imposing building in any street in London, but in that obscure mean quarter of London in which they had built it it appeared unduly enormous. Lifting right up above those grotesque houses, and built in that Greek style that we call Georgian, there was something Olympian about it. To my host an unfashionable street could have meant nothing, through all his youth wherever he had gone had become fashionable the moment he went there: words like the East End could have had no meaning to him.

Whoever built that house had enormous wealth and cared nothing for fashion, perhaps despised it. As I stood gazing at the magnificent upper windows draped with great curtains, indistinct in the evening, on which huge shadows flickered, my host attracted my attention from the doorway, and so I went in and met for the second time the ex-King of Eritivaria.

In front of us a stairway of rare marble led upwards. He took me through a side-door and downstairs and we came to a banqueting-hall of great magnificence. A long table ran up the middle of it, laid for quite twenty people, and I noticed the peculiarity that instead of chairs there were thrones, for everyone except me, who was the only guest and for whom there was an ordinary chair. My host explained to me when we all sat down that everyone who belonged to that club was by rights a king.

In fact none was permitted, he told me, to belong to the club until his claim to a kingdom, made out in writing, had been examined and allowed by those whose duty it was. The whim of a populace or the candidate's own misrule were never considered by the investigators, nothing counted with them but heredity and lawful descent from kings, all else was ignored. At that table there were those who had once reigned themselves, others lawfully claimed descent from kings that the world had forgotten, the kingdoms claimed by some had even changed their names. Hatzgurh, the mountain Kingdom, is almost regarded as mythical.

I have seldom seen greater splendour than that long hall provided below the level of the street. No doubt by day it was a little sombre, as all basements are, but at night with its great crystal chandeliers, and the glitter of heirlooms that had gone into exile, it surpassed the splendour of palaces that have only one king. They had come to London suddenly, most of those kings, or their fathers before them or forefathers; some had come away from their kingdoms by night, in a light sleigh, flogging the horses, or had galloped clear with morning over the border; some had trudged roads for days from their capital in disguise, yet many had had time just as they left to snatch up some small thing without price in markets, for the sake of old times as they said, but quite as much, I thought, with an eye to the future. And there these treasures glittered on that long table in the banqueting-hall of the basement of that strange club. Merely to see them was much, but to hear their story that their owners told was to go back in fancy to epic times on the romantic border of fable and fact, where the heroes of history fought with the gods of myth. The famous silver horses of Gilgianza were there, climbing their sheer mountain, which they did by miraculous means before the time of the Goths. It was not a large piece of silver, but its workmanship out-rivalled the skill of the bees.

A yellow Emperor had brought out of the East a piece of that incomparable porcelain that had made his dynasty famous though all their deeds are forgotten; it had the exact shade of the right purple.

And there was a little golden statuette of a dragon stealing a diamond from a lady, the dragon had the diamond in his claws, large and of the first water. There had been a kingdom whose whole constitution and history were founded on the legend, from which alone its kings had claimed their right to the sceptre, that a dragon stole a diamond from a lady. When its last king left that country, because his favourite general used a peculiar formation under the fire of artillery, he brought with him the little ancient image that no longer proved him a king outside that singular club.

There was the pair of amethyst cups of the turbaned King of Foo, the one that he drank from himself, and the one that he gave to his enemies: eye could not tell which was which.

All these things the ex-King of Eritivaria showed me, telling me a marvellous tale of each; of his own he had brought nothing, except the mascot that used once to sit on the top of the water tube of his favourite motor.

I have not outlined a tenth of the splendour of that table, I had meant to come again and examine each piece of plate and make notes of its history; had I known that this was the last time I should wish to enter that club I should have looked at its treasures more attentively, but now as the wine went round and the exiles began to talk I took my eyes from the table and listened to strange tales of their former state.

He that has seen better times has usually a poor tale to tell, some mean and trivial thing has been his undoing, but they that dined in that basement had mostly fallen like oaks on nights of abnormal tempest, had fallen mightily and shaken a nation. Those who had not been kings themselves, but claimed through an exiled ancestor, had stories to tell of even grander disaster, history seeming to have mellowed their dynasty's fate as moss grows over an oak a great while fallen. There were no jealousies there as so often there are among kings, rivalry must have ceased with the loss of their navies and armies, and they showed no bitterness against those that had turned them out, one speaking of the error of his Prime Minister by which he had lost his throne as "poor old Friedrich's heaven-sent gift of tactlessness."

They gossiped pleasantly of many things, the tittle-tattle we all had to know when we were learning history, and many a wonderful story I might have heard, many a sidelight on mysterious wars, had I not made use of one unfortunate word. That word was "upstairs."

The ex-King of Eritivaria having pointed out to me those unparalleled heirlooms to which I have alluded, and many more besides, hospitably asked me if there was anything else that I would care to see; he meant the pieces of plate that they had in the cupboards, the curiously graven swords of other princes, historic jewels, legendary seals; but I who had had a glimpse of their marvellous staircase, whose balustrade I believed to be solid gold, and wondering why in such a stately house they chose to dine in the basement, mentioned the word "upstairs." A hush as at sacrilege came down on the whole assembly, the hush that might greet levity in a cathedral.

"Upstairs!" he gasped. "We cannot go upstairs."

I perceived that what I had said was an ill-chosen thing. I tried to excuse myself but knew not how.

"Of course," I muttered, "members may not take guests upstairs."

"Members!" he said to me. "We are not the members!"

There was such reproof in his voice that I said no more, I looked at him questioningly, perhaps my lips moved, I may have said, "What are you?" A great surprise had come on me at their attitude.

"We are the waiters," he said.

That I could not have known, here at least was honest ignorance that I had no need to be ashamed of, the very opulence of their table denied it.

"Then who are the members?" I asked.

Such a hush fell at that question, such a hush of genuine awe, that all of a sudden a wild thought entered my head, a thought strange and fantastic and terrible. I gripped my host by the wrist and hushed my voice.

"Are they too exiles?" I asked.

Twice as he looked in my face he gravely nodded his head.

I left that club very swiftly indeed, never to see it again, scarcely pausing to say farewell to those menial kings, and as I left the door a great window opened far up at the top of the house and a flash of lightning streamed from it and killed a dog.

# H. P. Lovecraft

Howard Phillips Lovecraft (1890–1937), who spent his life in relative poverty and obscurity, has become in the years since his death the most popular and renowned American writer of horror stories since Poe. He is appreciated not only for his literary ability, but also for the imaginative quality that enabled him to conceive a new and original theme for the terror tale.

Despite his popularity, Lovecraft remains a controversial figure. His work has been attacked by those "mainstream" critics who remain steadfastly hostile to fantasy, and even among devotees there is a dispute regarding his merits. The early phases of his writing produced fine tales like "The Outsider," "The Rats in the Walls," and "The Music of Erich Zann"; some commentators believe that these represent his finest work, and that the later development of his career is best forgotten. Still, much of his fame derives from a scant dozen of his later stories, which taken together comprise what has been called the "Cthulhu mythos." These are based on the idea that alien entities from other galaxies and dimensions once controlled our planet and intend to do so again.

This concept, a cross between fantasy and science fiction, so impressed readers and other writers that several of Lovecraft's colleagues among the contributors to the pulp magazine *Weird Tales* began to work on it, with his encouragement. Such efforts have continued to the present day, and the manufactured mythology of menacing monsters has become a stock device, with the result that an author may now produce a "Cthulhu" story as readily as one about a traditional terror like the vampire or the werewolf. The myth has become so convincing and so widespread that a supposedly serious Satanist recently published a ritual for the worship of the fictitious Cthulhu, something that would surely have dismayed the skeptical Lovecraft.

"The Call of Cthulhu" was written in 1926 and published in *Weird Tales* in February 1928. As its title indicates, it is the cornerstone of Lovecraft's concept, and as such it is the most influential horror story of the twentieth century. Yet it tends to be neglected, even by the most enthusiastic Cthulhu cultists, apparently because the tales that followed it contain more details about the appearance and behavior of the Old Ones. This information delights devotees, but less committed critics have noted with some justice that the results of such elaborations are sometimes ponderous and ludicrous. Also, whereas many of Lovecraft's stories are set in imaginary locales whose very names thrill certain readers, this one is firmly placed in the real world, with settings that make it more convincing, if less mythical. It is in fact unusual for such a comparatively short work to cover so much of the earth's surface, and this spaciousness contributes considerably to its effect, at once creating a credible picture of a worldwide conspiracy and placing the conflict on a cosmic scale. Another technique involves the introduction of several artists' conceptions of Cthulhu, each larger in size, so that the loathsome creature seems to be growing as the tale progresses.

Lovecraft had a deep distaste for all forms of underwater life, and this seems to have intensified the horror dripping from the monster and its minions. His idea appears to owe something to William Hope Hodgson, as well as to others such as Arthur Machen, Lord Dunsany, Robert W. Chambers, and Algernon Blackwood, whose remarks preface this tale. These writers were repaid by his enthusiastic advocacy of their fiction in the pages of his brief but significant study *Supernatural Horror in Literature,* which has been an important influence in bringing their work to the attention of American audiences.

---

# THE CALL OF CTHULHU

---

# H. P. Lovecraft

*Of such great powers or beings there may be conceivably a survival . . . a survival of a hugely remote period when . . . consciousness was manifested, perhaps, in shapes and forms long since withdrawn before the tide of advancing humanity . . . forms of which poetry and legend alone have caught a flying memory and called them gods, monsters, mythical beings of all sorts and kinds . . .*

—ALGERNON BLACKWOOD

## 1. THE HORROR IN CLAY

The most merciful thing in the world, I think, is the inability of the human mind to correlate all its contents. We live on a placid island of ignorance in the midst of black seas of infinity, and it was not meant that we should voyage far. The sciences, each straining in its own direction, have hitherto harmed us little; but some day the piecing together of dissociated knowledge will open up such terrifying vistas of reality, and of our frightful position therein, that we shall either go mad from the revelation or flee from the deadly light into the peace and safety of a new dark age.

Theosophists have guessed at the awesome grandeur of the cosmic cycle wherein our world and human race form transient incidents. They have hinted at strange survivals in terms which would freeze the blood if not masked by a bland optimism. But it is not from them that there came the single glimpse of forbidden eons which chills me when I think of it and maddens me when I dream of it. That glimpse, like all dread glimpses of truth, flashed out from an accidental piecing together of separated things—in this case an old newspaper item and the notes of a dead professor. I hope that no one else will accomplish this piecing out; certainly, if I live, I shall never knowingly supply a link in so hideous a chain. I think that the professor, too, intended to keep silent regarding the part he knew, and that he would have destroyed his notes had not sudden death seized him.

My knowledge of the thing began in the winter of 1926-27 with the death of my granduncle, George Gammell Angell, Professor Emeritus of Semitic Languages in Brown University, Providence, Rhode Island. Professor Angell was widely known as an authority on ancient inscriptions, and had frequently been resorted to by the heads of prominent museums; so that his passing at the age of ninety-two may be recalled by many. Locally, interest was intensified by the obscurity of the cause of death. The professor had been stricken whilst returning from the Newport boat; falling suddenly, as witnesses said, after having been jostled by a nautical-looking negro who had come from one of the queer dark courts on the precipitous hillside which formed a short cut from the waterfront to the deceased's home in Williams Street. Physicians were unable to find any visible disorder, but concluded after perplexed debate that some obscure lesion of the heart, induced by the brisk ascent of so steep a hill by so elderly a man, was responsible for the end. At the time I saw no reason to dissent from this dictum, but latterly I am inclined to wonder —and more than wonder.

As my granduncle's heir and executor, for he died a childless widower, I was expected to go over his papers with some thoroughness; and for that purpose moved his entire set of files and boxes to my quarters in Boston. Much of the material which I correlated will be later published by the American Archaeological Society, but there was one box which I found exceedingly puzzling, and which I felt much averse from showing to other eyes. It had been locked, and I did not find the key till it occurred to me to examine the personal ring which the professor carried always in his pocket. Then, indeed, I succeeded in opening it, but when I did so seemed only to be confronted by a greater and more closely locked barrier. For what could be the meaning of the queer clay bas-relief and the disjointed jottings, ramblings, and cuttings which I found? Had my uncle, in his latter years, become credulous of the most superficial impostures? I resolved to search out the eccentric sculptor responsible for this apparent disturbance of an old man's peace of mind.

The bas-relief was a rough rectangle less than an inch thick and about five by six inches in area; obviously of modern origin. Its designs, however, were far from modern in atmosphere and suggestion; for, although the vagaries of cubism and futurism are many and wild, they do not often reproduce that cryptic regularity which lurks in prehistoric writing. And writing of some kind the bulk of these designs seemed certainly to be; though my memory, despite much familiarity with the papers and collections of my uncle, failed in any way to identify this particular species, or even hint at its remotest affiliations.

Above these apparent hieroglyphics was a figure of evidently pictorial intent, though its impressionistic execution forbade a very clear idea of its nature. It seemed to be a sort of monster, or symbol representing a monster, of a form which only a diseased fancy could conceive. If I say that my somewhat extravagant imagination yielded simultaneous pictures of an octopus, a dragon, and a human caricature, I shall not be unfaithful to the spirit of the thing. A pulpy, tentacled head surmounted a grotesque and scaly body with rudimentary wings; but it was the *general outline* of the whole which made it most shockingly frightful. Behind the figure was a vague suggestion of a Cyclopean architectural background.

The writing accompanying this oddity was, aside from a stack of press cuttings, in Professor Angell's most recent hand; and made no pretense to literary style. What seemed to be the main document was headed "CTHULHU CULT" in characters painstakingly printed to avoid the erroneous reading of a word so unheard-of. This manuscript was divided into two sections, the first of which was headed "1925—Dream and Dream Work of H. A. Wilcox, 7 Thomas St., Providence, R. I.," and the second, "Narrative of Inspector John R. Legrasse, 121 Bienville St., New Orleans, La., at 1908 A. A. S. Mtg.—Notes on Same, & Prof. Webb's Acct." The other manuscript papers were all brief notes, some of them accounts of the queer dreams of different persons, some of them citations from theosophical books and magazines (notably W. Scott-Elliott's *Atlantis and the Lost Lemuria*), and the rest comments on long-surviving secret societies and hidden cults, with references to passages in such mythological and anthropological source-books as Frazer's *Golden Bough* and Miss Murray's *Witch-Cult in Western Europe*. The cuttings largely alluded to outré mental illness and outbreaks of group folly or mania in the spring of 1925.

The first half of the principal manuscript told a very peculiar tale. It appears that on March 1st, 1925, a thin, dark young man of neurotic and excited aspect had called upon Professor Angell bearing the singular clay bas-relief, which was then exceedingly damp and fresh. His card bore the name of Henry Anthony Wilcox, and my uncle had recognized him as the youngest son of an excellent family slightly known to him, who had latterly been studying sculpture at the Rhode Island School of Design and living alone at the Fleur-de-Lys Building near that institution. Wilcox was a precocious youth of known genius but great eccentricity, and had from childhood excited attention through the strange stories and odd dreams he was in the habit of relating. He called himself "psychically hypersensitive," but the staid folk of the ancient commercial city dismissed him as merely "queer." Never mingling much with his kind, he had dropped gradually from social visibility, and was now known only to a small group of esthetes from other towns. Even the Providence Art Club, anxious to preserve its conservatism, had found him quite hopeless.

On the occasion of the visit, ran the professor's manuscript, the sculptor abruptly asked for the benefit of his host's archeological knowledge in identifying the hieroglyphics on the bas-relief. He spoke in a dreamy, stilted manner which suggested pose and alienated sympathy; and my uncle showed some sharpness in replying, for the conspicuous freshness of the tablet implied kinship with anything but archeology. Young Wilcox's rejoinder, which impressed my uncle enough to make him recall and record it verbatim, was of a fantastically poetic cast which must have typified his whole conversation, and which I have since found highly characteristic of him. He said, "It is new, indeed, for I made it last night in a dream of strange cities; and dreams are older than brooding Tyre, or the contemplative Sphinx, or garden-girdled Babylon."

It was then that he began that rambling tale which suddenly played upon a sleeping memory and won the fevered interest of my uncle. There had been a slight earthquake tremor the night before, the most considerable felt in New England for some years; and Wilcox's imagination had been keenly affected. Upon retiring, he had had an unprecedented dream of great Cyclopean cities of Titan blocks and sky-flung monoliths, all dripping with green ooze and sinister with latent horror. Hieroglyphics had covered the walls and pillars, and from some undetermined point below had come a voice that was not a voice; a chaotic sensation which only fancy could transmute into sound, but which he attempted to render by the almost unpronounceable jumble of letters, *"Cthulhu fhtagn."*

This verbal jumble was the key to the recollection which excited and disturbed Professor Angell. He questioned the sculptor with scientific minuteness; and studied with almost frantic intensity the bas-relief on which the youth had found himself working, chilled and clad only in his nightclothes, when waking had stolen bewilderingly over him. My uncle blamed his old age, Wilcox afterward said, for his slowness in recognizing both hieroglyphics and pictorial design. Many of his questions seemed highly out of place to his visitor, especially those which tried to connect the latter with strange cults or societies; and Wilcox could not understand the repeated promises of silence which he was offered in exchange for an admission of membership in some widespread mystical or paganly religious body. When Professor Angell became convinced that the sculptor was indeed ignorant of any cult or system of cryptic lore, he besieged his visitor with demands for future reports of dreams. This bore regular fruit, for after the first interview the manuscript records daily calls of the young man, during which he related startling fragments of nocturnal imagery whose burden was always some terrible Cyclopean vista of dark and dripping stone, with a subterrene voice or intelligence shouting monotonously in enigmatical sense-impacts uninscribable save as gibberish. The two sounds most frequently repeated are those rendered by the letters *"Cthulhu"* and *"R'lyeh."*

On March 23, the manuscript continued, Wilcox failed to appear; and inquiries at his quarters revealed that he had been stricken with an obscure sort of fever and taken to the home of his family in Waterman Street. He had cried out in the night, arousing several other artists in the building, and had manifested since then only alternations of unconsciousness and delirium. My uncle at once telephoned the family, and from that time forward kept close watch of the case; calling often at the Thayer Street office of Dr. Tobey, whom he learned to be in charge. The youth's febrile mind, apparently, was dwelling on strange things; and the doctor shuddered now and then as he spoke of them. They included not only a repetition of what he had formerly dreamed, but touched wildly on a gigantic thing "miles high" which walked or lumbered about. He at no time fully described this object but occasional frantic words, as repeated by Dr. Tobey, convinced the professor that it must be identical with the nameless monstrosity he had sought to depict in his dream-sculpture. Reference to this object, the doctor added, was invariably a prelude to the young man's subsidence into lethargy. His temperature, oddly enough, was not greatly above normal; but the whole condition was otherwise such as to suggest true fever rather than mental disorder.

On April 2 at about 3 P.M. every trace of Wilcox's malady suddenly ceased. He sat upright in bed, astonished to find himself at home and completely ignorant of what had happened in dream or reality since the night of March 22. Pronounced well by his physician, he returned to his quarters in three days; but to Professor Angell he was of no further assistance. All traces of strange dreaming had vanished with his recovery, and my uncle kept no record of his night-thoughts after a week of pointless and irrelevant accounts of thoroughly usual visions.

Here the first part of the manuscript ended, but references to certain of the scattered notes gave me much material for thought—so much, in fact, that only the ingrained skepticism then forming my philosophy can account for my continued distrust of the artist. The notes in question were those descriptive of the dreams of various persons covering the same period as that in which young Wilcox had had his strange visitations. My uncle, it seems, had quickly instituted a prodigiously far-flung body of inquiries amongst nearly all the friends whom he could question without impertinence, asking for nightly reports of their dreams, and the dates of any notable visions for some time past. The reception of his request seems to have been varied; but he must, at the very least, have received more responses than any ordinary man could have handled without a secretary. This original correspondence was not preserved, but his notes formed a thorough and really significant digest. Average people in society and business—New England's traditional "salt of the earth"—gave an almost completely negative result, though scattered cases of uneasy but formless nocturnal impressions appear here and there, always between March 23 and April 2—the period of young Wilcox's delirium. Scientific men were little more affected, though four cases of vague description suggest fugitive glimpses of strange landscapes, and in one case there is mentioned a dread of something abnormal.

It was from the artists and poets that the pertinent answers came, and I know that panic would have broken loose had they been able to compare notes. As it was, lacking their original letters, I half suspected the compiler of having asked leading questions, or of having edited the correspondence in corroboration of what he had latently resolved to see. That is why I continued to feel that Wilcox, somehow cognizant of the old data which my uncle had possessed, had been imposing on the veteran scientist. These responses from esthetes told a disturbing tale. From February 28 to April 2 a large proportion of them had dreamed very bizarre things, the intensity of the dreams being immeasurably the stronger during the period of the sculptor's delirium. Over a fourth of those who reported anything, reported scenes and half-sounds not unlike those which Wilcox had described; and some of the dreamers confessed acute fear of the gigantic nameless thing visible toward the last. One case, which the note describes with emphasis, was very sad. The subject, a widely known architect with leanings toward theosophy and occultism, went violently insane on the date of young Wilcox's seizure, and expired several months later after incessant screamings to be saved from some escaped denizen of hell. Had my uncle referred to these cases by name instead of merely by number, I should have attempted some corroboration and personal investigation; but as it was, I succeeded in tracing down only a few. All of these, however, bore out the notes in full. I have often wondered if all the objects of the professor's questioning felt as puzzled as did this fraction. It is well that no explanation shall ever reach them.

The press cuttings, as I have intimated, touched on cases of panic, mania, and eccentricity during the given period. Professor Angell must have employed a cutting bureau, for the number of extracts was tremendous, and the sources scattered throughout the globe. Here was a nocturnal suicide in London, where a lone sleeper had leaped from a window after a shocking cry. Here likewise a rambling letter to the editor of a paper in South America, where a fanatic deduces a dire future from visions he has seen. A dispatch from California describes a theosophist colony as donning white robes en masse for some "glorious fulfilment" which never arrives, whilst items from India speak guardedly of serious native unrest toward the end of March. Voodoo orgies multiply in Haiti, and African outposts report ominous mutterings. American officers in the Philippines find certain tribes bothersome about this time, and New York policemen are mobbed by hysterical Levantines on the night of March 22–23. The west of Ireland, too, is full of wild rumour and legendry, and a fantastic painter named Ardois-Bonnot hangs a blasphemous *Dream Landscape* in the Paris spring salon of 1926. And so numerous are the recorded troubles in insane asylums that only a miracle can have stopped the medical fraternity from noting strange parallelisms and drawing mystified conclusions. A weird bunch of cuttings, all told; and I can at this date scarcely envisage the callous rationalism with which I set them aside. But I was then convinced that young Wilcox had known of the older matters mentioned by the professor.

## 2. THE TALE OF INSPECTOR LEGRASSE

The older matters which had made the sculptor's dream and bas-relief so significant to my uncle formed the subject of the second half of his long manuscript. Once before, it appears, Professor Angell had seen the hellish outlines of the nameless monstrosity, puzzled over the unknown hieroglyphics, and heard the ominous syllables which can be rendered only as *"Cthulhu"*; and all this in so stirring and horrible a connection that it is small wonder he pursued young Wilcox with queries and demands for data.

This earlier experience had come in 1908, seventeen years before, when the American Archaeological Society held its annual meeting in St. Louis. Professor Angell, as befitted one of his authority and attainments, had had a prominent part in all the deliberations; and was one of the first to be approached by the several outsiders who took advantage of the convocation to offer questions for correct answering and problems for expert solution.

The chief of these outsiders, and in a short time the focus of interest for the entire meeting, was a commonplace-looking middle-aged man who had travelled all the way from New Orleans for certain special information unobtainable from any local source. His name was John Raymond Legrasse, and he was by profession an inspector of police. With him he bore the subject of his visit, a grotesque, repulsive, and apparently very ancient stone statuette whose origin he was at a loss to determine.

It must not be fancied that Inspector Legrasse had the least interest in archeology. On the contrary, his wish for enlightenment was prompted by purely professional considerations.

The statuette, idol, fetish, or whatever it was, had been captured some months before in the wooded swamps south of New Orleans during a raid on a supposed voodoo meeting; and so singular and hideous were the rites connected with it, that the police could not but realize that they had stumbled on a dark cult totally unknown to them, and infinitely more diabolic than even the blackest of the African voodoo circles. Of its origin, apart from the erratic and unbelievable tales extorted from the captured members, absolutely nothing was to be discovered; hence the anxiety of the police for any antiquarian lore which might help them to place the frightful symbol, and through it track down the cult to its fountain-head.

Inspector Legrasse was scarcely prepared for the sensation which his offering created. One sight of the thing had been enough to throw the assembled men of science into a state of tense excitement, and they lost no time in crowding around him to gaze at the diminutive figure whose utter strangeness and air of genuinely abysmal antiquity hinted so potently at unopened and archaic vistas. No recognized school of sculpture had animated this terrible object, yet centuries and even thousands of years seemed recorded in its dim and greenish surface of unplaceable stone.

The figure, which was finally passed slowly from man to man for close and careful study, was between seven and eight inches in height, and of exquisitely artistic workmanship. It represented a monster of vaguely anthropoid outline, but with an octopuslike head whose face was a mass of feelers, a scaly, rubbery-looking body, prodigious claws on hind and fore feet, and long, narrow wings behind. This thing, which seemed instinct with a fearsome and unnatural malignancy, was of a somewhat bloated corpulence, and squatted evilly on a rectangular block or pedestal covered with undecipherable characters. The tips of the wings touched the back edge of the block, the seat occupied the center, whilst the long, curved claws of the doubled-up, crouching hind legs gripped the front edge and extended a quarter of the way down toward the bottom of the pedestal. The cephalopod head was bent forward, so that the ends of the facial feelers brushed the backs of huge forepaws which clasped the croucher's elevated knees. The aspect of the whole was abnormally lifelike, and the more subtly fearful because its source was so totally unknown. Its vast, awesome, and incalculable age was unmistakable; yet not one link did it show with any known type of art belonging to civilization's youth—or indeed to any other time.

Totally separate and apart, its very material was a mystery; for the soapy, greenish-black stone with its golden or iridescent flecks and striations resembled nothing familiar to geology or mineralogy. The characters along the base were equally baffling; and no member present, despite a representation of half the world's expert learning in this field, could form the least notion of even their remotest linguistic kinship. They, like the subject and material, belonged to something horribly remote and distinct from mankind as we know it; something frightfully suggestive of old and  unhallowed cycles of life in which our world and our conceptions have no part.

And yet, as the members severally shook their heads and confessed defeat at the inspector's problem, there was one man in that gathering who suspected a touch of bizarre familiarity in the monstrous shape and writing, and who presently told with some diffidence of the odd trifle he knew. This person was the late William Channing Webb, professor of anthropology in Princeton University, and an explorer of no slight note.

Professor Webb had been engaged, forty-eight years before, in a tour of Greenland and Iceland in search of some Runic inscriptions which he failed to unearth; and whilst high up on the West Greenland coast had encountered a singular tribe or cult of degenerate Eskimos whose religion, a curious form of devil-worship, chilled him with its deliberate bloodthirstiness and repulsiveness. It was a faith of which other Eskimos knew little, and which they mentioned only with shudders, saying that it had come down from horribly ancient eons before ever the world was made. Besides nameless rites and human sacrifices there were certain queer hereditary rituals addressed to a supreme elder devil or *tornasuk;* and of this Professor Webb had taken a careful phonetic copy from an aged *angekok* or wizard-priest, expressing the sounds in Roman letters as best he knew how. But just now of prime significance was the fetish which this cult had cherished, and around which they danced when the aurora leaped high over the ice cliffs. It was, the professor stated, a very crude bas-relief of stone, comprising a hideous picture and some cryptic writing. And as far as he could tell, it was a rough parallel in all essential features of the bestial thing now lying before the meeting.

These data, received with suspense and astonishment by the assembled members, proved doubly exciting to Inspector Legrasse; and he began at once to ply his informant with questions. Having noted and copied an oral ritual among the swamp cult-worshipers his men had arrested, he besought the professor to remember as best he might the syllables taken down amongst the diabolist Eskimos. There then followed an exhaustive comparison of details, and a moment of really awed silence when both detective and scientist agreed on the virtual identity of the phrase common to two hellish rituals so many worlds of distance apart. What, in substance, both the Eskimo wizards and the Louisiana swamp-priests had chanted to their kindred idols was something very like this—the word-divisions being guessed at from traditional breaks in the phrase as chanted aloud:

*"Ph'nglui mglw'nafh Cthulhu R'lyeh wgah'nagl fhtagn."*

Legrasse had one point in advance of Professor Webb, for several among his mongrel prisoners had repeated to him what older celebrants had told them the words meant. This text, as given, ran something like this:

"In his house at R'lyeh dead Cthulhu waits dreaming."

And now, in response to a general urgent demand, Inspector Legrasse related as fully as possible his experience with the swamp worshipers; telling a story to which I could see my uncle attached profound significance. It savored of the wildest dreams of mythmaker and theosophist, and disclosed an astonishing degree of cosmic imagination among such half-castes and pariahs as might be least expected to possess it.

On November 1, 1907, there had come to New Orleans police a frantic summons from the swamp and lagoon country to the south. The squatters there, mostly primitive but good-natured descendants of Lafitte's men, were in the grip of stark terror from an unknown thing which had stolen upon them in the night. It was voodoo, apparently, but voodoo of a more terrible sort than they had ever known; and some of their women and children had disappeared since the malevolent tom-tom had begun its incessant beating far within the black haunted woods where no dweller ventured. There were insane shouts and harrowing screams, soul-chilling chants and dancing devil-flames; and, the frightened messenger added, the people could stand it no more.

So a body of twenty police, filling two carriages and an automobile, had set out in the late afternoon with the shivering squatter as a guide. At the end of the passable road they alighted, and for miles splashed on in silence through the terrible cypress woods where day never came. Ugly roots and malignant hanging nooses of Spanish moss beset them, and now and then a pile of dank stones or fragments of a rotting wall intensified by its hint of morbid habitation a depression which every malformed tree and every fungous islet combined to create. At length the squatter settlement, a miserable huddle of huts, hove in sight; and hysterical dwellers ran out to cluster around the group of bobbing lanterns. The muffled beat of tom-toms was now faintly audible far, far ahead; and a curdling shriek came at infrequent intervals when the wind shifted. A reddish glare, too, seemed to filter through the pale undergrowth beyond endless avenues of forest night. Reluctant even to be left alone again, each one of the cowed squatters refused point-blank to advance another inch toward the scene of unholy worship, so Inspector Legrasse and his nineteen colleagues plunged on unguided into black arcades of horror that none of them had ever trod before.

The region now entered by the police was one of traditionally evil repute, substantially unknown and untraversed by white men. There were legends of a hidden lake unglimpsed by mortal sight, in which dwelt a huge, formless white polypous thing with luminous eyes; and squatters whispered that bat-winged devils flew up out of caverns in inner earth to worship it at midnight. They said it had been there before D'Iberville, before La Salle, before the Indians, and before even the wholesome beasts and birds of the woods. It was nightmare itself, and to see it was to die. But it made men dream, and so they knew enough to keep away. The present voodoo orgy was, indeed, on the merest fringe of this abhorred area, but that location was bad enough; hence perhaps the very place of the worship had terrified the squatters more than the shocking sounds and incidents.

Only poetry or madness could do justice to the noises heard by Legrasse's men as they plowed on through the black morass toward the red glare and the muffled tom-toms. There are vocal qualities peculiar to men, and vocal qualities peculiar to beasts; and it is terrible to hear the one when the source should yield the other. Animal fury and orgiastic license here whipped themselves to demoniac heights by howls and squawking ecstasies that tore and reverberated through those nighted woods like pestilential tempests from the gulfs of hell. Now and then the less organized ululations would cease, and from what seemed a well-drilled chorus of hoarse voices would rise in singsong chant that hideous phrase or ritual:

*"Ph'nglui mglw'nafh Cthulhu R'lyeh wgah'nagl fhtagn."*

Then the men, having reached a spot where the trees were thinner, came suddenly in sight of the spectacle itself. Four of them reeled, one fainted, and two were shaken into a frantic cry which the mad cacophony of the orgy fortunately deadened. Legrasse dashed swamp water on the face of the fainting man, and all stood trembling and nearly hypnotized with horror.

In a natural glade of the swamp stood a grassy island of perhaps an acre's extent, clear of trees and tolerably dry. On this now leaped and twisted a more indescribable horde of human abnormality than any but a Sime or an Angarola could paint. Void of clothing, this hybrid spawn were braying, bellowing and writhing about a monstrous ring-shaped bonfire; in the center of which, revealed by occasional rifts in the curtain of flame, stood a great granite monolith some eight feet in height; on top of which, incongruous in its diminutiveness, rested the noxious carven statuette. From a wide circle of ten scaffolds set up at regular intervals with the flame-girt monolith as a center hung, head downward, the oddly marred bodies of the helpless squatters who had disappeared. It was inside this circle that the ring of worshipers jumped and roared, the general direction of the mass motion being from left to right in endless bacchanale between the ring of bodies and the ring of fire.

It may have been only imagination and it may have been only echoes which induced one of the men, an excitable Spaniard, to fancy he heard antiphonal responses to the ritual from some far and unillumined spot deeper within the wood of ancient legendry and horror. This man, Joseph D. Galvez, I later met and questioned; and he proved distractingly imaginative. He indeed went so far as to hint of the faint beating of great wings, and of a glimpse of shining eyes and mountainous white bulk beyond the remotest trees —but I suppose he had been hearing too much native superstition.

Actually, the horrified pause of the men was of comparatively brief duration. Duty came first; and although there must have been nearly a hundred mongrel celebrants in the throng, the police relied on their firearms and plunged determinedly into the nauseous rout. For five minutes the resultant din and chaos were beyond description. Wild blows were struck, shots were fired, and escapes were made; but in the end Legrasse was able to count some forty-seven sullen prisoners, whom he forced to dress in haste and fall into line between two rows of policemen. Five of the worshipers lay dead, and two severely wounded ones were carried away on improvised stretchers by their fellow-prisoners. The image on the monolith, of course, was carefully removed and carried back by Legrasse.

Examined at headquarters after a trip of intense strain and weariness, the prisoners all proved to be men of a very low, mixed-blooded, and mentally aberrant type. Most were seamen, and a sprinkling of negroes and mulattoes, largely West Indians or Brava Portuguese from the Cape Verde Islands, gave a coloring of voodooism to the heterogeneous cult. But before many questions were asked, it became manifest that something far deeper and older than negro fetishism was involved. Degraded and ignorant as they were, the creatures held with surprising consistency to the central idea of their loathsome faith.

They worshiped, so they said, the Great Old Ones who lived ages before there were any men, and who came to the young world out of the sky. These Old Ones were gone now, inside the earth and under the sea; but their dead bodies had told their secrets in dreams to the first man, who formed a cult which had never died. This was that cult, and the prisoners said it had always existed and always would exist, hidden in distant wastes and dark places all over the world until the time when the great priest Cthulhu, from his dark house in the mighty city of R'lyeh under the waters, should rise and bring the earth again beneath his sway. Some day he would call, when the stars were ready, and the secret cult would always be waiting to liberate him.

Meanwhile no more must be told. There was a secret which even torture could not extract. Mankind was not absolutely alone among the conscious things of earth, for shapes came out of the dark to visit the faithful few. But these were not the Great Old Ones. No man had ever seen the Old Ones. The carven idol was great Cthulhu, but none might say whether or not the others were precisely like him. No one could read the old writing now, but things were told by word of mouth. The chanted ritual was not the secret—that was never spoken aloud, only whispered. The chant meant only this: "In his house at R'lyeh dead Cthulhu waits dreaming."

Only two of the prisoners were found sane enough to be hanged, and the rest were committed to various institutions. All denied a part in the ritual murders, and averred that the killing had been done by Black-winged Ones which had come to them from their immemorial meeting-place in the haunted wood. But of those mysterious allies no coherent account could ever be gained. What the police did extract came mainly from an immensely aged mestizo named Castro, who claimed to have sailed to strange ports and talked with undying leaders of the cult in the mountains of China.

Old Castro remembered bits of hideous legend that paled the speculations of theosophists and made man and the world seem recent and transient indeed. There had been eons when other Things ruled on the earth, and They had had great cities. Remains of Them, he said the deathless Chinamen had told him, were still to be found as Cyclopean stones on islands in the Pacific. They all died vast epochs of time before man came, but there were arts which could revive Them when the stars had come round again to the right positions in the cycle of eternity. They had, indeed, come themselves from the stars, and brought Their images with Them.

These Great Old Ones, Castro continued, were not composed altogether of flesh and blood. They had shape—for did not this star-fashioned image prove it?—but that shape was not made of matter. When the stars were right, They could plunge from world to world through the sky; but when the stars were wrong, They could not live. But although They no longer lived, They would never really die. They all lay in stone houses in Their great city of R'lyeh, preserved by the spells of mighty Cthulhu for a glorious resurrection when the stars and the earth might once more be ready for Them. But at that time some force from outside must serve to liberate Their bodies. The spells that preserved Them intact likewise prevented Them from making an initial move, and They could only lie awake in the dark and think whilst uncounted millions of years rolled by. They knew all that was occurring in the universe, for Their mode of speech was transmitted thought. Even now They talked in Their tombs. When, after infinities of chaos, the first men came, the Great Old Ones spoke to the sensitive among them by molding their dreams; for only thus could Their language reach the fleshy minds of mammals.

Then, whispered Castro, those first men formed the cult around small idols which the Great Ones showed them; idols brought in dim eras from dark stars. That cult would never die till the stars came right again, and the secret priests would take great Cthulhu from His tomb to revive His subjects and resume His rule of earth. The time would be easy to know, for then mankind would have become as the Great Old Ones; free and wild and beyond good and evil, with laws and morals thrown aside and all men shouting and killing and reveling in joy. Then the liberated Old Ones would teach them new ways to shout and kill and revel and enjoy themselves, and all the earth would flame with a holocaust of ecstasy and freedom. Meanwhile the cult, by appropriate rites, must keep alive the memory of those ancient ways and shadow forth the prophecy of their return.

In the elder time chosen men had talked with the entombed Old Ones in dreams, but then something had happened. The great stone city R'lyeh, with its monoliths and sepulchers, had sunk beneath the waves; and the deep waters, full of the one primal mystery through which not even thought can pass, had cut off the spectral intercourse. But memory never died, and high priests said that the city would rise again when the stars were right. Then came out of the earth the black spirits of earth, moldy and shadowy, and full of dim rumors picked up in caverns beneath forgotten sea-bottoms. But of them old Castro dared not speak much. He cut himself off hurriedly, and no amount of persuasion or subtlety could elicit more in this direction. The *size* of the Old Ones, too, he curiously declined to mention. Of the cult, he said that he thought the center lay amid the pathless deserts of Arabia, where Irem, the City of Pillars, dreams hidden and untouched. It was not allied to the European witch-cult, and was virtually unknown beyond its members. No book had ever really hinted of it, though the deathless Chinamen said that there were double meanings in the *Necronomicon* of the mad Arab Abdul Alhazred which the initiated might read as they chose, especially the much-discussed couplet:

> *That is not dead which can eternal lie,*
> *And with strange eons even death may die.*

Legrasse, deeply impressed and not a little bewildered, had inquired in vain concerning the historic affiliations of the cult. Castro, apparently, had told the truth when he said that it was wholly secret. The authorities at Tulane University could shed no light upon either cult or image, and now the detective had come to the highest authorities in the country and met with no more than the Greenland tale of Professor Webb.

The feverish interest aroused at the meeting by Legrasse's tale, corroborated as it was by the statuette, is echoed in the subsequent correspondence of those who attended; although scant mention occurs in the formal publication of the society. Caution is the first care of those accustomed to face occasional charlatanry and imposture. Legrasse for some time lent the image to Professor Webb, but at the latter's death it was returned to him and remains in his possession, where I viewed it not long ago. It is truly a terrible thing, and unmistakably akin to the dream-sculpture of young Wilcox.

That my uncle was excited by the tale of the sculptor I did not wonder, for what thoughts must arise upon hearing, after a knowledge of what Legrasse had learned of the cult, of a sensitive young man who had *dreamed* not only the figure and exact hieroglyphics of the swamp-found image and the Greenland devil tablet, but had come *in his dreams* upon at least three of the precise words of the formula uttered alike by Eskimo diabolists and mongrel Louisianans? Professor Angell's instant start on an investigation of the utmost thoroughness was eminently natural; though privately I suspected young Wilcox of having heard of the cult in some indirect way, and of having invented a series of dreams to heighten and continue the mystery at my uncle's expense. The dream-narratives and cuttings collected by the professor were, of course, strong corroboration; but the rationalism of my mind and the extravagance of the whole subject led me to adopt what I thought the most sensible conclusions. So, after thoroughly studying the manuscript again and correlating the theosophical and anthropological notes with the cult narrative of Legrasse, I made a trip to Providence to see the sculptor and give him the rebuke I thought proper for so boldly imposing upon a learned and aged man.

Wilcox still lived alone in the Fleur-de-Lys Building in Thomas Street, a hideous Victorian imitation of Seventeenth Century Breton architecture which flaunts its stuccoed front amidst the lovely Colonial houses on the ancient hill, and under the very shadow of the finest Georgian steeple in America. I found him at work in his rooms, and at once conceded from the specimens scattered about that his genius is indeed profound and authentic. He will, I believe, be heard from sometime as one of the great decadents; for he has crystallized in clay and will one day mirror in marble those nightmares and fantasies which Arthur Machen evokes in prose, and Clark Ashton Smith makes visible in verse and in painting.

Dark, frail, and somewhat unkempt in aspect, he turned languidly at my knock and asked me my business without rising. When I told him who I was, he displayed some interest; for my uncle had excited his curiosity in probing his strange dreams, yet had never explained the reason for the study. I did not enlarge his knowledge in this regard, but sought with some subtlety to draw him out.

In a short time I became convinced of his absolute sincerity for he spoke of the dreams in a manner none could mistake. They and their subconscious residuum had influenced his art profoundly, and he showed me a morbid statue whose contours almost made me shake with the potency of its black suggestion. He could not recall having seen the original of this thing except in his own dream bas-relief, but the outlines had formed themselves insensibly under his hands. It was, no doubt, the giant shape he had raved of in delirium. That he really knew nothing of the hidden cult, save from what my uncle's relentless catechism had let fall, he soon made clear; and again I strove to think of some way in which he could possibly have received the weird impressions.

He talked of his dreams in a strangely poetic fashion; making me see with terrible vividness the damp Cyclopean city of slimy green stone—whose *geometry,* he oddly said, was *all wrong*—and hear with frightened expectancy the ceaseless, half-mental calling from underground: *"Cthulhu fhtagn," "Cthulhu fhtagn."*

These words had formed part of that dread ritual which told of dead Cthulhu's dream-vigil in his stone vault at R'lyeh, and I felt deeply moved despite my rational beliefs. Wilcox, I was sure, had heard of the cult in some casual way, and had soon forgotten it amidst the mass of his equally weird reading and imagining. Later, by virtue of its sheer impressiveness, it had found subconscious expression in dreams, in the bas-relief, and in the terrible statue I now beheld; so that his imposture upon my uncle had been a very innocent one. The youth was of a type, at once slightly affected and slightly ill-mannered, which I could never like; but I was willing enough now to admit both his genius and his honesty. I took leave of him amicably, and wish him all the success his talent promises.

The matter of the cult still remained to fascinate me, and at times I had visions of personal fame from researches into its origin and connections. I visited New Orleans, talked with Legrasse and others of that old-time raiding-party, saw the frightful image, and even questioned such of the mongrel prisoners as still survived. Old Castro, unfortunately, had been dead for some years. What I now heard so graphically at first hand, though it was really no more than a detailed confirmation of what my uncle had written, excited me afresh; for I felt sure that I was on the track of a very real, very secret, and very ancient religion whose discovery would make me an anthropologist of note. My attitude was still one of absolute materialism *as I wish it still were,* and I discounted with a most inexplicable perversity the coincidence of the dream notes and odd cuttings collected by Professor Angell.

One thing which I began to suspect, and which I now fear I *know,* is that my uncle's death was far from natural. He fell on a narrow hill street leading up from an ancient waterfront swarming with foreign mongrels, after a careless push from a negro sailor. I did not forget the mixed blood and marine pursuits of the cult-members in Louisiana, and would not be surprised to learn of secret methods and poison needles as ruthless and as anciently known as the cryptic rites and beliefs. Legrasse and his men, it is true, have been let alone; but in Norway a certain seaman who saw things is dead. Might not the deeper inquiries of my uncle after encountering the sculptor's data have come to sinister ears? I think Professor Angell died because he knew too much, or because he was likely to learn too much. Whether I shall go as he did remains to be seen, for I have learned much now.

## 3. THE MADNESS FROM THE SEA

If heaven ever wishes to grant me a boon, it will be a total effacing of the results of a mere chance which fixed my eye on a certain stray piece of shelf-paper. It was nothing on which I would naturally have stumbled in the course of my daily round, for it was an old number of an Australian journal, *Sydney Bulletin* for April 18, 1925. It had escaped even the cutting bureau which had at the time of its issuance been avidly collecting material for my uncle's research.

I had largely given over my inquiries into what Professor Angell called the "Cthulhu Cult," and was visiting a learned friend of Paterson, New Jersey; the curator of a local museum and a mineralogist of note. Examining one day the reserve specimens roughly set on the storage shelves in a rear room of the museum, my eye was caught by an odd picture in one of the old papers spread beneath the stones. It was the *Sydney Bulletin* I have mentioned, for my friend has wide affiliations in all conceivable foreign parts; and the picture was a half-tone cut of a hideous stone image almost identical with that which Legrasse had found in the swamp.

Eagerly clearing the sheet of its precious contents, I scanned the item in detail; and was disappointed to find it of only moderate length. What it suggested, however, was of portentous significance to my flagging quest; and I carefully tore it out for immediate action. It read as follows:

MYSTERY DERELICT FOUND AT SEA

*Vigilant* Arrives with Helpless Armed New Zealand Yacht in Tow. One Survivor and Dead Man Found Aboard. Tale of Desperate Battle and Deaths at Sea. Rescued Seaman Refuses Particulars of Strange Experience. Odd Idol Found in His Possession. Inquiry to Follow.

The Morrison Co.'s freighter *Vigilant,* bound from Valparaiso, arrived this morning at its wharf in Darling Harbour, having in tow the battled and disabled but heavily armed steam yacht *Alert* of Dunedin, N. Z., which was sighted April 12th in S. Latitude 34° 21', W. Longitude 152° 17', with one living and one dead man aboard.

The *Vigilant* left Valparaiso March 25th, and on April 2d was driven considerably south of her course by exceptionally heavy storms and monster waves. On April 12th the derelict was sighted; and though apparently deserted, was found upon boarding to contain one survivor in a half-delirious condition and one man who had evidently been dead for more than a week.

The living man was clutching a horrible stone idol of unknown origin, about a foot in height, regarding whose nature authorities at Sydney University, the Royal Society, and the museum in College Street all profess complete bafflement, and which the survivor says he found in the cabin of the yacht, in a small carved shrine of common pattern.

This man, after recovering his senses, told an exceedingly strange story of piracy and slaughter. He is Gustaf Johansen, a Norwegian of some intelligence, and had been second mate of the two-masted schooner *Emma* of Auckland, which sailed for Callao February 20th, with a complement of eleven men.

The *Emma,* he says, was delayed and thrown widely south of her course by the great storm of March 1st, and on March 22d, in S. Latitude 49° 51', W. Longitude 128° 34', encountered the *Alert,* manned by a queer and evil-looking crew of Kanakas and half-castes. Being ordered peremptorily to turn back, Capt. Collins refused; whereupon the strange crew began to fire savagely and without warning upon the schooner with a peculiarly heavy battery of brass cannon forming part of the yacht's equipment.

The *Emma*'s men showed fight, says the survivor, and though the schooner began to sink from shots beneath the waterline they managed to heave alongside their enemy and board her, grappling with the savage crew on the yacht's deck, and being forced to kill them all, the number being slightly superior, because of their particularly abhorrent and desperate though rather clumsy mode of fighting.

Three of the *Emma*'s men, including Capt. Collins and First Mate Green, were killed; and the remaining eight under Second Mate Johansen proceeded to navigate the captured yacht, going ahead in their original direction to see if any reason for their ordering back had existed.

The next day, it appears, they raised and landed on a small island, although none is known to exist in that part of the ocean; and six of the men somehow died ashore, though Johansen is queerly reticent about this part of his story and speaks only of their falling into a rock chasm.

Later, it seems, he and one companion boarded the yacht and tried to manage her, but were beaten about by the storm of April 2d.

From that time till his rescue on the 12th, the man remembers little, and he does not even recall when William Briden, his companion, died. Briden's death reveals no apparent cause, and was probably due to excitement or exposure.

Cable advices from Dunedin report that the *Alert* was well known there as an island trader, and bore an evil reputation along the waterfront. It was owned by a curious group of half-castes whose frequent meetings and night trips to the woods attracted no little curiosity; and it had set sail in great haste just after the storm and earth tremors of March 1st.

Our Auckland correspondent gives the *Emma* and her crew an excellent reputation, and Johansen is described as a sober and worthy man.

The admiralty will institute an inquiry on the whole matter beginning tomorrow, at which every effort will be made to induce Johansen to speak more freely than he has done hitherto.

This was all, together with the picture of the hellish image; but what a train of ideas it started in my mind! Here were new treasuries of data on the Cthulhu Cult, and evidence that it had strange interests at sea as well as on land. What motive prompted the hybrid crew to order back the *Emma* as they sailed about with their hideous idol? What was the unknown island on which six of the *Emma*'s crew had died, and about which the mate Johansen was so secretive? What had the vice-admiralty's investigation brought out, and what was known of the noxious cult in Dunedin? And most marvelous of all, what deep and more than natural linkage of dates was this which gave a malign and now undeniable significance to the various turn of events so carefully noted by my uncle?

March 1st—our February 28th according to the International Date Line—the earthquake and storm had come. From Dunedin the *Alert* and her noisome crew had darted eagerly forth as if imperiously summoned, and on the other side of the earth poets and artists had begun to dream of a strange, dank Cyclopean city whilst a young sculptor had molded in his sleep the form of the dreaded Cthulhu. March 23rd the crew of the *Emma* landed on an unknown island and left six men dead; and on that date the dreams of sensitive men assumed a heightened vividness and darkened with dread of a giant monster's malign pursuit, whilst an architect had gone mad and a sculptor had lapsed suddenly into delirium! And what of this storm of April 2nd—the date on which all dreams of the dank city ceased, and Wilcox emerged unharmed from the bondage of strange fever? What of all this—and of those hints of old Castro about the sunken, star-born Old Ones and their coming reign; their faithful cult *and their mastery of dreams?* Was I tottering on the brink of cosmic horrors beyond man's power to bear? If so, they must be horrors of the mind alone, for in some way the second of April had put a stop to whatever monstrous menace had begun its siege of mankind's soul.

That evening, after a day of hurried cabling and arranging, I bade my host adieu and took a train for San Francisco. In less than a month I was in Dunedin; where, however, I found that little was known of the strange cult-members who had lingered in the old sea taverns. Waterfront scum was far too common for special mention; though there was vague talk about one inland trip these mongrels had made, during which faint drumming and red flame were noted on the distant hills.

In Auckland I learned that Johansen had returned *with yellow hair turned white* after a perfunctory and inconclusive questioning at Sydney, and had thereafter sold his cottage in West Street and sailed with his wife to his old home in Oslo. Of his stirring experience he would tell his friends no more than he had told the admiralty officials, and all they could do was to give me his Oslo address.

After that I went to Sydney and talked profitlessly with seamen and members of the vice-admiralty court. I saw the *Alert*, now sold and in commercial use, at Circular Quay in Sydney Cove, but gained nothing from its noncommittal bulk. The crouching image with its cuttlefish head, dragon body, scaly wings, and hieroglyphed pedestal, was preserved in the Museum at Hyde Park; and I studied it long and well, finding it a thing of balefully exquisite workmanship, and with the same utter mystery, terrible antiquity, and unearthly strangeness of material which I had noted in Legrasse's smaller specimen. Geologists, the curator told me, had found it a monstrous puzzle; for they vowed that the world held no rock like it. Then I thought with a shudder of what old Castro had told Legrasse about the primal Great Ones: "They had come from the stars, and had brought Their images with Them."

Shaken with such a mental revolution as I had never before known, I now resolved to visit Mate Johansen in Oslo. Sailing for London, I re-embarked at once for the Norwegian capital; and one autumn day landed at the trim wharves in the shadow of the Egeberg.

Johansen's address, I discovered, lay in the Old Town of King Harold Haardrada, which kept alive the name of Oslo during all the centuries that the greater city masqueraded as "Christiania." I made the brief trip by taxicab, and knocked with palpitant heart at the door of a neat and ancient building with plastered front. A sad-faced woman in black answered my summons, and I was stung with disappointment when she told me in halting English that Gustaf Johansen was no more.

He had not long survived his return, said his wife, for the doings at sea in 1925 had broken him. He had told her no more than he had told the public, but had left a long manuscript—of "technical matters" as he said—written in English evidently in order to safeguard her from the peril of casual perusal. During a walk through a narrow lane near the Gothenburg dock, a bundle of papers falling from an attic window had knocked him down. Two Lascar sailors at once helped him to his feet, but before the ambulance could reach him he was dead. Physicians found no adequate cause for the end, and laid it to heart trouble and a weakened constitution.

I now felt gnawing at my vitals that dark terror which will never leave me till I, too, am at rest; "accidentally" or otherwise. Persuading the widow that my connection with her husband's "technical matters" was sufficient to entitle me to his manuscript, I bore the document away and began to read it on the London boat.

It was a simple, rambling thing—a naive sailor's effort at a post-facto diary—and strove to recall day by day that last awful voyage. I can not attempt to transcribe it verbatim in all its cloudiness and redundance, but I will tell its gist enough to show why the sound of the water against the vessel's sides became so unendurable to me that I stopped my ears with cotton.

Johansen, thank God, did not know quite all, even though he saw the city and the Thing, but I shall never sleep calmly again when I think of the horrors that lurk ceaselessly behind life in time and in space, and of those unhallowed blasphemies from elder stars which dream beneath the sea, known and favored by a nightmare cult ready and eager to loose them on the world whenever another earthquake shall heave their monstrous stone city again to the sun and air.

Johansen's voyage had begun just as he told it to the vice-admiralty. The *Emma,* in ballast, had cleared Auckland on February 20th, and had felt the full force of that earthquake-born tempest which must have heaved up from the sea-bottom the horrors that filled men's dreams. Once more under control, the ship was making good progress when held up by the *Alert* on March 22nd, and I could feel the mate's regret as he wrote of her bombardment and sinking. Of the swarthy cult-fiends on the *Alert* he speaks with significant horror. There was some peculiarly abominable quality about them which made their destruction seem almost a duty, and Johansen shows ingenuous wonder at the charge of ruthlessness brought against his party during the proceedings of the court of inquiry. Then, driven ahead by curiosity in their captured yacht under Johansen's command, the men sight a great stone pillar sticking out of the sea, and in S. Latitude 47° 9′, W. Longitude 126° 43′, come upon a coastline of mingled mud, ooze, and weedy Cyclopean masonry which can be nothing less than the tangible substance of earth's supreme terror—the nightmare corpse-city of R'lyeh, that was built in measureless eons behind history by the vast, loathsome shapes that seeped down from the dark stars. There lay great Cthulhu and his hordes, hidden in green slimy vaults and sending out at last, after cycles incalculable, the thoughts that spread fear to the dreams of the sensitive and called imperiously to the faithful to come on a pilgrimage of liberation and restoration. All this Johansen did not suspect, but God knows he soon saw enough!

I suppose that only a single mountain-top, the hideous monolith-crowned citadel whereon great Cthulhu was buried, actually emerged from the waters. When I think of the *extent* of all that may be brooding down there I almost wish to kill myself forthwith. Johansen and his men were awed by the cosmic majesty of this dripping Babylon of elder demons, and must have guessed without guidance that it was nothing of this or of any sane planet. Awe at the unbelievable size of the greenish stone blocks, at the dizzying height of the great carven monolith, and at the stupefying identity of the colossal statues and bas-reliefs with the queer image found in the shrine on the *Alert,* is poignantly visible in every line of the mate's frightened description.

Without knowing what futurism is like, Johansen achieved something very close to it when he spoke of the city; for instead of describing any definite structure or building, he dwells only on the broad impressions of vast angles and stone surfaces—surfaces too great to belong to any thing right or proper for this earth, and impious with horrible images and hieroglyphs. I mention his talk about *angles* because it suggests something Wilcox had told me of his awful dreams. He had said that the *geometry* of the dream-place he saw was abnormal, non-Euclidean, and loathsomely redolent of spheres and dimensions apart from ours. Now an unlettered seaman felt the same thing whilst gazing at the terrible reality.

Johansen and his men landed at a sloping mud-bank on this monstrous acropolis, and clambered slipperily up over titan oozy blocks which could have been no mortal staircase. The very sun of heaven seemed distorted when viewed through the polarizing miasma welling out from this sea-soaked perversion, and twisted menace and suspense lurked leeringly in those crazily elusive angles of carven rock where a second glance showed concavity after the first showed convexity.

Something very like fright had come over all the explorers before anything more definite than rock and ooze and weed was seen. Each would have fled had he not feared the scorn of the others, and it was only half-heartedly that they searched—vainly, as it proved—for some portable souvenir to bear away.

It was Rodriguez the Portuguese who climbed up the foot of the monolith and shouted of what he had found. The rest followed him, and looked curiously at the immense carved door with the now familiar squid-dragon bas-relief. It was, Johansen said, like a great barn-door; and they all felt that it was a door because of the ornate lintel, threshold, and jambs around it, though they could not decide whether it lay flat like a trap door or slantwise like an outside cellar-door. As Wilcox would have said, the geometry of the place was all wrong. One could not be sure that the sea and the ground were horizontal, hence the relative position of everything else seemed fantasmally variable.

Briden pushed at the stone in several places without result. Then Donovan felt over it delicately around the edge, pressing each point separately as he went. He climbed interminably along the grotesque stone molding—that is, one would call it climbing if the thing was not after all horizontal—and the men wondered how any door in the universe could be so vast. Then, very softly and slowly, the acre-great panel began to give inward at the top; and they saw that it was balanced.

Donovan slid or somehow propelled himself down or along the jamb and rejoined his fellows, and everyone watched the queer recession of the monstrously carven portal. In this fantasy of prismatic distortion it moved anomalously in a diagonal way, so that all the rules of matter and perspective seemed upset.

The aperture was black with a darkness almost material. That tenebrousness was indeed a *positive quality;* for it obscured such parts of the inner walls as ought to have been revealed, and actually burst forth like smoke from its eon-long imprisonment, visibly darkening the sun as it slunk away into the shrunken and gibbous sky on flapping membranous wings. The odor arising from the newly opened depths was intolerable, and at length the quick-eared Hawkins thought he heard a nasty, slopping sound down there. Everyone listened, and everyone was listening still when It lumbered slobberingly into sight and gropingly squeezed Its gelatinous green immensity through the black doorway into the tainted outside air of that poison city of madness.

Poor Johansen's handwriting almost gave out when he wrote of this. Of the six men who never reached the ship, he thinks two perished of pure fright in that accursed instant. The Thing can not be described—there is no language for such abysms of shrieking and immemorial lunacy, such eldritch contradictions of all matter, force, and cosmic order. A mountain

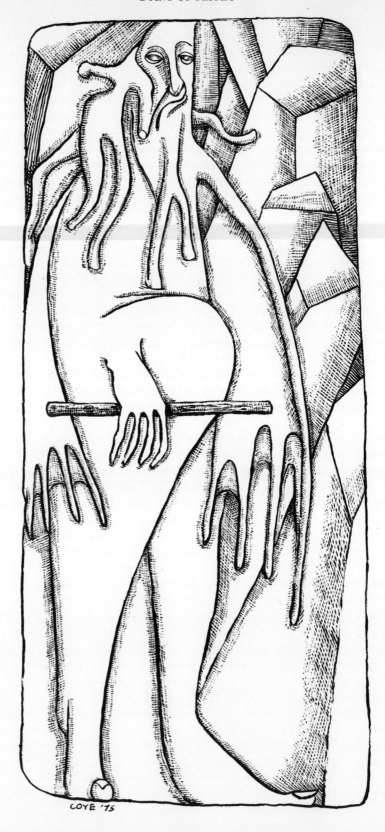

walked or stumbled. God! What wonder that across the earth a great architect went mad, and poor Wilcox raved with fever in that telepathic instant? The Thing of the idols, the green, sticky spawn of the stars, had awaked to claim his own. The stars were right again, and what an age-old cult had failed to do by design, a band of innocent sailors had done by accident. After vigintillions of years great Cthulhu was loose again, and ravening for delight.

Three men were swept up by the flabby claws before anybody turned. God rest them, if there be any rest in the universe. They were Donovan, Guerrera and Angstrom. Parker slipped as the other three were plunging frenziedly over endless vistas of green-crusted rock to the boat, and Johansen swears he was swallowed up by an angle of masonry which shouldn't have been there; an angle which was acute, but behaved as if it were obtuse. So only Briden and Johansen reached the boat, and pulled desperately for the *Alert* as the mountainous monstrosity flopped down the slimy stones and hesitated, floundering at the edge of the water.

Steam had not been suffered to go down entirely, despite the departure of all hands for the shore; and it was the work of only a few moments of feverish rushing up and down between wheels and engines to get the *Alert* under way. Slowly, amidst the distorted horrors of that indescribable scene, she began to churn the lethal waters; whilst on the masonry of that charnel shore that was not of earth the titan Thing from the stars slavered and gibbered like Polypheme cursing the fleeing ship of Odysseus. Then, bolder than the storied Cyclops, great Cthulhu slid greasily into the water and began to pursue with vast wave-raising strokes of cosmic potency. Briden looked back and went mad, laughing at intervals till death found him one night in the cabin whilst Johansen was wandering deliriously.

But Johansen had not given out yet. Knowing that the Thing could surely overtake the *Alert* until steam was fully up, he resolved on a desperate chance; and, setting the engine for full speed, ran lightning-like on deck and reversed the wheel. There was a mighty eddying and foaming in the noisome brine, and as the steam mounted higher and higher the brave Norwegian drove his vessel head on against the pursuing jelly which rose above the unclean froth like the stern of a demon galleon. The awful squid-head with writhing feelers came nearly up to the bowsprit of the sturdy yacht, but Johansen drove on relentlessly.

There was a bursting as of an exploding bladder, a slushy nastiness as of a cloven sunfish, a stench as of a thousand opened graves, and a sound that the chronicler would not put on paper. For an instant the ship was befouled by an acrid and blinding green cloud, and then there was only a venomous seething astern; where—God in heaven!—the scattered plasticity of that nameless sky-spawn was nebulously *recombining* in its hateful original form, whilst its distance widened every second as the *Alert* gained impetus from its mounting steam.

That was all. After that Johansen only brooded over the idol in the cabin and attended to a few matters of food for himself and the laughing maniac by his side. He did not try to navigate after the first bold flight; for the reaction had taken something out of his soul. Then came the storm of April 2nd, and a gathering of the clouds about his consciousness. There is a sense of spectral whirling through liquid gulfs of infinity, of dizzying rides through reeling universes on a comet's tail, and of hysterical plunges from the pit to the moon and from the moon back again to the pit, all livened by a cachinnating chorus of the distorted, hilarious elder gods and the green, bat-winged mocking imps of Tartarus.

Out of that dream came rescue—the *Vigilant*, the vice-admiralty court, the streets of Dunedin, and the long voyage back home to the old house by the Egeberg. He could not tell—they would think him mad. He would write of what he knew before death came, but his wife must not guess. Death would be a boon if only it could blot out the memories.

That was the document I read, and now I have placed it in the tin box beside the bas-relief and the papers of Professor Angell. With it shall go this record of mine—this test of my own sanity, wherein is pieced together that which I hope may never be pieced together again. I have looked upon all that the universe has to hold of horror, and even the skies of spring and the flowers of summer must ever afterward be poison to me. But I do not think my life will be long. As my uncle went, as poor Johansen went, so I shall go. I know too much, and the cult still lives.

Cthulhu still lives, too, I suppose, again in that chasm of stone which has shielded him since the sun was young. His accursed city is sunken once more, for the *Vigilant* sailed over the spot after the April storm; but his ministers on earth still bellow and prance and slay around idol-capped monoliths in lonely places. He must have been trapped by the sinking whilst within his black abyss, or else the world would by now be screaming with fright and frenzy. Who knows the end? What has risen may sink, and what has sunk may rise. Loathsomeness waits and dreams in the deep, and decay spreads over the tottering cities of men. A time will come—but I must not and can not think! Let me pray that, if I do not survive this manuscript, my executors may put caution before audacity and see that it meets no other eye.

# Frank Belknap Long

Frank Belknap Long (1903– ) is one of the most important authors whose interest in the macabre was inspired by an association with H. P. Lovecraft. Although many of these writers knew Lovecraft only through their correspondence, the young Long was a close personal friend, and the older author was a frequent visitor to the Long residence in New York. There can be little doubt that Long's friendship contributed significantly to the personal and professional growth of his reclusive mentor.

More important than his association with Lovecraft, though, is the contribution Long has made as a creator of fantasy and science fiction. He added several vivid tales to the burgeoning Cthulhu mythos, the best of them being "The Hounds of Tindalos" (1929), in which the protagonist ingests an exotic drug in a disastrous attempt to reach another dimension. An enthusiastic French critic, Jacques Bergier, called it "one of the ten most terrifying and significant short stories in all literature." Long's first novel, *The Horror from the Hills* (1931), is based on one of Lovecraft's nightmares, recounted to the author in an extensive letter.

Among Long's finest supernatural stories are "Second Night Out," "The Black Druid," "Two Face," and the recent "Cottage Tenant," along with such melodramatic but brilliantly visualized pieces as "The Space-Eaters" and "The Ocean Leech." Twenty of his horror tales were collected in the 1946 volume *The Hounds of Tindalos*, which has since been reprinted several times. His early work appeared in such magazines as *Weird Tales*, *Unknown*, *Astounding Science Fiction*, and *Startling Stories*, and across the years his stories have been included in many important anthologies. He was for several years associate editor of *Satellite Science Fiction*, *Mike Shayne Mystery Magazine*, and *Short Stories*.

In recent years Long has devoted more time to science fiction, perhaps a logical outgrowth of his interest in what Lovecraft described as "cosmic horror." Long has written seven hardback and more than a dozen paperback novels in the genre, including *Mars Is My Destination*, *Space Station Number One*, *It Was the Day of the Robot*, *Lest Earth Be Conquered*, *The Martian Visitors*, and *Survival World*. His recent publications include a science fiction and supernatural story collection called *The Rim of the Unknown*, a memoir entitled *Howard Phillips Lovecraft: Dreamer on the Night Side*, and *The Early Long*, a major compilation of fiction that also includes a considerable amount of autobiographical material.

"A Visitor from Egypt," one of his most gripping terror tales, has been performed as a radio play and was selected by the discerning mystery author Dashiell Hammett for his 1931 anthology *Creeps by Night*. It is one of the best stories inspired by that ancient and eternal culture that heralded the dawn of civilization and that has also spawned such artifacts as an apparently endless stream of films about reanimated mummies. Long's story, which views the question of existence after extinction on a more esoteric level, is a remarkable performance, free from literary antecedents, yet imbued with the atmosphere of a primitive and vindictive cult. It first appeared in a 1930 issue of *Weird Tales*.

# A VISITOR FROM EGYPT

# Frank Belknap Long

On a dismal rainy afternoon in August a tall, very thin gentleman tapped timidly on the frosted glass window of the curator's office in a certain New England museum. He wore a dark blue Chinchilla overcoat, olive-green Homburg hat with high tapering crown, yellow gloves, and spats. A blue silk muffler with white dots encircled his neck and entirely concealed the lower portion of his face and virtually all of his nose. Only a small expanse of pink and very wrinkled flesh was visible above the muffler and below his forehead, but as this exposed portion of his physiognomy contained his eyes it was as arresting as it was meager. So arresting indeed was it that it commanded instant respect, and the attendants, who were granted liberal weekly emoluments for merely putting yards of red tape between the main entrance and the narrow corridor that led to the curator's office, waived all of their habitual and asinine inquiries and conducted the muffled gentleman straight to what a Victorian novelist would have called the sacred precincts.

Having tapped, the gentleman waited. He waited patiently, but something in his manner suggested that he was extremely nervous and perturbed and decidedly on edge to talk to the curator. And yet when the door of the office at last swung open, and the curator peered out fastidiously from behind gold-rimmed spectacles, he merely coughed and extended a visiting card.

The card was conservatively fashionable in size and exquisitely engraved, and as soon as the curator perused it his countenance underwent an extraordinary alteration. He was ordinarily a supremely reticent individual with long, pale face and lugubrious, condescending eyes, but he suddenly became preposterously friendly and greeted his visitor with an effusiveness that was almost hysterical. He seized his visitor's somewhat flabby gloved hand and gave it a Babbittesque squeeze. He nodded and bowed and smirked and seemed almost beside himself with gratification.

"If only I had known, Sir Richard, that you were in America! The papers were unusually silent—outrageously silent, you know. I can not imagine how you managed to elude the reporters. They are usually so persistent, so indecently curious. I really can not imagine how you achieved it!"

"I did not wish to talk to idiotic old women, to lecture before mattoids, to have my photo reproduced in your absurd papers." Sir Richard's voice was oddly high-pitched, almost effeminate, and it quivered with the intensity of his emotion. "I *detest* publicity, and I regret that I am not utterly unknown in this—er—region."

"I quite understand, Sir Richard," murmured the curator soothingly. "You naturally desired leisure for research, for discussion. You were not interested in what the vulgar would

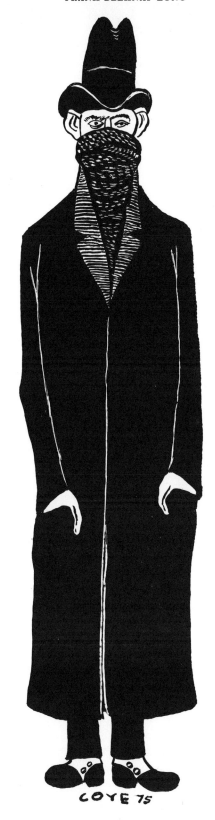

say or think about you. A commendable and eminently scholarly attitude to take, Sir Richard! A splendid attitude! I quite understand and sympathize. We Americans have to be polite to the press occasionally, but you have no idea how it cramps our style, if I may use an expressive but exceedingly coarse colloquialism. It really does, Sir Richard. You have no idea —but do come in. Come in, by all means. We are honored immeasurably by the visit of so eminent a scholar."

Sir Richard bowed stiffly and preceded the curator into the office. He selected the most comfortable of the five leather-backed chairs that encircled the curator's desk and sank into it with a faintly audible sigh. He neither removed his hat nor withdrew the muffler from his pinkish visage.

The curator selected a seat on the opposite side of the table and politely extended a box of Havana panatelas. "Extremely mild," he murmured. "Won't you try one, Sir Richard?"

Sir Richard shook his head. "I have never smoked," he said, and coughed.

There ensued a silence. Then Sir Richard apologized for the muffler. "I had an unfortunate accident on the ship," he explained. "I stumbled in one of the deck games and cut my face rather badly. It's in a positively unpresentable condition. I know you'll pardon me if I don't remove this muffler."

The curator gasped. "How horrible, Sir Richard! I can sympathize, believe me. I hope that it will not leave a scar. One should have the most expert advice in such matters. I hope— Sir Richard, have you consulted a specialist, may I ask?"

Sir Richard nodded. "The wounds are not deep—nothing serious, I assure you. And now, Mr. Buzzby, I should like to discuss with you the mission that has brought me to Boston. Are the predynastic remains from Luxor on exhibition?"

The curator was a trifle disconcerted. He had placed the Luxor remains on exhibition that very morning, but he had not as yet arranged them to his satisfaction, and he would have preferred that his distinguished guest should view them at a later date. But he very clearly perceived that Sir Richard was so intensely interested that nothing that he could say would induce him to wait, and he *was* proud of the remains and flattered that England's ablest Egyptologist should have come to the city expressly to see them. So he nodded amiably and confessed that the bones were on exhibition, and he added that he would be delighted and honored if Sir Richard would view them.

"They are truly marvelous," he explained. "The pure Egyptian type—dolichocephalic, with relatively primitive features. And they date—Sir Richard, they date from at least 8,000 B.C."

"Are the bones tinted?"

"I should say so, Sir Richard! They are wonderfully tinted, and the original colors have scarcely faded at all. Blue and red, Sir Richard, with red predominating."

"Hm. A most absurd custom," murmured Sir Richard.

Mr. Buzzby smiled. "I have always considered it pathetic, Sir Richard. Infinitely amusing, but pathetic. They thought that by painting the bones they could preserve the vitality of the corruptible body. Corruption putting on incorruption, as it were."

"It was blasphemous!" Sir Richard had arisen from his chair. His face, above the muffler, was curiously white, and there was a hard, metallic glitter in his small dark eyes. "They sought to cheat Osiris! They had no conception of hyperphysical realities!"

The curator stared curiously. "Precisely what do you mean, Sir Richard?"

Sir Richard started a trifle at the question, as though he were awakening from some strange nightmare, and his emotion ebbed as rapidly as it had arisen. The glitter died out of his eyes and he sank listlessly back in his chair. "I—I was merely amused by your comment.

As though by merely painting their mummies they could restore the circulation of the blood!''

"But that, as you know, Sir Richard, would occur in the other world. It was one of the most distinctive prerogatives of Osiris. He alone could restore the dead.''

"Yes, I know,'' murmured Sir Richard. "They counted a good deal on Osiris. It is curious that it never occurred to them that the god might be offended by their presumptions.''

"You are forgetting the Book of the Dead, Sir Richard. The promises in that are very definite. And it is an inconceivably ancient book. I am strongly convinced that it was in existence in 10,000 B.C. You have read my brochure on the subject?''

Sir Richard nodded. "A very scholarly work. But I believe that the Book of the Dead as we know it was a forgery!''

"Sir Richard!''

"Parts of it are undoubtedly predynastic, but I believe that the Judgment of the Dead, which defines the judicial prerogatives of Osiris, was inserted by some meddling priest as late as the historical period. It is a deliberate attempt to modify the relentless character of Egypt's supreme deity. Osiris does not judge, he *takes*.''

"He takes, Sir Richard?''

"Precisely. Do you imagine any one can ever cheat death? Do you imagine that, Mr. Buzzby? Do you imagine for one moment that Osiris would restore to life the fools that returned to him?''

Mr. Buzzby colored. It was difficult to believe that Sir Richard was really in earnest. "Then you honestly believe that the character of Osiris as we know it is——''

"A myth, yes. A deliberate and childish evasion. No man can ever comprehend the character of Osiris. He is the Dark God. *But he treasures his own*.''

"Eh?'' Mr. Buzzby was genuinely startled by the tone of ferocity in which the last remark was uttered. "What did you say, Sir Richard?''

"Nothing.'' Sir Richard had risen and was standing before a small revolving bookcase in the center of the room. "Nothing, Mr. Buzzby. But your taste in fiction interests me extremely. I had no idea you read young Finchley!''

Mr. Buzzby blushed and looked genuinely distressed. "I don't ordinarily,'' he said. "I despise fiction ordinarily. And young Finchley's romances are unutterably silly. He isn't even a passable scholar. But that book has—well, there are a few good things in it. I was reading it this morning on the train and put it with the other books temporarily because I had no other place to put it. You understand, Sir Richard? We all have our little foibles, eh? A work of fiction now and then is sometimes—er—well, suggestive. And H. E. Finchley is rather suggestive occasionally.''

"He is, indeed. His Egyptian redactions are imaginative masterpieces!''

"You amaze me, Sir Richard. Imagination in a scholar is to be deplored. But of course, as I said, H. E. Finchley is not a scholar and his work is occasionally illuminating if one doesn't take it too seriously.''

"He knows his Egypt.''

"Sir Richard, I can't believe you really approve of him. A mere fictionist——''

Sir Richard had removed the book and opened it casually. "May I ask, Mr. Buzzby, if you are familiar with Chapter 13, *The Transfiguration of Osiris*?''

"Bless me, Sir Richard, I am not. I skipped that portion. Such purely grotesque rubbish repelled me.''

"Did it, Mr. Buzzby? But the repellent is usually arresting. Just listen to this:

"It is beyond dispute that Osiris made his worshipers dream strange things of him, and that he possessed their bodies and souls forever. There is a devilish wrath against mankind with which Osiris was for Death's sake inspired. In the cool of the evening he walked among men, and upon his head was the Crown of Upper Egypt, and his cheeks were inflated with a wind that slew. His face was veiled so that no man could see it, but assuredly it was an old face, very old and dead and dry, for the world was young when tall Osiris died."

Sir Richard snapped the book shut and replaced it in the shelf. "What do you think of that, Mr. Buzzby?" he inquired.

"Rot," murmured the curator. "Sheer, unadulterated rot."

"Of course, of course. Mr. Buzzby, did it ever occur to you that a god may live, figuratively, a dog's life?"

"Eh?"

"Gods are transfigured, you know. They go up in smoke, as it were. In smoke and flame. They become pure flame, pure spirit, creatures with no visible body."

"Dear, dear, Sir Richard, that had not occurred to me." The curator laughed and nudged Sir Richard's arm. "Beastly sense of humor," he murmured, to himself. "The man is unutterably silly."

"It would be dreadful, for example," continued Sir Richard, "if the god had no control over his transfiguration; if the change occurred frequently and unexpectedly; if he shared, as it were, the ghastly fate of a Dr. Jekyll and Mr. Hyde."

Sir Richard was advancing toward the door. He moved with a curious, shuffling gait and his shoes scraped peculiarly upon the floor. Mr. Buzzby was instantly at his elbow. "What is the matter, Sir Richard? What has happened?"

"Nothing!" Sir Richard's voice rose in hysterical denial. "Nothing. Where is the lavatory, Mr. Buzzby?"

"Down one flight of stairs on your left as you leave the corridor," muttered Mr. Buzzby. "Are—are you ill?"

"It is nothing, nothing," murmured Sir Richard. "I must have a drink of water, that is all. The injury has—er—affected my throat. When it becomes too dry it pains dreadfully."

"Good heavens!" murmured the curator. "I can send for water, Sir Richard. I can indeed. I beg you not to disturb yourself."

"No, no, I insist that you do not. I shall return immediately. Please do not send for anything."

Before the curator could renew his protestations Sir Richard had passed through the door and disappeared down the corridor.

Mr. Buzzby shrugged his shoulders and returned to his desk. "A most extraordinary person," he muttered. "Erudite and original, but queer. Decidedly queer. Still, it is pleasant to reflect that he has read my brochure. A scholar of his distinction might very pardonably have overlooked it. He called it a scholarly work. A scholarly work. Hmm. Very gratifying, I'm sure."

Mr. Buzzby clipped and lit a cigar.

"Of course he is wrong about the Book of the Dead," he mused. "Osiris was a most benevolent god. It is true that the Egyptians feared him, but only because he was supposed to judge the dead. There was nothing essentially evil or cruel about him. Sir Richard is quite wrong about that. It is curious that a man so eminent could go so sensationally astray. I can use no other phrase. Sensationally astray. I really believe that my arguments impressed him, though. I could see that he was impressed."

The curator's pleasant reflections were coarsely and unexpectedly interrupted by a shout in the corridor. "Get them extinguishers down! Quick, you b——"

The curator gasped and rose hastily to his feet. Profanity violated all the rules of the museum and he had always firmly insisted that the rules should be obeyed. Striding quickly to the door he threw it open and stared incredulously down the corridor.

"What was that?" he cried. "Did any one call?"

He heard hurried steps and the sound of someone shouting, and then an attendant appeared at the end of the corridor. "Come quickly, sir!" he exclaimed. "There's fire and smoke comin' out of the basement!"

Mr. Buzzby groaned. What a dreadful thing to happen when he had such a distinguished guest! He raced down the corridor and seized the attendant angrily by the arm. "Did Sir Richard get out?" he demanded. "Answer me! Is Sir Richard down there now?"

"Who?" gasped the attendant.

"The gentleman who went down a few minutes ago, you idiot. A tall gentleman wearing a blue coat?"

"I dunno, sir. I didn't see nobody come up."

"Good God!" Mr. Buzzby was frantic. "We must get him out immediately. I believe that he was ill. He's probably fainted."

He strode to the end of the corridor and stared down the smoke-filled staircase leading to the lavatory. Immediately beneath him three attendants were cautiously advancing. Wet handkerchiefs, bound securely about their faces, protected them from the acrid fumes, and each held at arm's length a cylindrical fire extinguisher. As they descended the stairs they squirted the liquid contents of the extinguishers into the rapidly rising spirals of lethal blue smoke.

"It was much worse a minute ago," exclaimed the attendant at Mr. Buzzby's elbow. "The smoke was thicker and had a most awful smell. Like them dinosaur eggs smelt when you first unpacked 'em last spring, sir."

The attendants had now reached the base of the staircase and were peering cautiously into the lavatory. For a moment they peered in silence, and then one of them shouted up at Mr. Buzzby. "The smoke's dreadfully dense here, sir. We can't see any flames. Shall we go in, sir?"

"Yes, do!" Mr. Buzzby's voice was tragically shrill. "Do all you can. Please!"

The attendants disappeared into the lavatory and the curator waited with an agonized and expectant air. His heart was wrung at the thought of the fate which had in all probability overtaken his distinguished guest, but he could not think of anything further to do. Sinister forebodings crowded into his mind, but he was powerless to act.

Then it was that the shrieks commenced. From whatever cause arising they were truly ghastly, but they began so suddenly, so unexpectedly, that at first the curator could form no theory as to what had caused them. They issued so horribly and suddenly from the lavatory, echoing and reechoing through the empty corridors, that the curator could only stare and gasp.

But when they became fairly coherent, when the screams of affright turned to appeals for mercy, for pity, and when the language in which they found grim expression changed too, becoming familiar to the curator but incomprehensible to the man beside him, a dreadful incident occurred which the latter has never been able to consign to a merciful mnemonic oblivion.

The curator fell upon his knees, literally went down upon his knees at the head of the staircase and raised both arms in an unmistakable gesture of supplication. And then from his ashen lips there poured a torrent of grotesque gibberish:

"sdmw stn Osiris! sdmw stn Osiris! sdmw stn Osiris! sdm-f Osiris! Oh, sdm-f Osiris! sdmw stn Osiris!"

"Fool!" A muffled form emerged from the lavatory and ponderously ascended the stairs. "Fool! You—you have sinned irretrievably!" The voice was guttural, harsh, remote, and seemed to come from an immeasurable distance.

"Sir Richard! Sir Richard!" The curator got stumblingly to his feet and staggered toward the ascending figure. "Protect me, Sir Richard. There's something unspeakable down there. I thought—for a moment I thought—Sir Richard, did you *see* it? Did you hear anything? those shrieks——"

But Sir Richard did not reply. He did not even look at the curator. He brushed past the unfortunate man as though he were a mere meddling fool, and grimly began to climb the stairs that led to the Hall of Egyptian Antiquities. He ascended so rapidly that the curator could not catch up with him, and before the frightened man had reached the half-way landing his steps were resounding on the tiled floor above.

"Wait, Sir Richard!" shrieked Buzzby. "Wait, please! I am sure that you can explain everything. I am afraid. Please wait for me!"

A spasm of coughing seized him, and at that moment there ensued a most dreadful crash. Fragments of broken glass tinkled suggestively upon the stone floor, and awoke ominous echoes in the corridor and up and down the winding stairway. Mr. Buzzby clung to the banisters and moaned. His face was purplish and distorted with fear and beads of sweat glistened on his high forehead. For a moment he remained thus cowering and whimpering on the staircase. Then, miraculously, his courage returned. He ascended the last flight three steps at a time and dashed wildly forward.

An intolerable thought had abruptly been born in the poor, bewildered brain of Mr. Buzzby. It had suddenly occurred to him that Sir Richard was an impostor, a murderous madman intent only upon destruction, and that his collections were in immediate danger. Whatever Mr. Buzzby's human deficiencies, in his professional capacity he was conscientious and aggressive to an almost abnormal degree. And the crash had been unmistakable and susceptible of only one explanation. Mr. Buzzby completely forgot his fear in his concern for his precious collections. Sir Richard had smashed one of the cases and was extracting its contents! There was little doubt in Mr. Buzzby's mind as to which of the cases Sir Richard had smashed. "The Luxor remains can never be duplicated," he moaned. "I have been horribly duped!"

Suddenly he stopped, and stared. At the very entrance to the Hall lay an assortment of garments which he instantly recognized. There was the blue Chinchilla coat and the Alpine Homburg with its high tapering crown, and the blue silk muffler that had concealed so effectively the face of his visitor. And on the very top of the heap lay a pair of yellow suede gloves.

"Good God!" muttered Mr. Buzzby. "The man has shed all of his clothes!"

He stood there for a moment staring in utter bewilderment and then with long, hysterical strides he advanced into the hall. "A hopeless maniac," he muttered, under his breath. "A sheer, raving lunatic. Why did I not——"

Then, abruptly, he ceased to reproach himself. He forgot entirely his folly, the heap of clothes, and the smashed case. Everything that had up to that moment occupied his mind was instantly extruded and he shriveled and shrank with fear. Never had the unwilling gaze of Mr. Buzzby encountered such a sight.

Mr. Buzzby's visitor was bending over the shattered case and only his back was visible. But it was not an ordinary back. In a lucid, unemotional moment Mr. Buzzby would have called it a nasty, malignant back, but in juxtaposition with the crown that topped it there is no Aryan polysyllable suggestive enough to describe it. For the crown was very tall and ponderous with jewels and unspeakably luminous, and it accentuated the vileness of the back. It was a green back. *Sapless* was the word that ran through Mr. Buzzby's mind as he stood and stared at it. And it was wrinkled, too, horribly wrinkled, all crisscrossed with centuried grooves.

Mr. Buzzby did not even notice his visitor's neck, which glistened and was as thin as a beanpole, nor the small round scaly head that bobbed and nodded ominously. He saw only the hideous back, and the unbelievably awesome crown. The crown shed a fiery radiance upon the reddish tiles of the dim, vast hall, and the starkly nude body twisted and turned and writhed shockingly.

Black horror clutched at Mr. Buzzby's throat and his lips trembled as though he were about to cry out. But he spoke no word. He had staggered back against the wall and was making curious futile gestures with his arms, as though he sought to embrace the darkness, to wrap the darkness in the hall about him, to make himself as inconspicuous as possible and invisible to the thing that was bending over the case. But apparently he soon found to his infinite dismay that the thing was aware of his presence, and as it turned slowly toward him he made no further attempt to obliterate himself, but went down on his knees and screamed and screamed and screamed.

Silently the figure advanced toward him. It seemed to glide rather than to walk, and in its terribly lean arms it held a queer assortment of brilliant scarlet bones. And it cackled loathsomely as it advanced.

And then it was that Mr. Buzzby's sanity departed utterly. He groveled and gibbered and dragged himself along the floor like a man in the grip of an instantaneous catalepsy. And all the while he murmured incoherently about how spotless he was and would Osiris spare him and how he longed to reconcile himself with Osiris.

But the figure, when it got to him, merely stooped and breathed on him. Three times it breathed on his ashen face and one could almost see the face shrivel and blacken beneath its warm breath. For some time it remained in a stooping posture, glaring glassily, and when it arose Mr. Buzzby made no effort to detain it. Holding the scarlet bones very firmly in its horribly thin arms it glided rapidly away in the direction of the stairs. The attendants did not see it descend. No one ever saw it again.

And when the coroner, arriving in response to the tardy summons of an attendant, examined Mr. Buzzby's body, the conclusion was unavoidable that the curator had been dead for a long, long time.

# Henry Kuttner

Henry Kuttner (1914–1958) is not only an important fantasy author in his own right, he is also a significant transition figure between the *Weird Tales* school of the nineteen thirties and modern writers. He was one of the young writers who came under the influence of H. P. Lovecraft, and he worked in the Cthulhu mythos vein, producing such stories as "The Salem Horror" and "Hydra." In later years, Kuttner in turn provided inspiration for a new generation. Ray Bradbury reports that his first professionally published horror story, "The Candle," was completed by Kuttner. And Richard Matheson dedicated his famous novel *I Am Legend* to Kuttner, "with my grateful thanks for his help and encouragement on this book."

After Lovecraft's death, Kuttner did a few stories in the manner of Robert E. Howard, who had originated the popular prehistoric adventurer Conan. Kuttner's character was Elak of Atlantis, who first appeared in the 1938 story "Thunder in the Dawn." It was in the pages of the pulp magazine *Unknown,* however, that he really established his own unique style, beginning with the humorous fantasy "The Misguided Halo" and continuing with such ironic tales as "Compliments of the Author," "A Gnome There Was," "Design for Dreaming," and "The Devil We Know." Later, he concentrated on the science fiction genre, producing memorable stories like "The Twonky" and "Exit the Professor."

In 1940, Kuttner married Catherine L. Moore, a fantasy writer of no small reputation, perhaps most renowned for her story "Shambleau." It is said that this wedding resulted in so many collaborations that virtually every story appearing subsequently under either name was the result of their combined efforts. They even created a new pseudonym, "Lewis Padgett," under which name appeared mysteries, fantasies, and science fiction.

Kuttner's characteristic tone in his mature work usually involves a flavoring of wry comedy. Yet several of his stories are grim, and one of them, "The Graveyard Rats," is truly horrendous. It appeared in *Weird Tales* in March 1936 and was his first published work. This tale, which has haunted so many readers, haunted its author as well. He was a teenager when he wrote it, but it proved so unforgettable that he was constantly reminded of it, even after decades of other writing. Kuttner may have come to consider it a youthful indiscretion, but it is certainly more than that.

The repulsive rodents featured in this story are, along with spiders and snakes, the most popular pets in terror tales. Among the most important works to feature these belligerent beasts are J. Sheridan Le Fanu's "An Account of Some Strange Disturbances in Aungier Street," Bram Stoker's "The Judge's House," H. P. Lovecraft's "The Rats in the Walls,"

189

and Stephen Gilbert's *Ratman's Notebooks,* which became the film *Willard.* The story is also part of a recent American tradition ascribing the most terrible motives to people professionally involved in looking after the dead, a tradition that has produced such tales as Lovecraft's "In the Vault," Bradbury's "The Handler," and C. M. Eddy's "The Loved Dead." And yet, although there are many stories with which it can be compared, "The Graveyard Rats," with its overtones of isolation and claustrophobia, is one of a kind.

# THE GRAVEYARD RATS

# Henry Kuttner

Old Masson, the caretaker of one of Salem's oldest and most neglected cemeteries, had a feud with the rats. Generations ago they had come up from the wharves and settled in the graveyard, a colony of abnormally large rats, and when Masson had taken charge after the inexplicable disappearance of the former caretaker, he decided that they must go. At first he set traps for them and put poisoned food by their burrows, and later he tried to shoot them, but it did no good. The rats stayed, multiplying and overrunning the graveyard with their ravenous hordes.

They were large, even for the *mus decumanus,* which sometimes measures fifteen inches in length, exclusive of the naked pink and gray tail. Masson had caught glimpses of some as large as good-sized cats, and when, once or twice, the grave-diggers had uncovered their burrows, the malodorous tunnels were large enough to enable a man to crawl into them on his hands and knees. The ships that had come generations ago from distant ports to the rotting Salem wharves had brought strange cargoes.

Masson wondered sometimes at the extraordinary size of these burrows. He recalled certain vaguely disturbing legends he had heard since coming to ancient, witch-haunted Salem—tales of a moribund, inhuman life that was said to exist in forgotten burrows in the earth. The old days, when Cotton Mather had hunted down the evil cults that worshipped Hecate and the dark Magna Mater in frightful orgies, had passed; but dark gabled houses still leaned perilously toward each other over narrow cobbled streets, and blasphemous secrets and mysteries were said to be hidden in subterranean cellars and caverns, where forgotten pagan rites were still celebrated in defiance of law and sanity. Wagging their gray heads wisely, the elders declared that there were worse things than rats and maggots crawling in the unhallowed earth of the ancient Salem cemeteries. .

And then, too, there was this curious dread of the rats. Masson disliked and respected the ferocious little rodents, for he knew the danger that lurked in their flashing, needle-sharp fangs; but he could not understand the inexplicable horror which the oldsters held for deserted, rat-infested houses. He had heard vague rumors of ghoulish beings that dwelt far underground, and that had the power of commanding the rats, marshaling them like horrible armies. The rats, the old men whispered, were messengers between this world and the grim and ancient caverns far below Salem. Bodies had been stolen from graves for nocturnal subterranean feasts, they said. The myth of the Pied Piper is a fable that hides a blasphemous horror, and the black pits of Avernus have brought forth hell-spawned monstrosities that never venture into the light of day.

Masson paid little attention to these tales. He did not fraternize with his neighbors, and, in fact, did all he could to hide the existence of the rats from intruders. Investigation, he realized, would undoubtedly mean the opening of many graves. And while some of the gnawed, empty coffins could be attributed to the activities of the rats, Masson might find it difficult to explain the mutilated bodies that lay in some of the coffins.

The purest gold is used in filling teeth, and this gold is not removed when a man is buried. Clothing, of course, is another matter; for usually the undertaker provides a plain broadcloth suit that is cheap and easily recognizable. But gold is another matter; and sometimes, too, there were medical students and less reputable doctors who were in need of cadavers, and not over-scrupulous as to where these were obtained.

So far Masson had successfully managed to discourage investigation. He had fiercely denied the existence of the rats, even though they sometimes robbed him of his prey. Masson did not care what happened to the bodies after he had performed his gruesome thefts, but the rats inevitably dragged away the whole cadaver through the hole they gnawed in the coffin.

The size of these burrows occasionally worried Masson. Then, too, there was the curious circumstance of the coffins always being gnawed open at the end, never at the side or top. It was almost as though the rats were working under the direction of some impossibly in-telligent leader.

Now he stood in an open grave and threw a last sprinkling of wet earth on the heap beside the pit. It was raining, a slow, cold drizzle that for weeks had been descending from soggy black clouds. The graveyard was a slough of yellow, sucking mud, from which the rain-washed tombstones stood up in irregular battalions. The rats had retreated to their burrows, and Masson had not seen one for days. But his gaunt, unshaved face was set in frowning lines; the coffin on which he was standing was a wooden one.

The body had been buried several days earlier, but Masson had not dared to disinter it before. A relative of the dead man had been coming to the grave at intervals, even in the drenching rain. But he would hardly come at this late hour, no matter how much grief he might be suffering, Masson thought, grinning wryly. He straightened and laid the shovel aside.

From the hill on which the ancient graveyard lay he could see the lights of Salem flickering dimly through the downpour. He drew a flashlight from his pocket. He would need light now. Taking up the spade, he bent and examined the fastenings of the coffin.

Abruptly he stiffened. Beneath his feet he sensed an unquiet stirring and scratching, as though something were moving within the coffin. For a moment a pang of superstitious fear shot through Masson, and then rage replaced it as he realized the significance of the sound. The rats had forestalled him again!

In a paroxysm of anger Masson wrenched at the fastenings of the coffin. He got the sharp edge of the shovel under the lid and pried it up until he could finish the job with his hands. Then he sent the flashlight's cold beam darting down into the coffin.

Rain spattered against the white satin lining; the coffin was empty. Masson saw a flicker of movement at the head of the case, and darted the light in that direction.

The end of the sarcophagus had been gnawed through, and a gaping hole led into dark-ness. A black shoe, limp and dragging, was disappearing as Masson watched, and abruptly he realized that the rats had forestalled him by only a few minutes. He fell on his hands and knees and made a hasty clutch at the shoe, and the flashlight incontinently fell into the coffin and went out. The shoe was tugged from his grasp, he heard a sharp, excited squealing, and then he had the flashlight again and was darting its light into the burrow.

It was a large one. It had to be, or the corpse could not have been dragged along it. Masson wondered at the size of the rats that could carry away a man's body, but the thought of the loaded revolver in his pocket fortified him. Probably if the corpse had been an ordinary one Masson would have left the rats with their spoils rather than venture into the narrow burrow, but he remembered an especially fine set of cuff-links he had observed, as well as a stickpin that was undoubtedly a genuine pearl. With scarcely a pause he clipped the flashlight to his belt and crept into the burrow.

It was a tight fit, but he managed to squeeze himself along. Ahead of him in the flashlight's glow he could see the shoes dragging along the wet earth of the bottom of the tunnel. He crept along the burrow as rapidly as he could, occasionally barely able to squeeze his lean body through the narrow walls.

The air was overpowering with its musty stench of carrion. If he could not reach the corpse in a minute, Masson decided, he would turn back. Belated fears were beginning to crawl, maggot-like, within his mind, but greed urged him on. He crawled forward, several times passing the mouths of adjoining tunnels. The walls of the burrow were damp and slimy, and twice lumps of dirt dropped behind him. The second time he paused and screwed his head around to look back. He could see nothing, of course, until he had unhooked the flashlight from his belt and reversed it.

Several clods lay on the ground behind him, and the danger of his position suddenly became real and terrifying. With thoughts of a cave-in making his pulse race, he decided to abandon the pursuit, even though he had now almost overtaken the corpse and the invisible things that pulled it. But he had overlooked one thing: the burrow was too narrow to allow him to turn.

Panic touched him briefly, but he remembered a side tunnel he had just passed, and backed awkwardly along the tunnel until he came to it. He thrust his legs into it, backing until he found himself able to turn. Then he hurriedly began to retrace his way, although his knees were bruised and painful.

Agonizing pain shot through his leg. He felt sharp teeth sink into his flesh, and kicked out frantically. There was a shrill squealing and the scurry of many feet. Flashing the light behind him, Masson caught his breath in a sob of fear as he saw a dozen great rats watching him intently, their slitted eyes glittering in the light. They were great misshapen things, as large as cats, and behind them he caught a glimpse of a dark shape that stirred and moved swiftly aside into the shadow; and he shuddered at the unbelievable size of the thing.

The light had held them for a moment, but they were edging closer, their teeth dull orange in the pale light. Masson tugged at his pistol, managed to extricate it from his pocket, and aimed carefully. It was an awkward position, and he tried to press his feet into the soggy sides of the burrow so that he should not inadvertently send a bullet into one of them.

The rolling thunder of the shot deafened him, for a time, and the clouds of smoke set him coughing. When he could hear again and the smoke had cleared, he saw that the rats were gone. He put the pistol back and began to creep swiftly along the tunnel, and then with a scurry and a rush they were upon him again.

They swarmed over his legs, biting and squealing insanely, and Masson shrieked horribly as he snatched for his gun. He fired without aiming, and only luck saved him from blowing a foot off. This time the rats did not retreat so far, but Masson was crawling as swiftly as he could along the burrow, ready to fire again at the first sound of another attack.

There was patter of feet and he sent the light stabbing back of him. A great gray rat paused and watched him. Its long ragged whiskers twitched, and its scabrous, naked tail was moving slowly from side to side. Masson shouted and the rat retreated.

He crawled on, pausing briefly, the black gap of a side tunnel at his elbow, as he made out a shapeless huddle on the damp clay a few yards ahead. For a second he thought it was a mass of earth that had been dislodged from the roof, and then he recognized it as a human body.

It was a brown and shriveled mummy, and with a dreadful unbelieving shock Masson realized that it was moving.

It was crawling toward him, and in the pale glow of the flashlight the man saw a frightful gargoyle face thrust into his own. It was the passionless, death's-head skull of a long-dead corpse, instinct with hellish life; and the glazed eyes swollen and bulbous betrayed the thing's blindness. It made a faint groaning sound as it crawled toward Masson, stretching its ragged and granulated lips in a grin of dreadful hunger. And Masson was frozen with abysmal fear and loathing.

Just before the Horror touched him, Masson flung himself frantically into the burrow at his side. He heard a scrambling noise at his heels, and the thing groaned dully as it came after him. Masson, glancing over his shoulder, screamed and propelled himself desperately through the narrow burrow. He crawled along awkwardly, sharp stones cutting his hands and knees. Dirt showered into his eyes, but he dared not pause even for a moment. He scrambled on, gasping, cursing, and praying hysterically.

Squealing triumphantly, the rats came at him, horrible hunger in their eyes. Masson almost succumbed to their vicious teeth before he succeeded in beating them off. The passage was narrowing, and in a frenzy of terror he kicked and screamed and fired until the hammer clicked on an empty shell. But he had driven them off.

He found himself crawling under a great stone, embedded in the roof, that dug cruelly into his back. It moved a little as his weight struck it, and an idea flashed into Masson's fright-crazed mind. If he could bring down the stone so that it blocked the tunnel!

The earth was wet and soggy from the rains, and he hunched himself half upright and dug away at the dirt around the stone. The rats were coming closer. He saw their eyes glowing in the reflection of the flashlight's beam. Still he clawed frantically at the earth. The stone was giving. He tugged at it and it rocked in its foundation.

A rat was approaching—the monster he had already glimpsed. Gray and leprous and hideous it crept forward with its orange teeth bared, and in its wake came the blind dead thing, groaning as it crawled. Masson gave a last frantic tug at the stone. He felt it slide downward, and then he went scrambling along the tunnel.

Behind him the stone crashed down, and he heard a sudden frightful shriek of agony. Clods showered upon his legs. A heavy weight fell on his feet and he dragged them free with difficulty. The entire tunnel was collapsing!

Gasping with fear, Masson threw himself forward as the soggy earth collapsed at his heels. The tunnel narrowed until he could barely use his hands and legs to propel himself; he wriggled forward like an eel and suddenly felt satin tearing beneath his clawing fingers, and then his head crashed against something that barred his path. He moved his legs, discovering that they were not pinned under the collapsed earth. He was lying flat on his stomach, and when he tried to raise himself he found that the roof was only a few inches from his back. Panic shot through him.

When the blind horror had blocked his path, he had flung himself desperately into a side tunnel, a tunnel that had no outlet. He was *in a coffin,* an empty coffin into which he had crept through the hole the rats had gnawed in its end!

He tried to turn on his back and found that he could not. The lid of the coffin pinned him down inexorably. Then he braced himself and strained at the coffin lid. It was immovable, and even if he could escape from the sarcophagus, how could he claw his way up through five feet of hard-packed earth?

He found himself gasping. It was dreadfully fetid, unbearably hot. In a paroxysm of terror he ripped and clawed at the satin until it was shredded. He made a futile attempt to dig with his feet at the earth from the collapsed burrow that blocked his retreat. If he were only able to reverse his position he might be able to claw his way through to air . . . air. . . .

White-hot agony lanced through his breast, throbbed in his eyeballs. His head seemed to be swelling, growing larger and larger; and suddenly he heard the exultant squealing of the rats. He began to scream insanely but could not drown them out. For a moment he thrashed about hysterically within his narrow prison, and then he was quiet, gasping for air. His eyelids closed, his blackened tongue protruded, and he sank down into the blackness of death with the mad squealing of the rats dinning in his ears.

# John Collier

John Collier (1901– ) is the author of dozens of devilishly witty and devastatingly weird short stories. He is one of those very rare masters of the sardonically sinister tale, achieving again and again an impeccable balance between horror and hilarity. Some critics are inclined to regard this as a minor achievement, but Collier's consistency makes his collected short stories a major work, even as a string of small gems can be collected into a magnificent necklace.

He is also a novelist, best known for the bizarre *His Monkey Wife: or, Married to a Chimp* (1930). The self-explanatory title can hardly convey the combination of delicacy and depravity with which he expresses his theme. His other novels include *Defy the Foul Fiend* and *Full Circle* (1933), the latter a futuristic fantasy about an England ravaged by war.

Migrating from his native land to Hollywood, Collier worked on a number of motion pictures. Probably his finest work in the field, although he is not usually identified with it, is the script of the award-winning film *The African Queen*. More recently, he has concocted a screenplay from John Milton's epic of heaven and hell, *Paradise Lost*. This effort is all the more remarkable because the script was published as a book, rather than produced as a movie.

Still, it is as a teller of tales that Collier will be best remembered. He has published them in several volumes, of which the most important are *Presenting Moonshine* (1941), *A Touch of Nutmeg* (1943), *Fancies and Goodnights* (1951), and *The John Collier Reader* (1972). Some of the best stories, originally published in magazines like *The New Yorker, Harper's, Atlantic Monthly,* and *Esquire,* have appeared again and again in each successive Collier collection.

A few of his early tales were, in their day, considered somewhat sexually suggestive, and they originally appeared in private printings. Although these are hardly shocking by today's standards, they have retained their entertainment value unimpaired. He has also written a few unrelievedly grim narratives, including "Bird of Prey" and "Special Delivery." His finest fiction, though, is likely to elicit a mixture of chills and uneasy chuckles. Among his best are such tales of crime as "Back for Christmas," "Over Insurance," and "Wet Saturday." His fantasies include "Thus I Refute Beelzy," "Bottle Party," "The Lady on the Gray," "The Devil, George and Rosie," and "Green Thoughts."

"Rope Enough," one of Collier's most startling stories, draws its inspiration from accounts of the notorious "Indian Rope Trick." Numerous historical documents assert that this trick has been seen, exactly as described in the story, but no modern magician has been able to duplicate it. A committee of English conjurors studied the matter in 1934 and concluded that producing such an illusion was impossible and that its performance was only a legend. The *Times of India* offered 10,000 rupees for a single demonstration, but nobody collected it. So perhaps the hero of this story has reason to sneer, even as he will certainly have cause to regret it.

# ROPE ENOUGH

# John Collier

Henry Fraser, well assured that almost everything is done by mirrors, was given a job in India. No sooner had he set foot on shore than he burst into a horse-laugh. Those who were meeting him asked in some alarm the cause of this merriment. He replied he was laughing at the mere idea of the Indian Rope Trick.

He emitted similar startling sounds, and gave the same explanation, at a tiffin where he was officially made welcome; likewise on the Maidan, over *chota peg,* in rickshaws, in bazaars, in the Club, and on the polo ground. Soon he was known from Bombay to Calcutta as the man who laughed at the Indian Rope Trick, and he gloried in the well-deserved publicity.

There came a day, however, when he was sitting in his bungalow, bored to death. His boy entered, and, with suitable salaams, announced that a mountebank was outside, who craved the honor of entertaining the *sahib* with a performance of the Indian Rope Trick. Laughing heartily, Henry consented, and moved out to his chair upon the veranda.

Below, in the dusty compound, stood a native who was emaciated to a degree, and who had with him a spry youngster, a huge mat basket, and a monstrous great sword. Out of the basket he dragged some thirty feet of stout rope, made a pass or two, and slung it up into the air. It stayed there. Henry chuckled.

The boy then, with a caper, sprang at the rope, clutched it, and went up hand over hand, like a monkey. When he reached the top he vanished into thin air. Henry guffawed.

Soon the man, looking upwards with an anxious expression, began to hoot and holler after the boy. He called him down, he ordered him down, he begged him down, he began to swear and curse horribly. The boy, it seemed, took no notice at all. Henry roared.

Now the black, clapping his abominable great scimitar between his teeth, took hold of the rope himself, and went up it like a sailor. He, also, disappeared at the top. Henry's mirth increased.

Pretty soon some yelps and squeals were heard coming out of the empty air, and then a blood-curdling scream. Down came a leg, thump on to the ground, then an arm, a thigh, a head and other joints, and finally (no ladies being present), a bare backside, which struck the earth like a bomb. Henry went into fits.

Then the black came sliding down, holding on with one hand, fairly gibbering with excitement. He presented to Henry, with a salaam, his reeking blade for inspection. Henry rocked in his chair.

The black, seemingly overwhelmed with remorse, gathered up the fragments of his little stooge, lavishing a hundred lamentations and endearments upon each grisly member, and he stowed them all in the giant basket.

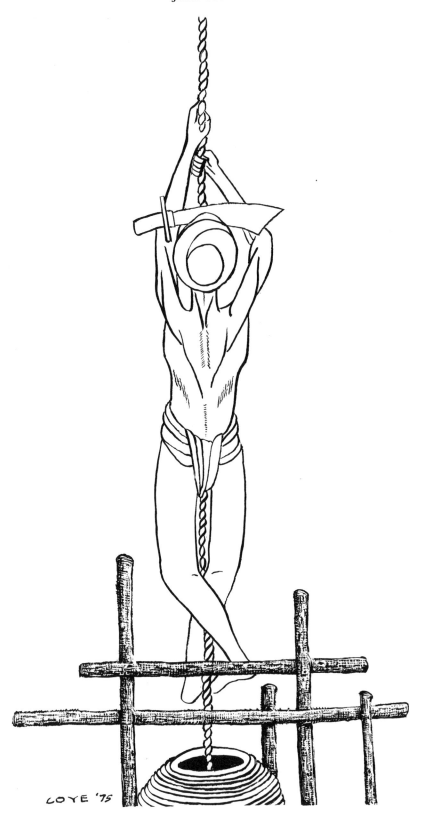

LOYE '75

At that moment Henry, feeling the time had come for a showdown, and willing to bet a thousand to one they'd planted the whole compound full of mirrors before calling him out there, pulled out his revolver, and blazed away all six chambers in different directions, in the expectation of splintering at least one of those deceiving glasses.

Nothing of that sort happened, but the black, doing a quick pirouette in alarm, looked down in the dust at his feet, and held up a villainous little snake, no thicker than a lead pencil, which had been killed by one of Henry's stray bullets. He gave a gasp of relief, touched his turban very civilly, turned round again, and made a pass or two over the basket. At once, with a wiggle and a frisk, the boy sprang out, whole, alive, smiling, full of health and wickedness.

The black hastily hauled down the rope, and came cringing up to Henry, overflowing with gratitude for having been saved from that villainous little snake, which was nothing more nor less than a krait—one nip and a man goes round and round like a Catherine wheel for eleven seconds; then he is as dead as mutton.

"But for the Heavenborn," said the black, "I should have been a goner, and my wicked little boy here, who is my pride and delight, must have lain dismembered in the basket till the *sahib's* servants condescended to throw him to the crocodiles. Our worthless lives, our scanty goods, are all at the *sahib's* disposal."

"That's all right," said Henry. "All I ask is, show me how the trick is worked, or the laugh will be on me from now on."

"Would not the *sahib*," said the black diffidently, "prefer the secret of a superb hair-restorer?"

"No. No," said Henry. "Nothing but the trick."

"I have," said the black, "the secret of a very peculiar tonic, which the *sahib* (not now, of course, but in later life) might find——"

"The trick," said Henry, "and without further delay."

"Very well," said the black. "Nothing in the world could be more simple. You make a pass, like that——"

"Wait a minute," said Henry. "Like that?"

"Exactly," said the black. "You then throw up the rope—so. You see? It sticks."

"So it does," said Henry.

"Any boy can climb," said the black. "Up boy! Show the *sahib*."

The boy, smiling, climbed up and disappeared.

"Now," said the black, "if the *sahib* will excuse me, I shall be back immediately." And with that he climbed up himself, threw down the boy in sections, and speedily rejoined Henry on the ground.

"All that," said he, scooping up legs and arms as he spoke, "all that can be done by anyone. There is a little knack, however, to the pass I make at this juncture. If the *sahib* will deign to observe closely—like that."

"Like that?" said Henry.

"You have it to perfection," said the black.

"Very interesting," said Henry. "Tell me, what's up there at the top of the rope?"

"Ah, *sahib*," said the black with a smile, "that is something truly delightful."

With that he salaamed and departed, taking with him his rope, his giant basket, his tremendous great scimitar, and his wicked little boy. Henry was left feeling rather morose: he was known from the Deccan to the Khyber Pass as the man who laughed at the Indian Rope Trick, and now he could laugh no more.

He decided to keep very quiet about it, but this unfortunately was not enough. At tiffin, at *chota peg,* at the Club, on the Maidan, in the bazaar, and at polo, he was expected to laugh like a horse, and in India one has to do what is expected of one. Henry became extremely unpopular, cabals were formed against him, and soon he was hoofed out of the Service.

This was the more distressing as in the meantime he had married a wife, strong-featured, upstanding, well groomed, straight-eyed, a little peremptory in manner, and as jealous as a demon, but in all respects a *mem-sahib* of the highest type, who knew very well what was due to her. She told Henry he had better go to America and make a fortune. He agreed, they packed up, and off they went to America.

"I hope," said Henry, as they stood looking at the skyline of New York, "I hope I shall make that fortune."

"Of course," said she. "You must insist upon it."

"Very well, my dear," said he.

On landing, however, he discovered that all the fortunes had already been made, a discovery which very generally awaits those who visit America on this errand, and after some weeks of drifting about from place to place, he was prepared to cut his demand down to a mere job, then to a lesser job, and finally to the price of a meal and a bed for the night.

They reached this extremity in a certain small town in the Middle West. "There is nothing for it, my dear," said Henry. "We shall have to do the Indian Rope Trick."

His wife cried out very bitterly at the idea of a *mem-sahib* performing this native feat in a Middle Western town, before a Middle Western audience. She reproached him with the loss of his job, the poor quality of his manhood, with the time he let her little dog get run over on the Bund, and with a glance he had cast at a Parsee maiden at Bombay. Nevertheless, reason and hunger prevailed: they pawned her last trinket, and invested in a rope, a roomy grip, and a monstrous old rusty scimitar they discovered in a junk-shop.

When she saw this last, Henry's wife flatly refused to go on, unless she was given the star part and Henry took that of the stooge. "But," said Henry, drawing an apprehensive thumb down the notched and jagged edge of the grim and rusty bilbo. "But," said he, "you don't know how to make the passes."

"You shall teach me," she said, "and if anything goes wrong you will have only yourself to blame."

So Henry showed her. You may be sure he was very thorough in his instructions. In the end she mastered them perfectly, and there was nothing left to do but to stain themselves with coffee. Henry improvised a turban and loin-cloth: she wore a *sari* and a pair of ash-trays borrowed from the hotel. They sought out a convenient waste lot, a large crowd collected, and the show began.

Up went the rope. Sure enough, it stuck. The crowd, with a multiple snigger, whispered that everything was done by mirrors. Henry, not without a good deal of puffing, went up hand over hand. When he got to the top, he forgot the crowd, the act, his wife, and even himself, so surprised and delighted was he by the sight that met his eyes.

He found himself crawling out of something like a well, on to what seemed to be solid ground. The landscape about him was not at all like that below: it was like an Indian paradise, full of dells, bowers, scarlet ibises, and heaven knows what all. However, his surprise and delight came less from these features of the background than from the presence of a young female in the nearest of these bowers or arbors, which happened to be all wreathed, canopied, overgrown and intertwined with passion flowers. This delightful creature, who was a positive houri, and very lightly attired, seemed to be expecting Henry, and greeted him with rapture.

Henry, who had a sufficiently affectionate nature, flung his arms round her neck and gazed deeply into her eyes. These were surprisingly eloquent: they seemed to say, "Why not make hey hey while the sun shines?"

He found the notion entirely agreeable, and planted a lingering kiss on her lips, noting only with a dim and careless annoyance that his wife was hooting and hollering from below. "What person of any tact or delicacy," thought he, "could hoot and holler at such a moment?" and he dismissed her from his mind.

You may imagine his mortification when his delicious damsel suddenly repulsed him from her arms. He looked over his shoulder, and there was his wife, clambering over the edge, terribly red in the face, with the fury of a demon in her eye, and the mighty scimitar gripped well between her teeth.

Henry tried to rise, but she was beforehand with him, and while yet he had but one foot on the ground, she caught him one across the loins with the huge and jagged bilbo, which effectually hamstrung him, so that he fell grovelling at her feet. "For heaven's sake!" he cried. "It's all a trick. Part of the act. It means nothing. Remember our public. The show must go on."

"It shall," said she, striking at his arms and legs.

"Oh, those notches!" cried he. "I beg you, my dear, sharpen it a little upon a stone."

"It is good enough for you, you viper," said she, hacking away all the time. Pretty soon Henry was a limbless trunk.

"For the love of God," said he, "I hope you remember the passes. I can explain everything."

"To hell with the passes!" said she, and with a last swipe she sent his head rolling like a football.

She was not long in picking up the scattered fragments of poor Henry, and flinging them down to earth, amid the applause and laughter of the crowd, who were more than ever convinced it was all done by mirrors.

Then, gripping her scimitar, she was about to swarm down after him, not from any softhearted intention of reassembling her unfortunate spouse, but rather to have another hack or two at some of the larger joints. At that moment she became aware of someone behind her, and, looking round, there was a divine young man, with the appearance of a Maharaja of the highest caste, an absolute Valentino, in whose eyes she seemed to read the words, "It is better to burn upon the bed of passion than in the chair of electricity."

This idea presented itself with an overwhelming appeal. She paused only to thrust her head through the aperture, and cry, "That's what happens to a pig of a man who betrays his wife with a beastly native," before hauling up the rope and entering into conversation with her charmer.

The police soon appeared upon the scene. There was nothing but a cooing sound above, as if invisible turtle doves were circling in amorous flight. Below, the various portions of Henry were scattered in the dust, and the blue-bottle flies were already settling upon them.

The crowd explained it was nothing but a trick, done with mirrors.

"It looks to me," said the sergeant, "as if the biggest one must have splintered right on top of him."

# Anthony Boucher

Anthony Boucher is the most renowned of the pseudonyms adopted by William Anthony Parker White (1911–1968). As Boucher, he had a remarkably rich and varied career as an author, an editor, and a critic. What is more surprising is that he practiced these three professions in three related but distinct genres: mystery, fantasy, and science fiction, fields whose followers have often been at odds with each other. Boucher rose above such arbitrary divisions, earning the respect and affection of both public and professionals, while at the same time demonstrating that all of these genres share a common interest in excitement and imagination.

For seventeen years, Boucher wrote the "Criminals at Large" column reviewing mysteries for the *New York Times*. His first detective novel was published in 1937; his most unusual was *Rocket to the Morgue* (1942), which appeared under another of his aliases, "H. H. Holmes." It is a clever locked-room mystery in which most of the suspects are writers or fans of science fiction, and many of the characters are based on real people. "I hope," wrote Boucher, "that some of the regular readers of whodunits may find this picture of the field provocative enough to make them investigate further."

In 1949, he assumed editorship (with J. Francis McMoas) of the *Magazine of Fantasy and Science Fiction*, a publication that made a successful effort to raise the literary quality in the latter field. It also provided a showcase for supernatural stories during an era when such forums were all too infrequent. The first issue included an H. H. Holmes terror tale, "Review Copy"; and in 1952 the magazine featured another of Boucher's important borderline stories, "The Anamoly of the Empty Man," in which he combined detection and the demonic in a problem about mysteriously missing men that has two solutions, one scientific and one supernatural.

Boucher's first published fantasy, "Snulbug," appeared in the magazine *Unknown Worlds* in 1941. This is a story about an incompetent imp without the power to grant useful wishes, and it is typical of the whimsical themes with which the magazine, previously known as *Unknown*, helped to revolutionize the supernatural story. Among his other contributions in the same vein was the novelette *The Compleat Werewolf*, which became the title of Boucher's entertaining collection of fantasies, published in 1969.

*Unknown* had a darker side, too, and it was never better represented than by "They Bite," first published in June 1942. It is set against a background of World War II espionage, in keeping with the magazine's policy of presenting traditional terrors in modern dress. Boucher touches on an ancient horror that has been rarely treated in recent fiction, the legendary ogre. He manages to create something even more gruesome than the old stories, cited in the text, from which he drew his inspiration. Some of these citations are factual, and some are mythical. As Boucher wrote in 1962, "It is a regrettable but demonstrable fact that there never was a monster named Sawney Bean who lived in a cave in Scotland some four centuries ago, bred a large family by compound incest, and fed his brood with the flesh of helpless travelers," yet Bean's actual existence has been asserted by several eminent if gullible authorities. And if there were no Carkers, at least none gifted with the incredible powers described by Boucher, it is hardly a matter for regret.

---

# THEY BITE

---

# Anthony Boucher

There was no path, only the almost vertical ascent. Crumbled rock for a few yards, with the roots of sage finding their scanty life in the dry soil. Then jagged outcroppings of crude crags, sometimes with accidental footholds, sometimes with overhanging and untrustworthy branches of greasewood, sometimes with no aid to climbing but the leverage of your muscles and the ingenuity of your balance.

The sage was as drably green as the rock was drably brown. The only color was the occasional rosy spikes of a barrel cactus.

Hugh Tallant swung himself up onto the last pinnacle. It had a deliberate, shaped look about it—a petrified fortress of Lilliputians, a Gibraltar of pygmies. Tallant perched on its battlements and unslung his field glasses.

The desert valley spread below him. The tiny cluster of buildings that was Oasis, the exiguous cluster of palms that gave name to the town and shelter of his own tent and the shack he was building, the dead-ended highway leading straightforwardly to nothing, the oiled roads diagraming the vacant blocks of an optimistic subdivision.

Tallant saw none of these. His glasses were fixed beyond the oasis and the town of Oasis on the dry lake. The gliders were clear and vivid to him, and the uniformed men busy with them were as sharply and minutely visible as a nest of ants under glass. The training school was more than usually active. One glider in particular, strange to Tallant, seemed the focus of attention. Men would come and examine it and glance back at the older models in comparison.

Only the corner of Tallant's left eye was not preoccupied with the new glider. In that corner something moved, something little and thin and brown as the earth. Too large for a rabbit, much too small for a man. It darted across that corner of vision, and Tallant found gliders oddly hard to concentrate on.

He set down the bifocals and deliberately looked about him. His pinnacle surveyed the narrow, flat area of the crest. Nothing stirred. Nothing stood out against the sage and rock but one barrel of rosy spikes. He took up the glasses again and resumed his observations. When he was done, he methodically entered the results in the little black notebook.

His hand was still white. The desert is cold and often sunless in winter. But it was a firm hand, and as well trained as his eyes, fully capable of recording faithfully the designs and dimensions which they had registered so accurately.

Once his hand slipped, and he had to erase and redraw, leaving a smudge that displeased him. The lean, brown thing had slipped across the edge of his vision again. Going toward the east edge, he would swear, where that set of rocks jutted like the spines on the back of a stegosaur.

Only when his notes were completed did he yield to curiosity, and even then with cynical self-reproach. He was physically tired, for him an unusual state, from this daily climbing and from clearing the ground for his shack-to-be. The eye muscles play odd nervous tricks. There could be nothing behind the stegosaur's armor.

There was nothing. Nothing alive and moving. Only the torn and half-plucked carcass of a bird, which looked as though it had been gnawed by some small animal.

It was halfway down the hill—hill in Western terminology, though anywhere east of the Rockies it would have been considered a sizable mountain—that Tallant again had a glimpse of a moving figure.

But this was no trick of a nervous eye. It was not little nor thin nor brown. It was tall and broad and wore a loud red-and-black lumberjacket. It bellowed, "Tallant!" in a cheerful and lusty voice.

Tallant drew near the man and said, "Hello." He paused and added, "Your advantage, I think."

The man grinned broadly. "Don't know me? Well, I daresay ten years is a long time, and the California desert ain't exactly the Chinese rice fields. How's stuff? Still loaded down with Secrets for Sale?"

Tallant tried desperately not to react to that shot, but he stiffened a little. "Sorry. The prospector getup had me fooled. Good to see you again, Morgan."

The man's eyes narrowed. "Just having my little joke," he smiled. "Of course you wouldn't have no serious reason for mountain climbing around a glider school, now, would you? And you'd kind of need field glasses to keep an eye on the pretty birdies."

"I'm out here for my health." Tallant's voice sounded unnatural even to himself.

"Sure, sure. You were always in it for your health. And come to think of it, my own health ain't been none too good lately. I've got me a little cabin way to hell-and-gone around here, and I do me a little prospecting now and then. And somehow it just strikes me, Tallant, like maybe I hit a pretty good lode today."

"Nonsense, old man. You can see—"

"I'd sure hate to tell any of them Army men out at the field some of the stories I know about China and the kind of men I used to know out there. Wouldn't cotton to them stories a bit, the Army wouldn't. But if I was to have a drink too many and get talkative-like—"

"Tell you what," Tallant suggested brusquely. "It's getting near sunset now, and my tent's chilly for evening visits. But drop around in the morning and we'll talk over old times. Is rum still your tipple?"

"Sure is. Kind of expensive now, you understand—"

"I'll lay some in. You can find the place easily—over by the oasis. And we . . . we might be able to talk about your prospecting, too."

Tallant's thin lips were set firm as he walked away.

The bartender opened a bottle of beer and plunked it on the damp-circled counter. "That'll be twenty cents," he said, then added as an afterthought, "Want a glass? Sometimes tourists do."

Tallant looked at the others sitting at the counter—the red-eyed and unshaven old man, the flight sergeant unhappily drinking a Coke—it was after Army hours for beer—the young man with the long, dirty trench coat and the pipe and the new-looking brown beard —and saw no glasses. "I guess I won't be a tourist," he decided.

This was the first time Tallant had had a chance to visit the Desert Sport Spot. It was as well to be seen around in a community. Otherwise people begin to wonder and say, "Who is that man out by the oasis? Why don't you ever see him anyplace?"

The Sport Spot was quiet that night. The four of them at the counter, two Army boys shooting pool, and a half-dozen of the local men gathered about a round poker table, soberly and wordlessly cleaning a construction worker whose mind seemed more on his beer than on his cards.

"You just passing through?" the bartender asked sociably.

Tallant shook his head. "I'm moving in. When the Army turned me down for my lungs, I decided I better do something about it. Heard so much about your climate here I thought I might as well try it."

"Sure thing," the bartender nodded. "You take up until they started this glider school, just about every other guy you meet in the desert is here for his health. Me, I had sinus, and look at me now. It's the air."

Tallant breathed the atmosphere of smoke and beer suds, but did not smile. "I'm looking forward to miracles."

"You'll get 'em. Whereabouts you staying?"

"Over that way a bit. The agent called it 'the old Carker place.' "

Tallant felt the curious listening silence and frowned. The bartender had started to speak and then thought better of it. The young man with the beard looked at him oddly. The old man fixed him with red and watery eyes that had a faded glint of pity in them. For a moment, Tallant felt a chill that had nothing to do with the night air of the desert.

The old man drank his beer in quick gulps and frowned as though trying to formulate a sentence. At last he wiped beer from his bristly lips and said, "You wasn't aiming to stay in the adobe, was you?"

"No. It's pretty much gone to pieces. Easier to rig me up a lttle shack than try to make the adobe livable. Meanwhile, I've got a tent."

"That's all right, then, mebbe. But mind you don't go poking around that there adobe."

"I don't think I'm apt to. But why not? Want another beer?"

The old man shook his head reluctantly and slid from his stool to the ground. "No thanks. I don't rightly know as I —"

"Yes?"

"Nothing. Thanks all the same." He turned and shuffled to the door.

Tallant smiled. "But why should I stay clear of the adobe?" he called after him.

The old man mumbled.

"What?"

"They bite," said the old man, and went out shivering into the night.

The bartender was back at his post. "I'm glad he didn't take that beer you offered him," he said. "Along about this time in the evening I have to stop serving him. For once he had the sense to quit."

Tallant pushed his own empty bottle forward. "I hope I didn't frighten him away."

"Frighten? Well, mister, I think maybe that's just what you did do. He didn't want beer that sort of came, like you might say, from the old Carker place. Some of the old-timers here, they're funny that way."

Tallant grinned. "Is it haunted?"

"Not what you'd call haunted, no. No ghosts there that I ever heard of." He wiped the counter with a cloth and seemed to wipe the subject away with it.

The flight sergeant pushed his Coke bottle away, hunted in his pocket for nickels, and went over to the pinball machine. The young man with the beard slid onto his vacant stool. "Hope old Jake didn't worry you," he said.

Tallant laughed. "I suppose every town has its deserted homestead with a grisly tradition. But this sounds a little different. No ghosts, and they bite. Do you know anything about it?"

"A little," the young man said seriously. "A little. Just enough to—"

Tallant was curious. "Have one on me and tell me about it."

The flight sergeant swore bitterly at the machine.

Beer gurgled through the beard. "You see," the young man began, "the desert's so big you can't be alone in it. Ever notice that? It's all empty and there's nothing in sight, but there's always something moving over there where you can't quite see it. It's something very dry and thin and brown, only when you look around it isn't there. Ever see it?"

"Optical fatigue—" Tallant began.

"Sure. I know. Every man to his own legend. There isn't a tribe of Indians hasn't got some way of accounting for it. You've heard of the Watchers? And the twentieth-century white man comes along, and it's optical fatigue. Only in the nineteenth century things weren't quite the same, and there were the Carkers."

"You've got a special localized legend?"

"Call it that. You glimpse things out of the corner of your mind, same like you glimpse lean, dry things out of the corner of your eye. You encase 'em in solid circumstance and they're not so bad. That is known as the Growth of Legend. The Folk Mind in Action. You take the Carkers and the things you don't quite see and you put 'em together. And they bite."

Tallant wondered how long that beard had been absorbing beer. "And what were the Carkers?" he prompted politely.

"Ever hear of Sawney Bean? Scotland—reign of James First, or maybe the Sixth, though I think Roughead's wrong on that for once. Or let's be more modern—ever hear of the Benders? Kansas in the 1870s? No? Ever hear of Procrustes? Or Polyphemus? Or Fee fi-fo-fum?"

"There are ogres, you know. They're no legend. They're fact, they are. The inn where nine guests left for every ten that arrived, the mountain cabin that sheltered travelers from the snow, sheltered them all winter till the melting spring uncovered their bones, the lonely stretches of road that so many passengers traveled halfway—you'll find 'em everywhere. All over Europe and pretty much in this country too before communications became what they are. Profitable business. And it wasn't just the profit. The Benders made money, sure; but that wasn't why they killed all their victims as carefully as a kosher butcher. Sawney Bean got so he didn't give a damn about the profit; he just needed to lay in more meat for the winter.

"And think of the chances you'd have at an oasis."

"So these Carkers of yours were, as you call them, ogres?"

"Carkers, ogres—maybe they were Benders. The Benders were never seen alive, you know, after the townspeople found those curiously butchered bones. There's a rumor they got this far west. And the time checks pretty well. There wasn't any town here in the eighties. Just a couple of Indian families, last of a dying tribe living on at the oasis. They vanished after the Carkers moved in. That's not so surprising. The white race is a sort of super-ogre, anyway. Nobody worried about them. But they used to worry about why so many travelers never got across this stretch of desert. The travelers used to stop over at the Carkers', you see, and somehow they often never got any farther. Their wagons'd be found maybe fifteen miles beyond in the desert. Sometimes they found the bones, too, parched and white. Gnawed-looking, they said sometimes."

"And nobody ever did anything about these Carkers?"

"Oh, sure. We didn't have King James Sixth—only I still think it was First—to ride up on a great white horse for a gesture, but twice Army detachments came here and wiped them all out."

"Twice? One wiping-out would do for most families." Tallant smiled.

"Uh-uh. That was no slip. They wiped out the Carkers twice because, you see, once didn't do any good. They wiped 'em out and still travelers vanished and still there were gnawed bones. So they wiped 'em out again. After that they gave up, and people detoured the oasis. It made a longer, harder trip, but after all—"

Tallant laughed. "You mean to say these Carkers were immortal?"

"I don't know about immortal. They somehow just didn't die very easy. Maybe, if they were the Benders—and I sort of like to think they were—they learned a little more about what they were doing out here on the desert. Maybe they put together what the Indians knew and what they knew, and it worked. Maybe Whatever they made their sacrifices to understood them better out here than in Kansas."

"And what's become of them—aside from seeing them out of the corner of the eye?"

"There's forty years between the last of the Carker history and this new settlement at the oasis. And people won't talk much about what they learned here in the first year or so. Only that they stay away from that old Carker adobe. They tell some stories— The priest says he was sitting in the confessional one hot Saturday afternoon and thought he heard a penitent come in. He waited a long time and finally lifted the gauze to see was anybody there. Something was there, and it bit. He's got three fingers on his right hand now, which looks funny as hell when he gives a benediction."

Tallant pushed their two bottles toward the bartender. "That yarn, my young friend, has earned another beer. How about it, bartender? Is he always cheerful like this, or is this just something he's improvised for my benefit?"

The bartender set out the fresh bottles with great solemnity. "Me, I wouldn't've told you all that myself, but then, he's a stranger too and maybe don't feel the same way we do here. For him it's just a story."

"It's more comfortable that way," said the young man with the beard, and he took a firm hold on his beer bottle.

"But as long as you've heard that much," said the bartender, "you might as well— It was last winter, when we had that cold spell. You heard funny stories that winter. Wolves coming into prospectors' cabins just to warm up. Well, business wasn't so good. We don't have a license for hard liquor, and the boys don't drink much beer when it's that cold. But they used to come in anyway because we've got that big oil burner.

"So one night there's a bunch of 'em in here—old Jake was here, that you was talking to, and his dog Jigger—and I think I hear somebody else come in. The door creaks a little. But I don't see nobody, and the poker game's going, and we're talking just like we're talking now, and all of a sudden I hear a kind of a noise like crack! over there in that corner behind the juke box near the burner.

"I go over to see what goes and it gets away before I can see it very good. But it was little and thin and it didn't have no clothes on. It must've been damned cold that winter."

"And what was the cracking noise?" Tallant asked dutifully.

"That? That was a bone. It must've strangled Jigger without any noise. He was a little dog. It ate most of the flesh, and if it hadn't cracked the bone for the marrow it could've finished. You can still see the spots over there. The blood never did come out."

There had been silence all through the story. Now suddenly all hell broke loose. The flight sergeant let out a splendid yell and began pointing excitedly at the pinball machine and yelling for his payoff. The construction worker dramatically deserted the poker game, knocking his chair over in the process, and announced lugubriously that these guys here had their own rules, see?

Any atmosphere of Carker-inspired horror was dissipated. Tallant whistled as he walked over to put a nickel in the jukebox. He glanced casually at the floor. Yes, there was a stain, for what that was worth.

He smiled cheerfully and felt rather grateful to the Carkers. They were going to solve his blackmail problem very neatly.

Tallant dreamed of power that night. It was a common dream with him. He was a ruler of the new American Corporate State that would follow the war; and he said to this man, "Come!" and he came, and to that man, "Go!" and he went, and to his servants, "Do this!" and they did it.

Then the young man with the beard was standing before him, and the dirty trench coat was like the robes of an ancient prophet. And the young man said, "You see yourself riding high, don't you? Riding the crest of the wave—the Wave of the Future, you call it. But there's a deep, dark undertow that you don't see, and that's a part of the Past. And the Present and even your Future. There is evil in mankind that is blacker even than your evil, and infinitely more ancient."

And there was something in the shadows behind the young man, something little and lean and brown.

Tallant's dream did not disturb him the following morning. Nor did the thought of the approaching interview with Morgan. He fried his bacon and eggs and devoured them cheerfully. The wind had died down for a change, and the sun was warm enough so that he could strip to the waist while he cleared land for his shack. His machete glinted brilliantly as it swung through the air and struck at the roots of the brush.

When Morgan arrived his full face was red and sweating.

"It's cool over there in the shade of the adobe," Tallant suggested. "We'll be more comfortable." And in the comfortable shade of the adobe he swung the machete once and clove Morgan's full, red, sweating face in two.

It was so simple. It took less effort than uprooting a clump of sage. And it was so safe. Morgan lived in a cabin way to hell-and-gone and was often away on prospecting trips. No one would notice his absence for months, if then. No one had any reason to connect him with Tallant. And no one in Oasis would hunt for him in the Carker-haunted adobe.

The body was heavy, and the blood dripped warm on Tallant's bare skin. With relief he dumped what had been Morgan on the floor of the adobe. There were no boards, no flooring. Just the earth. Hard, but not too hard to dig a grave in. And no one was likely to come poking around in this taboo territory to notice the grave. Let a year or so go by, and the grave and the bones it contained would be attributed to the Carkers.

The corner of Tallant's eye bothered him again. Deliberately he looked about the interior of the adobe.

The little furniture was crude and heavy, with no attempt to smooth down the strokes of the ax. It was held together with wooden pegs or half-rotted thongs. There were age-old cinders in the fireplace, and the dusty shards of a cooking jar among them.

And there was a deeply hollowed stone, covered with stains that might have been rust, if stone rusted. Behind it was a tiny figure, clumsily fashioned of clay and sticks. It was something like a man and something like a lizard, and something like the things that flit across the corner of the eye.

Curious now, Tallant peered about further. He penetrated to the corner that the one unglassed window lighted but dimly. And there he let out a little choking gasp. For a moment

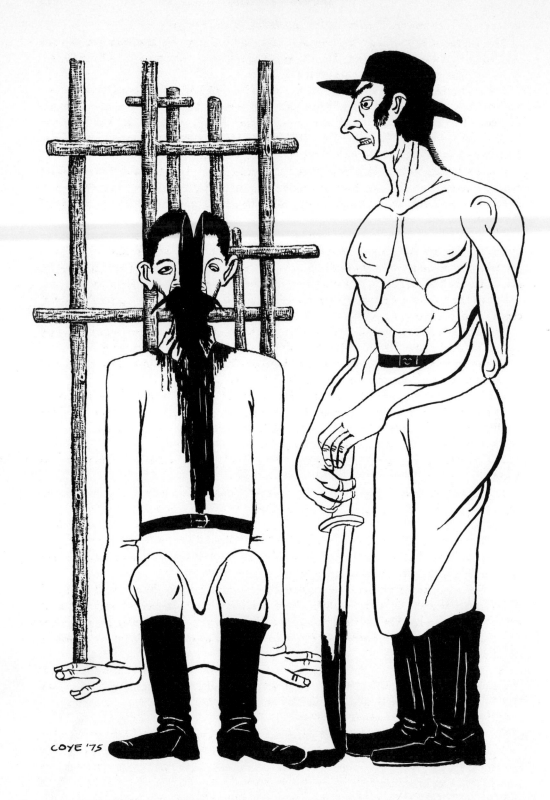

he was rigid with horror. Then he smiled and all but laughed aloud.

This explained everything. Some curious individual had seen this, and from his accounts had burgeoned the whole legend. The Carkers had indeed learned something from the Indians, but that secret was the art of embalming.

It was a perfect mummy. Either the Indian art had shrunk bodies, or this was that of a ten-year-old boy. There was no flesh. Only skin and bone and taut, dry stretches of tendon between. The eyelids were closed; the sockets looked hollow under them. The nose was sunken and almost lost. The scant lips were tightly curled back from the long and very white teeth, which stood forth all the more brilliantly against the deep-brown skin.

It was a curious little trove, this mummy. Tallant was already calculating the chances for raising a decent sum of money from an interested anthropologist—murder can produce such delightfully profitable chance by-products—when he noticed the infinitesimal rise and fall of the chest.

The Carker was not dead. It was sleeping.

Tallant did not dare stop to think beyond the instant. This was no time to pause to consider if such things were possible in a well-ordered world. It was no time to reflect on the disposal of the body of Morgan. It was a time to snatch up your machete and get out of there.

But in the doorway he halted. There, coming across the desert, heading for the adobe, clearly seen this time, was another—a female.

He made an involuntary gesture of indecision. The blade of the machete clanged ringingly against the adobe wall. He heard the dry shuffling of a roused sleeper behind him.

He turned fully now, the machete raised. Dispose of this nearer one first, then face the female. There was no room even for terror in his thoughts, only for action.

The lean brown shape darted at him avidly. He moved lightly away and stood poised for its second charge. It shot forward again. He took one step back, machete arm raised, and fell headlong over the corpse of Morgan. Before he could rise, the thin thing was upon him. Its sharp teeth had met through the palm of his left hand.

The machete moved swiftly. The thin dry body fell headless to the floor. There was no blood.

The grip of the teeth did not relax. Pain coursed up Tallant's left arm—a sharper, more bitter pain than you would expect from a bite. Almost as though venom—

He dropped the machete, and his strong white hand plucked and twisted at the dry brown lips. The teeth stayed clenched, unrelaxing. He sat bracing his back against the wall and gripped the head between his knees. He pulled. His flesh ripped, and blood formed dusty clots on the dirt floor. But the bite was firm.

His world had become reduced now to that hand and that head. Nothing outside mattered. He must free himself. He raised his aching arm to his face, and with his own teeth he tore at that unrelenting grip. The dry flesh crumbled away in desert dust, but the teeth were locked fast. He tore his lip against their white keenness, and tasted in his mouth the sweetness of blood and something else.

He staggered to his feet again. He knew what he must do. Later he could use cautery, a tourniquet, see a doctor with a story about a Gila monster—their heads grip too, don't they?—but he knew what he must do now.

He raised the machete and struck again.

His white hand lay on the brown floor, gripped by the white teeth in the brown face. He propped himself against the adobe wall, momentarily unable to move. His open wrist hung over the deeply hollowed stone. His blood and his strength and his life poured out before the little figure of sticks and clay.

The female stood in the doorway now, the sun bright on her thin brownness. She did not move. He knew that she was waiting for the hollow stone to fill.

# Robert Bloch

Robert Bloch (1917– ) is perhaps the foremost living writer in the field of the macabre, and his long career exemplifies most of the important trends in the genre. He began as a teen‑aged disciple of H. P. Lovecraft, contributing to the pages of *Weird Tales* such effective tales of the Cthulhu mythos as "The Faceless God." Later, he was an important author for John W. Campbell's magazine *Unknown,* which specialized in lighter, more urbane fantasies, a style that Bloch helped to create. And he wrote the scripts for the radio series "Stay Tuned for Terror."

When radio drama and pulp magazines were discontinued in the 1950s, Bloch was able to inject a note of terror into a number of powerful mystery and science fiction stories, thus helping to keep the genre alive during a difficult period. He achieved a major breakthrough in 1960 when his novel *Psycho* was turned into a brilliant film by Alfred Hitchcock; since then Bloch has penned the screenplays for a number of motion pictures, including such critically praised productions as *The House That Dripped Blood* (1971) and *Asylum* (1972). He has also provided stories and scripts for most of the better television programs specializing in mystery, science fiction, and the supernatural.

Bloch has written countless short tales of terror, and they have been collected in numerous volumes; the first of these was *The Opener of the Way,* published in 1945. Others include *Pleasant Dreams, Tales in a Jugular Vein, The Living Demons,* and *Dragons and Nightmares.* Among his best stories are "Enoch," "The Cheaters," "The Sorceror's Apprentice," "Nursemaid to Nightmares," "One Way to Mars," and "The Cloak."

Bloch's achievements have been recognized by his colleagues, who elected him national president of the Mystery Writers of America in 1971; he also received the major science fiction award, the "Hugo," for his powerful story "That Hell-Bound Train" (1958). Yet he often deprecates his own work, perhaps because his writing does not duplicate the elaborately literary style prevalent in many great terror tales of the past. What Bloch offers instead is an important innovation and a major achievement: the effective use of modern American idiom to create macabre moods.

"Yours Truly, Jack the Ripper," perhaps his most celebrated tale, first appeared in *Weird Tales,* July 1943, and achieved wider recognition through radio and television broadcasts. It is an ingenious treatment of a subject that has fascinated writers for almost a century. Jack was a real person, one of the most vicious mass murderers in history, and has become a subject of much interest for several reasons. A flamboyant character, "Jack the Ripper" provided his own colorful alias in the poem, reproduced in this story, that was in fact delivered to the authorities. His decision to choose his victims among what his contemporaries might have called "fallen women" seems to have titillated countless commentators. Most of all, he (or possibly she) was never apprehended, and speculation about the identity of the killer has run rampant.

Bloch's story transcends its sources by making its villain not only a master criminal, but the very embodiment of the spirit of blood lust. Harlan Ellison's anthology of new science fiction and fantasy stories, *Dangerous Visions* (1967), elicited a sequel by Bloch, "A Toy for Juliette," and a further one by Ellison, "The Prowler in the City at the Edge of the World." The theme also inspired a Bloch script for the popular television series "Star Trek."

In 1975, Bloch received the Lifetime Achievement Award at the First World Fantasy Convention.

# YOURS TRULY, JACK THE RIPPER

## Robert Bloch

### 1

I looked at the stage Englishman. He looked at me.

"Sir Guy Hollis?" I asked.

"Indeed. Have I the pleasure of addressing John Carmody, the psychiatrist?"

I nodded. My eyes swept over the figure of my distinguished visitor. Tall, lean, sandy-haired—with the traditional tufted mustache. And the tweeds. I suspected a monocle concealed in a vest pocket, and wondered if he'd left his umbrella in the outer office.

But more than that, I wondered what the devil had impelled Sir Guy Hollis of the British Embassy to seek out a total stranger here in Chicago.

Sir Guy didn't help matters any as he sat down. He cleared his throat, glanced around nervously, tapped his pipe against the side of the desk. Then he opened his mouth.

"Mr. Carmody," he said, "have you ever heard of—Jack the Ripper?"

"The murderer?" I asked.

"Exactly. The greatest monster of them all. Worse than Springheel Jack or Crippen. Jack the Ripper. Red Jack."

"I've heard of him," I said.

"Do you know his history?"

"Listen, Sir Guy," I muttered. "I don't think we'll get any place swapping old wives' tales about famous crimes of history."

Another bulls-eye. He took a deep breath.

"This is no old wives' tale. It's a matter of life or death."

He was so wrapped up in his obsession he even talked that way. Well—I was willing to listen. We psychiatrists get paid for listening.

Reprinted by permission of the author and the author's agents, Scott Meredith Literary Agency, Inc., 580 Fifth Avenue, New York, New York 10036.

"Go ahead," I told him. "Let's have the story."

Sir Guy lit a cigarette and began to talk.

"London, 1888," he began. "Late summer and early fall. That was the time. Out of nowhere came the shadowy figure of Jack the Ripper—a stalking shadow with a knife, prowling through London's East End. Haunting the squalid dives of Whitechapel, Spitalfields. Where he came from no one knew. But he brought death. Death in a knife.

"Six times that knife descended to slash the throats and bodies of London's women. Drabs and alley sluts. August 7th was the date of the first butchery. They found her body lying there with 39 stab wounds. A ghastly murder. On August 31st, another victim. The press became interested. The slum inhabitants were more deeply interested still.

"Who was this unknown killer who prowled in their midst and struck at will in the deserted alley-ways of night-town? And what was more important—when would he strike again?

"September 8th was the date. Scotland Yard assigned special deputies. Rumors ran rampant. The atrocious nature of the slayings was the subject for shocking speculation.

"The killer used a knife—expertly. He cut throats and removed—certain portions—of the bodies after death. He chose victims and settings with a fiendish deliberation. No one saw him or heard him. But watchmen making their gray rounds in the dawn would stumble across the hacked and horrid thing that was the Ripper's handiwork.

"Who was he? What was he? A mad surgeon? A butcher? An insane scientist? A pathological degenerate escaped from an asylum? A deranged nobleman? A member of the London police?

"Then the poem appeared in the newspapers. The anonymous poem, designed to put a stop to speculations—but which only aroused public interest to a further frenzy. A mocking little stanza:

> *I'm not a butcher, I'm not a Yid*
> *Nor yet a foreign skipper,*
> *But I'm your own true loving friend,*
> *Yours truly—Jack the Ripper.*

"And on September 30th, two more throats were slashed open."

I interrupted Sir Guy for a moment.

"Very interesting," I commented. I'm afraid a faint hint of sarcasm crept into my voice.

He winced, but didn't falter in his narrative.

"There was silence, then, in London for a time. Silence, and a nameless fear. When would Red Jack strike again? They waited through October. Every figment of fog concealed his phantom presence. Concealed it well—for nothing was learned of the Ripper's identity, or his purpose. The drabs of London shivered in the raw wind of early November. Shivered, and were thankful for the coming of each morning's sun.

"November 9th. They found her in her room. She lay there very quietly, limbs neatly arranged. And beside her, with equal neatness, were laid her head and heart. The Ripper had outdone himself in execution.

"Then, panic. But needless panic. For though press, police, and populace alike waited in sick dread, Jack the Ripper did not strike again.

"Months passed. A year. The immediate interest died, but not the memory. They said Jack had skipped to America. That he had committed suicide. They said—and they wrote. They've written ever since. Theories, hypotheses, arguments, treatises. But to this day no one knows who Jack the Ripper was. Or why he killed. Or why he stopped killing."

Sir Guy was silent. Obviously he expected some comment from me.

"You tell the story well," I remarked. "Though with a slight emotional bias."

"I've got all the documents," said Sir Guy Hollis. "I've made a collection of existing data and studied it."

I stood up. "Well," I yawned, in mock fatigue, "I've enjoyed your little bedtime story a great deal, Sir Guy. It was kind of you to abandon your duties at the British Embassy to drop in on a poor psychiatrist and regale him with your anecdotes."

Goading him always did the trick.

"I suppose you want to know why I'm interested?" he snapped.

"Yes. That's exactly what I'd like to know. Why are you interested?"

"Because," said Sir Guy Hollis, "I am on the trail of Jack the Ripper now. I think he's here—in Chicago!"

I sat down again. This time I did the blinking act.

"Say that again," I stuttered.

"Jack the Ripper is alive, in Chicago, and I'm out to find him."

"Wait a minute," I said. "Wait—a—minute!"

He wasn't smiling. It wasn't a joke.

"See here," I said. "What was the date of these murders?"

"August to November, 1888."

"1888? But if Jack the Ripper was an able-bodied man in 1888, he'd surely be dead today! Why look, man—if he were merely born in that year, he'd be 57 years old today!"

"Would he?" smiled Sir Guy Hollis. "Or should I say, 'Would she?' Because Jack the Ripper may have been a woman. Or any number of things."

"Sir Guy," I said. "You came to the right person when you looked me up. You definitely need the services of a psychiatrist."

"Perhaps. Tell me, Mr. Carmody, do you think I'm crazy?"

I looked at him and shrugged. But I had to give him a truthful answer.

"Frankly—no."

"Then you might listen to the reasons I believe Jack the Ripper is alive today."

"I might."

"I've studied these cases for thirty years. Been over the actual ground. Talked to officials. Talked to friends and acquaintances of the poor drabs who were killed. Visited with men and women in the neighborhood. Collected an entire library of material touching on Jack the Ripper. Studied all the wild theories or crazy notions.

"I learned a little. Not much, but a little. I won't bore you with my conclusions. But there was another branch of inquiry that yielded more fruitful return. I have studied unsolved crimes. Murders.

"I could show you clippings from the papers of half the world's great cities. San Francisco. Shanghai. Calcutta. Omsk. Paris. Berlin. Pretoria. Cairo. Milan. Adelaide.

"The trail is there, the pattern. Unsolved crimes. Slashed throats of women. With the peculiar disfigurations and removals. Yes, I've followed a trail of blood. From New York westward across the continent. Then to the Pacific. From there to Africa. During the World War of 1914-18 it was Europe. After that, South America. And since 1930, the United States again. Eighty-seven such murders—and to the trained criminologist, all bear the stigma of the Ripper's handiwork.

"Recently there were the so-called Cleveland torso slayings. Remember? A shocking series. And finally, two recent deaths in Chicago. Within the past six months. One out on South Dearborn. The other somewhere up on Halsted. Same type of crime, same technique. I tell you, there are unmistakable indications in all these affairs—indications of the work of Jack the Ripper!"

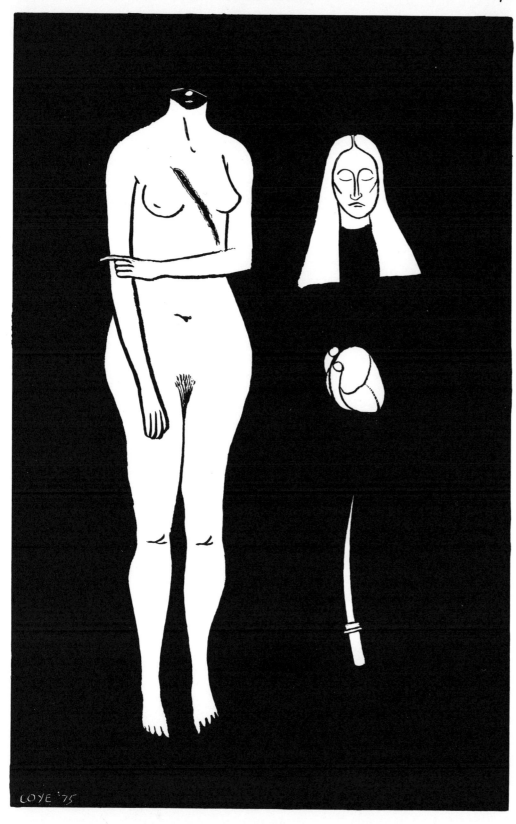

COYE '75

I smiled.

"A very tight theory," I said. "I'll not question your evidence at all, or the deductions you draw. You're the criminologist, and I'll take your word for it. Just one thing remains to be explained. A minor point perhaps, but worth mentioning."

"And what is that?" asked Sir Guy.

"Just how could a man of, let us say, 85 years commit these crimes? For if Jack the Ripper was around 30 in 1888 and lived, he'd be 85 today."

Sir Guy Hollis was silent. I had him there. But—

"*Suppose he didn't get any older?*" whispered Sir Guy.

"What's that?"

"Suppose Jack the Ripper didn't grow old? Suppose he is still a young man today?"

"All right," I said. "I'll suppose for a moment. Then I'll stop supposing and call for my nurse to restrain you."

"I'm serious," said Sir Guy.

"They all are," I told him. "That's the pity of it all, isn't it? They know they hear voices and see demons. But we lock them up just the same."

It was cruel, but it got results. He rose and faced me.

"It's a crazy theory, I grant you," he said. "All the theories about the Ripper are crazy. The idea that he was a doctor. Or a maniac. Or a woman. The reasons advanced for such beliefs are flimsy enough. There's nothing to go by. So why should my notion be any worse?"

"Because people grow older," I reasoned with him. "Doctors, maniacs, and women alike."

"What about—*sorcerers?*"

"Sorcerers?"

"Necromancers. Wizards. Practicers of Black Magic?"

"What's the point?"

"I studied," said Sir Guy. "I studied everything. After awhile I began to study the dates of the murders. The pattern those dates formed. The rhythm. The solar, lunar, stellar rhythm. The sidereal aspect. The astrological significance."

He was crazy. But I still listened.

"Suppose Jack the Ripper didn't murder for murder's sake alone? Suppose he wanted to make—a sacrifice?"

"What kind of a sacrifice?"

Sir Guy shrugged. "It is said that if you offer blood to the dark gods that they grant boons. Yes, if a blood offering is made at the proper time—when the moon and the stars are right— and with the proper ceremonies—they grant boons. Boons of youth. Eternal youth."

"But that's nonsense!"

"No. That's—Jack the Ripper."

I stood up. "A most interesting theory," I told him. "But Sir Guy—there's just one thing I'm interested in. Why do you come here and tell it to me? I'm not an authority on witchcraft. I'm not a police official or criminologist. I'm a practicing psychiatrist. What's the connection?"

Sir Guy smiled.

"You are interested, then?"

"Well, yes. There must be some point."

"There is. But I wished to be assured of your interest first. Now I can tell you my plan."

"And just what is that plan?"

Sir Guy gave me a long look. Then he spoke.

"John Carmody," he said, "you and I are going to capture Jack the Ripper."

# 2

That's the way it happened. I've given the gist of that first interview in all its intricate and somewhat boring detail, because I think it's important. It helps to throw some light on Sir Guy's character and attitude. And in view of what happened after that—

But I'm coming to those matters.

Sir Guy's thought was simple. It wasn't even a thought. Just a hunch.

"You know the people here," he told me. "I've inquired. That's why I came to you as the ideal man for my purpose. You number amongst your acquaintances many writers, painters, poets. The so-called intelligentsia. The Bohemians. The lunatic fringe from the near north side.

"For certain reasons—never mind what they are—my clues lead me to infer that Jack the Ripper is a member of that element. He chooses to pose as an eccentric. I've a feeling that with you to take me around and introduce me to your set, I might hit upon the right person."

"It's all right with me," I said. "But just how are you going to look for him? As you say, he might be anybody, anywhere. And you have no idea what he looks like. He might be young or old. Jack the Ripper—a Jack of all trades? Rich man, poor man, beggar man, thief, doctor, lawyer—how will you know?"

"We shall see." Sir Guy sighed heavily. "But I must find him. At once."

"Why the hurry?"

Sir Guy sighed again. "Because in two days he will kill again."

"Are you sure?"

"Sure as the stars. I've plotted this chart, you see. All of the murders correspond to certain astrological rhythm patterns. If, as I suspect, he makes a blood sacrifice to renew his youth, he must murder within two days. Notice the pattern of his first crimes in London. August 7th. Then August 31. September 8th. September 30th. November 9th. Intervals of 24 days, 9 days, 22 days—he killed two this time—and then 40 days. Of course there were crimes in between. There had to be. But they weren't discovered and pinned on him.

"At any rate, I've worked out a pattern for him, based on all my data. And I say that within the next two days he kills. So I must seek him out, somehow, before then."

"And I'm still asking you what you want me to do."

"Take me out," said Sir Guy. "Introduce me to your friends. Take me to parties."

"But where do I begin? As far as I know, my artistic friends, despite their eccentricities, are all normal people."

"So is the Ripper. Perfectly normal. Except on certain nights." Again that faraway look in Sir Guy's eyes. "Then he becomes an ageless pathological monster, crouching to kill, on evenings when the stars blaze down in the blazing patterns of death."

"All right," I said. "All right. I'll take you to parties, Sir Guy. I want to go myself, anyway. I need the drinks they'll serve there, after listening to your kind of talk."

We made our plans. And that evening I took him over to Lester Baston's studio.

As we ascended to the penthouse roof in the elevator I took the opportunity to warn Sir Guy.

"Baston's a real screwball," I cautioned him. "So are his guests. Be prepared for anything and everything."

"I am." Sir Guy Hollis was perfectly serious. He put his hand in his trousers pocket and pulled out a gun.

"What the—" I began.

"If I see him I'll be ready," Sir Guy said. He didn't smile, either.

"But you can't go running around at a party with a loaded revolver in your pocket, man!"

"Don't worry, I won't behave foolishly."

I wondered. Sir Guy Hollis was not, to my way of thinking, a normal man.

We stepped out of the elevator, went toward Baston's apartment door.

"By the way," I murmured, "just how do you wish to be introduced? Shall I tell them who you are and what you are looking for?"

"I don't care. Perhaps it would be best to be frank."

"But don't you think that the Ripper—if by some miracle he or she is present—will immediately get the wind up and take cover?"

"I think the shock of the announcement that I am hunting the Ripper would provoke some kind of betraying gesture on his part," said Sir Guy.

"You'd make a pretty good psychiatrist yourself," I conceded. "It's a fine theory. But I warn you, you're going to be in for a lot of ribbing. This is a wild bunch."

Sir Guy smiled.

"I'm ready," he announced "I have a little plan of my own. Don't be shocked at anything I do," he warned me.

I nodded and knocked on the door.

Baston opened it and poured out into the hall. His eyes were as red as the maraschino cherries in his Manhattan. He teetered back and forth regarding us very gravely. He squinted at my square-cut homburg hat and Sir Guy's mustache.

"Aha," he intoned. "The Walrus and the Carpenter."

I introduced Sir Guy.

"Welcome," said Baston, gesturing us inside with over-elaborate courtesy. He stumbled after us into the garish parlor.

I stared at the crowd that moved restlessly through the fog of cigarette smoke.

It was the shank of the evening for this mob. Every hand held a drink. Every face held a slightly hectic flush. Over in one corner the piano was going full blast, but the imperious strains of the *March* from *The Love for Three Oranges* couldn't drown out the profanity from the crap-game in the other corner.

Prokofieff had no chance against African polo, and one set of ivories rattled louder than the other.

Sir Guy got a monocle-full right away. He saw LaVerne Gonnister, the poetess, hit Hymie Kralik in the eye. He saw Hymie sit down on the floor and cry until Dick Pool accidentally stepped on his stomach as he walked through to the dining room for a drink.

He heard Nadia Vilinoff the commercial artist tell Johnny Odcutt that she thought his tattooing was in dreadful taste, and he saw Barclay Melton crawl under the dining room table with Johnny Odcutt's wife.

His zoological observations might have continued indefinitely if Lester Baston hadn't stepped to the center of the room and called for silence by dropping a vase on the floor.

"We have distinguished visitors in our midst," bawled Lester, waving his empty glass in our direction. "None other than the Walrus and the Carpenter. The Walrus is Sir Guy Hollis, a something-or-other from the British Embassy. The Carpenter, as you all know, is our own John Carmody, the prominent dispenser of libido liniment."

He turned and grabbed Sir Guy by the arm, dragging him to the middle of the carpet. For a moment I thought Hollis might object, but a quick wink reassured me. He was prepared for this.

"It is our custom, Sir Guy," said Baston, loudly, "to subject our new friends to a little cross-examination. Just a little formality at these very formal gatherings, you understand. Are you prepared to answer questions?"

Sir Guy nodded and grinned.

"Very well," Baston muttered. "Friends—I give you this bundle from Britain. Your witness."

Then the ribbing started. I meant to listen, but at that moment Lydia Dare saw me and dragged me off into the vestibule for one of those Darling-I-waited-for-your-call-all-day routines.

By the time I got rid of her and went back, the impromptu quiz session was in full swing. From the attitude of the crowd, I gathered that Sir Guy was doing all right for himself.

Then Baston himself interjected a question that upset the apple-cart.

"And what, may I ask, brings you to our midst tonight? What is your mission, oh Walrus?"

"I'm looking for Jack the Ripper."

Nobody laughed.

Perhaps it struck them all the way it did me. I glanced at my neighbors and began to *wonder*.

LaVerne Connister. Hymie Kralik. Harmless. Dick Pool. Nadia Vilinoff. Johnny Odcutt and his wife. Barclay Melton. Lydia Dare. All harmless.

But what a forced smile on Dick Pool's face! And that sly, self-conscious smirk that Barclay Melton wore!

Oh, it was absurd, I grant you. But for the first time I saw these people in a new light. I wondered about their lives—their secret lives beyond the scenes of parties.

How many of them were playing a part, concealing something?

Who here would worship Hecate and grant that horrid goddess the dark boon of blood?

Even Lester Baston might be masquerading.

The mood was upon us all, for a moment. I saw questions flicker in the circle of eyes around the room.

Sir Guy stood there, and I could swear he was fully conscious of the situation he'd created, and enjoyed it.

I wondered idly just what was *really* wrong with him. Why he had this odd fixation concerning Jack the Ripper. Maybe he was hiding secrets, too. . . .

Baston, as usual, broke the mood. He burlesqued it.

"The Walrus isn't kidding, friends," he said. He slapped Sir Guy on the back and put his arm around him as he orated. "Our English cousin is really on the trail of the fabulous Jack the Ripper. You all remember Jack the Ripper, I presume? Quite a cutup in the old days, as I recall. Really had some ripping good times when he went out on a tear.

"The Walrus has some idea that the Ripper is still alive, probably prowling around Chicago with a Boy Scout knife. In fact"—Baston paused impressively and shot it out in a rasping stage-whisper—"in fact he has reason to believe that Jack the Ripper might even be right here in our midst tonight."

There was the expected reaction of giggles and grins. Baston eyed Lydia Dare reprovingly. "You girls needn't laugh," he smirked. "Jack the Ripper might be a woman, too, you know. Sort of a Jill the Ripper."

"You mean you actually suspect one of us?" shrieked LaVerne Gonnister, simpering up to Sir Guy. "But that Jack the Ripper person disappeared ages ago, didn't he? In 1888?"

"Aha!" interrupted Baston. "How do you know so much about it, young lady? Sounds suspicious! Watch her, Sir Guy—she may not be as young as she appears. These lady poets have dark pasts."

The tension was gone, the mood was shattered, and the whole thing was beginning to degenerate into a trivial party joke. The man who had played the *March* was eyeing the piano with a *Scherzo* gleam in his eye that augured ill for Prokofieff. Lydia Dare was glancing at the kitchen, waiting to make a break for another drink.

Then Baston caught it.

"Guess what?" he yelled. "The Walrus has a gun."

His embracing arm had slipped and encountered the hard outline of the gun in Sir Guy's pocket. He snatched it out before Hollis had the opportunity to protest.

I stared hard at Sir Guy, wondering if this thing had carried far enough. But he flicked a wink my way and I remembered he had told me not to be alarmed.

So I waited as Baston broached a drunken inspiration.

"Let's play fair with our friend the Walrus," he cried. "He came all the way from England to our party on this mission. If none of you is willing to confess, I suggest we give him a chance to find out—the hard way."

"What's up?" asked Johnny Odcutt.

"I'll turn out the lights for one minute. Sir Guy can stand here with his gun. If anyone in this room is the Ripper he can either run for it or take the opportunity to—well, eradicate his pursuer. Fair enough?"

It was even sillier than it sounds, but it caught the popular fancy. Sir Guy's protests went unheard in the ensuing babble. And before I could stride over and put in my two cents' worth, Lester Baston had reached the light switch.

"Don't anybody move," he announced, with fake solemnity. "For one minute we will remain in darkness—perhaps at the mercy of a killer. At the end of that time, I'll turn up the lights again and look for bodies. Choose your partners, ladies and gentlemen."

The lights went out.

Somebody giggled.

I heard footsteps in the darkness. Mutterings.

A hand brushed my face.

The watch on my wrist ticked violently. But even louder, rising above it, I heard another thumping. The beating of my heart.

Absurd. Standing in the dark with a group of tipsy fools. And yet there was real terror lurking here, rustling through the velvet blackness.

Jack the Ripper prowled in darkness like this. And Jack the Ripper had a knife. Jack the Ripper had a madman's brain and a madman's purpose.

But Jack the Ripper was dead, dead and dust these many years—by every human law.

Only there are no human laws when you feel yourself in the darkness, when the darkness hides and protects and the outer mask slips off your face and you feel something welling up within you, a brooding shapeless purpose that is brother to the blackness.

Sir Guy Hollis shrieked.

There was a gristly thud.

Baston had the lights on.

Everybody screamed.

Sir Guy Hollis lay sprawled on the floor in the center of the room. The gun was still clutched in his hand.

I glanced at the faces, marveling at the variety of expressions human beings can assume when confronting horror.

All the faces were present in the circle. Nobody had fled. And yet Sir Guy Hollis lay there. . . .

LaVerne Gonnister was wailing and hiding her face.

"All right."

Sir Guy rolled over and jumped to his feet. He was smiling.

"Just an experiment, eh? If Jack the Ripper *were* among those present, and thought I had been murdered, he would have betrayed himself in some way when the lights went on and he saw me lying there.

"I am convinced of your individual and collective innocence. Just a gentle spoof, my friends."

Hollis stared at the goggling Baston and the rest of them crowding in behind him.

"Shall we leave, John?" he called to me. "It's getting late, I think."

Turning, he headed for the closet. I followed him. Nobody said a word.

It was a pretty dull party after that.


# 3

I met Sir Guy the following evening as we agreed, on the corner of 29th and South Halsted.

After what had happened the night before, I was prepared for almost anything. But Sir Guy seemed matter-of-fact enough as he stood huddled against a grimy doorway and waited for me to appear.

"Boo!" I said, jumping out suddenly. He smiled. Only the betraying gesture of his left hand indicated that he'd instinctively reached for his gun when I startled him.

"All ready for our wild goose chase?" I asked.

"Yes." He nodded. "I'm glad that you agreed to meet me without asking questions," he told me. "It shows you trust my judgment." He took my arm and edged me along the street slowly.

"It's foggy tonight, John," said Sir Guy Hollis. "Like London."

I nodded.

"Cold, too, for November."

I nodded again and half-shivered my agreement.

"Curious," mused Sir Guy. "London fog and November. The place and the time of the Ripper murders."

I grinned through darkness. "Let me remind you, Sir Guy, that this isn't London, but Chicago. And it isn't November, 1888. It's over fifty years later."

Sir Guy returned my grin, but without mirth. "I'm not so sure, at that," he murmured. "Look about you. These tangled alleys and twisted streets. They're like the East End. Mitre Square. And surely they are as ancient as fifty years, at least."

"You're in the colored neighborhood off South Clark Street," I said, shortly. "And why you dragged me down here I still don't know."

"It's a hunch," Sir Guy admitted. "Just a hunch on my part, John. I want to wander around down here. There's the same geographical conformation in these streets as in those courts where the Ripper roamed and slew. That's where we'll find him, John. Not in the bright lights of the Bohemian neighborhood, but down here in the darkness. The darkness where he waits and crouches."

"Is that why you brought a gun?" I asked. I was unable to keep a trace of sarcastic nervousness from my voice. All of this talk, this incessant obsession with Jack the Ripper, got on my nerves more than I cared to admit.

"We may need a gun," said Sir Guy, gravely. "After all, tonight is the appointed night."

I sighed. We wandered on through the foggy, deserted streets. Here and there a dim light burned above a gin-mill door-way. Otherwise, all was darkness and shadow. Deep, gaping alley-ways loomed as we proceeded down a slanting side-street.

We crawled through that fog, alone and silent, like two tiny maggots floundering within a shroud.

When that thought hit me, I winced. The atmosphere was beginning to get *me*, too. If I didn't watch my step I'd go as loony as Sir Guy.

"Can't you see there's not a soul around these streets?" I said, tugging at his coat impatiently.

"He's bound to come," said Sir Guy. "He'll be drawn here. This is what I've been looking for. A *genius loci*. An evil spot that attracts evil. Always, when he slays, it's in the slums.

"You see, that must be one of his weaknesses. He has a fascination for squalor. Besides, the women he needs for sacrifice are more easily found in the dives and stewpots of a great city."

I smiled. "Well, let's go into one of the dives or stewpots," I suggested. "I'm cold. Need a drink. This damned fog gets into your bones. You Britishers can stand it, but I like warmth and dry heat."

We emerged from our side-street and stood upon the threshold of an alley.

Through the white clouds of mist ahead, I discerned a dim blue light, a naked bulb dangling from a beer sign above an alley tavern.

"Let's take a chance," I said. "I'm beginning to shiver."

"Lead the way," said Sir Guy. I led him down the alley passage. We halted before the door of the dive.

"What are you waiting for?" he asked.

"Just looking in," I told him. "This is a tough neighborhood, Sir Guy. Never know what you're liable to run into. And I'd prefer we didn't get into the wrong company. Some of these Negro places resent white customers."

"Good idea, John."

I finished my inspection through the doorway. "Looks deserted," I murmured. "Let's try it."

We entered a dingy bar. A feeble light flickered above the counter and railing, but failed to penetrate the further gloom of the back booths.

A gigantic Negro lolled across the bar—a black giant with prognathous jaw and ape-like torso. He scarcely stirred as we came in, but his eyes flicked open quite suddenly and I knew he noted our presence and was judging us.

"Evening," I said.

He took his time before replying. Still sizing us up. Then, he grinned.

"Evening, gents. What's your pleasure?"

"Gin," I said. "Two gins. It's a cold night."

"That's right, gents."

He poured, I paid, and took the glasses over to one of the booths. We wasted no time in emptying them. The fiery liquor warmed.

I went over to the bar and got the bottle. Sir Guy and I poured ourselves another drink. The big Negro went back into his doze, with one wary eye half-open against any sudden activity.

The clock over the bar ticked on. The wind was rising outside, tearing the shroud of fog to ragged shreds. Sir Guy and I sat in the warm booth and drank our gin.

He began to talk, and the shadows crept up about us to listen.

He rambled a great deal. He went over everything he'd said in the office when I met him, just as though I hadn't heard it before. The poor devils with obsessions are like that.

I listened very patiently. I poured Sir Guy another drink. And another.

# Ray Bradbury

Ray Bradbury (1920– ) is, among all living authors of fantasy and science fiction, the one whose work has found most favor with reviewers and readers who usually ignore this type of writing. As a result, he is a subject of controversy among devotees of the fantastic: a source of pride because of his reputation, and yet a source of annoyance because his writing is removed from the mainstream of work in the genre. He is, in short, an individualist, less interested in abiding by arbitrary rules than in expressing his own outlook. His science fiction is often unscientific, and his horrors are often homey, but his stories are always unique and interesting.

Although most of his work is science fiction, Bradbury began as a teller of terror tales. He once stated that this early work was an attempt to exorcise his childhood fears, as though it were merely a preparation for more relevant writing, but he has continued to return to such themes in recent novels like *Something Wicked This Way Comes* (1962) and *The Hallowe'en Tree* (1972). Most of his horrors, however, were published in his first book, *Dark Carnival* (1947), which was later revised and reissued as *The October Country* (1955). The stories in these collections include "Skeleton," "The Small Assassin," "The Next in Line," "The Jar," and "The Handler."

Bradbury admits that his youthful interest in fantasy was inspired in large measure by such colorful comic strips as "Buck Rogers" by Phil Nowlan and Dick Calkins, "Tarzan" by Harold Foster, and "Flash Gordon" by Alex Raymond. Years later, many of his stories were adapted into this form by the editors and artists of the unusual E.C. comic book line, which included such titles as *Tales from the Crypt, The Vault of Horror,* and *Weird Science.* These adaptations were subsequently collected in book form.

The demise of the E.C. comics, and of pulp magazines like *Weird Tales,* was a loss to which Bradbury reacted personally, partly because their disappearance was attributable to misguided attempts at suppression and censorship. "Without all this splendid mediocrity, this sublime and wondrous trash in my background," he wrote, "I don't think I would be any sort of writer today."

One of the results was his novel *Fahrenheit 451* (1953), about a future society dedicated to the destruction of books, and thus ideas. This book was filmed by François Truffaut in 1966. The 1953 movie *The Beast from 20,000 Fathoms* was based on Bradbury's tale about a lovesick sea serpent, "The Fog Horn." And the episodic film *The Illustrated Man* (1969) was based on his short story collection of the same name. Bradbury's other major story collections include the celebrated *The Martian Chronicles* (1950), *The Golden Apples of the Sun* (1953), *A Medicine for Melancholy* (1959), and *I Sing the Body Electric* (1969).

227

"Homecoming," one of Bradbury's strangest supernatural stories, was first published in 1946 in, of all places, *Mademoiselle*. It involves such a reversal of expectations that it is almost a commentary on the terror tale and on the sources of its appeal. The story suggests that however horrible demons and monsters may be, they are at least endowed with powers that it might be pleasant to possess, and they might be inclined to pity something as human and helpless as a mere mortal.

# HOMECOMING

## Ray Bradbury

"Here they come," said Cecy, lying there flat in her bed.

"Where are they?" cried Timothy from the doorway.

"Some of them are over Europe, some over Asia, some of them over the Islands, some over South America!" said Cecy, her eyes closed, the lashes long, brown, and quivering.

Timothy came forward upon the bare plankings of the upstairs room. "Who are they?"

"Uncle Einar and Uncle Fry, and there's Cousin William, and I see Frulda and Helgar and Aunt Morgiana and Cousin Vivian, and I see Uncle Johann! They're all coming fast!"

"Are they up in the sky?" cried Timothy, his little gray eyes flashing. Standing by the bed, he looked no more than his fourteen years. The wind blew outside, the house was dark and lit only by starlight.

"They're coming through the air and traveling along the ground, in many forms," said Cecy, in her sleeping. She did not move on the bed; she thought inward on herself and told what she saw. "I see a wolflike thing coming over a dark river—at the shallows—just above a waterfall, the starlight shining up his pelt. I see a brown oak leaf blowing far up in the sky. I see a small bat flying. I see many other things, running through the forest trees and slipping through the highest branches; and they're *all* coming this way!"

"Will they be here by tomorrow night?" Timothy clutched the bedclothes. The spider on his lapel swung like a black pendulum, excitedly dancing. He leaned over his sister. "Will they all be here in time for the Homecoming?"

"Yes, yes, Timothy, yes," sighed Cecy. She stiffened. "Ask no more of me. Go away now. Let me travel in the places I like best."

"Thanks, Cecy," he said. Out in the hall, he ran to his room. He hurriedly made his bed. He had just awakened a few minutes ago, at sunset, and as the first stars had risen he had gone to let his excitement about the party run with Cecy. Now she slept so quietly there was not a sound. The spider hung on a silvery lasso about Timothy's slender neck as he washed his face. "Just think, Spid, tomorrow night is Allhallows Eve!"

He lifted his face and looked into the mirror. His was the only mirror allowed in the house. It was his mother's concession to his illness. Oh, if only he were not so afflicted! He opened his mouth, surveyed the poor, inadequate teeth nature had given him. No more than so many corn kernels—round, soft and pale in his jaws. Some of the high spirit died in him.

It was now totally dark and he lit a candle to see by. He felt exhausted. This past week the whole family had lived in the fashion of the old country. Sleeping by day, rousing at sunset to move about. There were blue hollows under his eyes. "Spid, I'm no good," he said, quietly, to the little creature. "I can't even get used to sleeping days like the others."

He took up the candleholder. Oh, to have strong teeth, with incisors like steel spikes. Or strong hands, even, or a strong mind. Even to have the power to send one's mind out, free, as Cecy did. But, no, he was the imperfect one, the sick one. He was even—he shivered and drew the candle flame closer—afraid of the dark. His brothers snorted at him. Bion and Leonard and Sam. They laughed at him because he slept in a bed. With Cecy it was different; her bed was part of her comfort for the composure necessary to send her mind abroad to hunt. But Timothy, did he sleep in the wonderful polished boxes like the others? He did not! Mother let him have his own bed, his own room, his own mirror. No wonder the family skirted him like a holy man's crucifix. If only the wings would sprout from his shoulder blades. He bared his back, stared at it. And sighed again. No chance. Never.

Downstairs were exciting and mysterious sounds, the slithering black crape going up in all the halls and on the ceilings and doors. The sputter of burning black tapers in the banistered stair well. Mother's voice, high and firm. Father's voice, echoing from the damp cellar. Bion walking from outside the old country house lugging vast two-gallon jugs.

"I've just got to go to the party, Spid," said Timothy. The spider whirled at the end of its silk, and Timothy felt alone. He would polish cases, fetch toadstools and spiders, hang crape, but when the party started he'd be ignored. The less seen or said of the imperfect son the better.

All through the house below, Laura ran.

"The Homecoming!" she shouted gaily. "The Homecoming!" Her footsteps everywhere at once.

Timothy passed Cecy's room again, and she was sleeping quietly. Once a month she went belowstairs. Always she stayed in bed. Lovely Cecy. He felt like asking her, "Where are you now, Cecy? And *in* who? And what's happening? Are you beyond the hills? And what goes on there?" But he went on to Ellen's room instead.

Ellen sat at her desk, sorting out many kinds of blond, red and black hair and little scimitars of fingernail gathered from her manicurist job at the Mellin Village beauty parlor fifteen miles over. A sturdy mahogany case lay in one corner with her name on it.

"Go away," she said, not even looking at him. "I can't work with you gawking."

"Allhallows Eve, Ellen; just think!" he said, trying to be friendly.

"Hunh!" She put some fingernail clippings in a small white sack, labeled them. "What can it mean to you? What do you know of it? It'll scare the hell out of you. Go back to bed."

His cheeks burned. "I'm needed to polish and work and help serve."

"If you don't go, you'll find a dozen raw oysters in your bed tomorrow," said Ellen, matter-of-factly. "Good-by, Timothy."

In his anger, rushing downstairs, he bumped into Laura.

"Watch where you're going!" she shrieked from clenched teeth.

She swept away. He ran to the open cellar door, smelled the channel of moist earthy air rising from below. "Father?"

"It's about time," Father shouted up the steps. "Hurry down, or they'll be here before we're ready!"

Timothy hesitated only long enough to hear the million other sounds in the house. Brothers came and went like trains in a station, talking and arguing. If you stood in one spot long enough the entire household passed with their pale hands full of things. Leonard with his little black medical case, Samuel with his large, dusty ebon-bound book under his arm, bearing more black crape, and Bion excursioning to the car outside and bringing in many more gallons of liquid.

Father stopped polishing to give Timothy a rag and a scowl. He thumped the huge mahogany box. "Come on, shine this up, so we can start on another. Sleep your life away."

While waxing the surface, Timothy looked inside.

"Uncle Einar's a big man, isn't he, Papa?"

"Unh."

"How big is he?"

"The size of the box'll tell you."

"I was only asking. Seven feet tall?"

"You talk a lot."

About nine o'clock Timothy went out into the October weather. For two hours in the now-warm, now-cold wind he walked the meadows collecting toadstools and spiders. His heart began to beat with anticipation again. How many relatives had Mother said would come? Seventy? One hundred? He passed a farmhouse. If only you knew what was happening at our house, he said to the glowing windows. He climbed a hill and looked at the town, miles away, settling into sleep, the town-hall clock high and round white in the distance. The town did not know, either. He brought home many jars of toadstools and spiders.

In the little chapel belowstairs a brief ceremony was celebrated. It was like all the other rituals over the years, with Father chanting the dark lines, mother's beautiful white ivory hands moving in the reverse blessings, and all the children gathered except Cecy, who lay upstairs in bed. But Cecy was present. You saw her peering, now from Bion's eyes, now Samuel's, now Mother's, and you felt a movement and now she was in you, fleetingly and gone.

Timothy prayed to the Dark One with a tightened stomach. "Please, please, help me grow up, help me be like my sisters and brothers. Don't let me be different. If only I could put the hair in the plastic images as Ellen does, or make people fall in love with me as Laura does with people, or read strange books as Sam does, or work in a respected job like Leonard and Bion do. Or even raise a family one day, as mother and father have done. . . ."

At midnight a storm hammered the house. Lightning struck outside in amazing, snow-white bolts. There was a sound of an approaching, probing, sucking tornado, funneling and nuzzling the moist night earth. Then the front door, blasted half off its hinges, hung stiff and discarded, and in trooped Grandmama and Grandpapa, all the way from the old country!

From then on people arrived each hour. There was a flutter at the side window, a rap on the front porch, a knock at the back. There were fey noises from the cellar; autumn wind piped down the chimney throat, chanting. Mother filled the large crystal punch bowl with a scarlet fluid poured from the jugs Bion had carried home. Father swept from room to room lighting more tapers. Laura and Ellen hammered up more wolfsbane. And Timothy stood amidst this wild excitement, no expression to his face, his hands trembling at his sides, gazing now here, now there. Banging of doors, laughter, the sound of liquid pouring, darkness, sound of wind, the webbed thunder of wings, the padding of feet, the welcoming bursts of talk at the entrances, the transparent rattlings of casements, the shadows passing, coming, going, wavering.

"Well, well, and *this* must be Timothy!"

"What?"

A chilly hand took his hand. A long hairy face leaned down over him. "A good lad, a fine lad," said the stranger.

"Timothy," said his mother. "This is Uncle Jason."

"Hello, Uncle Jason."

"And over here——" Mother drifted Uncle Jason away. Uncle Jason peered back at Timothy over his caped shoulder, and winked.

Timothy stood alone.

From off a thousand miles in the candled darkness, he heard a high fluting voice; that was Ellen. "And my brothers, they *are* clever. Can you guess their occupations, Aunt Morgiana?"

"I have no idea."

"They operate the undertaking establishment in town."

"What!" A gasp.

"Yes!" Shrill laughter. "Isn't that priceless!"

Timothy stood very still.

A pause in the laughter. "They bring home sustenance for Mama, Papa and all of us," said Laura. "Except, of course, Timothy. . . ."

An uneasy silence. Uncle Jason's voice demanded. "Well? come now. What about Timothy?"

"Oh, Laura, your tongue," said mother.

Laura went on with it. Timothy shut his eyes. "Timothy doesn't—well—doesn't *like* blood. He's delicate."

"He'll learn," said mother. "He'll learn," she said very firmly. "He's my son, and he'll learn. He's only fourteen."

"But I was raised on the stuff," said Uncle Jason, his voice passing from one room on into another. The wind played the trees outside like harps. A little rain spatted on the windows—"raised on the stuff," passing away into faintness.

Timothy bit his lips and opened his eyes.

"Well, it was all my fault." Mother was showing them into the kitchen now. "I tried forcing him. You can't force children, you only make them sick, and then they never get a taste for things. Look at Bion, now, he was thirteen before he . . ."

"I understand," murmured Uncle Jason. "Timothy will come around."

"I'm sure he will," said mother, defiantly.

Candle flames quivered as shadows crossed and recrossed the dozen musty rooms. Timothy was cold. He smelled the hot tallow in his nostrils and instinctively he grabbed at a candle and walked with it around and about the house, pretending to straighten the crape.

*"Timothy,"* someone whispered behind a patterned wall, hissing and sizzling and sighing the words, *"Timothy is afraid of the dark."*

Leonard's voice. Hateful Leonard!

"I like the candle, that's all," said Timothy in a reproachful whisper.

More lightning, more thunder. Cascades of roaring laughter. Bangings and clickings and shouts and rustles of clothing. Clammy fog swept through the front door. Out of the fog, settling his wings, stalked a tall man.

"Uncle Einar!"

Timothy propelled himself on his thin legs, straight through the fog, under the green webbing shadows. He threw himself across Einar's arms. Einar lifted him.

"You've wings, Timothy!" He tossed the boy light as thistles. "Wings, Timothy: fly!" Faces wheeled under. Darkness rotated. The house blew away. Timothy felt breezelike. He flapped his arms. Einar's fingers caught and threw him once more to the ceiling. The ceiling rushed down like a charred wall. "Fly, Timothy!" shouted Einar, loud and deep. "Fly with wings! Wings!"

He felt an exquisite ecstasy in his shoulder blades, as if roots grew, burst to explode and blossom into new, moist membrane. He babbled wild stuff; again Einar hurled him high.

The autumn wind broke in a tide on the house, rain crashed down, shaking the beams, causing chandeliers to tilt their enraged candle lights. And the one hundred relatives peered out from every black, enchanted room, circling inward, all shapes and sizes, to where Einar balanced the child like a baton in the roaring spaces.

"Enough!" shouted Einar, at last.

Timothy, deposited on the floor timbers, exaltedly, exhaustedly fell against Uncle Einar, sobbing happily. "Uncle, uncle, uncle!"

"Was it good, flying? Eh, Timothy?" said Uncle Einar, bending down, patting Timothy's head. "Good, good."

It was coming toward dawn. Most had arrived and were ready to bed down for the daylight, sleep motionlessly with no sound until the following sunset, when they would shout out of their mahogany boxes for the revelry.

Uncle Einar, followed by dozens of others, moved toward the cellar. Mother directed them downward to the crowded row on row of highly polished boxes. Einar, his wings like sea-green tarpaulins tented behind him, moved with a curious whistling down the passageway; where his wings touched they made a sound of drumheads gently beaten.

Upstairs, Timothy lay wearily thinking, trying to like the darkness. There was so much you could do in darkness that people couldn't criticize you for, because they never saw you. He *did* like the night, but it was a qualified liking: sometimes there was so much night he cried out in rebellion.

In the cellar, mahogany doors sealed downward, drawn in by pale hands. In corners, certain relatives circled three times to lie, heads on paws, eyelids shut. The sun rose. There was a sleeping.

Sunset. The revel exploded like a bat nest struck full, shrieking out, fluttering, spreading. Box doors banged wide. Steps rushed up from cellar damp. More late guests, kicking on front and back portals, were admitted.

It rained, and sodden visitors laid their capes, their water-pelleted hats, their sprinkled veils upon Timothy who bore them to a closet. The rooms were crowd-packed. The laughter of one cousin, shot from one room, angled off the wall of another, ricocheted, banked and returned to Timothy's ears from a fourth room, accurate and cynical.

A mouse ran across the floor.

"I know you, Niece Leibersrouter!" exclaimed father.

The mouse spiraled three women's feet and vanished into a corner. Moments later a beautiful woman rose up out of nothing and stood in the corner, smiling her white smile at them all.

Something huddled against the flooded pane of the kitchen window. It sighed and wept and tapped continually, pressed against the glass, but Timothy could make nothing of it, he saw nothing. In imagination he was outside staring in. The rain was on him, the wind at him, and the taper-dotted darkness inside was inviting. Waltzes were being danced; tall thin figures pirouetted to outlandish music. Stars of light flickered off lifted bottles; small clods of earth crumbled from casques, and a spider fell and went silently legging over the floor.

Timothy shivered. He was inside the house again. Mother was calling him to run here, run there, help, serve, out to the kitchen now, fetch this, fetch that, bring the plates, heap the food—on and on—the party happened around him but not to him. The dozens of towering people pressed in against him, elbowed him, ignored him.

Finally, he turned and slipped away up the stairs.

He called softly. "Cecy. Where are you now, Cecy?"

She waited a long while before answering. "In the Imperial Valley," she murmured faintly. "Beside the Salton Sea, near the mud pots and the steam and the quiet. I'm inside a farmer's wife. I'm sitting on a front porch. I can make her move if I want, or do anything or think anything. The sun's going down."

"What's it like, Cecy?"

"You can hear the mud pots hissing," she said, slowly, as if speaking in a church. "Little gray heads of steam push up the mud like bald men rising in the thick syrup, head first, out in the broiling channels. The gray heads rip like rubber fabric, collapse with noises like wet lips moving. And feathery plumes of steam escape from the ripped tissue. And there is a smell of deep sulphurous burning and old time. The dinosaur has been abroiling here ten million years."

"Is he done yet, Cecy?"

"Yes, he's done. Quite done." Cecy's calm sleeper's lips turned up. The languid words fell slowly from her shaping mouth. "Inside this woman's skull I am, looking out, watching the sea that does not move, and is so quiet it makes you afraid. I sit on the porch and wait for my husband to come home. Occasionally, a fish leaps, falls back, starlight edging it. The valley, the sea, the few cars, the wooden porch, my rocking chair, myself, the silence."

"What now, Cecy?"

"I'm getting up from my rocking chair," she said.

"Yes?"

"I'm walking off the porch, toward the mud pots. Planes fly over, like primordial birds. Then it is quiet, so quiet."

"How long will you stay inside her, Cecy?"

"Until I've listened and looked and felt enough: until I've changed her life some way. I'm walking off the porch and along the wooden boards. My feet knock on the planks, tiredly, slowly."

"And now?"

"Now the sulphur fumes are all around me. I stare at the bubbles as they break and smooth. A bird darts by my temple, shrieking. Suddenly I am in the bird and fly away! And as I fly, inside my new small glass-bead eyes I see a woman below me, on a boardwalk, take one two three steps forward into the mud pots. I hear a sound as of a boulder plunged into molten depths. I keep flying, circle back. I see a white hand, like a spider, wriggle and disappear into the gray lava pool. The lava seals over. Now I'm flying home, swift, swift, swift!"

Something clapped hard against the window, Timothy started.

Cecy flicked her eyes wide, bright, full, happy, exhilarated.

"Now I'm *home!*" she said.

After a pause, Timothy ventured, "The Homecoming's on. And everybody's here."

"Then why are you upstairs?" She took his hand. "Well, ask me." She smiled slyly. "Ask me what you came to ask."

"I didn't come to ask anything," he said. "Well, almost nothing. Well—oh, Cecy!" It came from him in one long rapid flow. "I want to do something at the party to make them look at me, something to make me good as them, something to make me belong, but there's nothing I can do and I feel funny and, well, I thought you might  . . ."

"I might," she said, closing her eyes, smiling inwardly. "Stand up straight. Stand very still." He obeyed. "Now, shut your eyes and blank out your thought."

He stood very straight and thought of nothing, or at least thought of thinking nothing.

She sighed. "Shall we go downstairs now, Timothy?" Like a hand into a glove, Cecy was within him.

"Look everybody!" Timothy held the glass of warm red liquid. He held up the glass so that the whole house turned to watch him. Aunts, uncles, cousins, brothers, sisters!

He drank it straight down.

He jerked a hand at his sister Laura. He held her gaze, whispering to her in a subtle voice that kept her silent, frozen. He felt tall as the trees as he walked to her. The party now slowed. It waited on all sides of him, watching. From all the room doors the faces peered. They were not laughing. Mother's face was astonished. Dad looked bewildered, but pleased and getting prouder every instant.

He nipped Laura, gently, over the neck vein. The candle flames swayed drunkenly. The wind climbed around on the roof outside. The relatives stared from all the doors. He popped toadstools into his mouth, swallowed, then beat his arms against his flanks and circled. "Look, Uncle Einar! I can fly, at last!" Beat went his hands. Up and down pumped his feet. The faces flashed past him.

At the top of the stairs flapping, he heard his mother cry, "Stop, Timothy!" far below. "Hey!" shouted Timothy, and leaped off the top of the well, thrashing.

Halfway down, the wings he thought he owned dissolved. He screamed. Uncle Einar caught him.

Timothy flailed whitely in the receiving arms. A voice burst out of his lips, unbidden. "This is Cecy! This is Cecy! Come see me, all of you, upstairs, first room on the left!" Followed by a long trill of high laughter. Timothy tried to cut if off with his tongue.

Everybody was laughing. Einar set him down. Running through the crowding blackness as the relatives flowed upstairs toward Cecy's room to congratulate her, Timothy banged the front door open.

"Cecy, I hate you, I hate you!"

By the sycamore tree, in deep shadow, Timothy spewed out his dinner, sobbed bitterly and threshed in a pile of autumn leaves. Then he lay still. From his blouse pocket, from the protection of the matchbox he used for his retreat, the spider crawled forth. Spid walked along Timothy's arm. Spid explored up his neck to his ear and climbed in the ear to tickle it. Timothy shook his head. "Don't, Spid. Don't."

The feathery touch of a tentative feeler probing his eardrum set Timothy shivering. "Don't, Spid!" He sobbed somewhat less.

The spider traveled down his cheek, took a station under the boy's nose, looked up into the nostrils as if to seek the brain, and then clambered softly up over the rim of the nose to sit, to squat there peering at Timothy with green gem eyes until Timothy filled with ridiculous laughter. "Go away, Spid!"

Timothy sat up, rustling the leaves. The land was very bright with the moon. In the house he could hear the faint ribaldry as Mirror, Mirror was played. Celebrants shouted, dimly muffled, as they tried to identify those of themselves whose reflections did not, had not ever appeared in a glass.

"Timothy." Uncle Einar's wings spread and twitched and came in with a sound like kettledrums. Timothy felt himself plucked up like a thimble and set upon Einar's shoulder. "Don't feel badly, Nephew Timothy. Each to his own, each in his own way. How much better things are for you. How rich. The world's dead for us. We've seen so much of it, believe me. Life's best to those who live the least of it. It's worth more per ounce, Timothy, remember that."

The rest of the black morning, from midnight on, Uncle Einar led him about the house, from room to room, weaving and singing. A horde of late arrivals set the entire hilarity off afresh. Great-great-great-great and a thousand more great-greats Grandmother was there, wrapped in Egyptian cerements. She said not a word, but lay straight as a burnt ironing board against the wall, her eye hollows cupping a distant, wise, silent glimmering. At the breakfast, at four in the morning, one-thousand-odd-greats Grandmama was stiffly seated at the head of the longest table.

The numerous young cousins caroused at the crystal punch bowl. Their shiny olive-pit eyes, their conical, devilish faces and curly bronze hair hovered over the drinking table, their hard-soft, half-girl half-boy bodies wrestling against each other as they got unpleasantly, sullenly drunk. The wind got higher, the stars burned with fiery intensity, the noises redoubled, the dances quickened, the drinking became more positive. To Timothy there were thousands of things to hear and watch. The many darknesses roiled, bubbled, the many faces passed and repassed. . . .

"Listen!"

The party held its breath. Far away the town clock struck its chimes, saying six o'clock. The party was ending. In time to the rhythm of the striking clock, their one hundred voices began to sing songs that were four hundred years old, songs Timothy could not know. Arms twined, circling slowly, they sang, and somewhere in the cold distance of morning the town clock finished out its chimes and quieted.

Timothy sang. He knew no words, no tune, yet the words and tune came round and high and good. And he gazed at the closed door at the top of the stairs.

"Thanks Cecy," he whispered. "You're forgiven. Thanks."

Then he just relaxed and let the words move, with Cecy's voice, free from his lips.

Good-bys were said, there was a great rustling. Mother and Father stood at the door to shake hands and kiss each departing relative in turn. The sky beyond the open door colored in the east. A cold wind entered. And Timothy felt himself seized and settled in one body after another, felt Cecy press him into Uncle Fry's head so he stared from the wrinkled leather face, then leaped in a flurry of leaves up over the house and awakening hills. . . .

Then, loping down a dirt path, he felt his red eyes burning, his fur pelt rimed with morning, as inside Cousin William he panted through a hollow and dissolved away. . . .

Like a pebble in Uncle Einar's mouth, Timothy flew in a webbed thunder, filling the sky. And then he was back for all time, in his own body.

In the growing dawn, the last few were embracing and crying and thinking how the world was becoming less a place for them. There had been a time when they had met every year, but now decades passed with no reconciliation. "Don't forget," someone cried, "we meet in Salem in 1970!"

Salem. Timothy's numbed mind turned the words over. Salem, 1970. And there would be Uncle Fry and a thousand-times-great Grandmother in her withered cerements, and Mother and Father and Ellen and Laura and Cecy and all the rest. But would he be there? Could he be certain of staying alive until then?

With one last withering blast, away they all went, so many scarves, so many fluttery mammals, so many sere leaves, so many whining and clustering noises, so many midnights and insanities and dreams.

Mother shut the door. Laura picked up a broom. "No," said Mother. "We'll clean tonight. Now we need sleep." And the Family vanished down cellar and upstairs. And Timothy moved in the crape-littered hall, his head down. Passing a party mirror, he saw the pale mortality of his face all cold and trembling.

"Timothy," said Mother.

She came to touch her hand on his face. "Son," she said, "We love you. Remember that. We all love you. No matter how different you are, no matter if you leave us one day." She kissed his cheek. "And if and when you die, your bones will lie undisturbed, we'll see to that. You'll lie at ease forever, and I'll come visit every Allhallows Eve and tuck you in the more secure."

The house was silent. Far away the wind went over a hill with its last cargo of dark bats, echoing, chittering.

Timothy walked up the steps, one by one, crying to himself all the way.

# Carter Dickson

Carter Dickson is the alias of John Dickson Carr (1905– ), who has, under both names, earned an admirable reputation as one of the twentieth century's finest writers of detective stories. Although he has never known the wild popularity of colleagues like Agatha Christie and Erle Stanley Gardner, critics and colleagues alike have recognized that he is unsurpassed for ingenious plotting and atmospheric presentation. Howard Haycraft, in his definitive study *Murder for Pleasure*, confesses that his favorite fictional detective is Sir Henry Merrivale, the hero of "The House in Goblin Wood."

Carr specializes in imagining apparently impossible crimes, in which the problem is not only identifying the criminal but also explaining how the dastardly deed was done. The puzzles are often intensified by the possibility of a supernatural explanation, and Carr's culprits frequently rely on legends of hauntings and horrors in their efforts to baffle the authorities. The result is a series of macabre mysteries that demonstrate that this author is as great a master of the terror tale as many who have devoted themselves exclusively to the attempt to provoke shudders. Carr also manages to inject scenes of robust slapstick comedy without ever striking a false note.

His first mystery novel was *It Walks by Night* (1930), a story about a homicidal maniac with a fondness for beheading his victims. He later wrote, "I think it's pretty terrible, but I hope it's entertaining—to me the one unforgivable sin is being dull." Its hero is Bencolin, a French detective of satanic appearance, who also appeared in sinister stories like *The Lost Gallows* (1931) and *The Corpse in the Waxworks* (1932). Carr really hit his stride in 1933 with *Hag's Nook,* which introduced Dr. Gideon Fell. He has since solved many macabre murder mysteries, including *The Three Coffins* (1935), *The Crooked Hinge* (1938), *The Man Who Could Not Shudder* (1940), and *The Case of the Constant Suicides* (1941). Sir Henry Merrivale was introduced, under the transparent pseudonym Carter Dickson, in *The Plague Court Murders* (1934); Sir Henry's other uncanny cases include *The Reader Is Warned* (1939), *The Curse of the Bronze Lamp* (1945), and *The Skeleton in the Clock* (1948).

Sir Henry and Dr. Fell are cut from the same cloth. Both are overbearing, overweight old Englishmen of unexpected imagination. Most of their adventures take place in Great Britain; Carr himself is a native American who emigrated to England before beginning his literary career. Considering the weird cases he encounters, it is not surprising that Dr. Fell is described in one book as the author of a study of the supernatural in fiction or that his appearance and personality are based on those of G. K. Chesterton, Carr's principal predecessor in the description of bizarre puzzles.

Occasionally, Carr moves directly into the realm of the supernatural. *The Burning Court* (1937) is a tale of genuine witchcraft, in which one sorcerer protects another by offering a logical theory for a crime that was really committed by magic. *The Devil in Velvet* (1951) concerns a scholar whose devilish deal transports him back to the seventeenth century, where he attempts to solve the murder of an ancestor.

John Dickson Carr is one of the great masters of what has been called the "formal" detective story, which he describes as "a hoodwinking contest, a duel between author and reader," in short, a mystery in which all the clues are presented and there is a fair opportunity to arrive at a solution. Unfortunately, in these days of lurid spy thrillers and fist-fighting private eyes, the pure mystery, as devised by Poe, seems to be in eclipse.

"The House in Goblin Wood" received a "Special Award of Merit" when it appeared in *Ellery Queen's Mystery Magazine* in 1947. This story demonstrates Carr's skill at evoking the uncanny and then dispelling it with a solution that is equally unnerving. It is also, as Queen asserted, "almost a complete manual of detective story theory and practice."

# THE HOUSE IN GOBLIN WOOD

## Carter Dickson

In Pall Mall, that hot July afternoon three years before the war, an open saloon car was drawn up to the curb just opposite the Senior Conservatives' Club.

And in the car sat two conspirators.

It was the drowsy post-lunch hour among the clubs, where only the sun remained brilliant. The Rag lay somnolent; the Athaneum slept outright. But these two conspirators, a dark-haired young man in his early thirties and a fair-haired girl perhaps half a dozen years younger, never moved. They stared intently at the Gothic-like front of the Senior Conservatives'.

"Look here, Eve," muttered the young man, and punched at the steering wheel. "Do you think this is going to work?"

"I don't know," the fair-haried girl confessed. "He absolutely *loathes* picnics."

"Anyway, we've probably missed him."

"Why so?"

"He can't have taken as long over lunch as that!" her companion protested, looking at a wrist watch. The young man was rather shocked. "It's a quarter to four! Even if . . ."

"Bill! There! Look there!"

Their patience was rewarded by an inspiring sight.

Out of the portals of the Senior Conservatives' Club, in awful majesty, marched a large, stout, barrel-shaped gentleman in a white linen suit.

His corporation preceded him like the figurehead of a man-of-war. His shell-rimmed spectacles were pulled down on a broad nose, all being shaded by a Panama hat. At the top of the stone steps he surveyed the street, left and right, with a lordly sneer.

"Sir Henry!" called the girl.

"Hey?" said Sir Henry Merrivale.

"I'm Eve Drayton. Don't you remember me? You knew my father!"

"Oh, ah," said the great man.

"We've been waiting here a terribly long time," Eve pleaded. "Couldn't you see us for just five minutes?—The thing to do," she whispered to her companion, "is to keep him in a good humor. Just keep him in a good humor!"

As a matter of fact, H.M. was in a good humor, having just triumphed over the Home Secretary in an argument. But not even his own mother could have guessed it. Majestically, with the same lordly sneer, he began in grandeur to descend the steps of the Senior Conservatives'. He did this, in fact, until his foot encountered an unnoticed object lying some three feet from the bottom.

It was a banana skin.

"Oh, dear!" said the girl.

Now it must be stated with regret that in the old days certain urchins, of what were then called the "lower orders," had a habit of placing such objects on the steps in the hope that some eminent statesman would take a toss on his way to Whitehall. This was a venial but deplorable practice, probably accounting for what Mr. Gladstone said in 1882.

In any case, it accounted for what Sir Henry Merrivale said now.

From the pavement, where H.M. landed in a seated position, arose, in H.M.'s bellowing voice such a torrent of profanity, such a flood of invective and vile obscenities, as has seldom before blasted the holy calm of Pall Mall. It brought the hall porter hurrying down the steps, and Eve Drayton flying out of the car.

Heads were now appearing at the windows of the Atheneum across the street.

"Is it all right?" cried the girl, with concern in her blue eyes. "Are you hurt?"

H.M. merely looked at her. His hat had fallen off, disclosing a large bald head; and he merely sat on the pavement and looked at her.

"Anyway, H.M., get up! Please get up!"

"Yes, sir," begged the hall porter, "for heaven's sake get up!"

"Get up?" bellowed H.M., in a voice audible as far as St. James's Street. "Burn it all, how *can* I get up?"

"But why not?"

"My behind's out of joint," said H.M. simply. "I'm hurt awful bad. I'm probably goin' to have spinal dislocation for the rest of my life."

"But, sir, people are looking!"

H.M. explained what these people could do. He eyed Eve Drayton with a glare of indescribable malignancy over his spectacles.

"I suppose, my wench, *you're* responsible for this?"

Eve regarded him in consternation.

"You don't mean the banana skin?" she cried.

"Oh, yes, I do," said H.M., folding his arms like a prosecuting counsel.

"But we—we only wanted to invite you to a picnic!"

H.M. closed his eyes.

"That's fine," he said in a hollow voice. "All the same, don't you think it'd have been a subtler kind of hint just to pour mayonnaise over my head or shove ants down the back of my neck? Oh, lord love a duck!"

"I didn't mean that! I meant . . ."

"Let me help you up, sir," interposed the calm, reassuring voice of the dark-haired and blue-chinned young man who had been with Eve in the car.

"So you want to help too, hey? And who are *you*?"

"I'm awfully sorry!" said Eve. "I should have introduced you! This is my fiancé. Dr. William Sage."

H.M.'s face turned purple.

"I'm glad to see," he observed, "you had the uncommon decency to bring along a doctor. I appreciate that, I do. And the car's there, I suppose, to assist with the examination when I take off my pants?"

The hall porter uttered a cry of horror.

Bill Sage, either from jumpiness and nerves or from sheer inability to keep a straight face, laughed loudly.

"I keep telling Eve a dozen times a day," he said, "that I'm not to be called 'doctor.' I happen to be a surgeon—"

(Here H.M. really did look alarmed.)

"—but I don't think we need operate. Nor, in my opinion," Bill gravely addressed the hall porter, "will it be necessary to remove Sir Henry's trousers in front of the Senior Conservatives' Club."

"Thank you very much, sir."

"We had an infernal nerve to come here," the young man confessed to H.M. "But I honestly think, Sir Henry, you'd be more comfortable in the car. What about it? Let me give you a hand up?"

Yet even ten minutes later, when H.M. sat glowering in the back of the car and two heads were craned round towards him, peace was not restored.

"All right!" said Eve. Her pretty, rather stolid face was flushed; her mouth looked miserable. "If you won't come to the picnic, you won't. But I did believe you might do it to oblige me."

"Well . . . now!" muttered the great man uncomfortably.

"And I did think, too, you'd be interested in the other person who was coming with us. But Vicky's—difficult. She won't come either, if you don't."

"Oh? And who's this other guest?"

"Vicky Adams."

H.M.'s hand, which had been lifted for an oratorical gesture, dropped to his side.

"Vicky Adams? That's not the gal who . . .?"

"Yes!" Eve nodded. "They say it was one of the great mysteries, twenty years ago, that the police failed to solve."

"It was, my wench," H.M. agreed sombrely. "It was."

"And now Vicky's grown up. And we thought if you of all people went along, and spoke to her nicely, she'd tell us what really happened on that night."

H.M.'s small, sharp eyes fixed disconcertingly on Eve.

"I say, my wench. What's your interest in all this?"

"Oh, reasons." Eve glanced quickly at Bill Sage, who was again punching moodily at the steering wheel, and checked herself. "Anyway, what difference does it make now? If you won't go with us . . ."

H.M. assumed a martyred air.

"I never said I *wasn't* goin' with you, did I?" he demanded. (This was inaccurate, but no matter.) "Even after you practically made a cripple of me, I never said I *wasn't* goin?" His manner grew flurried and hasty. "But I got to leave now," he added apologetically. "I got to get back to my office."

"We'll drive you there, H.M."

"No, no, no," said the practical cripple, getting out of the car with surprising celerity. "Walkin' is good for my stomach if it's not so good for my behind. I'm a forgivin' man. You pick me up at my house tomorrow morning. G'bye."

And he lumbered off in the direction of the Haymarket.

It needed no close observer to see that H.M. was deeply abstracted. He remained so abstracted, indeed, as to be nearly murdered by a taxi at the Admiralty Arch; and he was halfway down Whitehall before a familiar voice stopped him.

"Afternoon, Sir Henry!"

Burly, urbane, buttoned up in blue serge, with his bowler hat and his boiled blue eye, stood Chief Inspector Masters.

"Bit odd," the Chief Inspector remarked affably, "to see you taking a constitutional on a day like this. And how are you, sir?"

"Awful," said H.M. instantly. "But that's not the point. Masters, you crawlin' snake! You're the very man I wanted to see."

Few things startled the Chief Inspector. This one did.

"You," he repeated, "wanted to see *me*?"

"Uh-huh."

"And what about?"

"Masters, do you remember the Victoria Adams case about twenty years ago?"

The Chief Inspector's manner suddenly changed and grew wary.

"Victoria Adams case?" he ruminated. "No, sir, I can't say I do."

"Son, you're lyin'! You were sergeant to old Chief Inspector Rutherford in those days, and well I remember it!"

Masters stood on his dignity.

"That's as may be, sir. But twenty years ago . . ."

"A little girl of twelve or thirteen, the child of very wealthy parents, disappeared one night out of a country cottage with all the doors and windows locked on the inside. A week later, while everybody was havin' screaming hysterics, the child reappeared again: through the locks and bolts, tucked up in her bed as usual. And to this day nobody's ever known what really happened."

There was a silence, while Masters shut his jaws hard.

"This family, the Adamses," persisted H.M., "owned the cottage, down Aylesbury way, on the edge of Goblin Wood, opposite the lake. Or was it?"

"Oh, ah," growled Masters. "It was."

H.M. looked at him curiously.

"They used the cottage as a base for bathin' in summer, and ice-skatin' in winter. It was black winter when the child vanished, and the place was all locked up inside against drafts. They say her old man nearly went loopy when he found her there a week later, lying asleep under the lamp. But all she'd say, when they asked her where she'd been, was, '*I don't know.*' "

Again there was a silence, while red buses thundered through the traffic press of Whitehall.

"You've got to admit, Masters, there was a flaming public rumpus. I say: did you ever read Barrie's *Mary Rose*?"

"No."

"Well, it was a situation straight out of Barrie. Some people, y'see, said that Vicky Adams was a child of faërie who'd been spirited away by the pixies . . ."

Whereupon Masters exploded.

He removed his bowler hat and wiped his forehead. He made remarks about pixies, in detail, which could not have been bettered by H.M. himself.

"I know, son, I know." H.M. was soothing. Then his big voice sharpened. "Now tell me. Was all this talk strictly true?"

"What talk?"

"Locked windows? Bolted doors? No attic-trap? No cellar? Solid walls and floor?"

"Yes, sir," answered Masters, regaining his dignity with a powerful effort, "I'm bound to admit it *was* true."

"Then there wasn't any jiggery-pokery about the cottage?"

"In your eye there wasn't," said Masters.

"How d'ye mean?"

"Listen, sir." Masters lowered his voice. "Before the Adamses took over that place, it was a hideout for Chuck Randall. At that time he was the swellest of the swell mob; we lagged him a couple of years later. Do you think Chuck wouldn't have rigged up some gadget for a getaway? Just so! Only . . ."

"Well? Hey?"

"We couldn't find it," grunted Masters.

"And I'll bet that pleased old Chief Inspector Rutherford?"

"I tell you straight: he was fair up the pole. Especially as the kid herself was a pretty kid, all big eyes and dark hair. You couldn't help trusting her."

"Yes," said H.M. "That's what worries me."

"Worries you?"

"Oh, my son!" said H.M. dismally. "Here's Vicky Adams, the spoiled daughter of dotin' parents. She's supposed to be 'odd' and 'fey.' She's even encouraged to be. During her adolescence, the most impressionable time of her life, she gets wrapped round with the gauze of a mystery that people talk about even yet. What's that woman like now, Masters? What's that woman like now?"

"Dear Sir Henry!" murmured Miss Vicky Adams in her softest voice.

She said this just as William Sage's car, with Bill and Eve Drayton in the front seat, and Vicky and H.M. in the back seat, turned off the main road. Behind them lay the smoky-red roofs of Aylesbury, against a brightness of late afternoon. The car turned down a side road, a damp tunnel of greenery, and into another road which was little more than a lane between hedgerows.

H.M.—though cheered by three good-sized picnic hampers from Fortnum & Mason, their wickerwork lids bulging with a feast—did not seem happy. Nobody in that car was happy, with the possible exception of Miss Adams herself.

Vicky, unlike Eve, was small and dark and vivacious. Her large light-brown eyes, with very black lashes, could be arch and coy; or they could be dreamily intense. The late Sir James Barrie might have called her a sprite. Those of more sober views would have recognized a different quality: she had an inordinate sex appeal, which was as palpable as a physical touch to any male within yards. And despite her smallness, Vicky had a full voice like Eve's. All these qualities she used even in so simple a matter as giving traffic directions.

"First right," she would say, leaning forward to put her hands on Bill Sage's shoulders. "Then straight on until the next traffic light. Ah, clever boy!"

"Not at all, not at all!" Bill would disclaim, with red ears and rather an erratic style of driving.

"Oh, yes, you are!" And Vicky would twist the lobe of his ear, playfully, before sitting back again.

(Eve Drayton did not say anything. She did not even turn round. Yet the atmosphere, even of that quiet English picnic party, had already become a trifle hysterical.)

"Dear Sir Henry!" murmured Vicky, as they turned down into the deep lane between the hedgerows. "I do wish you wouldn't be so materialistic! I do, really. Haven't you the tiniest bit of spirituality in your nature?"

"Me?" said H.M. in astonishment. "I got a very lofty spiritual nature. But what I want just now, my wench, is grub.—Oi!"

Bill Sage glanced round.

"By that speedometer," H.M. pointed, "we've now come forty-six miles and a bit. We didn't even leave town until people of decency and sanity were having their tea. Where are we *goin'*?"

"But didn't you know?" asked Vicky, with wide-open eyes. "We're going to the cottage where I had such a dreadful experience when I was a child."

"Was it such a dreadful experience, Vicky dear?" inquired Eve.

Vicky's eyes seemed far away.

"I don't remember, really. I was only a child, you see. I didn't understand. I hadn't developed the power for myself then."

"What power?" H.M. asked sharply.

"To dematerialize," said Vicky. "Of course."

In that warm sun-dusted lane, between the hawthorn hedges, the car jolted over a rut. Crockery rattled.

"Uh-huh. I see," observed H.M. without inflection. "And where do you go, my wench, when you dematerialize?"

"Into a strange country. Through a little door. You wouldn't understand. Oh, you *are* such Philistines!" moaned Vicky. Then, with a sudden change of mood, she leaned forward and her whole physical allurement flowed again towards Bill Sage. "*You* wouldn't like me to disappear, would you, Bill?"

(Easy! Easy!)

"Only," said Bill, with a sort of wild gallantry, "if you promised to reappear again straightaway."

"Oh, I should have to do that," Vicky sat back. She was trembling. "The power wouldn't be strong enough. But even a poor little thing like me might be able to teach you a lesson. Look there!"

And she pointed ahead.

On their left, as the lane widened, stretched the ten-acre gloom of what is fancifully known as Goblin Wood. On their right lay a small lake, on private property and therefore deserted.

The cottage—set well back into a clearing of the wood so as to face the road, screened from it by a line of beeches—was in fact a bungalow of rough-hewn stone, with a slate roof. Across the front of it ran a wooden porch. It had a seedy air, like the long yellow-green grass of its front lawn. Bill parked the car at the side of the road, since there was no driveway.

"It's a bit lonely, ain't it?" demanded H.M. His voice boomed out against that utter stillness, under the hot sun.

"Oh, yes!" breathed Vicky. She jumped out of the car in a whirl of skirts. "That's why *they* were able to come and take me. When I was a child."

"They?"

"Dear Sir Henry! Do I need to explain?"

Then Vicky looked at Bill.

"I must apologize," she said, "for the state the house is in. I haven't been out here for months and months. There's a modern bathroom, I'm glad to say. Only paraffin lamps, of course. But then," a dreamy smile flashed across her face, "you won't need lamps, will you? Unless . . ."

"You mean," said Bill, who was taking a black case out of the car, "unless you disappear again?"

"Yes, Bill. And promise me you won't be frightened when I do."

The young man uttered a ringing oath which was shushed by Sir Henry Merrivale, who austerely said he disapproved of profanity. Eve Drayton was very quiet.

"But in the meantime," Vicky said wistfully, "let's forget it all, shall we? Let's laugh and dance and sing and pretend we're children! And surely our guest must be even more hungry by this time?"

It was in this emotional state that they sat down to their picnic.

H.M., if the truth must be told, did not fare too badly. Instead of sitting on some hummock of ground, they dragged a table and chairs to the shaded porch. All spoke in strained voices. But no word of controversy was said. It was only afterwards, when the cloth was cleared, the furniture and hampers pushed indoors, the empty bottles flung away, that danger tapped a warning.

From under the porch Vicky fished out two half-rotted deck chairs, which she set up in the long grass of the lawn. These were to be occupied by Eve and H.M., while Vicky took Bill Sage to inspect a plum tree of some remarkable quality she did not specify.

Eve sat down without comment. H.M., who was smoking a black cigar opposite her, waited some time before he spoke.

"Y' know," he said, taking the cigar out of his mouth, "you're behaving remarkably well."

"Yes," Eve laughed. "Aren't I?"

"Are you pretty well acquainted with this Adams gal?"

"I'm her first cousin," Eve answered simply. "Now that her parents are dead, I'm the only relative she's got. I know *all* about her."

From far across the lawn floated two voices saying something about wild strawberries. Eve, her fair hair and fair complexion vivid against the dark line of Goblin Wood, clenched her hands on her knees.

"You see, H.M.," she hesitated, "there was another reason why I invited you here. I—I don't quite know how to approach it."

"I'm the old man," said H.M., tapping himself impressively on the chest. "You tell me."

"Eve, darling!" interposed Vicky's voice, crying across the ragged lawn. "Coo-ee! Eve!"

"Yes, dear?"

"I've just remembered," cried Vicky, "that I haven't shown Bill over the cottage! You don't mind if I steal him away from you for a little while?"

"No, dear! Of course not!"

It was H.M., sitting so as to face the bungalow, who saw Vicky and Bill go in. He saw Vicky's wistful smile as she closed the door after them. Eve did not even look round. The sun was declining, making fiery chinks through the thickness of Goblin Wood behind the cottage.

"I won't let her have him," Eve suddenly cried. "I won't! I won't! I won't!"

"Does she want him, my wench? Or, which is more to the point, does he want her?"

"He never has," Eve said with emphasis. "Not really. And he never will."

H.M., motionless, puffed out cigar smoke.

"Vicky's a faker," said Eve. "Does that sound catty?"

"Not necessarily. I was just thinkin' the same thing myself."

"I'm patient," said Eve. Her blue eyes were fixed. "I'm terribly, terribly patient. I can wait years for what I want. Bill's not making much money now, and I haven't got a bean. But Bill's got great talent under that easy-going manner of his. He *must* have the right girl to help him. If only . . ."

"If only the elfin sprite would let him alone. Hey?"

"Vicky acts like that," said Eve, "towards practically every man she ever meets. That's why she never married. She says it leaves her soul free to commune with other souls. This occultism—"

Then it all poured out, the family story of the Adamses. This repressed girl spoke at length, spoke as perhaps she had never spoken before. Vicky Adams, the child who wanted to attract attention, her father, Uncle Fred, and her mother, Aunt Margaret, seemed to walk in vividness as the shadows gathered.

"I was too young to know her at the time of the 'disappearance,' of course. But, oh, I knew her afterwards! And I thought . . ."

"Well?"

"If I could get *you* here," said Eve, "I thought she'd try to show off with some game. And then you'd expose her. And Bill would see what an awful faker she is. But it's hopeless! It's hopeless!"

"Looky here," observed H.M., who was smoking his third cigar. He sat up. "Doesn't it strike you those two are being a rummy-awful long time just in lookin' through a little bungalow?"

Eve, roused out of a dream, stared back at him. She sprang to her feet. She was not now, you could guess, thinking of any disappearance.

"Excuse me a moment," she said curtly.

Eve hurried across to the cottage, went up on the porch, and opened the front door. H.M. heard her heels rap down the length of the small passage inside. She marched straight back again, closed the front door, and rejoined H.M.

"All the doors of the rooms are shut," she announced in a high voice. "I really don't think I ought to disturb them."

"Easy, my wench!"

"I have absolutely no interest," declared Eve, with the tears coming into her eyes, "in what happens to either of them now. Shall we take the car and go back to town without them?"

H.M. threw away his cigar, got up, and seized her by the shoulders.

"I'm the old man," he said, with a leer like an ogre. "Will you listen to me?"

"No!"

"If I'm any reader of the human dial," persisted H.M., "that young feller's no more gone on Vicky Adams than I am. He was scared, my wench, Scared." Doubt, indecision crossed H.M.'s face. "I dunno what he's scared of. Burn me, I don't! But . . ."

"Hoy!" called the voice of Bill Sage.

It did not come from the direction of the cottage.

They were surrounded on three sides by Goblin Wood, now blurred with twilight. From the north side the voice bawled at them, followed by crackling in dry undergrowth. Bill, his hair and sports coat and flannels more than a little dirty, regarded them with a face of bitterness.

"Here are her blasted wild strawberries," he announced, extending his hand. "Three of 'em. The fruitful (excuse me) result of three quarters of an hour's hard labor. I absolutely refuse to chase 'em in the dark."

For a moment Eve Drayton's mouth moved without speech.

"Then you weren't . . . in the cottage all this time?"

"In the cottage?" Bill glanced at it. "I was in that cottage," he said, "about five minutes. Vicky had a woman's whim. She wanted some wild strawberries out of what she called the 'forest.' "

"Wait a minute, son!" said H. M. very sharply. "You didn't come out that front door. Nobody did."

"No! I went out the back door! It opens straight on the wood."

"Yes. And what happened then?"

"Well, I went to look for these damned . . ."

"No, no! What did *she* do?"

"Vicky? She locked and bolted the back door on the inside. I remember her grinning at me through the glass panel. She—"

Bill stopped short. His eyes widened, and then narrowed, as though at the impact of an idea. All three of them turned to look at the rough-stone cottage.

"By the way," said Bill. He cleared his throat vigorously. "By the way, have you seen Vicky since then?"

"No."

"This couldn't be . . . ?"

"It could be, son," said H.M. "We'd all better go in there and have a look."

They hesitated for a moment on the porch. A warm, moist fragrance breathed up from the ground after sunset. In half an hour it would be completely dark.

Bill Sage threw open the front door and shouted Vicky's name. That sound seemed to penetrate, reverberating, through every room. The intense heat and stuffiness of the cottage, where no window had been raised in months, blew out at them. But nobody answered.

"Get inside," snapped H.M. "And stop yowlin'." The Old Maestro was nervous. "I'm dead sure she didn't get out by the front door; but we'll just make certain there's no slippin' out now."

Stumbling over the table and chairs they had used on the porch, he fastened the front door. They were in a narrow passage, once handsome with parquet floor and pine-paneled walls, leading to a door with a glass panel at the rear. H.M. lumbered forward to inspect this door and found it locked and bolted, as Bill had said.

Goblin Wood grew darker.

Keeping well together, they searched the cottage. It was not large, having two good-sized rooms on one side of the passage, and two small rooms on the other side, so as to make space for bathroom and kitchenette. H.M., raising fogs of dust, ransacked every inch where a person could possibly hide.

And all the windows were locked on the inside. And the chimney-flues were too narrow to admit anybody.

And Vicky Adams wasn't there.

"Oh, my eye!" breathed Sir Henry Merrivale.

They had gathered, by what idiotic impulse not even H.M. could have said, just outside the open door of the bathroom. A bath tap dripped monotonously. The last light through a frosted-glass window showed three faces hung there as though disembodied.

"Bill," said Eve in an unsteady voice, "this is a trick. Oh, I've longed for her to be exposed! This is a trick!"

"Then where is she?"

"H.M. can tell us! Can't you, H.M.?"

"Well . . . now," muttered the great man.

Across H.M.'s Panama hat was a large black handprint, made there when he had pressed down the hat after investigating the chimney. He glowered under it.

"Son," he said to Bill, "there's just one question I want you to answer in all this hokey-pokey. When you went out pickin' wild strawberries, will you swear Vicky Adams didn't go with you?"

"As God is my judge, she didn't," returned Bill, with fervency and obvious truth. "Besides, how the devil could she? Look at the lock and bolt on the back door!"

H.M. made two more violent black handprints on his hat.

He lumbered forward, his head down, two or three paces in the narrow passage. His foot half skidded on something that had been lying there unnoticed, and he picked it up. It was a large, square section of thin, waterproof oilskin, jagged at one corner.

"Have you found anything?" demanded Bill in a strained voice.

"No. Not to make any sense, that is. But just a minute!"

At the rear of the passage, on the left-hand side, was the bedroom from which Vicky Adams had vanished as a child. Though H.M. had searched this room once before, he opened the door again.

It was now almost dark in Goblin Wood.

He saw dimly a room of twenty years before: a room of flounces, of lace curtains, of once-polished mahogany, its mirrors glimmering against white-papered walls. H.M. seemed especially interested in the windows.

He ran his hands carefully round the frame of each, even climbing laboriously up on a chair to examine the tops. He borrowed a box of matches from Bill; and the little spurts of light, following the rasp of the match, rasped against nerves as well. The hope died out of his face, and his companions saw it.

"H.M.," Bill said for the dozenth time, "where is she?"

"Son," replied H.M. despondently, "I don't know."

"Let's get out of here," Eve said abruptly. Her voice was a small scream. "I kn-know it's all a trick! I know Vicky's a faker! But let's get out of here. For God's sake let's get out of here!"

"As a matter of fact," Bill cleared his throat, "I agree. Anyway, we won't hear from Vicky until tomorrow morning."

"*Oh, yes, you will,*" whispered Vicky's voice out of the darkness.

Eve screamed.

They lighted a lamp.

But there was nobody there.


Their retreat from the cottage, it must be admitted, was not very dignified.

How they stumbled down that ragged lawn in the dark, how they piled rugs and picnic hampers into the car, how they eventually found the main road again, is best left undescribed.

Sir Henry Merrivale has since sneered at this—"a bit of a goosy feeling; nothin' much"— and it is true that he has no nerves to speak of. But he can be worried, badly worried; and that he was worried on this occasion may be deduced from what happened later.

H.M., after dropping in at Claridge's for a modest late supper of lobster and *Pêche Melba*, returned to his house in Brook Street and slept a hideous sleep. It was three o'clock in the morning, even before the summer dawn, when the ringing of the bedside telephone roused him.

What he heard sent his blood pressure soaring.

"Dear Sir Henry!" crooned a familiar and sprite-like voice.

H.M. was himself again, full of gall and bile. He switched on the bedside lamp and put on his spectacles with care, so as adequately to address the phone.

"Have I got the honor," he said with dangerous politeness, "of addressin' Miss Vicky Adams?"

"Oh, yes!"

"I sincerely trust," said H.M., "you've been havin' a good time? Are you materialized yet?"

"Oh, yes!"

"Where are you now?"

"I'm afraid," there was coy laughter in the voice, "that must be a little secret for a day or two. I want to teach you a really *good* lesson. Blessings, dear."

And she hung up the receiver.

H.M. did not say anything. He climbed out of bed. He stalked up and down the room, his corporation majestic under an old-fashioned nightshirt stretching to his heels. Then, since he himself had been waked up at three o'clock in the morning, the obvious course was to wake up somebody else; so he dialed the home number of Chief Inspector Masters.

"No, sir," retorted Masters grimly, after coughing the frog out of his throat, "I do *not* mind you ringing up. Not a bit of it!" He spoke with a certain pleasure. "Because I've got a bit of news for you."

H.M. eyed the phone suspiciously.

"Masters, are you trying to do me in the eye again?"

"It's what you always try to do to me, isn't it?"

"All right, all right!" growled H.M. "What's the news?"

"Do you remember mentioning the Vicky Adams case to me yesterday?"

"Sort of. Yes."

"Oh, ah! Well, I had a word or two round among our people. I was tipped the wink to go and see a certain solicitor. He was old Mr. Fred Adams's solicitor before Mr. Adams died about six or seven years ago."

Here Masters's voice grew suave with triumph.

"I always said, Sir Henry, that Chuck Randall had planted some gadget in that cottage for a quick getaway. And I was right. The gadget was . . ."

"You were quite right, Masters. The gadget was a trick window."

The telephone, so to speak, gave a start.

"What's that?"

"A trick window." H.M. spoke patiently. "You press a spring. And the whole frame of the window, two leaves locked together, slides down between the walls far enough so you can climb over. Then you push it back up again."

*"How in lum's name do you know that?"*

"Oh, my son! They used to build windows like it in country houses during the persecution of Catholic priests. It was a good enough *second* guess. Only . . . it won't work."

Masters seemed annoyed. "It won't work now," Masters agreed. "And do you know why?"

"I can guess. Tell me."

"Because, just before Mr. Adams died, he discovered how his darling daughter had flummoxed him. He never told anybody except his lawyer. He took a handful of four-inch nails, and sealed up the top of that frame so tight an orangoutang couldn't move it, and painted 'em over so they wouldn't be noticed."

"Uh-huh. You can notice 'em now."

"I doubt if the young lady herself ever knew. But, by George!" Masters said savagely. "I'd like to see anybody try the same game now!"

"You would, hey? Then will it interest you to know that the same gal has just disappeared out of the same house AGAIN?"

H.M. began a long narrative of the facts, but he had to break off because the telephone was raving.

"Honest, Masters," H.M. said seriously, "I'm not joking. She didn't get out through the window. But she did get out. You'd better meet me," he gave directions, "tomorrow morning. In the meantime, son, sleep well."

It was, therefore, a worn-faced Masters who went into the Visitors' Room at the Senior Conservatives' Club just before lunch on the following day.

The Visitors' Room is a dark sepulchral place, opening on an air well, where the visitor is surrounded by pictures of dyspeptic-looking gentlemen with beards. It has a pervading mustiness of wood and leather. Though whiskey and soda stood on the table, H.M. sat in a leather chair far away from it, ruffling his hands across his bald head.

"Now, Masters, keep your shirt on!" he warned. "This business may be rummy. But it's not a police matter—yet."

"I know it's not a police matter," Masters said grimly. "All the same, I've had a word with the Superintendent at Aylesbury."

"Fowler?"

"You know him?"

"Sure. I know everybody. Is he goin' to keep an eye out?"

"He's going to have a look at that ruddy cottage. I've asked for any telephone calls to be put through here. In the meantime, sir—"

It was at this point, as though diabolically inspired, that the telephone rang. H.M. reached it before Masters.

"It's the old man," he said, unconsciously assuming a stance of grandeur. "Yes, yes! Masters is here, but he's drunk. You tell me first. What's that?"

The telephone talked thinly.

"Sure I looked in the kitchen cupboard," bellowed H.M. "Though I didn't honestly expect to find Vicky Adams hidin' there. What's that? Say it again! Plates? Cups that had been . . ."

An almost frightening change had come over H.M.'s expression. He stood motionless. All the posturing went out of him. He was not even listening to the voice that still talked thinly, while his eyes and his brain moved to put together facts. At length (though the voice still talked) he hung up the receiver.

H.M. blundered back to the center table, where he drew out a chair and sat down.

"Masters," he said very quietly, "I've come close to makin' the silliest mistake of my life."

Here he cleared his throat.

"I shouldn't have made it, son. I really shouldn't. But don't yell at me for cuttin' off Fowler. I can tell you now how Vicky Adams disappeared. And she said one true thing when she said she was going into a strange country."

"How do you mean?"

"She's dead," answered H.M.

The word fell with heavy weight into that dingy room, where the bearded faces looked down.

"Y'see," H.M. went on blankly, "a lot of us were right when we thought Vicky Adams was a faker. She was. To attract attention to herself, she played that trick on her family with the hocused window. She's lived and traded on it ever since. That's what sent me straight in the wrong direction. I was on the alert for some *trick* Vicky Adams might play. So it never occurred to me that this elegant pair of beauties, Miss Eve Drayton and Mr. William Sage, were deliberately conspirin' to murder *her*."

Masters got slowly to his feet.

"Did you say . . . murder?"

"Oh, yes."

Again H.M. cleared his throat.

"It was all arranged beforehand for me to be a witness. They knew Vicky Adams couldn't resist a challenge to disappear, especially as Vicky always believed she could get out by the trick window. They wanted Vicky to *say* she was goin' to disappear. They never knew anything about the trick window, Masters. But they knew their own plan very well.

"Eve Drayton even told me the motive. She hated Vicky, of course. But that wasn't the main point. She was Vicky Adams's only relative; she'd inherit an awful big scoopful of money. Eve said she could be patient. (And, burn me, how her eyes meant it when she said that!) Rather than risk any slightest suspicion of murder, she was willing to wait seven years until a disappeared person can be presumed dead.

"Our Eve, I think, was the fiery drivin' force of that conspiracy. She was only scared part of the time. Sage was scared all of the time. But it was Sage who did the real dirty work. He lured Vicky Adams into that cottage, while Eve kept me in close conversation on the lawn . . ."

H.M. paused.

Intolerably vivid in the mind of Chief Inspector Masters, who had seen it years before, rose the picture of the rough-stone bungalow against the darkening wood.

"Masters," said H.M., "why should a bath tap be dripping in a house that hadn't been occupied for months?"

"Well?"

"Sage, y'see, is a surgeon. I saw him take his black case of instruments out of the car. He took Vicky Adams into that house. In the bathroom he stabbed her, he stripped her, and *he dismembered her body in the bath tub. —Easy, son!*"

"Go on," said Masters without moving.

"The head, the torso, the folded arms and legs, were wrapped up in three large square pieces of thin transparent oilskin. Each was sewed up with coarse thread so the blood wouldn't drip. Last night I found one of the oilskin pieces he'd ruined when his needle slipped at the corner. Then he walked out of the house, with the back door still standin' unlocked, to get his wild-strawberry alibi."

"Sage went out of there," shouted Masters, "leaving the body in the house?"

"Oh, yes," agreed H.M.

"But where did he leave it?"

H.M. ignored this.

"In the meantime, son, what about Eve Drayton? At the end of the arranged three quarters of an hour, she indicated there was hanky-panky between her fiancé and Vicky Adams. She flew into the house. But what did she do?

"She walked to the back of the passage. I heard her. *There she simply locked and bolted the back door.* And then she marched out to join me with tears in her eyes. And these two beauties were ready for investigation."

"Investigation?" said Masters. *"With that body still in the house?"*

"Oh, yes."

Masters lifted both fists.

"It must have given young Sage a shock," said H.M., "when I found that piece of waterproof oilskin he'd washed but dropped. Anyway, these two had only two more bits of hokeypokey. The 'vanished' gal had to speak — to show she was still alive. If you'd been there, son, you'd have noticed that Eve Drayton's got a voice just like Vicky Adams's. If somebody speaks in a dark room, carefully imitatin' a coy tone she never uses herself, the illusion's goin' to be pretty good. The same goes for a telephone.

"It was finished, Masters. All that had to be done was remove the body from the house, and get it far away from there . . ."

"But that's just what I'm asking you, sir! Where was the body all this time? And who in blazes *did* remove the body from the house?"

"All of us did," answered H.M.

"What's that?"

"Masters," said H.M., "aren't you forgettin' the picnic hampers?"

And now, the Chief Inspector saw, H.M. was as white as a ghost. His next words took Masters like a blow between the eyes.

"Three good-sized wickerwork hampers, with lids. After our big meal on the porch, those hampers were shoved inside the house where Sage could get at 'em. He had to leave most of the used crockery behind, in the kitchen cupboard. But three wickerwork hampers from a picnic, and three butcher's parcels to go inside 'em. I carried one down to the car myself. It felt a bit funny . . ."

H.M. stretched out his hand, not steadily, towards the whiskey.

"Y'know," he said, "I'll always wonder whether I was carrying the — head."

# Fritz Leiber

Fritz Leiber, Jr. (1910– ), who began his career with supernatural stories, has since become one of the most acclaimed authors of science fiction. Yet, unlike many others who have followed the same path, he has never abandoned his interest in pure fantasy. His most important science fiction novels include *Gather, Darkness!* and *The Big Time.* The respect Leiber has earned from his colleagues is indicated by the fact that his 1967 story "Gonna Roll the Bones" won both major science fiction awards, the "Hugo" and the "Nebula," even though its theme is essentially supernatural.

He achieved early popularity with a series of stories that has continued for over thirty years, recounting the adventures of Fafhrd and the Gray Mouser, two rogues who roam an ancient world full of sin and sorcery, a backward realm known as Nehwon. Their exploits have been featured in several books, including *Swords Against Death* and *Swords Against Wizardry.* This series, which began in the pages of *Unknown,* is at least the best sword and sorcery saga since the Robert E. Howard tales that appeared in *Weird Tales.* In a genre that tolerates a depressing amount of hack writing, Leiber's stories are distinguished by their wit and imagination. The characters were originally conceived with the aid of Harry Fischer.

His tales of terror are equally outstanding. The novel *Conjure Wife* is remarkably effective, all the more so in view of its unusually unlikely idea that all the women in the world are secretly practicing magic. It has been filmed twice, in 1944 and 1962. *You're All Alone* is a nightmare based on the paranoid premise that the world is in reality a malevolent machine designed to suppress individuality.

Leiber is the son of a Shakespearean actor, and he himself has performed under a stage name. This background has obviously influenced such of his stories as "Little Old Miss Macbeth" and "Four Ghosts in Hamlet." And most of his work is theatrical in the best sense of the term, vividly staged and dramatically unified.

His first book, *Night's Black Agents* (1947), contains many of his best horror stories, some of them from the pages of *Weird Tales* and *Unknown.* "Smoke Ghost" and "The Hound" are especially evocative examples of Leiber's interest in imagining metropolitan menaces. "There are terrors in the modern city," he has written, "in comparison to which the darks of Gothic castles and haunted woods are light."

"The Man Who Never Grew Young," which first appeared in *Night's Black Agents,* is a fantasy about a reaction to the overwhelming fears that haunt contemporary civilization. Although it might be considered less of a horror story than a story about horror, it is nevertheless one of the most grotesque tales in English, and one that is difficult to dislodge from the memory. Leiber claims that it almost wrote itself, presumably without any consideration on his part as to whether its theme was scientific or supernatural. As he says, "All I ever try to write is a good story with a good measure of strangeness in it. The supreme goddess of the universe is Mystery, and being well entertained is the highest joy."

# THE MAN WHO NEVER GREW YOUNG

## Fritz Leiber

Maot is becoming restless. Often toward evening she trudges to where the black earth meets the yellow sand and stands looking across the desert until the wind starts.

But I sit with my back to the reed screen and watch the Nile.

It isn't just that she's growing young. She is wearying of the fields. She leaves their tilling to me and lavishes her attentions on the flock. Every day she takes the sheep and goats farther to pasture.

I have seen it coming for a long time. For generations the fields have been growing scantier and less diligently irrigated. There seems to be more rain. The houses have become simpler—mere walled tents. And every year some family gathers its flocks and wanders off west.

Why should I cling so tenaciously to these poor relics of civilization—I, who have seen king Cheops' men take down the Great Pyramid block by block and return it to the hills?

I often wonder why I never grow young. It is still as much a mystery to me as to the brown farmers who kneel in awe when I walk past.

I envy those who grow young. I yearn for the sloughing of wisdom and responsibility, the plunge into a period of lovemaking and breathless excitement, the carefree years before the end.

But I remain a bearded man of thirty-odd, wearing the goatskin as I once wore the doublet or the toga, always on the brink of that plunge yet never making it.

It seems to me that I have always been this way. Why, I cannot even remember my own disinterment, and everyone remembers that.

Maot is subtle. She does not ask for what she wants, but when she comes home at evening she sits far back from the fire and murmurs disturbing fragments of song and rubs her eyelids with green pigment to make herself desirable to me and tries in every way to infect me with her restlessness. She tempts me from the hot work at midday and points out how hardy our sheep and goat are becoming.

There are no young men among us any more. All of them start for the desert with the approach of youth, or before. Even toothless, scrawny patriarchs uncurl from their grave-holes, and hardly pausing to refresh themselves with the food and drink dug up with them, collect their flocks and wives and hobble off into the west.

I remember the first disinterment I witnessed. It was in a country of smoke and machines and constant news. But what I am about to relate occurred in a backwater where there were still small farms and narrow roads and simple ways.

There were two old women named Flora and Helen. It could not have been more than a few years since their own disinterments, but those I cannot remember. I think I was some sort of nephew, but I cannot be sure.

They began to visit an old grave in the cemetery a half mile outside town. I remember the little bouquets of flowers they would bring back with them. Their prim, placid faces became troubled. I could see that grief was entering their lives.

The years passed. Their visits to the cemetery became more frequent. Accompanying them once, I noted that the worn inscription on the headstone was growing clearer and sharper, just as was happening to their own features. "John, loving husband of Flora. . . ."

Often Flora would sob through half the night, and Helen went about with a set look on her face. Relatives came and spoke comforting words, but these seemed only to intensify their grief.

Finally the headstone grew brand-new and the grass became tender green shoots which disappeared into the raw brown earth. As if these were the signs their obscure instincts had been awaiting, Flora and Helen mastered their grief and visited the minister and the mortician and the doctor and made certain arrangements.

On a cold autumn day, when the brown curled leaves were whirling up into the trees, the procession set out—the empty hearse, the dark silent automobiles. At the cemetery we found a couple of men with shovels turning away unobstrusively from the newly opened grave. Then, while Flora and Helen wept bitterly and the minister spoke solemn words, a long narrow box was lifted from the grave and carried to the hearse.

At home the lid of the box was unscrewed and slid back, and we saw John, a waxen old man with a long life before him.

Next day, in obedience to what seemed an age-old ritual, they took him from the box, and the mortician undressed him and drew a pungent liquid from his veins and injected the red blood. Then they took him and laid him in bed. After a few hours of stoney-eyed waiting, the blood began to work. He stirred and his first breath rattled in his throat. Flora sat down on the bed and strained him to her in a fearful embrace.

But he was very sick and in need of rest, so the doctor waved her from the room. I remember the look on her face as she closed the door.

I should have been happy too, but I seem to recall that I felt there was something unwholesome about the whole episode. Perhaps our first experiences of the great crises of life always affect us in some such fashion.

I love Maot. The hundreds I have loved before her in my wanderings down the world do not take away from the sincerity of my affection. I did not enter her life, or theirs, as lovers ordinarily do—from the grave or in the passion of some terrible quarrel. I am always the drifter.

Maot knows there is something strange about me. But she does not let that interfere with her efforts to make me do the thing she wants.

I love Maot and eventually I will accede to her desire. But first I will linger a while by the Nile and the mighty pageantry conjured up by its passage.

My first memories are always the most difficult and I struggle the hardest to interpret them. I have the feeling that if I could get back a little beyond them, a terrifying understanding would come to me. But I never seem able to make the necessary effort.

They begin without antecedent in cloud and turmoil, darkness and fear. I am a citizen of a great country far away, beardless and wearing ugly confining clothing, but no different in age and appearance from today. The country is a hundred times bigger than Egypt, yet it is only one of many. All the peoples of the world are known to each other, and the world is round,

not flat, and it floats in an endless immensity dotted with islands of suns, not confined under a star-speckled bowl.

Machines are everywhere, and news goes round the world like a shout, and desires are many. There is undreamed-of abundance, unrivaled opportunities. Yet men are not happy. They live in fear. The fear, if I recall rightly, is of a war that will engulf and perhaps destroy us all. It overhangs us like the dark.

The weapons they have ready for that war are terrible. Great engines that sail pilotless, not through the water but the air, halfway around the world to destroy some enemy city. Others that dart up beyond the air itself, to come in attacking from the stars. Poisoned clouds. Deadly motes of luminous dust.

But worst of all are the weapons that are only rumored.

For months that seem eternities we wait on the brink of that war. We know that the mistakes have been made, the irrevocable steps taken, the last chances lost. We only await the event.

It would seem that there must have been some special reason for the extremity of our hopelessness and horror. As if there had been previous worldwide wars and we had struggled back from each desperately promising ourselves that it would be the last. But of any such, I can remember nothing. I and the world might well have been created under the shadow of that catastrophe, in a universal disinterment.

The months wear on. Then, miraculously, unbelievably, the war begins to recede. The tension relaxes. The clouds lift. There is great activity, conferences and plans. Hopes for lasting peace ride high.

This does not last. In sudden holocaust, there arises an oppresser named Hitler. Odd, how that name should come back to me after these millennia. His armies fan out across the globe.

But their success is short-lived. They are driven back, and Hitler trails off into oblivion. In the end he is an obscure agitator, almost forgotten.

Another peace then, but neither does it last. Another war, less fierce than the preceding, and it too trails off into a quieter era.

And so on.

I sometimes think (I must hold on to this) that time once flowed in the opposite direction, and that, in revulsion from the ultimate war, it turned back upon itself and began to retrace its former course. That our present lives are only a return and an unwinding. A great retreat.

In that case time may turn again. We may have another chance to scale the barrier.

But no. . .

The thought has vanished in the rippling Nile.

Another family is leaving the valley today. All morning they have toiled up the sandy gorge. And now, returning perhaps for a last glimpse, to the verge of the yellow cliffs, they are outlined against the morning sky—upright specks for men, flat specks for animals.

Maot watches beside me. But she makes no comment. She is sure of me.

The cliff is bare again. Soon they will have forgotten the Nile and its disturbing ghosts of memories.

All our life is a forgetting and a closing in. As the child is absorbed by its mother, so great thoughts are swallowed up in the mind of genius. At first they are everywhere. They environ us like the air. Then there is a narrowing in. Not all men know them. Then there comes one great man, and he takes them to himself, and they are a secret. There only remains the disturbing conviction that something worthy has vanished.

I have seen Shakespeare unwrite the great plays, I have watched Socrates unthink the great thoughts. I have heard Jesus unsay the great words.

There is an inscription in stone, and it seems eternal. Coming back centuries later I find it the same, only a little less worn, and I think that it, at least, may endure. But some day a scribe comes and laboriously fills in the grooves until there is only blank stone.

Then only he knows what was written there. And as he grows young, that knowledge dies forever.

It is the same in all we do. Our houses grow new and we dismantle them and stow the materials inconspicuously away, in mine and quarry, forest and field. Our clothes grow new and we put them off. And we grow new and forget and blindly seek a mother.

All the people are gone now. Only I and Maot linger.

I had not realized it would come so soon. Now that we are near the end, Nature seems to hurry.

I suppose that there are other stragglers here and there along the Nile, but I like to think that we are the last to see the vanishing fields, the last to look upon the river with some knowledge of what it once symbolized, before oblivion closes in.

Ours is a world in which lost causes conquer. After the second war of which I spoke, there was a long period of peace in my native country across the sea. There were among us at that time a primitive people called Indians, neglected and imposed upon and forced to live apart in unwanted areas. We gave no thought to these people. We would have laughed at anyone who told us they had power to hurt us.

But from somewhere a spark of rebellion appeared among them. They formed bands, armed themselves with bows and inferior guns, took the warpath against us.

We fought them in little unimportant wars that were never quite conclusive. They persisted, always returning to the fight, laying ambushes for our men and wagons, harrying us continually, eventually making sizable inroads.

Yet we still considered them of such trifling importance that we found time to engage in a civil war among ourselves.

The issue of this war was sad. A dusky portion of our citizenry were enslaved and made to toil for us in house and field.

The Indians grew formidable. Step by step they drove us back across the wide midwestern rivers and plains, through the wooded mountains to eastward.

On the eastern coast we held for a while, chiefly by leaguing with a transoceanic island nation, to whom we surrendered our independence.

There was an enheartening occurrence. The enslaved Negroes were gathered together and crowded in ships and taken to the southern shores of this continent, and there liberated or given into the hands of warlike tribes who eventually released them.

But the pressure of the Indians, sporadically aided by foreign allies, increased. City by city, town by town, settlement by settlement, we pulled up our stakes and took ship ourselves across the sea. Toward the end the Indians became strangely pacific, so that the last boatloads seemed to flee not so much in physical fear as in supernatural terror of the green silent forests that had swallowed up their homes.

To the south the Aztecs took up their glass knives and flint-edged swords and drove out the . . . I think they were called Spaniards.

In another century the whole western continent was forgotten, save for dim, haunting recollections.

Growing tyranny and ignorance, a constant contraction of frontiers, rebellions of the downtrodden, who in turn became oppressors—these constituted the next epoch of history.

Once I thought the tide had turned. A strong and orderly people, the Romans, arose and put most of the diminished world under their sway.

But this stability proved transitory. Once again the governed rose against the governors. The Romans were driven back—from England, from Egypt, from Gaul, from Asia, from

Greece. Rising from barren fields came Carthage to contest successfully Rome's preeminence. The Romans took refuge in Rome, became unimportant, dwindled, were lost in a maze of migrations.

Their energizing thoughts flamed up for one glorious century in Athens, then ceased to carry weight.

After that, the decline continued at a steady pace. Never again was I deceived into thinking the trend had changed.

Except this one last time.

Because she was stony and sun-drenched and dry, full of temples and tombs, given to custom and calm, I thought Egypt would endure. The passage of almost changeless centuries encouraged me in this belief. I thought that if we had not reached the turning point, we had at least come to rest.

But the rains have come, the temples and tombs fill the scars in the cliffs, and the custom and calm have given way to the restless urges of the nomad.

If there is a turning point, it will not come until man is one with the beasts.

And Egypt must vanish like the rest.

Tomorrow Maot and I set out. Our flock is gathered. Our tent is rolled.

Maot is afire with youth. She is very loving.

It will be strange in the desert. All too soon we will exchange our last and sweetest kiss and she will prattle to me childishly and I will look after her until we find her mother.

Or perhaps some day I will abandon her in the desert, and her mother will find her.

And I will go on.

# Richard Matheson

Richard Matheson (1926– ) is one of the most active and visible writers working today in the field of fantasy. He has produced a number of fine short stories and three important novels that have been turned into motion pictures. His adaptations of fiction by other authors have provided the screenplays for some of the most important horror movies of recent years.

Matheson's scripts include several of the Poe films produced by American International, directed by Roger Corman, and starring Vincent Price: *House of Usher* (1960), *The Pit and the Pendulum* (1961), *Tales of Terror* (1962), and *The Raven* (1963). For England's Hammer Films, he adapted novels by Anne Blaisdell and Dennis Wheatley for *Fanatic* (1965) and the excellent *The Devil's Bride* (1967).

His novel of a vampire plague, *I Am Legend* (1954), has been filmed twice, as *The Last Man on Earth* (1964) and *The Omega Man* (1971). Matheson wrote neither of these scripts, but he did do the screenplays for the 1957 film of his 1956 novel *The Shrinking Man* and for the 1973 film of his 1971 novel *Hell House*.

All of the novels and most of the movies have won critical praise for Matheson, who also wrote the scripts for such popular television films as *The Night Stalker* and *Duel*. In the midst of such prolific production, his impressive short stories are sometimes overlooked. Among the best are such clever variations on the vampire theme as "The Funeral," "Dress of White Silk," and the frequently reprinted "Blood Son." Another of his important stories is the wrenching "Mad House," in which the protagonist's bad temper infects his home until the furnishings rise up against him. Matheson's collections of tales include *Born of Man and Woman* (1954) and *The Shores of Space* (1957).

The title story of the first collection, "Born of Man and Woman," was the author's first published work. It appeared in 1950 in the *Magazine of Fantasy and Science Fiction;* Matheson was one of the most important discoveries of editors Anthony Boucher and J. Francis McMoas. The tale created an immediate sensation and was anthologized several times within a year of its original appearance, but it has been neglected in recent years in comparison with the author's more widely publicized achievements.

Still, this story remains one of his most imaginative and accomplished works. It is rare for a writer successfully to present a narrative through the eyes of a monster, yet Matheson succeeds here. He also demonstrates his ability to project himself into the half-formed mind of a child, a technique more frequently associated with his contemporary Ray Bradbury. Exactly what the narrator of the story may be is anybody's guess, and therein lies half the charm of the tale. Followers of fantasy might opt for the changeling legend, while science fiction fans

263

will insist on the mutant theory. Regardless, the story is a powerful one, of two human beings faced with an insoluble problem and an inhuman being determined to find a solution.

# BORN OF MAN AND WOMAN

## Richard Matheson

X—This day when it had light mother called me retch. You retch she said. I saw in her eyes the anger. I wonder what it is a retch.

This day it had water falling from upstairs. It fell all around. I saw that. The ground of the back I watched from the little window. The ground it sucked up the water like thirsty lips. It drank too much and it got sick and runny brown. I didnt like it.

Mother is a pretty I know. In my bed place with cold walls around I have a paper things that was behind the furnace. I says on it SCREENSTARS. I see in the pictures faces like of mother and father. Father says they are pretty. Once he said it.

And also mother he said. Mother so pretty and me decent enough. Look at you he said and didnt have the nice face. I touched his arm and said it is alright father. He shook and pulled away where I couldnt reach.

Today mother let me off the chain a little so I could look out the little window. Thats how I saw the water falling from upstairs.

XX—This day it had goldness in the upstairs. As I know when I looked at it my eyes hurt. After I look at it the cellar is red.

I think this was church. They leave the upstairs. The big machine swallows them and rolls out past and is gone. In the back part is the little mother. She is much small than me. I am I can see out the little window all I like.

In this day when it got dark I had eat my food and some bugs. I hear laughs upstairs. I like to know why there are laughs for. I took the chain from the wall and wrapped it around me. I walked squish to the stairs. They creak when I walk on them. My legs slip on them because I dont walk on stairs. My feet stick to the wood.

I went up and opened a door. It was a white place. White as white jewels that come from upstairs sometime. I went in and stood quiet. I hear the laughing some more. I walk to the sound and look through to the people. More people than I thought was. I thought I should laugh with them.

Mother came out and pushed the door in. It hit me and hurt. I fell back on the smooth floor and the chain made noise. I cried. She made a hissing noise into her and put her hand on her mouth. Her eyes got big.

She looked at me. I heard father call. What fell he called. She said a iron board. Come help pick it up she said. He came and said now is *that* so heavy you need. He saw me and grew big. The anger came in his eyes. He hit me. I spilled some of the drip on the floor from one arm. It was not nice. It made ugly green on the floor.

Father told me to go to the cellar. I had to go. The light it hurt some now in my eyes. It is not so like that in the cellar.

Father tied my legs and arms up. He put me on my bed. Upstairs I heard laughing while I

was quiet there looking on a black spider that was swinging down to me. I thought what father said. Ohgod he said. And only eight.

XXX—This day father hit in the chain again before it had light. I have to try pull it out again. He said I was bad to come upstairs. He said never do that again or he would beat me hard. That hurts.

I hurt. I slept the day and rested my head against the cold wall. I thought of the white place upstairs.

XXXX—I got the chain from the wall out. Mother was upstairs. I heard little laughs very high. I looked out the window. I saw all little people like the little mother and little fathers too. They are pretty.

They were making nice noise and jumping around the ground. Their legs was moving hard. They are like mother and father. Mother says all right people look like they do.

One of the little fathers saw me. He pointed at the window. I let go and slid down the wall in the dark. I curled up as they would not see. I heard their talks by the window and foots running. Upstairs there was a door hitting. I heard the little mother call upstairs. I heard heavy steps and I rushed in my bed place. I hit the chain in the wall and lay down on my front.

I heard mother come down. Have you been at the window she said. I heard the anger. *Stay* away from the window. You have pulled the chain out again.

She took the stick and hit me with it. I didnt cry. I cant do that. But the drip ran all over the bed. She saw it and twisted away and made a noise. Oh mygodmygod she said why have you *done* this to me? I heard the stick go bounce on the stone floor. She ran upstairs. I slept the day.

XXXXX—This day it had water again. When mother was upstairs I heard the little one come slow down the steps. I hidded myself in the coal bin for mother would have anger if the little mother saw me.

She had a little live thing with her. It walked on the arms and had pointy ears. She said things to it.

It was all right except the live thing smelled me. It ran up the coal and looked down at me. The hairs stood up. In the throat it made an angry noise. I hissed but it jumped on me.

I didnt want to hurt it. I got fear because it bit me harder than the rat does. I hurt and the little mother screamed. I grabbed the live thing tight. It made sounds I never heard. I pushed it all together. It was all lumpy and red on the black coal.

I hid there when mother called. I was afraid of the stick. She left. I crept over the coal with the thing. I hid it under my pillow and rested on it. I put the chain in the wall again.

X—This is another times. Father chained me tight. I hurt because he beat me. This time I hit the stick out of his hands and made noise. He went away and his face was white. He ran out of my bed place and locked the door.

I am not so glad. All day it is cold in here. The chain comes slow out of the wall. And I have a bad anger with mother and father. I will show them. I will do what I did that once.

I will screech and laugh loud. I will run on the walls. Last I will hang head down by all my legs and laugh and drip green all over until they are sorry they didn't be nice to me.

If they try to beat me again Ill hurt them. I will.

# Joseph Payne Brennan

Joseph Payne Brennan (1918– ) is the last major author of supernatural stories to have been associated with *Weird Tales*. "The Green Parrot," his first story for the magazine, appeared in 1952, a scant two years before *Weird Tales* ceased publication after thirty-one years. Perhaps Brennan's most powerful contribution to the last issues of this important publication was the novelette "Slime," a tale about a protoplasmic monster's assault on the inhabitants of an isolated village.

If Brennan has not received the wider acclaim of contemporaries like Robert Bloch and Ray Bradbury, it is due in large measure to the fact that he was not a child prodigy and that for most of the twenty-five years during which he has been writing in the field, there has been no reliable commercial outlet for short tales of terror. Brennan's writing was interrupted by World War II, when he served in General Patton's Third Army; he earned four battle stars, one for the Battle of the Bulge. He now works at Yale University's Sterling Memorial Library.

Much of his time is devoted to his poetry, which has been published in five volumes, equaling his production of fiction. His work has appeared in the *New York Times, Esquire,* the *Christian Science Monitor,* the *Reader's Digest,* and the *American Scholar,* among many others. He also edits and publishes two little magazines: *Essence,* devoted to poetry, and *Macabre,* devoted to frightening fiction. In recent years, many of his sinister stories have appeared in *Alfred Hitchcock's Mystery Magazine.*

Brennan's latest books are the poetry collection *Edges of Night* (1974) and *Stories of Darkness and Dread* (1973). The latter includes a number of excellent stories; among them are "Zombique," "The Keeper of the Dust," and "City of the Seven Winds," some of the most chilling horror tales of recent years. He has also revived a long-standing fictional tradition with a series about the exploits of an occult investigator; many of these tales have appeared in *The Casebook of Lucius Leffing.* Two of the stories from *The Dark Returners* (1959) were adapted for the television program "Thriller," hosted by Boris Karloff.

His first volume of fiction, *Nine Horrors and a Dream* (1958), includes such stories as "Slime" and the tour de force "I'm Murdering Mr. Massington," in addition to four composed especially for the book. One of these is "Levitation." This brief but unforgettable tale is among Brennan's best, and it demonstrates one of his greatest strengths, a deceptively direct and simple prose style. Although he is capable of flights of fancy dependent on the witchery of words, many of Brennan's impressive effects are achieved without the obvious verbal pyrotechnics that often occur in supernatural stories, and his work is all the better for its restraint.

The conjuring trick known as levitation, a highly impressive stage illusion, seems to have been developed by John Neville Maskelyne, with later refinements by Harry Kellar and Howard Thurston. Unfortunately, it is done with wires. There are, however, apparently authentic cases of people who have actually succeeded in raising themselves into the air, among them the seventeenth-century Italian monk St. Joseph of Copertino and the nineteenth-century Scottish medium Daniel Dunglas Home.

# LEVITATION

## Joseph Payne Brennan

Morgan's Wonder Carnival moved into Riverville for an overnight stand, setting up its tents in the big ball park on the edge of the village. It was a warm evening in early October and by seven o'clock a sizable crowd had made its way to the scene of raucous amusement.

The traveling show was neither large nor particularly impressive of its type, but its appearance was eagerly welcomed in Riverville, an isolated mountain community many miles from the motion picture houses, vaudeville theatres and sports arenas situated in larger towns.

The natives of Riverville did not demand sophisticated entertainment; consequently the inevitable Fat Lady, the Tattooed Man and the Monkey Boy kept them chattering animatedly for many minutes at a time. They crammed peanuts and buttered popcorn into their mouths, drank cup after cup of pink lemonade, and got their fingers all but stuck together trying to scrape the paper wrappers off colored taffy candies.

Everyone appeared to be in a relaxed and tolerant state of mind when the barker for the Hypnotist began his spiel. The barker, a short stocky man wearing a checkered suit, bellowed through an improvised megaphone, while the Hypnotist himself remained aloof at the rear of the plank platform erected in front of his tent. He appeared disinterested, scornful, and he scarcely deigned to glance at the gathering crowd.

At length, however, when some fifty souls had assembled in front of the platform, he stepped forward into the light. A murmur went up from the crowd.

In the harsh overhead electric glare, the Hypnotist made a striking appearance. His tall figure, thin to the point of emaciation, his pale complexion, and most of all his dark, sunken eyes, enormous and brilliant, compelled immediate attention. His dress, a severe black suit and an archaic black string tie, added a final Mephistophelean touch.

He surveyed the crowd coolly, with an expression betraying resignation and a kind of quiet contempt.

His sonorous voice reached to the far edge of the throng. "I will require one volunteer from among you," he said. "If someone will kindly step up—"

Everyone glanced around, or nudged his neighbor, but nobody advanced toward the platform.

Reprinted by permission of the author and the author's agents, Scott Meredith Literary Agency, Inc., 580 Fifth Avenue, New York, New York 10036.

The Hypnotist shrugged. "There can be no demonstration," he said in a weary voice, "unless one of you is kind enough to come up. I assure you, ladies and gentlemen, the demonstration is quite harmless, quite without danger."

He looked around expectantly and presently a young man slowly elbowed through the crowd toward the platform.

The Hypnotist helped him up the steps and seated him in a chair.

"Relax," said the Hypnotist. "Presently you will be asleep and you will do exactly what I tell you to do."

The young man squirmed on the chair, grinning self-consciously toward the crowd.

The Hypnotist caught his attention, fixing his enormous eyes on him, and the young man stopped squirming.

Suddenly someone in the crowd threw a large ball of colored popcorn toward the platform. The popcorn arched over the lights, landing squarely atop the head of the young man sitting in the chair.

He jerked sideways, almost falling off the chair, and the crowd, quiet a moment before, guffawed boisterously.

The Hypnotist was furious. He turned scarlet and literally shook with rage as he glared at the crowd.

"Who threw that?" he demanded in a choking voice.

The crowd grew silent.

The Hypnotist continued to glare at them. At length the color left his face and he stopped trembling, but his brilliant eyes remained baleful.

Finally he nodded to the young man seated on the platform, dismissing him with brief thanks, and turned again toward the crowd.

"Due to the interruption," he announced in a low voice, "it will be necessary to recommence the demonstration—with a new subject. Perhaps the person who threw the popcorn would care to come up?"

At least a dozen people in the crowd turned to gaze at someone who stood half in shadow at the rear of the gathering.

The Hypnotist spotted him at once; his dark eyes seemed to smoulder. "Perhaps," he said in a purring, mocking voice, "the one who interrupted is afraid to come up. He prefers to hide in the shadows and throw popcorn!"

The culprit voiced a sudden exclamation and then pushed belligerently toward the platform. His appearance was not in any way remarkable; in fact, he somewhat resembled the first young man, and any casual observer would have placed the two of them in the farm-laborer class, neither more nor less capable than the average.

The second young man sat down in the platform chair with a distinct air of defiance and for some minutes visibly fought the Hypnotist's suggestion to relax. Presently, however, his aggressiveness disappeared and he dutifully stared into the smouldering eyes opposite his own.

In another minute or two he arose at the Hypnotist's command and lay flat on his back on the hard planks of the platform. The crowd gasped.

"You will fall asleep," the Hypnotist told him. "You will fall asleep. You are falling asleep. You are falling asleep. You are asleep and you will do anything which I command you to do. Anything which I command you to do. Anything. . . ."

His voice droned on, repeating repetitious phrases, and the crowd grew perfectly silent.

Suddenly a new note entered the Hypnotist's voice and the audience became tense.

"Do not stand up—but *rise from the platform!*" the Hypnotist commanded. *"Rise from the platform!"* His dark eyes became wild and luminous-looking and the crowd shivered.

*"Rise!"*

Then the crowd drew in its collective breath with an audible start.

The young man lying rigid on the platform, without moving a muscle, began to ascend horizontally. He arose slowly, almost imperceptively at first, but soon with a steady and unmistakable acceleration.

*"Rise!"* the Hypnotist's voice rang out.

The young man continued to ascend, until he was feet off the platform, and still he did not stop.

The crowd was sure it was some kind of trick, but in spite of themselves they stared openmouthed. The young man appeared to be suspended and moving in mid-air without any possible means of physical support.

Abruptly the focus of the crowd's attention was shifted; the Hypnotist clasped a hand to his chest, staggered, and crumpled to the platform.

There were calls for a doctor. The barker in the checkered suit appeared out of the tent and bent over the motionless form.

He felt for a pulse, shook his head and straightened up. Someone offered a bottle of whiskey, but he merely shrugged.

Suddenly a woman in the crowd screamed.

Everyone turned to look at her and a second later followed the direction of her gaze.

Immediately there were further cries—for the young man whom the Hypnotist had put to sleep was still ascending. While the crowd's attention had been distracted by the fatal collapse of the Hypnotist, he had continued to rise. He was now a good seven feet above the platform and moving inexorably upward. Even after the death of the Hypnotist, he continued to obey that final ringing command: *"Rise!"*

The barker, eyes all but popping out of his head, made a frantic upward leap, but he was too short. His fingers barely brushed the moving figure above and he fell heavily back to the platform.

The rigid form of the young man continued to float upward, as if he were being hoisted by some kind of invisible pulley.

Women began screaming hysterically; men shouted. But no one knew what to do. A look of terror crept over the face of the barker as he stared up. Once he glanced wildly toward the sprawled shape of the Hypnotist.

"Come down, Frank! Come down!" the crowd shrieked. "Frank! Wake up! Come down! Stop! Frank!"

But the rigid form of Frank moved ever upward. Up, up, until he was level with the top of the carnival tent, until he reached the height of the tallest trees—until he passed the trees and moved on into the soft moonlit sky of early October.

Many in the crowd threw hands over horror-stricken faces and turned away.

Those who continued to stare saw the floating form ascend into the sky until it was no more than a tiny speck, like a little cinder drifting far up near the moon.

Then it disappeared altogether.